# A Long Way from Home

# A Long Way from Home

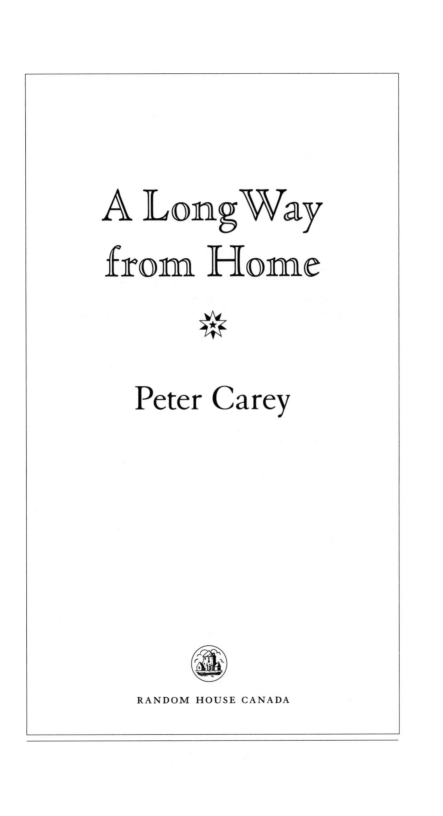

## Peter Carey

RANDOM HOUSE CANADA

PUBLISHED BY RANDOM HOUSE CANADA

Copyright © 2018 Peter Carey

www.penguinrandomhouse.ca

Library and Archives Canada Cataloguing in Publication

Carey, Peter, 1943–, author
A long way from home / Peter Carey.

Issued in print and electronic formats.
ISBN 978-0-7352-7386-3
eBook ISBN 978-0-7352-7388-7

I. Title.

PR9619.3.C36L66 2018          823'.914          C2017-905475-9
                              C2017-905476-7

Jacket design by gray318
Printed and bound in the United States of America

10  9  8  7  6  5  4  3  2  1

Penguin
Random House
RANDOM HOUSE CANADA

*For Frances Coady*

# Bacchus Marsh,
# 33 Miles from Melbourne

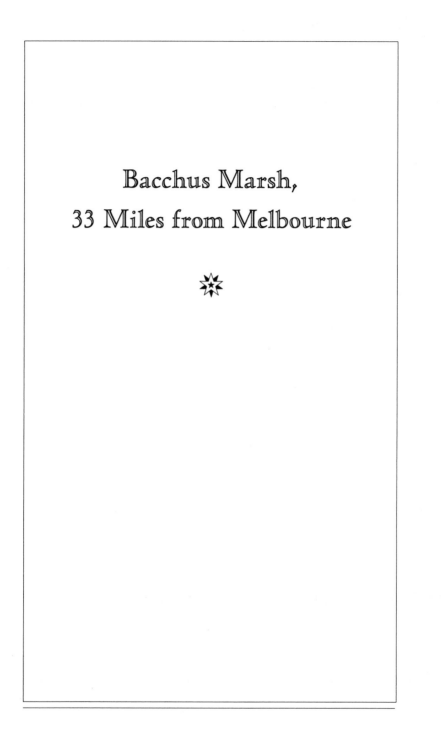

# 1

FOR A GIRL to defeat one father is a challenge, but there were two standing between me and what I wanted, which was—not to fiddle-faddle—a lovely little fellow named Titch Bobs.

The first father was my own. When he discovered that I, his teeny Irene, his little mouse, his petite sized mademoiselle, had, all by herself, proposed matrimony to a man of five foot three, he spat his Wheaties in his plate.

Titch's father was number two. He came out of the gate at a gallop, one hundred percent in favour. I was a beauty, a bobby-dazzler until, in the hallway by the coat stand, he gave me cause to slap his face.

My sister was older and more "experienced." She could not see why I would want so small a husband. Did I plan to breed a team of mice? Ha bloody ha. Beverly was five foot two and a half, and always breaking off engagements to lanky Lurch or gigantic Dino, or the famous football player whose name I am not ignorant enough to mention. I would have been afraid to shake his hand, forget the other business.

Beverly made her bed and got what you might expect i.e. thirty-hour labours and heads as big as pumpkins. My own children were as tiny and perfect as their daddy, ideal in their proportions, in the lovely co-ordination of their limbs, in the pink appley cheeks they inherited from Titch, the smile they got from me. My sister could not abide my happiness. She would spend years looking for evidence that it was "fake." When the first husband ran away to New Zealand she wrote me a spiteful letter saying I was more interested in my husband than in my kiddies. She said her boys were everything to her. She knew, she wrote, I only married Titch because of the money I could get from him. She was upset, of course. Why wouldn't she be? She had married a bastard. She was divorced "without a penny" so could she please go and live in the childhood home we had both inherited and whose sale she had always managed to impede? Could Titch and I have used the money? She didn't ask. Would it have changed our lives? Of course. I agreed on a peppercorn rent and kept my feelings to myself.

Beverly liked to say that I was wilful, which was an idea she had got from Mum. But Mum liked me being wilful. She got a real kick from seeing how I got my way. Of course she was a bit the same, Mum, and she was blessed with such neat level teeth and cheekbones, you would do anything to see her smile, even if you had to buy her a washing machine to make her do it. She got Dad to purchase the Ford which was what brought Titch to our door in Geelong, Victoria, Australia. It was Victory in Europe Day, May 8, 1945.

No-one will ever know how Mum planned to utilise the Ford. Drive down to Colac and see her sister after church? That was one story not even Dad could swallow. Didn't matter. He went on and wrote the cheque to the salesman, Dan Bobst who, as I discovered when I opened the front door on V-E Day, had thrown in "free" driving lessons which would be supplied by his sonny. Oh Lord, what a sight that sonny was, there on our front porch with his cardboard suitcase on a Tuesday morning. I learned he was to stay with us.

Poor Mum, alas, she never got to put the key in the ignition and everyone was so upset and busy with the funeral, no-one told the young man that he should leave. He had nowhere else to stay, so he unpacked his "port" and "awaited instructions" as he later liked to say. The Ford was parked in our drive, with no sign that it was now part of the deceased estate.

My mum was in the Mount Duneed Cemetery and the new boarder was the only one who helped me go through her things. He said nothing about the car or about the lessons he had been expecting to give to the deceased. He asked me if I knew how to drive. I told him that if he could be home by six at night he could have tea with us. In the midst of all the sadness the pretty red-cheeked man was a great comfort I could not do without. I held my breath. I cooked for him and he scraped his plate clean and helped with the drying up. He was neat. When I cried, he comforted me. He left talcum powder on the bathroom floor.

In the nights at Western Beach, when you could hear the forlorn anchor chains of the old warships anchored in Corio Bay, he told me stories of his father which he thought were funny. These were more important than I knew. In any case my eyes stung hot to hear that the lovely boy had broken his arm swinging the prop of the wretched father's monoplane, and that the old bully had taught him to land by sitting behind him in the navigator's seat and thumping his slender back with his fist until he pushed the stick down sufficiently, that he abandoned him to stay with a pair of old Irish bachelors at Bullenga-rook until they had learned to drive their purchase. The sonny was named Titch although he was sometimes Zac which was what they called a sixpence and a zac was therefore half a shilling or half a bob, which was, of course, his father's name. Forget it. He was always Titch, God Jesus, and it seemed I was put on earth to love your tortured body and your impy joyous soul.

How could I predict, dear Beverly, what sort of life my heart's desire would lead me to? Our dad was still alive on the day I first set eyes on Titch. My babies were not yet born. I couldn't drive a car. We had not yet arrived at the era of Holden Versus Ford. There was not even a Redex Around Australia Reliability Trial although that, the greatest Australian car race of the century, is the story I will get to in the end.

I was married the same day I got my driving licence. I drove us a hundred miles to Warragul myself. After that we moved to Sale, then Bairnsdale and Titch sold Fords for his father who always short-changed him on commission. My new husband was ideal in almost every way, and I knew that even before I understood his genius, which was the last thing you'd look for in a car salesman. He did not know how to lie, or so it seemed. He never exaggerated, unless to make a joke. He was funny, he was cheeky. He told me he had perfected the art of not being hit which was just as well, seeing the bars he did business in.

We lived in boarding houses and rented rooms and ate whole flocks of mutton but incredibly we were happy, even if his dad was in the room next door. Sometimes we made ourselves sick with laughing, rolling round the carpet on a Sunday afternoon. That should have been enough for anyone.

My father-in-law was always lurking. I did not tell Titch the disgusting things he had suggested to me. He never heard them, thank the Lord. Nor did my husband seem to notice the insults against himself. Dan Bobs was not a handsome fellow but he preened with his comb so constantly he finally lost his hair. Titch was blind to the vanity. He would sit and listen as the scoundrel bragged endlessly about his exploits. I endured all this for years until the old man found a Melbourne woman who would tolerate him. When he announced his retirement in the *Warragul Express,* I did not dare believe it.

Dan had a lifetime of cuttings in his scrapbook. He had the first pilot's licence in Australia. He had flown planes and got reported when he crashed them. He had raced Fords from Melbourne to Sydney. He had sold cars from farm to farm in the muddy dairy district of Gippsland and flat volcanic plains of Sunbury where he did business in the old-school style, that is, left his son behind to give the driving lessons. Was he giving up the game? Or was this "retirement" just another chance to be written up?

Edith was already seven. Ronnie had just been born. I tucked him in his pram so I could help shift his grandfather's possessions into his trailer. Ronnie woke up dirty and hungry but I would not go to him until I had lashed a tarpaulin over Dan's oily junk. Even then I waited, watching that red tail-light turn the corner by the Lodge.

Soon we had a postcard from "Mrs. Donaldson" who introduced herself as the old man's "housekeeper." Then there came an envelope containing a clipping from the *Mordialloc Advertiser.* He had set himself up as a scrap dealer. Mrs. Donaldson said they had a "grand" backyard. "Danny" had put a sign over the front gate: THE OLDEST AIRMAN IN THE WORLD. He sold war disposals and the occasional used car. He made another sign: IF YOU CAN'T FIND IT HERE, IT DOESN'T EXIST ON EARTH. A photograph was delivered: we saw he had "modified" the front verandah so it was now held up by aeroplane propellers.

AVIATOR RETIRES TO WATTLE STREET.

Dan would never ask us direct for money. He would, instead, turn up with, say, a water pump for a '46 Ford. Titch did not need it, but I could never get him to refuse his dad.

Beverly would say I always got my own way, but it was Beverly who got her way, refusing to get a job, or budge from our Geelong house. There was enough money locked up there to start a dealership, but Titch never questioned me, never argued, never insisted.

When Dan had left us to bully Mrs. Donaldson I found a property for rent in Bacchus Marsh, a small town in a rural district Titch was long familiar with. Titch had hopes to build up a used car business so we could finally be Ford dealers. I chose the house with this in mind. It had a huge yard and a big shed spanning the width of the back fence. Titch was tickled pink.

You could say that's where the story starts, at the site of our planned business, observed by the next door neighbour, a fair-haired bachelor with a strong jaw and absent bottom, cinched in trousers, crumply face, deep frown marks on his forehead. He found me in my overalls with a spanner in my hand. Himself, he held a colander, some sort of gift, and I saw the sad fond way he had with the kids and I thought it might be a bad idea to be too kind to him, for everything in life begins with kindness.

We had no plan to take advantage of him.

# 2

MRS. BOBS DID NOT KNOW the first thing about me, for instance that I was a chalk-and-talker, recently suspended for hanging a troublesome student out of a classroom window. She did not know that I was sought by bailiffs, that I was a regular on *Deasy's Radio Quiz Show* where my winnings were publicly announced each week. She did not know that I was a mess of carnal yearning and remorse, that my small weatherboard house was now legally a fire hazard, its floors and tables crammed with books and papers. A putative visitor would be compelled to travel crabwise down the hallway, between the illegal bookshelves, from front door to the sink. The kitchen table was a catastrophe, piled high with damp washing and academic quarterlies and musty pulp novels featuring Detective Inspector Napoleon Bonaparte ("Bony") of the Queensland Police Force.

Oh, a bookworm, she would later say.

I spent my entire life in Australia with the conviction that it was a mistake, that my correct place was elsewhere, located on a map with German names. I had lived with the expectation that something spectacular would happen to me, or would arrive, deus ex machina, and I was, in this sense, like a man crouched on a lonely platform ready to spring aboard a speeding train. I had run away from Adelaide when I should I have stayed home in the parsonage. I had married when I would have been happier single. I had fled my wife's adultery, left the only job that ever suited me and come to Bacchus Marsh to teach the notorious second form. And still I waited for my salvation, like the pastor's son I was, with an impatience that made my toes squirm inside my thirsty shoes. I had certainly been anticipating my new neighbours, although I could not have imagined anything like this.

The night before had been filled with awful portent. A horse float was driven past my bedroom window and two human figures then appeared. I rolled on my side, waiting for the horse to show its face but when the doors were opened nothing was revealed but kitchen chairs.

I drifted back to sleep and dreamed. In that other world I saw the doors of the float, now quilted and studded like a banquette. These swung slowly open and I saw a man and boy carry out a mattress. They staggered down the ramp, and I was slow to understand their unsteadiness was not caused by their burden but by laughter. I was sound asleep. I smiled as they danced out into the yard. They got just past the outhouse where they dropped their comic cargo beneath the walnut tree. It was only then I got the joke which was: the mattress was not a mattress. It was a huge fat snake, whiskery like a catfish, neatly folded up for travelling, wound round itself like a pastry snail. The man and boy uncoiled the serpent as if they were volunteer firefighters laying a canvas fire hose down the centre of Main Street.

Then the man charged ahead into the house holding the placid snake's head beneath his arm. Although this man was not Mr. Deasy from the radio quiz show, he had a similar military moustache. The boy tottered helplessly behind him, holding what he could, until he collapsed onto the floor, rolling as if tickled.

For several years I had paid attention to my dreams and I judged this is a very positive specimen. I thought, while still asleep, that there was a time when snakes had feathers.

I woke filled with light and happiness which was not ruined when I heard my complaining hens gathered outside my door. I was sorry they had been bred to be so stupid. I was sorry to keep the poor creatures waiting. I made it up to them, putting together a special treat, a pollard mix, bran, cod-liver oil, and added a good two bob's worth of cow's milk, stirring with my hand in the bucket. I washed. I opened the back door to find the rooster on the step. The hens must be fed first. The rooster knew that. It was his own principle, and he knew why I had to kick him across the yard. Sex is everywhere, most particularly when you have escaped it.

As I watched the chooks eat I became aware of the fuss next door, living children running through the previously abandoned house. I was in pyjamas. My feet were bare and the earth was cold. The horse float had disappeared. An extraordinary vehicle was now parked inside the cavernous open-sided shed.

I did not rush at my neighbours like a lunatic. I dressed as normal, in checked tweed gardening clothes and gumboots. I bumped the wheelbarrow off the front verandah and trundled out onto the street to collect whatever cow manure had been dropped by the beasts on their way to the sale yards. Back home, I cut a cauliflower. I collected what eggs my hens had laid for me. I took in my belt another notch. I washed the eggs and placed them in the remnants of my marriage, a chipped enamelled colander. I would not deliver this gift like a stranger, by walking down the driveway. Instead I used the vine-entangled gate in the side fence, a monument to the old friendship between a barber (whose estate owned my house) and the panelbeater who had become a landlord.

I was startled to confront a miniature boy and girl playing amongst the wild mint. They had found a fresh hen's egg, evidence my chooks were in the habit of trespassing. Perhaps I spoke to them, perhaps not. I turned to the former panelbeater's open-sided shed, a pavilion really, stretched across the back of the property. There, wrapped in shadow, was the vehicle: a two-tone Ford Customline. Of course I did not know the brand quite yet but it was so new and shiny that it contained an entire sky—towering white cumulus—in its bulbous fenders.

I could hear the voices of a man and woman, also the song of cooling metal.

"Hang on."

"No, the other one."

They might have been doing the dishes, she washing, he drying, at the kitchen sink.

I was drawn inevitably towards the automobile. I called first good morning and then coo-ee. Then I was inside the shed which had become the home of pigeons with alarming wings. Then came another awful noise, like a filing cabinet dragged across a concrete floor and there they were shooting out from under the Ford, the astonishing pair clad in faded coveralls, lying flat on mechanic's trollies, icons with bright silver spanners in their hands.

Mister must have been five foot two and she even smaller. Missus's hair was so tousled and curling she might have been, had not all the other evidence been so much to the contrary, a boy. Her husband's complexion was smooth and glowing, he could have been a girl. Yet to talk of boys and girls is to miss the point. The new arrivals stared at me and I somehow understood that they, being visions, were not required to speak.

I am Willie Bachhuber, I said, for the war was less than ten years over, and it was best to get the German business finished with at once.

# 3

I AM WILLIE BACHHUBER the stranger says, God bless him. Why did that make me grateful? Because he did not say he was William Bach or Billy Hubert. That is, he was in no way like my father-in-law Herr Daniel Bobst who lived his days in terror of being thought a kraut. Dan had changed Bobst to Bobs then acted out this airman nonsense as if he had really served the King of England. When he retired to his scrap yard he reinforced this false impression, filling it with bomb casings and other matériel from War Disposal.

But Dan was gone from our lives now, together with his belief that his son was put on earth to do his bidding. I had not taken an Aspro in a month and I knew the reason. No Dan. No more. Titch was finally his own man, at work pacing out the shed and he was understanding that it was true what I had told him: we could put three vehicles there. I loved so much to see him happy.

The autumn air was sweet with burning leaves. There was a white chook fossicking for worms. I didn't even wonder how it got there. White chook, green grass, blue sky. My Edith had said goodbye to her last boarding house meal. She had found canna lilies growing wild behind the laundry. Ronnie dug up a wet and slippery tennis ball with which he accidentally hit the neighbour. Mr. Bachhuber had a colander in his right hand but he caught the ball on the rebound off his chest. The colander contained a cauliflower and teetering eggs but he lobbed the ball gently back in the direction of my son who had already run away and was tracking a rusty coloured hen through unmown grass. I slipped my spanner into my pocket. Edith jumped at Ronnie's chook and the chook flew into the air. Whoever heard of such a thing? A hen with wings like a mighty eagle's. It landed on the tin roof of our house. You had to laugh.

"Sorry," said the neighbour and I understood the chook was his.

"Bachhuber," he repeated, reminding me I hadn't said my name.

"We are Bobs," I told him, nodding to my husband who was attending to our vehicle with his Belgian feather duster.

"Blind to everything but cars," I said. He could not help himself, dear Titchy. His vehicles must be clean. He could travel the dustiest road to the loneliest farm and he would always find a creek before he arrived and he would have a chamois and a bucket and roll his sleeves up. He presented his vehicles in the filthiest situations, always in showroom condition like himself.

The neighbour was tall and whippy with slender arms. He had not yet explained the colander and I did not like to presume it was for us, but he was a nice-looking man with fine fair hair he had to flick away. He had the most spectacular frown which pushed down around his schnoz. It made you want to comfort him some way.

He said, "Perhaps I can carry this inside for you?"

He meant the colander and I followed him inside trying to remember where I had packed the Kraft cheddar. It was a Sunday. All the shops were closed.

The house was a shambles and a pigsty and the movers had left the hydraulic jack in the hall and the kitchen table in the living room. There was a hole kicked in the bedroom plaster I hadn't noticed when I took the place. Only now did I learn that the oven was coated with rancid grease. I turned on the gas range but it would not light. I tried a dozen matches and burned my finger on the last one before I accepted that the gas was not connected.

Meanwhile the neighbour had vanished. Embarrassed for me, probably, but we would get our domestic situation into shape. The hydraulic jack was six feet long, weighed a ton, but I wheeled it out to the back door and across the threshold and down the garden path. Finally the gravel stopped all further movement.

Ronnie had commandeered next door's colander and was gathering eggs from amongst the canna lilies. The neighbour was standing at the fence again. He raised his eyebrows, perhaps referring to the tea towel on his shoulder. He was a comic turn, but not too much I hoped.

I had no heat to cook with, but we had bread and I knew we had cheese and some apples. I was so light and happy to be just us four.

Then I heard the crunch of tyres on gravel and saw, entering our establishment, a 1938 Plymouth equipped with one of those wood-burning gas producers, from the days of wartime petrol rationing. This one had a large cylindrical furnace. From this a pipe snaked across the roof and then down into the engine. Who would drive a thing like this in 1953?

As the window in the driver's door descended slowly, the vehicle cut rudely in front of me, laying white oil smoke across the yard.

My father-in-law was on the graveyard side of seventy, but he stepped into our yard clad in the usual cotton dustcoat, full of piss and vinegar. How had he tracked us down? He released a statuesque biddy in furs and high heeled shoes. That must be the Mrs. Donaldson. Ignorant, I thought, seeing how she gave the kiddies barley sugar.

No-one had invited Mr. Bachhuber but there he was standing on the Plymouth's running board, inspecting the dog's breakfast on the roof, amongst which, it seems, he had identified an old aircraft propeller. "Westland Wallace," he pronounced, as if I should applaud.

Both kids took my hand, dear babies.

The neighbour closed his eyes and spoke without invitation: "Mr. Dan Bobst, having engine trouble with his Westland Wallace, negotiated a clever landing by the Jarrahmond station, then transferred to his Malvern Star bicycle by which means he travelled four miles to Orbost for emergency supplies." He was like a clever child reciting poetry.

A look of cunning twisted my father-in-law's features. He grabbed for something in his trouser pocket, a business card which he would snatch back when it had served its purpose. The card would be green and faded. On it would be printed the likeness of the Westland Wallace which had appeared in the British Empire Trade Exhibition in Buenos Aires. Above this image, in the washed-out sky, would be a mous-tached aviator in leather helmet and goggles. *Dangerous Dan Bobs, the oldest airman in the world.*

"Thank you Mr. Bobs," said Mr. Bachhuber. I was upset to see how reverently he held the card. "But I do know exactly who you are."

But who could ever imagine the size of Dan Bobs' self-regard? A mood descended on me very bad indeed.

"A clever landing by the Jarrahmond station, then transferred to his ever-present bicycle by which means he travelled four miles to Orbost. Where—" Ronnie squeezed my hand and looked up at me, all teeth and worried eyes—"he purchased a bar of soap needed to repair the leaking petrol line."

You might expect Dan to be interested in how a total stranger could have this write-up off by heart, but curiosity was not his strong point. He puffed himself up like a cobra, glaring in triumph at those of us whose wallets he planned to lighten.

"I should like to introduce my colleague Mrs. Donaldson," he said.

As the housekeeper stepped forward, Titch removed a box from the boot of the Ford and escaped with it towards the house.

Dan and his female "colleague" hardly noticed. They were all over Bachhuber as if he were a feed of steak and kidney pudding.

"You in the motor game?" Dan asked.

"No, no, nothing so interesting."

I interrupted but it was as if a dog spoke, the way he looked at me. "The propeller is a real beauty," I said.

"Talk to your husband," he said but I was the one who must refuse this "gift." I smiled and grovelled and wagged my tail. I told him I wished we could afford it, that we had no place to even store it. I made myself feel sick. "It would be a crime," I said, "to expose it to the weather."

Dan turned away to Bachhuber. "What sort of vehicle do you have yourself?"

"Just the bike," said Bachhuber. "A Malvern Star."

Dangerous Dan then announced he had personally known Sir

Hubert Opperman. "Oppy" had ridden a Malvern Star to win the famous Paris–Brest–Paris race.

"In 1931," added the neighbour.

This unsettled Dan. "I was a mate of Tom Finnigan. You ever hear of him?"

"My word," said Bachhuber. "Mr. Malvern Star himself."

"Began business in Glenferrie Road."

"Yes, number 58."

Dan began searching urgently inside his wallet. Then he changed his mind. "Go get your bike," he ordered. "Let's see."

"It's just an old crate."

"You won't be sorry Bachhuber."

And off the innocent went, still carrying his tea towel, marching over the fallen autumn leaves, up the driveway to the street. There were bloody chooks lined up on the ridge line of the house.

"Dad," I said.

"Keep your panties on. Jeez."

"We're broke, Dad."

Mrs. Donaldson urgently produced more sweets, fancy chocolates from Darrell Lea. I had to take them.

"You're not setting up a pitch here?" said Dan. He was on the running board, his back towards me, releasing his white elephant. "You haven't got a hoist. You haven't even got a petrol pump. You should have told me."

"We wouldn't ask you for money," I said. "You've got trouble of your own."

That got his full attention. "What trouble?" He swung on me. "I've got no bloody troubles. I'm not like some people. I'm not going into business with no experience. I'm not sneaking off to go into competition with my father."

"You said you were retired."

"You shouldn't be so secretive," he said.

"We didn't have your number."

"The boy imagines he can be a Ford dealer? With a place like this?

With five quid in the bank? Does no-one have a clue? You think I don't still talk to the blokes at Ford?"

"They're assessing the application now. We filled it out."

"You just embarrassed them," Dan said. "Call your dog off, Dan, they said."

"Don't call your son a dog."

That was the wrong way to speak to Dan but fortunately Bachhuber came back with his bicycle and all his interest went that way.

"I like bikes," he announced, winding rope around his arm. "By Jove yes. I had a bike myself."

"Yes," the poor fellow recited, "you carried a Malvern Star bicycle on your plane."

"No, listen."

The neighbour smiled agreeably.

"I'd give you forty quid for the bike. I could tip you into a Ford Customline exactly like that one there. How's that? I'm not so far away. Any problems I can be here in a mo."

"Yes, but I brought something for you, Mr. Bobs."

The neighbour had a beautiful old book in the basket. There was a gold picture of an old plane on its cover and a title like *Aeronautics* except in some foreign language. Of course Dan wanted it but he stepped back, holding up his hands. "I could go as high as fifty for the bike," he said.

The neighbour held the book like a bible to his chest. "I can't drive."

"I'll teach you."

"I'm OK."

"Are you?" Dan asked and I recognised that nasty edge. "What do you do for a crust?"

"I'm a schoolteacher."

That was when Dan lost interest. I had seen him do this so many times before. He climbed to the running board and untied the final rope. He lifted the propeller free and with a grunt pivoted, and compelled the poor bloke to accept it. "You're what?"

"Schoolteacher."

Mr. Bachhuber was forced to kneel in order to set the propeller on the grass. He pointed out that it had been sheathed in copper which had once been secured by either screws or rivets soldered and then expertly smoothed down. "Lovely work."

Dan hid his smile behind his hand, an offensive gesture, there for all the world to see.

"A chalk-and-talker."

"That's me."

"And these are your chooks on the roof?"

"I'm afraid so, yes."

"You can't have them making their mess here, not now there are little kiddies. Their mother will tell you, won't you Mumsy? It's not hygienic. You kept chooks before? No? The trick is, mate, you need to clip their wings."

"Yes, I didn't get around to it."

"Any mug can do it. All we need is some clippers, which actually I have."

When I protested, he turned his hate on me. "Are you a mother or what?"

I heard the back door bang. Titch returned not knowing I had lit a fire. I had promised I would never again fight Dan, but now I didn't care. "If Mr. Bachhuber needs help with his chickens," I said, "I'll be happy to assist."

"You can clip wings?"

I smiled right in his nasty face.

"Dad," Titch said, "I'm sorry but we can't use the prop." This was a first. I could have cried.

"You need some signage, sonny. You can be a Ford dealer all you like, no-one will notice. The prop is what they call sales promotion."

"I can't afford it," Titch said.

"Fifteen quid? Of course you can afford it. You want people to know you're in business, don't you? You want the town to talk about you? Even if the council makes you take it down. Just dig a hole in the front lawn."

"Your dad says his mates at Ford have rejected our application."

"You shouldn't have gone behind my back to Ford," Dan said. "You're an embarrassment. You think they'll give you a Ford dealership? A place like this?"

Titch's colour had risen, but his smile was crisp and neat. "We'll help you tie it on again." Then he lifted the propeller and I thought, you lovely man.

Dan nodded to Mrs. D. Immediately she turned and, with a small apologetic smile to me, teetered across the gravel to the car. A moment later the Plymouth accelerated up the drive.

The propeller dwarfed my husband, and seemed to overpower him, but no, he lifted it like a barbell. And hurled it against the fence. "Fifteen quid," he cried.

Our neighbour's mouth was open.

"Thank God I was not born a strong man," my husband said, "or I would have killed someone by now."

# 4

AS A BABY in the Payneham parsonage, I had climbed up to the kitchen sink and tumbled out the window where, by sheer good fortune, I gouged a lump from beneath my shoulderblade and left my little head intact. Sometimes in later years, in the shower for instance, I would explore the crater in my flesh and amuse myself by thinking of what it prophesied: a lifetime of escaping my own dull nature, of seeking the thrill of energy by jumping when I should be safe and still. It was this desire, I am now certain, that physically attracted me to Adelina Koenig, that tall dark beauty with whom I had cut my high school classes and explored the musty mud and grasses by the River Torrens where it lived its sulky sullen life at what was still called Payneham then. I was a pastor's son with no interest in money. I was not excited by the Koenigs' wealth or status in the Deutscher Club, but to be in Adelina's presence was like being plugged into a power point, like becoming her subject, as vitally connected as an electric fan, or drill.

Mrs. Bobbsey was the same.

Her husband had pink cheeks, jet black hair, an unworldly vitality that made you think of the circus. How I envied him his life.

Mrs. Bobbsey struck matches and her failures were exhilarating. I had a week's worth of stew to offer, seven single meals for each inevitable night, just waiting in the fridge. My thoughts were on the mad side, obviously.

At home I put the dinner on my stove, removed books from my dining room table, replaced them with others. I doubted my personal library would be of much interest to this family but I also knew there were volumes anyone would love, French mostly, but illustrated with fine engravings: the beauty of the mechanical age, knitting machines, automata, aeroplanes with feathers on their wings. It was to my advantage there was no market for that language in my monolingual land.

Mrs. Bobbsey did not like her father-in-law. I could have listened to him all day. If he had tried to sell me a car, why would I mind? Given a chance, I would have paid for the propeller. I could have hung it from the ceiling, on the diagonal, suspended by piano wire. At the same time I was thrilled to see tiny shiny Mr. Bobbsey HURL the valuable item against the fence. What different lives they lived to mine, clipping chook wings, repairing aeroplanes with soap, deciding to be Ford dealers, asking no-one permission, alone, like tightrope walkers, with no summonses to hide from. I would have given everything to be like them.

What would Dangerous Dan have done about the summons? Would he pay support for a child that was not his? Would he endure the double insult of being laughed at as a cuckold as well as suffering the relentless punishment of paying for the fruit of adultery? I was not sorry to have removed myself from Adelina's world, but I was ashamed to have fled like a worm. I had crawled from the State Library of Victoria (where I had been wonderfully at home) and slunk to Bacchus Marsh where the high school was desperate to let me teach the worst class in the school.

Legal letters sought me c/- Mr. Deasy's quiz show but Deasy had much invested in me, and for this reason we always prerecorded at erratic times. The bailiffs arrived when the show was on air, and I was far away. When you understand the deceitful nature of the quiz show prizes, those huge cheques as big as a door which Deasy presented in public, you will bet he must have dodged a bailiff once or twice himself.

By the simple expedient of not reading my mail or answering my own door, I had been safe, until I hung young Bennett Ash by his ankles out the classroom window.

What would happen now? Would the disciplinary tribunal treat me as my father's church did pregnant girls, demanding they stand before the congregation?

Do you Adelina Koenig confess that you have manifestly sinned against God and given offence to his congregation?

Do you pray that God for Christ's sake will forgive your sin, and do you also ask the congregation to forgive you?

Do you also intend to amend your life and by the help of the Holy Spirit live according to God's will?

Or will you just run away and not tell anyone your trouble?

Bacchus Marsh High School was a two-storey red brick building in approximate Edwardian style, separated from the Maddingley oval by a two-lane road along which the five-ton colliery trucks, having spilled a little of their load on the railway crossing, accelerated on their way to no-one knew exactly where.

I had already broken my father's decent heart. Had he stood across this busy road on a certain afternoon in the early autumn of 1953, he would have been destroyed to learn that it was me, his beloved son, who was responsible for the bawling thirteen-year-old hanging from the second-storey window.

I was sorry. I am always sorry. I had arrived in Bacchus Marsh four years and three months previously. I seemed to have no wife or even girlfriend. My name was obviously German but I was not, as far as any-one could see, a sissy. In my first year I played on the wing for Bacchus Marsh where the *Express* reported me to be "fast and slippery as an eel."

Then Butch Daley called me a kraut.

My name was Bachhuber. Take a joke they said.

I smiled and was as misunderstood as I had wished to be. Soon I got a hamstring injury. That seemed the only safe response. And that is the creature I had spent my life becoming. I was so expert at avoiding con-flict that it still seems impossible that I was brought down by a child.

The second form of the high school had been, until my arrival, a notorious scene of rage and uproar, a simmering pot, ruled by boys who had been yearly denied promotion to the third form and were now in limbo, waiting for the day on which they could legally abandon their education. "I turned fourteen and you can't fucking touch me."

I had a degree but no teacher training. To my surprise I was a suc-cessful teacher of the untouchables. The headmaster was grateful, but what my amiable colleagues secretly thought of me I can never really know. The education department inspectors, however, loved me: *A very good teacher working earnestly and zealously in a challenging environment.*

So I had never expected to be vulnerable to Bennett Ash who I had long ago brought to heel. Bennett had dirt ingrained on his skinny wrists and lice eggs, doubtless, beneath his broken nails. It was Bennett, sitting in the front row where I kept him, who accused me of having "Balts" in the class.

Where would one start?

I asked him what he thought a Balt was.

He thought it was a reffo, sir. He meant a refugee, a person displaced by war.

I could have escorted him to the map of the world, that is the pink British Empire and the other bits. I could have shown him that Balt was short for Baltic, or a person from the Baltic states. But could he even recognise the Baltic Sea?

How could I possibly "teach" him that the Australian government had deliberately misnamed the displaced persons Balts? That was the path by which the word had entered his vocabulary. How many weeks might it take to have him understand that the Australian government were selecting light skinned "Nordic types" as future citizens and that they had, for the sake of obfuscation, named them Balts?

Of course I had my own ancient scars and fears, my deep sense of displacement, that I was not from here, that this was not my landscape, that I had been denied my natural land which had been accurately depicted by Caspar David Friedrich.

I asked Bennett did he know what a "Nordic type" was.

"You never taught us, sir."

"Then sit down. Put your hanky back in your pocket."

Then Suzy Winspear, whose father was a dentist with a slow old-fashioned drill, said that Sippe Van Hanraad was a Nordic type.

Sippe, in the second row, was actually Dutch. He was tall with fine blond hair and was quickly beginning to grasp the lessons.

"Yes," said Bennett Ash holding up a warty hand, "Sippe is a Balt, sir. You favour him."

His point was that Sippe's hair was pretty much like mine.

"Yes Bennett, what is a Balt?"

"What about you, sir? Why did they let you in?"

I am a calm man, have been so all my life. I grabbed the heel of the boy's hobnailed boot, and yanked him off balance and pushed his body out the window and held him there while he bawled and shouted.

He was not a big boy but he had mass. He squirmed and flapped and I felt the horror of my relentless dreams which were peopled not only by snakes but creatures like possums that would end up being born as children if I did not kill them. The rivers in my sleep were filled with fish which broke apart like wet cardboard. I often sleepwalked, but in my classroom I was wide awake, dangling a pupil out my window. There was no precedent for this except the unexpected fit that had me leave my marriage.

It would later be alleged that I had refused to haul Bennett Ash back to safety until he promised not to breed. This was never true. Once he was safe I gave dictation just to calm the situation. Anyone can now tell me I had ignored a valuable teaching moment, but Bennett lived in a world where the truth would die of thirst.

I had been a peaceful much-loved child with a great passion for atlases, but there would be no such thing, even of the musty cheaply printed variety, in the shadow of the condensed milk factory where Bennett Ash lived. Nor would anyone in that dark place discuss, in terms high or low, the government's thoughts on non-British migration into monocultural Australia. No-one would care what Nordic or Baltic meant, or see the parallels between the government's recruitment of "Nordic types" and their habit of removing the paler Aboriginal children from their mothers and giving them to white families with the total confidence that half-castes would never give birth to "throwbacks," wishful racial thinking with no basis in genetics.

The headmaster did not visit me until after the final bell when I found him blocking my exit, posing, I thought, running a large index finger along the disturbing vein in the pale eggshell head that I would see again, much later, in the work of George Grosz.

"You know a lot of idiots will be pleased to hear what you did?"

I suppose I must have sighed. If not I irritated him another way.

"You do know that, don't you Willie? The whole Marsh will be talking about it now."

"Yes."

"They'll love it," said Harry Huthnance, biting off the words while continuing to smile. "They'll say the boy deserved it. But none of them has my job."

"Sorry, Harry."

"There's a social worker involved with the Ash family. Did you know that? She'll want to advocate for her client."

"Client?"

"It's not funny. Yes, Bennett is her client. She will want to address our disciplinary tribunal."

"Harry, don't do this."

"Willie, I don't have a choice. You didn't give me one."

"Perhaps I could have a chat to the dad."

"You will not go near that family. Luckily I have a little influence with the tribunal."

I had no way of knowing if this was true. But Huthnance surely wouldn't want to lose a teacher who could actually handle the second-form boys. My predecessor had punched him in the nose before departure.

"I will have to suspend you, Will. Please don't frown like that."

"With pay?"

He gave me a sharp look and I knew what he was thinking. Bachhuber is rich. He gets these big prizes from his quiz show.

"You wouldn't believe the bloody paperwork involved in a tribunal."

"What sort of suspension is it?"

"Maybe you could think about the wool syllabus while you're off?"

It was typical that he should wish to trade with me. The wool syllabus was his chore, not mine. It was bureaucratic not pedagogic. He had been directed to remedy *the total ignorance of high school students on the issue of wool and its vital role in the history of the state.* The source of this correspondence was the state education department in Melbourne, but what political forces were behind this aberration? Who would know?

"It's rubbish," I told him. "You said so yourself. This is more your sort of thing Harry."

"If you remain on the payroll, you must do something. You'll make something of it. I know you will. You can design this better than anyone else in the school, certainly better than me."

"You'll only rewrite it afterwards."

"I won't have the time. You have my word. You'll give me time to concentrate on the tribunal. Come on, give me a break. Full pay, OK?"

He was disgusted by my imagined greed. I couldn't really blame him. He was not privy to the value of all Deasy's phoney cheques. He straightened up and buttoned his shiny suit and held out his damp hand.

"I can save your bacon. You have my word."

He was weak and his word was worthless, and I didn't believe him for a second. So why was it that I rode home in such a strange light mood? Was I finally in that state Sebastian Laski had spoken of? Was I now empty of myself, formless, like water? Was it possible that I was happy to have once again destroyed my scaffolding, to be hanging from another window, tremulous and giddy on the brink of my real life?

# 5

I HAD RELINQUISHED our children to one more foreign school but all I could think about was that damn propeller. Clearly I was not a normal mother. And yet the propeller was a danger to us all, not least because *someone* had woken in the middle of the night and dragged the damn thing inside the shed. Was I meant to think it walked in there? Had it been transported there by elves? Or was my husband still his father's slave?

"Out of the weather," Titch said. And looked at me, with his mouth wobbly.

Out of the bloody weather? Why had we carted our kids a hundred miles from anything they knew? Not to see their father carrying Dan's propeller like the Holy Cross. I loved Titch, of course I did, but we were not returning to our former servitude.

"I have a mind to dump it up the tip," I said.

In reply he kissed my hand and I saw he would let my temper run its course. Like a grassfire by the road, he would have said. Very bloody funny. Ha ha. But not all grassfires stay by the verge as is well known. They can rage for miles, for acres, destroying all the fences as they go, all the way from the Marsh to Mordialloc to burn a certain scrap yard to the ground.

My father-in-law had owned stables and taxi services and had maybe sold a lot of Fords but he had never been within spitting distance of a franchise. His mates at Ford would drink with him, and listen to his airman stories, but he was an artful dodger and would go to the grave without ever being an authorised dealer in anything. At seventy-five years of age he was still in competition with his son.

Dan worshipped Henry Ford to an extreme degree. Titch had the same disease. He was therefore happy to let the Ford Motor Company go snooping through our bank account, our debts, our credit history, and now, while they were deciding if we were good enough to be their authorised dealer, while there were no new vehicles released to us, Titch would take the train to Ballarat to buy used stock from Joe Thacker. You would fear for Titch to see him walk into the pub that Joe Thacker called "my office": all those windburnt faces, cow cockies, racecourse touts, bookmakers, cockroaches living off the smell of spilled beer and last night's cigarettes. I only saw it once and I thought he would be killed in there, my Titchy. He was too small, too neat, and his shoes were far too dainty, but, as I was compelled to accept and understand, he was at home in Craig's Hotel. He was a strange and unexpected creature, unlike anything you could imagine, controlled and well dressed, then like a crazy little animal when the lights were off. No-one would believe it, if they ever knew, or heard, good grief. His mouth.

So I drove him to the station and parked the car and walked hand in hand onto the platform and I wrapped his tartan scarf around his neck and buttoned it inside his camel overcoat. I kissed him. He kissed me. It was perhaps not the best occasion to say what I said, but I said it anyhow. We should not wait for Ford's approval. We were better off without them. We had arrived in the era of "Australia's Own Car" i.e. General Motors Holden. It was now Holden Versus Ford and Ford were set to lose. We should tell Ford to jump in the lake, snaffle the Bacchus Marsh Holden dealership while it was still available.

Titch listened to my blasphemy. He did not ask how I could be so confident of getting a Holden dealership. He said he would think about what I had said but clearly he couldn't wait to get away from my opinions. He kissed my eyes and said he loved me but he was hurt to be called a "nervous Nellie."

He boarded the train. I drove first to the co-op and then the butcher's where they tried to find out who I was. They were very eager to deliver but I wouldn't give them the address. Everybody wants to know your private business.

I drove home and straight into the shed. And there was the copper-tipped propeller catching the light like some disgusting Catholic saint. I had not really intended to dump it on the tip, today or ever, but now I ran inside and snatched the eiderdown off our marriage bed and returned to the shed where I tied it across the roof of the Customline, running binder twine through the open windows. My dad had been a stock and station agent and I had spent my childhood going from farm to farm at harvest time. I got the eiderdown tied down as firm as any bale of hay.

The sight of that pink quilt would have been more distressing to Titch than mud splashed on the hubcaps, but that would be a wifely secret now.

The propeller was heavier than I had imagined when I saw my husband hurl it through the air. But I would move it, first one inch, then another, across the concrete floor. Of course I had no idea how I would lift it to the roof. But if I had been so easily discouraged I would still be a virgin bride. That was not how I did things, by being defeated at the start. In less than half an hour I had the propeller leaning gently against the car.

I never really hoped to find Mr. Bachhuber home—he was a teacher, it was a weekday—but I went through the garden gate and I stood on his back doorstep and knocked. No-one answered. A more genteel woman might have given up, but I snuck around the side and, what a shock it gave me to find him staring out his bedroom window.

It would never have occurred to me that such a polite nice-looking man was hiding from the law. All I thought was: thank the Lord.

He met me at his kitchen door all shaved and shiny and I was in so much of a hurry to get his help that I inadvertently gave him the impression there had been an accident. I handed him the twine and, he told me later, he understood it was for a tourniquet and even when I brought him to our shed he was not inclined to look at the propeller.

"Can you lift it for me?" I asked him.

"This?"

What else? I thought. "Could you lay it on the roof?"

He said he could, but he didn't move.

I asked him did he need a hand.

No he didn't. He embraced the prop and swung it to the horizontal and laid it on the quilt and I saw I had given him an oil stain and was too guilty to mention it.

"That was all you wanted?"

"I can tie it on myself."

But he was running his long fingers along the prop as if he had sanded it himself. "Do you know what this timber is, Mrs. Bobs?"

"Not a clue," I said.

"It's laminated white oak. See how tight the grain is?"

I looked into those strange German eyes. "How do you know that?" I asked.

Of course I was completely unaware that my neighbour was famous on a quiz show. He knew everything, it turned out—the history of Egyptians and volcanoes—and when he saw I wanted to secure the prop he dismissed my binder twine and I let him fetch his own rope— why not?—and then it seemed ropes were made from hemp, cotton, coir, jute or straw. And I admit it was rather nice, the affectionate familiar way he talked about the rope. I stood back and let him lash the prop on.

When he was all done I asked could he direct me to the tip.

"The tip?" He raised his eyebrows. He stared at me. I got hot cheeks.

I told him he had a spot on his nice white shirt. I was sorry.

He didn't even look at it. "You can't take this to the tip," he said.

It was not his fault he didn't know my character. I explained I had to dump it. There was no choice.

"I'll look after it," he said. "I'd be happy to."

"No. I have to dispose of it."

He folded his arms across his chest and admired the propeller as if it were a statue of Our Lady. I said I was sorry. That was how it was.

"What does Mr. Bobs think?"

I asked him where was the tip.

"Someone will scavenge it," he said.

I saw his point. I located our hacksaw in our big green box. I put this in the boot. "Will you tell me where the tip is?"

"You're not going to cut it?"

He was smiling now, just a small smile. His nose was a little broad but in perfect proportion to his jaw. His head tilted to the side as if he finally got a glimpse of who I was.

"How will you lift that down off the roof?"

"I'll manage."

He clearly thought I couldn't, so he got in the passenger seat. I don't know why I trusted him. I just did. I took off up the drive and paused at the street. "Left or right?"

"Left."

I turned in the direction of the Catholic school then right on Gisborne Road where I left some rubber in my wake. He took it well.

"Does Mr. Bobs not need the car?"

Our neighbour knew nothing about us, so I told him how Titch had sold Henry Ford's cars since he was twelve years old. How he was the best country salesman in this state. He was the one who talked the Ford Motor Co into offering a very persuasive type of differential which would get a dairy farmer to the top of his muddy hill. Titch had come to the Marsh confident that Ford would appoint him a dealer. I wasn't worried. If that didn't come to pass, Ford were not the only pebble on the beach.

He directed me around the edges of the Darley oval, and I swung onto the gravel and dropped a cog and planted it to see what he would say. We were soon ascending a dusty cutting on the naked hill. There was a grand view across brown grass to the lush market gardens and the winding banks of the Lerderderg River.

In the very centre was a fenced off pit, the home of crows and blowflies and two men.

"Here we are," he said.

# 6

WHEN MRS. BOBS FOUND ME at my bedroom window she was wearing coveralls, shockingly becoming. I glimpsed a white singlet like a baby might have worn, crocheted around the neck.

Who would be a man locked inside his skin with only prayer and filthy thoughts for company? Is that God's plan, that good men should buy disgraceful photographs upstairs from the milliners on Little Bourke Street?

She was waiting at the back door and explained what she wanted of me. Astonishing how coveralls reveal a body when the intention is the very opposite. I was never a flirt or an adulterer. I said I must go to work. She didn't even hear me lie. She wished me to destroy a beautiful propeller that a good man would have saved for history. It should be in a vitrine in the Melbourne museum. I could have written the plaque myself: *Propeller from Westland Wallace. In 1933 this was the first aircraft to fly over Mount Everest, as part of the Houston Mount Everest Expedition.* It was a gorgeous thing to slice the air so high above the world.

I knew better but I would have done whatever she asked me, burned the blades of an Ader Éole, to which the maniac Ader had added feathers.

I got into her car as she suggested. The smell of Pears soap was familial. And then, dear Lord, she put down her little foot—size five or even four—sending gravel spraying back against the fence. I had hung a child out a classroom window. Not knowing that, she smiled at me.

Having rarely been a passenger in a motor car, I had little to compare her with. Mrs. Bobs piloted with her nose just above the wheel, checking her mirrors, left, right, centre. I was reminded of a sparrow eating.

"Hold onto your hat," she said and squealed her tyres on Gisborne Road. Her husband's train would already have left Ballan, she said. She insisted on him somewhat. She wrinkled her lovely nose, dropped a "cog," as it is called, and passed the five-ton truck heading for the Darley brickworks. She told me, in confidence, she wished her husband would sell Holden not Fords. The American firm of General Motors had recently begun to produce the Holden, which she said was "Australia's Own Car." Titch Bobbsey, I learned, was a lifetime soldier in the cause of Ford. Mrs. Bobbsey had just received information which would make him change his mind.

"You are a pair of powerhouses I would say."

"You can't know us from a bar of soap," she said (so happily) and by then we were at the Darley tip. It was a melancholy scene where the crime would be committed: a gate and, just inside, a small hut not much bigger than an outhouse. Here a smoking 44-gallon drum was tended by two men, Kelvin the manager (whose mighty stomach was corsetted by a leather apron) and a stringy little fellow with a battered hat, a shrunken sleeveless pullover, and a knotted rope belt. He sported dusty brickworks boots.

Mrs. Bobs did not pause to ask permission but drove straight to a place where she applied the handbrake vigorously. She was immediately out of the car and jumping to untie ropes she could not reach. If it must be done 'tis best it were done quickly.

I lifted the condemned propeller from its quilt and let Mrs. Bobs steer me to its final resting place: amidst tangled rusted wire, broken terracotta tiles, fresh two-by-four offcuts.

It was done, I thought. I turned my back and coiled my rope and untangled her binder twine and bedding before laying them tidily on the back seat. I had previously thought the tip an optimistic place, one of the great democratic institutions of the Marsh. You did not need to pay for entrance and you could remove anything you liked. On any weekend, you could see four generations of one family, ridding themselves of bottles or grass clippings or the final pram, or pursuing private treasure hunts in the open pit where they might find butter churns, or Laval separators, and other items (Mum, Mum, what's this?) of unknown provenance or purpose. The shire engineer served his fancy guests on a dinner service from the Darley tip. Its origin was no secret. He was as delighted with that prize as with the eight-inch pram wheels which had carried his son to victory in the Soapbox Derby.

I turned and saw she was at it with the hacksaw. Kelvin and his colleague were cooking sausages and seemed to have no interest in what was taking place. I was the witness to Mrs. Bobs' attempt to remove the tip from the propeller. She had chosen a vulnerable spot where the copper sheathing ended.

She had the wrong tool for the job. I could do nothing but watch and swat away the blowflies from my face, and she was halfway through when she gave up the hacksaw. Next she chose a house brick to attack the prop, her neck and cheeks all red in her enthusiasm. As she achieved the murderous separation of one part from the next, I thought how Lavoisier, when his head was separated from the guillotine, is said to have blinked twenty times in signal to his servant. I prayed that was not true.

"You don't know my father-in-law," she said. "Or you wouldn't look at me like that."

I would have been too emotional to speak about Lavoisier so I was not sorry to be interrupted by the Sanitation Disposal Supervisor and his colleague. Kelvin picked up the amputated tip, and for a moment I thought it had been saved, but then he hurled it into the abyss.

When Mrs. Bobbsey returned the hacksaw to the car, I found Kelvin's friend's hostile gaze on me and accepted what I took to be his judgement. I hurried to join my accomplice unaware that he was shadowing me.

"Barkhumper," he said, clearly delighted to see me jump. "You don't know who I am, do you?"

"I don't think I've had the pleasure."

"No pleasure," he said, and I recognised, in those familiar angry eyes, the father of Bennett Ash.

Mrs. Bobs started the engine.

"I know where you live," said Ash, opening the passenger door. "Get in," he said and I could hear the cruel way life had scraped the meat off him and left him with a rope belt and shrunken sweater.

"I'll hang you out the window you fucking Balt."

Mrs. Bobs engaged first gear. I slammed the door. The Ford attacked the puddles violently, sliding over the bulldozed earth and out the gate.

"What was that?" she asked.

I could not really trust my voice to answer.

"Jeez, what a mongrel."

Mrs. Bobbsey drove more thoughtfully than previously. She slowed, then slowed a little more. When she came round by the Darley oval she pulled off the road. "Here," she said. It was a handkerchief.

If she imagined I was crying, I was not, but neither could I look directly at her. Finally I confessed what I had resolved to never mention. "He is a parent just like you," I said. "If he had done what I did he would have gone to jail."

"I suppose he has a hateful son."

"He's just a boy."

I folded the handkerchief carefully and returned it to her. She took my hand and, in a gesture that surprised us both, raised it to her lips.

# 7

ONCE I KISSED old Father Slocomb on the top of his bald head.

Another time I kissed a telegram boy because I got proposed to. Nothing came of that. I kissed an iceman. I also rode from Geelong to Barwon Heads inside the spare wheel of a Model T and got roared up. I might have fallen off and died, but then they told the story whenever we had visitors. When Dad was a stock and station agent we were often at Kippenross which was owned by the Robinsons. During harvest time one year Mrs. Robinson sent me out into the paddock with billy tea and scones for the men. I found them in the middle of a hundred acres of paddock and stooks of wheat were everywhere. It was so hot I crawled into a stook for shade. Dad finally found me sound asleep— some part of my foot was sticking out from a stook. They had searched for me for hours.

My mother was a kisser. She would kiss the top of my head while I said my prayers.

It was not his hand, more his wrist in any case. My lips only brushed the fine blond hairs and I remarked his furrowed knuckles, as if his fingers were frowning too. The hand was slender, very shapely and shadowy in the knuckles and below the nails, but I did not need his confession on the Gisborne Road to feel pity for him. I had seen his pale blue eyes staring out his bedroom window. That was what I had in mind when I kissed his poor sad hand. I meant, you are a good man no matter what you did. I never was permitted to have a horse but I thought he was like a horse with its ears back, locked inside his stall.

Returning from the tip I had a pile of cardboard boxes to unpack and had two children who required their share of love, poor darlings. Edith would be OK, but Ronnie would do it hard. I knew that before

I saw his class dismissed and he came out the front gate wearing short pants and one long sock. How could you lose a sock and keep your shoe?

Edith stood behind him, shaking her head at me.

I asked Ronnie did someone pick on him.

In answer he did a silly dance, in the street, in front of everyone. He looked insane, pointing at his head and then his bottom, sticking out his tongue. You can't afford to care what people think of you, but I took his hand and dragged him home, Edith hurrying behind saying, what are you going to do?

Of course I should have sat down with them both and baked them biscuits and poured glasses of milk, but I had to call my contact at General Motors Holden before Titch got home. If I had been found out I would have got the scarlet letter or the dunce's cap.

You might not imagine a huge company like GMH would know all the men who sold the opposition's cars, but they knew my Titch, by reputation. By "they" I mean Mr. Dunstan. Dunstan said my husband was a "gun," like a gun shearer which is a man who can tally four hundred sheep a day. (The number for merinos is different, of course.) Somehow Mr. Dunstan knew all Titch's sales figures like cricket scores: so many runs in Warragul, so many in Sale. I was gratified, the first time I made contact, to hear Mr. Dunstan wanted Titch "on board." Like me, he believed the future was with the Holden.

He was very straight with me, or so I thought. He did not hide the money issue. If you are to be a dealer you have to have premises, a workshop, mechanics, spare parts inventory. He shared examples of their "floor plan" whereby they would finance our showroom inventory.

Titch had already had a similar conversation with Ford and as a result we had sat around the table filling out forms and collecting bank statements and tax returns. He never doubted we would get the Ford franchise. Who would say no to a salesman with his record?

I was fearful of his confidence, the hurt he would suffer if rejected. It occurred to me that I would improve our balance sheet if I forced Beverly to finally sell our joint inheritance. She had milked it long enough, and I had said this to Titch, but perhaps he thought he should not take money from a woman. In any case, it would have been no fun to deal with Beverly. I had let it drop.

But when I revealed this asset to Mr. Dunstan he became extremely positive. Clearly, he then had the old place valued because on the next call he knew that it was right on Corio Bay with "massive" views. Funny, Corio Bay had always made me melancholy.

I never actually saw Dunstan's office door but he emphasised the fact that it was open. We could get ninety-day terms through GMAC which was GMH's finance company. Ford, meanwhile, were wanting more and more information from us. It was time to bring Dunstan up to date so I got Ronnie listening to his *Superman* serial and Edith had a drawing to do for school and I closed myself in the kitchen.

"Yes?" said the operator.

I told her I had to make a trunk call to Melbourne. It was an HP number. Humbug Point.

"Are you Bacchus Marsh 29?"

I said I was.

"That must be Mrs. Bobs."

I didn't know Miss Hoare yet but every small town has that general type of character, listening in on everybody all day long. I could hear her breathing on the line while the phone rang in Dunstan's office at GMH. Titch would kill me if he knew.

"Hello?" said Dunstan.

Said Miss Hoare, "I have a trunk call for you."

I hung up.

We had scrambled eggs and toast and pea soup, the three of us together.

There was now a functioning gas fire but I did not like to waste it, and I tucked them up in bed and told them stories of the rascally wombat their father had invented. The rascally wombat had a huge bottom which made the children laugh. Was it really big? How big was it? The rascally wombat was always falling asleep in dangerous places. He was always hungry. The rascally wombat woke up one morning and smelled bacon cooking. Or it was Christmas and the rascally wombat sat on the chimney thinking how he would reach the biscuits left out for Santa Claus.

I had not a thought about the kiss. It was the propeller that concerned me. I should not have hurt the propeller. Is that what it is like to be a drunk? Do you wake up and think, dear Jesus, what have I done? What will people think of me? Can I still be loved?

I sat and waited for my husband. It is awful for a woman to wait for a salesman in the night, not knowing where he is. Of course the pubs had shut at six o'clock but there were bars still operating in their version of a wartime blackout. If you were a moth, you wouldn't know. You could drive through Balliang or Myrniong and never guess what illegal activity was going on. And good luck if you needed the police because they were hidden in the pub with everybody else. There were also other things I feared too obvious to mention. I turned on the wireless but could not pay attention. There was a quiz show but who wants to feel more stupid than they already are?

Then Edith came out and announced, "The rascally wombat just wet his bed."

Well, at least it kept me busy, washing the poor little fellow and finding dry sheets for him and reading *The House at Pooh Corner* until his sister stopped complaining and they both fell asleep.

I took the soiled linen to the laundry and rinsed it and put it in the copper. It was nine o'clock, then ten. I put the sheets through the mangle and found some pegs and hung them on the line.

I turned on the neon lights in the shed and went back into the kitchen and sat there looking out. The light flooded over the empty yard and a man on the wireless was doing *Crosby by Request*. I found my overcoat and sat shivering at the kitchen table.

I should never have done that to the propeller. I was asking for it now.

# 8

THERE ARE very sensible reasons why a man might be attracted to women who are inherently unstable. Their faces are more interesting to watch, their eyes so unpredictable. They are always more complex, dynamic, dangerous. Looked at in this way, my personal history had a certain logic.

I lay in bed alone with the pages of *Oceania* No. 3 Mar. 1953 but was distracted from the index (Berndt, Elkin etc.) by thoughts of Cloverdale, my co-contestant on Deasy's quiz show. Mr. Deasy called her Miss Clover.

"Listeners, we are in Clover." The "in" was offensive code which never failed to agitate the dormant ashes of her eyes, but neither she nor I could contest the power of Mr. Deasy who had been, long before his quiz show, a traveller for Rothmans cigarettes. He had us hooked in different ways.

Clover was about my own age, tall and slender as a flooded gum, her unstockinged skin very glossy on long straight legs with just sufficient calf. Sometimes, in the studio, she kicked her shoes off and I was allowed to see her toenails, like sea shells on the beach.

Each week she and I stood at our fluffy big microphones and Deasy suggested to the audience that she was about to "take the crown" or "topple the king." I knew he could not afford to do this. Clover, on the other hand, was like the audience in that she believed I took home thousands every month.

Clover saw me presented with my cheque. She had no idea that I was forced to tear it up, that the big money was bait for a growing audience and finally—touch wood—a national sponsor who could afford real prize money in their advertising budget. For now we advertised a

Christian Israelite car dealer, a chain of cut-price menswear, and a dry cleaning service with stores in seven suburbs. Deasy would fire them all as soon as he was able. He subscribed to the Nielsen rating service and watched as our numbers slowly rose. Meanwhile he spent "seed money" entertaining the advertising managers of Colgate, General Motors, Dunlop, the Dairy Board.

A time would come, he promised, when my ship came in. I was on the "ground floor," meaning, I presumed, the wharf.

"They will not let a woman win it," Clover had said last week when Deasy left to take a leak. "I am only on the show to lose."

We were always "live" one way or another. That is, Baby Deasy never took her headphones off and I could not have asked Clover to the pictures without her rejection being overheard. But even in the most secure environment I would never have dared reveal that I envied Clover her weekly cheque for twenty pounds which would end up as real cash money in her bank account.

"I don't think you're correct," I said.

"You are a nice man, Willie, but what you think about this really doesn't matter."

That may not seem alluring, but her true response was all voice, pure voice. Her face hardly moved at all. Why was this immobility so seductive?

"It is how the public wants it," she said to me, speaking, as usual like she was very tired, had been up all night reading Spinoza.

"Let me win one round," she pleaded. "It would change my life."

It would not change her life at all but she was immensely attractive, a little beatniky with a short and shaggy haircut, waves, soft curls, like Gina Lollobrigida in *Beauties of the Night*. The Problems of Desire, Volume XXI.

"If you really liked me," she said, "you would let me win a round."

I desired her, immensely. She was so slim she could move her skirt from back to front and back again. She sometimes did that in triumph, a sort of taunt and flourish you could only do on radio, in public and in secret both. Five points to Miss Clover. *And away she goes.*

"If you win the next round," I asked, "will you come out dancing with me?"

"If I win the next round I will do all sorts of things."

Baby Deasy might have heard this. I would find out soon enough. Now, lying in my bed with *Oceania,* I summoned up a vision of that alluring mouth. "I will do all sorts of things," she promised.

Who would be a bachelor? I thought. Headlights washed my bedroom ceiling and I saw a moth and heard the throaty engine of a powerful car. It passed slowly then throbbed and bobbled inside the shed where it was permitted to continue.

The night was cut by a woman's anguished cry.

Then, forgive me, I was a Peeping Tom in my dark kitchen and the hairs on my arms and neck were now electrified. The yard next door was washed with neon lights. The air was green like grass. And there, in the centre of the shed was what I would later learn was a Jaguar XK120: long, and slender, pearly white, with bulging mudguards capped by corner indicator lamps melding into headlamps and a long hood. It was so beautiful it might have come from outer space. The pilot then emerged in full view and I thought he must be freezing having driven with the hood down. Clearly he had worn his camelhair coat and yellow scarf, but that would be insufficient on the Pentland Hills. As to whether the car was sold or unsold, the question did not even enter my head. The nature of my thought was dictated by the curdled scream.

Mrs. Bobbsey came inside the shed as onto a bright stage, rushing, arms flailing, her dressing gown like a comet tail behind.

Good grief. She was striking him. On the head. On the chest. He was attempting to hold her wrists.

MYOB. Yes, mind my own business I thought, and was relieved when Mr. Bobbsey reached a switch and the stage was dark.

"You great moron," she cried. They could have heard her down in the sale yards, as far as the Catholic church, across the road at State School No. 28.

I retreated into *Oceania* No. 3 Mar. 1953. There I found a proposed survey of the archaeological structure of Melton East, just ten miles from Bacchus Marsh.

An owl cried mopoke.

I might have expected *archaeology* in Greece or Mesopotamia, never in the paddocks of dreary Melton. But here it was suggested that an investigation of the common or garden Kororoit Creek (which I would cross tomorrow on the train) would unearth "relics of the indigenous population in abundance." Thus an educated man, a schoolteacher, was surprised.

I returned to the kitchen for a glass of milk. There I accidentally saw the very natty Mr. Bobbsey, an actor in the back door spotlight, entering his house to lie with his wife.

Reading was my analgesic.

In *Oceania* I discovered the archaeologist proposing to excavate those famous properties Rockbank and Deanside which had once been the massive grazing lands of W.J.T. Clarke the richest man in Australia. On Clarke's Melton lands twenty thousand sheep had been shorn in a single year. Nearby, behind the present gunpowder factories, *Oceania* predicted evidence of ancient Aboriginal burials, artifacts, middens, scarred grey-box trees from which the indigenous peoples had cut canoes and shields.

"Idiot," I heard.

I sat up in my single bed and saw, through no fault of my own, the Bobbseys at their kitchen window, locked in combat it appeared. Then it was dark. Then the Bobbseys' screen door slammed and I saw what I took to be the female riding piggyback, laughing, or crying as she slapped her husband's head. This was not at all erotic, but there was sufficient light to see them on the lawn, stumbling, upright. Then they were racing round inside a bright parallelogram of garage light and now the male was hooting, mocking, fool, fool, fool and the female was laughing without a doubt. *Oceania* could not compete.

From the next door house there arose cries of unmistakable distress and then that screen door slammed again and then again and the two children ran into the light, the boy in front, the girl behind, white nightgown trailing like El Greco, weeping and begging, seeking their parents who soon collapsed onto the moony grass under the weight of their children's need and I, in the night air, in pyjamas and bedsocks, was unreasonably afraid.

What was said I did not hear. What was understood I could not guess. Now the father was piggybacking the tall fair haired girl whose feet almost touched the ground, and the little boy was riding monkey-high on his mother's shoulders and I was alarmed until it occurred to me that perhaps the Bobbseys were happy.

"You fool," cried Irene Bobs.

And kissed her husband's hand and mouth.

The children shrieked with laughter and entered the concrete-floored shrine in slippered feet. Titch took one high garage door and his wife the other and together they slowly blocked out the brilliant light.

All night I read. It calmed me down. I was still at it when the dunny man walked past my window to collect his weekly "honey bucket."

I slept and was back in my father's church in Adelaide. My mother was in great distress as the police had found strange wiring underneath the pews.

I woke to hear the sports car burble up the drive, see Mrs. Bobbsey capering beside it in her dressing gown.

The rooster was waiting with his girls at the back door. I made an egg sandwich for the train.

# 9

DEAR TITCHY WAS HONEST, although his truth was driven by his plentiful emotions, and his explanations of his actions could be a bit approximate, as in the case of his purchase of a Jaguar XK120.

He attested that he had first seen the Jaguar parked in Lydiard Street outside the Ballarat train station. He said he just "stumbled" upon it. Fair enough. But he refused to admit that an XK120 meant anything to him at all. In this he was like a husband admitting he had been staring at a woman's legs but insisting that it had not been with any special interest.

My husband had walked right past the world's fastest production car?

Excuse me, no. He had gawked with all the others. And his curly little Titchy mind would have thought the following: what bastard child of Ballarat has imported an XK120 and parked it here, to be drooled over by unlicensed drivers, drapers' clerks and butchers' boys? The Jag was a thing to die for. It had been abandoned naked, unprotected, with its hood down, so any apprentice plumber could touch the red leather upholstery and open the walnut glove box and see what was inside. Of course my husband wanted it, like he wanted a Ford dealership, whether that was wise or even possible. Who would not want him to have everything his heart desired? Who was presently engaged in persuading her sister that their shared inheritance must now be sold so Titch could be a dealer?

Clearly Joe Thacker had laid the Jag out like bait so Titch would walk past it on the way from the train to Craig's Hotel. That's what I said, to excuse him for doing such a stupid thing.

But no, oh no. My husband was *offended* by my excuses. And if I thought he was Whacker Thacker's victim, he said, I had no idea of who or what he was.

Fair enough. I had only been in Craig's the one time, in the saloon, not the public bar where women were forbidden so the men could swear and talk filth with no impediment. There I had met the famous Whacker Thacker, he with the peeled potato chin and grubby overcoat. He said he would put me in his coat pocket, the dirty flirt. He said he mistook Titch and me for Babes in Toyland and perhaps we looked like that to him. But compared to those muddy spud farmers and race-course touts we shone like clever jockeys on our way to win the cup.

This was the dirty water in which Titch had been taught to swim, the stale sour air he had fed on as a child. In this poison lake Joe Thacker waited for him.

Thacker was a hard man with large and handy fists. Titch was the most successful Ford salesman in rural Victoria. He made his way across the filthy carpet towards Joe Thacker's distant corner. Titch was gimlet-eyed, focused, pink cheeked and brilliantined with dainty shoes. We had both agreed that he would buy a Ford Customline from that big crook in the corner.

Thacker's drinking companion would turn out to be a bookmaker but he had the look, Titch said, of someone rich enough to employ others to do the bashing for him. He was larger than Thacker and he leaned on the bar with his stomach pushed against his waistcoat and a proper gold chain to keep his watch in place. He wore a silky grey tie and a white shirt a little looser than his neck demanded.

He, Mr. Green, was a hand crusher.

Joe was drinking his beer mixed with tomato juice for unknown reasons. He announced that he had three units for the visitor to choose from, all Ford Customlines, all parked around the block. One of them was two-tone. We wouldn't take a two-tone, Titch said. While discussing this aspect of the business, Titch felt himself to be the subject of the bookmaker's impolite examination.

"You're Bobs, that right? They call you Titch?"

This Mr. Green had a big head, thinning hair, rude red mouth. He lifted an eyebrow so tidy you could imagine his barber spent an hour preparing him.

"You're the son of the famous Dangerous Dan? You are the little whizzer who won my court case against your father."

Even I knew exactly what disgrace he was referring to. I appreciated how painful this was still, and if you want my view on it I can say that it had been typical of Dan to blame a boy for something not his fault. Even rude Green understood the situation had been ridiculous. They had asked a boy to be a witness for the defence and had not explained that he was required to lie.

Many years ago Dan had undertaken to fly this same Mr. Green to the races at Ballarat. I had heard the story many times. Titch had been at the airfield at Humbug Point when he saw Green climb into the Maurice Farman. It was this passenger's size that made the event so memorable, the huge tailored gut and big red lips, sixteen stone if he was anything. Titch watched the plane struggle to clear the fence at the end of the airstrip. A less desperate pilot would have turned back but Dan now had the money in his pocket and nothing would make him give it up.

Airman and bookmaker laboured on through drizzling rain and unexpected cold. Slowly they ascended through the altitude which separates the steeples of Melbourne from those of Ballarat. They gained two thousand feet but arrived no higher than the rooftops. Of course the bookie missed the race. He was two hours late.

Green then sued Dan for loss of income.

In the court Dan's barrister called Titch to the witness stand and said to him: "So your father could not have expected this difficulty?"

But of course, Titch said, he must have expected it. The minute he saw the passenger, the size of him.

"You told the truth," Green said and was still incredulous, years later in Craig's Hotel, that anyone would do such a thing.

The distinctive smell of the Alfredton sale yards entered the conversation. That is, Joe Thacker was shuffling his feet. Who could have predicted that this same feral creature would end his life a rich man with a huge house on Lake Wendouree and a Bentley and all the paintings that had once hung in Reid's Coffee Palace? (Who could imagine Green would die of shotgun wounds?)

"Which brings me to my point," said Joe. "Which is why I wanted Titch to meet you, Mr. Green."

Titch said he was here solely to look over these Customlines. That is, he was a Ford man, there to buy a Ford. He thought, why is Joe winking at me?

"Mr. Green," said Joe, "has a vehicle he needs to sell today."

Titch had a list of prospects in his pocket. His aim was to make a sale by bedtime. He repeated that he was only interested in a low mileage Ford Customline.

Mr. Green was laughing at the thought of such a thing. Titch did not connect him to the Jaguar. Green was checking his Windsor knot and buttoning and rebuttoning his posh suit. He was very pleased with who he was.

"But this is not a Customline you have?" Titch insisted.

Green confirmed that was correct.

"I'm a Ford bloke," Titch said.

"You seemed to have walked straight past your opportunity," said Green.

"Suit yourself."

"I will."

"No, no, you don't get it," cried Joe Thacker. "He's Titch. He's your only hope."

"That's your XK120?" Titch asked.

And of course it was.

I know my husband. I know what he was thinking. He didn't have authority to *buy* the Jaguar. He was only going to *drive* it. It was all desire. He could never ever sell this vehicle in the Marsh.

Joe was of the "go on" school of car salesman. *Go on, give it a spin. Go on, sit behind the wheel.* "Go on, mate, you can do it." With which he tossed a heavy brass key onto the bar. Titch did not touch it. You would never know, to look at him, how his heart was racing.

"Give me a number," he said to Green and the bookmaker's chin jutted as he felt the hook.

Green said, you know the book price Mr. Bobs, but Titch was already in that zone where he was unaware that these men were twelve inches taller. And he was only approximately aware of the book price. And it was thrilling for him not to even care.

"You want cash today, Mr. Green, then the number has to be realistic."

Green said he would take eight hundred but he was not smiling any more.

Titch could get very careless about numbers when they involved something like cashflow and capital for a dealership, but he was a calculating machine for this sort of thing. He did not know the exact number but he knew there were very few XK120s in all Australia. So if he could get this for seven hundred he could make three times the profit of a single Ford Customline. Of course, he was in love beyond his class, but even in the middle of this giddy fit, the arithmetic was simple.

"You going to float me?" he asked Joe Thacker.

"How much cash you got on you, Titch?"

He hadn't even driven the XK120, but he had the hundred and fifty quid I had given him and he staked it all. Joe offered to float him another five hundred and fifty, until tomorrow night. If the Jag was not sold by then, Titch could return the car and pay interest on the loan. They discussed percentages and did sums on a cigarette paper.

This was gambling which we had agreed we should never do.

It was not gambling, Titch insisted later. He had seen, in his mind's eye, in the midst of the negotiation, the prospect for this car i.e. Halloran the builder, who he could find, late any afternoon, in Dolan's Ballan Hotel sitting in the ladies' lounge with the licensee, Mrs. Maureen Haggerty. Halloran was a ladies' man and was driving a Citroën Light 15, a lovely piece of engineering, but without the show-off value of the Jag.

"How could you know this?" I wailed at him that night.

"It's a gift," he said. "I was born with it."

On another day that might be true. This time it would be a disaster. He would arrive late in Ballan. He would park the XK with its hood down, against the transformer shed which, no matter what an ugly lump it was, provided a flattering light. Showroom quality, he thought.

He would turn out to be wrong, so wrong, but I wasn't at Craig's Hotel to save us. My husband was enjoying himself. He saw how Thacker and Green were looking at him. He mistook their greed for admiration. They also misunderstood him, and I could have told them had I been allowed. The point was that he, Titch Bobs, resident of Bacchus Marsh, Victoria, would take the leaping cat roaring down the Pentland Hills, holding onto the suicide bends "like shit on a blanket" as he sometimes said. This was Titch's only fault, the belief he could have anything he wished. This is how birds fly into window glass, how women fall pregnant. There is no sense to it, only wanting what you are not allowed to have.

# 10

AS I PASSED the high school, my headmaster popped out like a cuckoo, waving, running between his roses, out into the path of coal trucks.

I thought, he will fire me now. I said, "What is happening with the tribunal?"

He was out of breath, his high forehead beaded with moisture like a refrigerated melon. "Have you written my syllabus?"

"I'm going to the city."

"You could almost write it on the train," he said. "One hour each way. Easy peasy."

Did he already know my fate? Was he sucking my blood before I got the chop? This made a certain sense except that he would never touch the sort of syllabus he could expect from me. This I pointed out.

"*You* will teach it obviously," he said.

And so I dared feel hope. I asked the date of the tribunal.

"Willie, trust me," he said and I thought, no, he is a scoundrel. "They will write to you in due course," he said. "Just look after the syllabus for me and I'll look after you."

"How can they send me a letter? I don't even have a letterbox."

Huthnance raised his pale ginger eyebrows and yes, of course, I was speaking nonsense. The postman would throw the envelope on the verandah together with the other threats where it would grow old and wrinkled amongst the windblown leaves.

"Do I have your promise you will write my syllabus?"

I could hear the train already at the Rowsley cemetery. I gave him my word as I jumped back on the bike.

Aboard the train I thought, why did I promise? I was such a pastor's son that I was already keeping my word, thinking about the merino sheep, wondering if the first Australian flock had been stolen from the king of Spain. No, as it turned out, but that would have been the basis for an interesting syllabus.

The ever shifting recording times of the quiz show (an accommodation that would cease being offered once Deasy had his national advertiser) took me to the city at different hours, but no matter the time, the light, the weather, the brown droughty summer, the damp green winter, the landscape beside the railway line was always dreary and denuded: rabbit burrows, erosion, L-shaped plantations of hard conifer windbreaks in the corners of the lonely paddocks, yellow gravel roads cutting through the red soil, dun coloured sheep country eventually giving way to the banal outer suburbs of western Melbourne.

The cover of *Oceania* No. 3, as I recall, was reliably unexciting, with no hint of its explosive nature. When I began to study the proposed survey of the archaeological structure of Melton East I had no foreknowledge, but I would soon see that same landscape outside the window for what it had always been: a forgotten colonial battleground, the blood-soaked site of a violent *"contact"* between the indigenous blacks and the imperial whites. If it was not a state secret, it might as well have been.

One hundred and twenty-one years ago, before the sheep arrived, before the factories, these volcanic plains—I learned it only now—had been covered with "luxuriant herbage" and "waving purplish-brown kangaroo grass," "shoulder high and thick as oats." The black skinned hunter-gatherers were unaware that the whites planned to stay for ever. None amongst them could credit that a human being might "own" an animal, particularly one as tasty as a sheep. Or that the sheep would eat everything that attracted the kangaroo and wallaby. And so on.

Very well, I thought, I will give you a bloody syllabus on the wool industry. It will be a pleasure to keep my word.

The hunter-gatherers killed the white men's sheep and ate them. What a treat for the education department of Victoria.

Bennett Ash, pay attention.

And here, just off the railway line, near the Massey Harris tractor works, the Darling flour silos, the dusty stone crushers and that threatening cluster of explosives factories, a cycle of murders had begun.

Deer Park, they called this place.

Sir, sir, I've been there, sir.

Yes, the Deer Park Hotel. Where are the deer?

I don't know, sir.

There were never any deer. Deer was a pretty synonym for murder. The Deer Park Hotel was now a "watering hole" for travelling salesmen, on the bank of the Kororoit Creek.

My planned class excursion would follow the creek behind the gunpowder factory and here inspect (Fig. I) the grey-box tree with footholds cut into its trunk. The young PhD suggested the steps might have been used for gathering honey. Where is the honey now?

The wool class could study archaeology, not only Fig. I but also Fig. III, the nearby red gum, whose high scar marked the shape of a canoe. With his warty fingers Bennett Ash could learn what wool had wrought.

As the train passed the Sunshine station I must have appeared both dull and diligent. I took pencil and paper and made a grid of thirteen squares, each one a history period of one hour and ten minutes. Who would guess that I was no more stable than a blowfly bouncing off the glass? Shall I blame Miss Clover?

It was Clover's unrealistic ambition to use Deasy's cheque to go to Florence, to spend three hours of every day at the Uffizi or the Pitti Palace. Unrealistic? But do not men fly through the sky and drive cars at one hundred and thirty miles an hour? Might a woman do that too? Might not Deasy get his sponsor, finally? Was it possible that, any day now, I might be permitted to bank my cheque? Would Clover come with me to Italy to start a life? In any case, there was Clover and there was the Pitti Palace as I wheeled my bicycle into the tea room of radio 3UZ.

I found her already in the studio, face framed by black turtleneck and curling Fellini hair. In Vermeer there would have been a window to bring out the light in her eyes. She narrowed hers, and her mouth moved a millimetre at the edges and I would have given her everything she asked.

I also thought, you are a total moron. You are inventing her completely. That is what you always do.

Just the same, I felt completely comfortable as she beheld me. I experienced a buzzy feeling, like a comb run through my hair.

I asked her what she was reading and she asked me the same and I told her about *Oceania* but all the time I was thinking, is this the day when I finally leap? I had no idea what I would do.

Deasy and Baby Deasy were in the control room. So what if they heard me say what I must? Would I die? I said, "Perhaps it is time for you and I to go dancing."

Clover's eyes gave off a light and energy which can be rationally understood as the reflection of the spotlight in the booth. She nodded at Deasy who had his questions stacked on yellow cards. She watched him shuffle as he was wont to do. He left the control room. Clover smiled at me and I thought I could look at that face for ever, in the Uffizi, or in the Pitti or George the Greek's in Bacchus Marsh. Deasy entered crying, "Up and away." He required no rejoinder. This up-and-away was his trade name, his call sign, his very self and when he placed his questions face down on the green felt table, he was here to work. In response to a signal from his heavily ringed finger, Baby Deasy began the prerecord.

Deasy cued his theme song and introduced himself and, for the eighth week in a row, made a big business about Miss Clover, who would, this time, perhaps, topple the king. For the moment this was cruel, but who knew what might happen next?

"Make it or break it," he cried. "Ladies first."

He flashed his cuffs and chose a card at "random," and I would never know if the question was by chance or not. He was duplicitous, of course, yet he always relied on me to know the answer and there had never been skulduggery of the expected sort.

"The first question is for Clover, for the challenger: who designed the first circular saw?"

Immediately she acted "thinking" which—she never seemed to quite get this—had no sound at all. Deasy told the listeners she was frowning "like a bloodhound" although her forehead was as smooth as marble. He held a noisy kitchen timer against his microphone. "The first . . . circular saw." He spoke in the same "intimate" voice he used on *Crosby by Request*. Then he began the countdown and Clover, without any warning, collapsed her shoulders and drew her finger across her Botticelli neck.

But of course she knew, I thought. She must. The circular saw had been designed by a *woman*. You could rely on her to know a thing like that and it was unforgivable, in this particular instance, that I should beat her to it. I would not be let off. I was my own worst enemy but I was also the show pony and I released the first answer in stages, in the way I had been coached.

"Designed by a Shaker," I said.

"Good grief," cried Deasy.

"A woman."

"And off he goes."

My opponent's eyes were now bright with emotion. She was nodding at me, smiling, encouraging. But what would that mean when the show was over? She had no idea how I wished to lose.

What Deasy understood I did not know. He slapped his head. *"Gee-up!"* he cried.

I cared only about Clover now. What was happening behind that furry microphone? I couldn't tell.

Deasy was frustrated with me, without a doubt. "Up up and away," he cried.

He asked a question about carbon paper. I looked to Clover who seemed to nod. Carbon paper had been created to help blind people write.

"Off he goes."

But I did not wish to be the winner.

"Why so glum oh genius?"

When the show was over I got my fake cheque and Clover received her real one and asked to use the lav.

I was slow to understand I could not invite her to a picture show today. She had left the key in the lavatory door and run down the stairs to the street. Then I, of course, was required to have sandwiches at the Windsor with Mr. Deasy who, in a strange fit, had once kissed me on the mouth.

We were both subdued. Mr. Deasy refrained from his usual reports, but I inferred Coca-Cola had stopped nibbling and become a "bait robber." Even when he revealed his eldest son had won preselection for a seat in parliament he remained forlorn.

I bolted my second egg sandwich of the day, and was back on the crowded train at 4:58 p.m., arriving in the Marsh at the so-called Wobbly Hour.

# 11

THE WOBBLY HOUR BEGAN at exactly six p.m. after which it was an offence for a pub to serve a single glass of beer. The parliamentary intention of that law had been to force the drinkers home to dinner and the bosom of their families. The accidental consequence was the "six o'clock swill," in which all those frothing glasses, purchased when still legal, were set in line and consumed, one after the other, in what was known as the "period of grace." *For sin will have no dominion over you, since you are not under law but under grace.*

When the period of grace expired, then began the Wobbly Hour. Thus Bennett Ash might explain to me, I couldn't do it sir, my dad had his wobbly boots on.

At the Wobbly Hour I cycled home through the dark streets. The fallen leaves were in piles and burning and the spitting rain produced sad odours of wet coal-dust and ash and mould. Dangerous headlights burned my back as I hunched against the drizzle. I passed over the bridge on the Werribee River, past the cold discoloured swimming pool with my mind flicking through the pages of *Oceania*.

Excepting some engravings and that postage stamp portraying One Pound Jimmy, I had never seen an Aboriginal. They were all far away in dusty history, or in hot places where they threw stones at passing cars. But if they had once dwelled on the Kororoit Creek, they had also been here on the Werribee, just there, behind the changing sheds below that empty chlorine swimming pool. They had walked where I was cycling now when Jesus hung upon the cross.

By Eric Redrop's isolated barber shop, I escaped the front bumper of a speeding truck, then pedalled illegally on the footpath as far as Simon's corner where a streetlight revealed a solitary boy, or so I imagined, sheltering beneath the butcher shop verandah. Was this one more teatime victim of the wobbly boot?

"Mr. Bachhuber."

Bless me, it was Mr. Bobs. I crossed the main street as a semitrailer descended on me, air brakes farting, gears changing, hurtling down Stamford Hill. As I reached safety, the high beam headlights revealed the Bobbsey with his brilliantined hair swept upwards in a comic book of shock. What on earth had happened to him?

"I am a man without a car," he cried.

"Then we are both in the same predicament." I spoke lightly, but I smelled the booze on him and thought, dear goodness, it is Icarus, crashed into the sea.

"It was impossible, Mr. Bachhuber. So the experts said."

"Hop on." I pointed the front wheel towards him, thereby indicating I could give him a ride home. Too late I saw he was attached to a hessian bag which he lifted with him as he sprang onto the bar. He almost tipped us into the gutter.

"Hold steady Mr. Bobs."

He could not have been a heavy man, but whatever he carried in his sack made him difficult to balance. I set off just the same.

"In the land of potato farmers, you can never sell an XK Jag." He turned his head to address me directly. "But ask me, where is the Jag?"

He was an adult, the father of children. It would be rude to instruct him to sit still.

"Ask me, is it up my sleeve? No. But there must be a trade-in. Where have I parked the trade-in?"

"Steady there, Mr. Bobs. There's a car behind us."

"No trade-in," he cried. "But that's impossible."

I could hear tyres hissing, windscreen wipers slapping. Then, as the car drew alongside, he kicked a leg at it. "But do you see a trade-in here? If you can find it, that's where I'd lose money on the deal."

We were opposite the shire chambers, by the crowded footpath outside the Royal Hotel. I lurched left, wobbled into Young Street, got safely to Bennett Street where he held his chaff bag high.

"I have done what cannot be done," he said, perhaps intending to make a magician's gesture, although the consequence was that the Malvern Star hit a deep concrete drain and we all flew, flesh and steel, landing hard, tangled up together.

Drain-water filled my shoes. I did not yet know that I had torn my new Fletcher Jones trousers but I could feel I had grazed my shin and palm. My neighbour crawled further along the drain, dragging his chaff bag behind him. There he sat, cross-legged beneath a streetlight, as blood descended from his brilliantine.

"Come on," I said. "I'll get you home."

"No home," he said. "You listen. First I thought I would sell it to Halloran. That was last night."

He would not budge no matter what I did. Finally we sat together, cross-legged in the drain. The rain continued. I learned that Halloran had been a perfect *prospect*, in every way, possessing not only income but a well-known passion for the latest vehicle. However the show-off builder was over six foot tall with the result that, once he had squeezed himself into the driver's seat, his "big boof-head" poked up above the windscreen.

His mates all barracked him unmercifully from the dark doorway of the pub.

"Pull in your head," they called. And: "Pull in your elbow."

But neither head nor elbow could be pulled inside the car and the prospect's knees pressed up under the dash and rubbed against the steering wheel. ("I'm not a bloody contortionist," he said.) He could not easily operate the clutch but he was, at the same time, a keen reader of *Wheels* and *Modern Motor* and could not deny himself the chance to unleash that legendary engine on the road. Alas, when truly tested, he lacked the ear and sensitivity to drive without synchromesh and his fellow drinkers cheered each time he crashed the gears. It was no deal, no sale, no luck and Bobs had to go home to the missus with a vehicle he could not easily explain.

"That was last night," he said. "I crashed and burned."

Stupidly I asked him to explain. So he continued with the story of his day until even I lost patience and got him propped against the sale yard fence. I gave him my hanky for the blood.

Then he was busy collecting the spilled contents of his chaff bag. "Pine cones," he explained. "Nothing like them to light a fire."

I straightened up the front wheel and together we set off, both drenched to the skin, me walking the bicycle, him dragging the pine cones behind.

Mrs. Bobs must have heard the gate. She met us red-eyed, weeping in her housecoat. The children were in great distress, the little boy howling in anguish, the pale daughter comforting her mother who seemed to believe, against all evidence, that she was now the mother of two orphans.

My presence did not staunch the widow's grief. She compelled her husband into a kitchen chair.

"Impossible," he said.

"Yes." She bathed his wound and anointed him with red salves and yellow tinctures, and kneeled beside him. "My darling little Titch, what have they done? What has happened to the vehicle?"

Only then did she see the bag which she kicked at with her little slippered foot. "What is this?"

"Pine cones," he said. "For the fire. If I can do this I can do anything."

"We have a gas fire," she said.

I sensed the necessity to flee a private scene but I was conscripted by the boy who rolled up his pyjama pants so I could apply to him his father's salve or sacrament.

The girl made tea.

The salesman's hair was now moulded flat upon his perfect head. His forehead and brow were painted red and yellow. He sat suddenly on the linoleum floor and pulled his snotty little son into his lap and wiped his face. The boy wanted the pine cones but his father removed a fat white envelope from inside his jacket.

"Get your sister to help you count it."

I remained at the table between the boy and girl as they counted out the largest amount of cash I had ever seen. Ten-pound notes, huge fivers, on the kitchen table.

"I could never sell it," said Titch, still on the floor. "Impossible."

Mrs. Bobbsey kneeled close by Mr. Bobbsey, alternately dabbing his head and kissing his hand.

"I thought you'd killed yourself in that horrid thing."

"What did I say I would do? This morning?"

"You said you'd take it back and pay the interest. Then you would chat to Ford about our franchise."

"And what did I do instead?"

"You made a brilliant deal, of course."

"Is this a deal?" the boy asked and although he continued to repeat his question, no-one answered him.

"But who?" his wife said. "Not Halloran, so who?"

In spite of his family's obvious adoration, the returning hero was, I slowly realised, reluctant to say who had provided these banknotes now stacked in three piles according to denomination.

Mrs. Bobbsey pushed his shoulder. "Who?"

"Can I have a cup of tea?"

"Was it Mrs. Markus?"

"Cuppa first."

But Mrs. Bobbsey's face had hardened. "What would she want with a car like that? Can she even drive it?"

Her husband shrugged.

"I suppose she wants driving lessons again."

"She has a licence."

"She had a licence last time."

"Irene," he pleaded.

"Were you drinking up there? With her? At Mount Egerton? Pine cones," she cried. "We have a gas fire."

"I'm a salesman."

"You left the car with her? What about the registration and insurance? She didn't drive you back to the Marsh?"

Something had happened. Everything had changed. Suddenly the children were to get to bed. Missus ushered them away, closed the door behind her, then opened it again.

"You bastard," she said. "She gave you pine cones for the fire? You were meant to be on the phone to Ford."

MYOB, I thought.

# 12

THE ARRIVAL OF the Bobbseys had placed a greater stress on both my normal and abnormal customs. For instance, no knock or thump would have previously persuaded me to show myself to any bailiffs lurking on my front verandah. Now I was drawn out of hiding by the Bobbsey boy playing with his wooden truck.

"Bobby," I cried.

He jumped off the verandah and considered if he would run out the gate. I pushed myself into full view and stood with dried hydrangea petals on my trousers.

"It is a race," he said at last.

"Who with?"

"A hundred trucks." He frowned. "Roundy bout that chair. I'm Ronnie."

"Can I play?"

He thought that might be possible, so I crawled around my verandah and soiled the knees of my second-best trousers.

A few days later I heard an extremely light, rather scratchy signal on my door. Clearly not a bailiff. More likely a boy with a truck to race. When I saw the mail pushed beneath my door, I smiled.

As I reached, the weathered envelope was snatched away. Ronnie was fishing for me, as if I were a yabby who could be drawn from his creek with lamb fat tied to a piece of string. Little bugger, I thought. And waited for the envelope to reappear and then I grabbed it.

"Got you," I cried, flinging open the door.

Dear Lord. There was Miss Cloverdale, her bare knees on that day's copy of the Melbourne *Sun*.

It was completely and totally inconceivable that she would ever be in this place. She should be forty miles away, teaching history at the Methodist Ladies' College. But now she saw me in these wretched slippers, in this house, in this street.

"Don't you pick up your mail?" The *Sun*'s front page showed a mushroom cloud. A-BOMB TEST AT WOOMERA. These were the catastrophic tests at Maralinga but I could not have been less interested. The top of my spine buzzed with excitement.

Then she, Clover, was inside my hall, then in my front room, selecting books like a customer in auction rooms. Her calves shone in the sombre light.

"So," she said. Her eyes were wild and sooty. "What is it you want of me?" she demanded. She had picked up my copy of Maurice Busset's *En Avion Vols et Combats,* and seemed to examine the frontispiece before laying it aside.

She chose another volume and dropped that too and I saw she was inexplicably angry, or possibly frightened. There was an intimate ferocity completely new to us.

"What about all this bloody dancing?"

"You ran away," I said.

"I waited."

"No."

"Yes, you came rushing out of the Windsor and looked straight at me. Then you pretended not to see me."

"For God's sake, it was dark."

She laid her cool hand on my cheek then withdrew it instantly. She returned her attention to my books. I saw my front room was a rat's nest and the floor was none too clean.

In this poor place I had dreamed of holding her slender body, had imagined her skirt slipping like a petal to my familiar floor. I had imagined saying "I love you" and here she was and I was no longer sure that I loved her, and I felt, not the intimacy of a beloved, but the shell of otherness. She moved from table to shelf, discarding the *Sun* and its mushroom cloud, examining my books, perhaps imagining their lonely owner with holes in his socks, at street stalls and auction houses, understanding that I was not who she had expected but a pathetic hoarder facing the abyss of an empty life.

"You should have a bookshop."

"Maybe I will."

"This one is from the State Library of Victoria."

Indeed. It had been a "gift" from the map librarian.

"Are you a thief then?" She removed her shoes as she so often did in the studio and I was shocked to see those gorgeous perfect feet touch my dirty floor.

"I really didn't see you outside the Windsor. I thought you had run away."

"Show me the house," she decided, and carried her shoes down the hallway.

"Don't go into the kitchen."

Of course she walked directly to the kitchen where the lino was as sticky as flypaper.

"Sugar," I explained.

And she was separating her perfect feet from my adhesive floor, making and breaking contact and looking out across my little garden.

"You should clip their wings."

I had a chipped enamel basin in which I was accustomed to washing the dirt off my potatoes and I now filled this with warm water from the tap. I shuffled around the borders of the sugar spill, placed the bowl on the table and brought a towel and bar of soap.

"Oh Willie," she said, and her upper lip looked slightly swollen. "Are you going to give me a bath?"

She was laughing at me, and I was so full of blood I could hardly see her. She sat on my least damaged kitchen chair. I boldly placed the bowl of water by her feet and she peered down curiously. When she handed me the soap I could not understand her eyes but they did not seem inclined to look away, not even as she placed her bare feet in the water.

I wished it had been new soap, not worn and old like this. I kneeled. I lifted her left foot. She permitted me this intimacy. I washed her pink soles and the soft shadows between her toes. I soaped her round slim heel and then her calf and when I finally looked up I found her thoughtful eyes. She reached to touch my cheek and then I stood and then she stood and I took her dry hand in my wet one and found myself not exactly present in the world.

"Can you see me, Willie?"

I led her back into the hallway.

"Are we dancing?"

"The floor is cleaner back here."

She showed nothing but curiosity about where I led her, to my unmade boy's bed, two foot six inches wide, books nestled in amongst the sheets.

"Read to me," she said, and there were practical reasons I was relieved, and I found the Persian poet and we lay together on my rumpled sheets and she rested her head upon my chest and I stroked her hair with my left hand while I held the slightly puffy water-damaged volume with my right. It was twelve ghazals by the Persian poet Hafiz.

I read and she kissed me on the cheek and my body arched in frank desire.

"Go on," she said.

I did.

> If I go after her, she stirs up a fuss.
> And if I hang back, she rises in wrath.
>
> And if, in desire, for a moment on the road,
> I fall as dust at her feet, she flees like the wind.
>
> And if I seek out but half a kiss, a hundred evasions
> pour out like sugar from the pearl case of her mouth.

"Sugar," she said. Then Hafiz was done, and I must read Neruda, then Christina Rossetti, then e e cummings, then Walt Whitman, then John Donne, then William Shakespeare and we rose to eat buttered toast until there was no more butter and it was getting dark. Our stomachs were rumbling. I left to feed the chooks and returned with eggs but she had grown up on a poultry farm and could not bear the taste of them. At dusk we walked down Gell Street in secret, past the hunch-back's bright fish and chip shop, thence into the main street. I had not pushed myself on her but I was a man and therefore overflowing with calculation and I had hoped against hope that Frank Benallack had not closed the door of his chemist shop. Too late. We walked slowly along the main street without touching. Clover folded her arms across her breasts and recalled certain stories to do with Giotto. We were thrilled to discover we were both admirers of the intemperate autobiography of Benvenuto Cellini. Outside the courthouse, her elbow bumped my arm. She was wonderfully infuriated that Vasari had so patronised Uccello.

It was now dark but the blacksmith was still working. The chime of his hammer was always, to my ears, the equal of the songs of mag-pies, the wrens and butcherbirds that gave the town its deceptive sense of peace. A single car travelled slowly past us. The second chemist shop was closed. It would have tested me in any case, to ask for what I wanted from people who knew me as a bachelor. After the chemist was the cruel dentist and after the dentist was Mrs. Hallowell's lolly shop, then Simon's garage with its forest of petrol pumps, all different species, some with glass reservoirs and hand pumps, Neptune, Caltex, Golden Fleece, Plume, Ampol, sad and faded, corner property for rent or sale.

On the opposite corner was the old Merrimu Cafe, known as The Greek's but owned by Ben Calvo, a Jew who had survived the homicidal German army in Salonika. Ben's haircut, courtesy of Eric Redrop, did no favours to his ears, and made no attempt to hide the deep creases up his neck and skull. As we entered the cafe it was clear he had seen us coming. His smile had taken possession of his swarthy face and his frown was rushed down towards the bump of his mighty nose. I was embarrassed already, before he demanded to be introduced. But then he made things worse.

When Clover said hello Ben cried, "The voice." He took her hand without a by-your-leave and led her to inspect the framed photographs of local legends: Carr the famous local bicyclist, Jackson who won the Stawell Gift, Dangerous Dan's crash on the Bacchus Marsh racecourse, the main street flooded, the Wool Pack Inn where they had changed horses for the stagecoaches of Cobb & Co, and there he pointed my place out, a pale patch on the wall.

"Tell him to let me put it back," he said now to Clover. "Why not let us admire him?"

"I think he's on the run," she said, a little flirty. I thought, please don't encourage him, he'll want to join us. But he was a nicer man than that. He knew I didn't drink but, perhaps in order to aid me in my wooing, served us illegal wine in teacups. We sat in the booth next to the Grant Street window and affected to believe the homemade plonk was chianti and we were in Firenze looking out at the Duomo rather than Simon's garage and that we, framed by the window, suspended above the footpath, were the Duke and Duchess of Urbino, Federico da Montefeltro and his wife Battista Sforza, in majestic profile.

We trod lightly around the edges of our pasts. We did not discuss the schismatic Lutheran churches of Adelaide or the poultry farms of Dandenong but we were, I believe, so very happy with each other that we failed to see Mrs. Bobbsey park her car opposite. Thus I was shocked to notice the light appear on the upper floor of Simon's garage and see quite a different painting, framed in a high bright window, of Mrs. Bobbsey in the arms of a strange man.

# 13

FROM THE TIME of her first marriage my sister cheated on her household expenses and maintained "rainy day" bank accounts not only in Geelong but in Colac and Winchelsea. She had kept her earlier engagement rings and knew their resale value. She was always married, then abandoned. It would have caused offence for me to say it was her fault i.e. you *keep* your husband because he is a treasure, and the more that is true, the more there will be other women after him. You "see off" the other women, is what I would have said.

So it was up to me to give Mrs. Markus her driving lesson and give her back her pine cones. I told her, to her face: I have no problem starting a fire in my own home.

I got home at lunchtime to find the heavy black telephone ringing. Below it were all Titch's worry papers: there was no handwriting quite like his, finance calculations, the names of prospects with the capital and smaller letters all jumbled together in a language of their own.

It was Mr. Dunstan.

"Your husband can never be the Ford dealer in Bacchus Marsh."

I thought, what have I done?

"The franchise is allocated elsewhere." He was so jubilant it made me ill.

"How can you know this?"

"If he wants to play now, he has to play with GMH. It's exactly what you wanted, Mrs. Bobs. It's everything we hoped. Ipso facto. QED. He's a Holden man today."

I thought, poor sweet Titch. Betrayed by your awful father, now your wife as well.

"We've bagged the number one country salesman in the state. We've bagged the little bugger."

"Don't call him that."

"No disrespect."

"And you haven't bagged him. He doesn't even like the Holden. You don't know him."

"It's not personal Mrs. Bobs, but this is what they call checkmate. You've been a major player on the team."

This was the actual point at which I wrecked our lives. Dunstan himself would play a major role, as would Thacker and Mr. Green, but I was the one who unlocked the door for them.

On top of that I got the capital. I had steeled my heart against my sister, because I thought it was my right to do so, because half the house was mine, because she had abused my generosity travelling up to Melbourne and running up bills at Myer's and Georges.

"You know your family's future is with Holden," said Dunstan. He had a deep slow voice. It would have calmed a yappy dog. "We're getting closer every day, Irene," he said. He had never called me Irene before and I didn't mind so much. He said he was driving up to Ballarat tonight and would pass through the Marsh at six o'clock. "You'll never guess what I have to show you," he said. "Everything is falling into place."

Whoa, I thought.

"My cousin is an Anderson," he said.

Anderson was a big Bacchus Marsh family. Of course I knew the name.

"She is married to George Halloran."

I knew Halloran, of course. He had built a scandalous "extension" for Mrs. Markus.

"Halloran is going to develop the site of Simon's garage."

He said Simon's garage was a perfect place for a dealership, a corner property, petrol tanks already in the ground, a hoist in place, and the failed bicycle factory just waiting to be a workshop. Plus there was a loft which, according to his cousin, could be turned into a cozy flat for "proprietor and family."

"The lease won't cost a penny until you take possession."

"We can't afford it."

"Yes you can. You'll have the cashflow of a major dealership and GMAC behind you with the financing."

In my defence: this was what Titch and I had both talked about when we were still living in a boarding house in Bairnsdale. Our own Bobs Motors with a display space for four vehicles with the lights on all night long.

"My husband would go nuts," I said. "He won't tolerate the debt."

"No, no. Don't worry. Come and look at the site."

"Don't underestimate him, Mr. Dunstan. He is not a timid man, believe me."

"I'll be in the Marsh at six tonight. Come by yourself. When you see it, you'll understand."

Oh Jesus, I thought. I didn't know where Titch was. He was meant to talk to Ford that morning, but he wasn't home.

"I don't think my husband heard from Ford."

"He did, yes."

Then why was he not here? What pub was he in now?

"Mrs. Bobs," Dunstan said, "if you were my wife, then I'd be very, very grateful. I'd know you had saved my life."

I arranged to meet Dunstan in the early evening expecting Titch would be there to go with me. At dusk he was still not home. Mrs. Wilson across the road was not exactly friendly but said the kids could sit at her kitchen table. So I went to meet with Dunstan alone.

His voice had suggested a tall slow man but in the murk of Simon's doorway he smelled of mint and whisky, a wiry bald fellow with a two-inch high moustache. He stamped his feet and clapped his hands and frightened me.

The beam of his torch swept across the heavy steel beams and concrete floors. What was I meant to think? I could make out a shadowy mess of chairs stacked to the ceiling. The lights came on. I saw tea chests and a workshop bench where someone had been turning bookends on a lathe. I told Dunstan that this was not for me to judge. I would have had a better idea if it was a cow.

He said I would grasp the value of the property if I came up the stairs and it was there he finally turned to face me. Dear God. Did he mean to propose to me? He was holding out a little velvet box.

"We want to thank you," he said.

I thought, it's pearls, but it was a fancy pen with my name engraved on it.

"No, I can't."

"You must."

"No-one must ever know," I said, and it was true.

"No-one need know," he agreed and grasped my hand and I said quit it but his mouth looked spoiled and sulky beneath its bed of hair. He was a married man. He wore a ring. He was kissing me, pushing his thing against my stomach, the idiot, with his awful tasting mouth. I pulled away but still he slobbered on my cheek and I looked down on Grant Street and saw, in the window of the Greek's, Mr. Bachhuber looking directly at me.

"We will go home now," I said. "You will tell this to my husband."

Dunstan took a step backwards, as if taking stock of me, and who I was, and what he might finally do to me, or I to him. I had a ladder in my stockings. Let him stare at that.

"You thought I was a cheat," I said. "You thought I was cheating on my husband by confiding in you. I was wrong. I never should have."

"Oh no, it's just a fountain pen, from all of us at GMH."

I didn't bother to call him a liar or make him more of my enemy than he already was. I told him to follow me in his car but when we turned the corner onto Gisborne Road I thought, what if Titch is still not home? Or if he's drunk?

I pulled off the road and waited for the pervert to come back and talk to me.

"You have to return later," I said. "I have to tell him what I have done with my sister."

He stood there in the darkness, staring at me. That was Dunstan. From the very start he thought I was a pain.

# 14

I WAITED FOR my husband. The silly quiz show finished and then *Crosby by Request* and then a pair of headlights washed down the drive and I stood at the back door and saw my Titchy was alive. In the bright light of the shed I watched him perform his customary inspection of the tyres and Duco.

He met me at the door and I hugged him, knowing how the rejection must be hurting.

"No Ford," was all he said.

"Good riddance," I said. "We'll do something even better."

I nuzzled my nose behind his perfect ear and before he even had his coat off I told him what I had done with my parents' estate. My share was all for him, I said so.

He said I was an amazing woman. I had changed the game completely.

It was lovely to see this was not the broken man I feared, but the one I married, the one I loved. He flipped the cap off a bottle. He grinned. He teased me. He found a penny in a private place and I let him be the way he was.

We finished our beers and I washed the glasses and we were husband and wife, warm in bed while the wind raged around us but he would not say what I had changed. I didn't worry very much. I expected he was going to buy more used vehicles from Joe Thacker. That was how he thought.

It was early morning when the phone rang and I thought it would be Thacker. But it was Dunstan asking for Mr. Bobs as if he didn't know me.

Ronnie was awake so I rushed him out to the shed to help me

blacken tyres. Then Titch finally appeared, in his striped pyjamas. I
sent Ronnie back inside.

"That was GMH," he said.

"What did they want?"

"Strange timing don't you think? Day after Ford?" He was looking
at me funny. "He knew all about me somehow."

I waited, nervous.

"His name is Dunstan."

"That was your game-changing idea? You're going to GMH?"

"Irene," said he, "I got the entry papers for the Redex Trial."

There was no money in the Redex Trial. It was all for skites and
show-offs, men who got drunk off printer's ink and headlines, public
heroes who could afford the luxury of fame. It was for publicity hounds
like Dangerous Dan. It was a so-called "reliability trial" which pun-
ished ordinary production cars and made them do things they were
never meant to do. Of course it was a big thrill for the so-called General Public. Two hundred lunatics circumnavigating the continent of
Australia, more than ten thousand miles over outback roads so rough
they might crack your chassis clean in half. I told my husband what I
thought.

"I knew you'd be like this," he said. "But it would make our name."

"We've got a name. It's Bobs. It's time to shift to Holden."

"But we've got the money from your parents' house."

I thought, now he's stuffed up everything I've done.

"I picked up the entry papers yesterday. When I left Ford I went
down to Melbourne. For Christ's sake listen. Ford cut my knackers off.
I need something to look forward to."

"I'm sorry about Ford," I said. "But we're not gambling. That's
agreed. We've got to make a living."

"Calm down."

"No, it's my money."

"You said it was for me."

"We've got two kids. It's around Australia, eighteen days. All you're
left with is a wreck."

"Don't you see? It could make us famous. That's the value. The fellow thought it was a good idea."

"What fellow?"

"Dunstan. He could see the business sense of it. If we were Holden dealers."

"He never."

And he was laughing. "We've got it," he said, and lifted me in the air and carried me, walking on gravel in bare feet. "Tell me it's impossible. Holden franchise. Redex Trial. You beauty bottler, Irene. You saved our bacon."

And he was kissing me and my feelings were all confused by what I knew and didn't know. How could we go in the Redex and leave the kids? What made him think we'd win?

"Talk to this Dunstan," he said. "Listen to what he says."

"We can't start a dealership and then run away."

"This is going to take months and months of prep. At the same time there's building to be done. We'll come back from the trial to open the new showroom."

I didn't ask him what "building" because of course I knew. "So this Mr. Dunstan. He's going to look after Ronnie and Edith? He's going to tuck them in and hear their prayers?"

"I'll solve it. I've got months to sort it out."

"You'll go away and leave me."

"We'll be co-drivers," he said, with those bright keen eyes and his thin pyjamas and I could feel how much he wanted me. "You watch," he said. "We're going to be a household name."

Who would have thought what the sight of us, this private moment, would do to someone else? Who might imagine that a well-educated schoolteacher might see this confusion as the ideal model for a modern life?

# 15

THAT WAS the first time I saw Dunstan. I did not know his name, of course, but I wished I never saw Mrs. Bobbsey in the mongrel's arms. It churned me up to think: Titch a cuckold. So I, who had previously coveted his wife, now wished to perform some act of unexpected kindness, to wash his car for instance, anything.

In the cafe, Clover had been unable to fathom why I was upset. "You're sweet on her?"

How could I explain? That I had been in love with the idea of Titch Bobbsey, his Jaguar, his wife, his children tumbling across the grass in the middle of the night. "Her husband is my friend."

Clover's upper lip contracted and I was moved to place my finger there, on that entrancing mole. She wished I wouldn't.

"Your beauty mark," I said, and she removed my hand.

"It is a mark of sin, according to my mother."

"It is certainly persuasive."

"No. It's not funny."

"Your sin?"

"I told my mother: if it's not my sin it must be yours. She slapped my face."

"Ha."

"Exactly."

I thought, what unknown winds have delivered our spirits to our bodies?

"Come on," she said. "It's time."

Time for what? As we rose from the booth I thought, you do not know her. You will say you love her because of something brainless like a lovely clavicle.

Bones, I thought, as we entered the darkness of Gisborne Road, up the hill where the air was damp and cool and smelled of rotting leaves and the excretions of cattle and attendant horses who had recently passed that way. Mare urine is an aphrodisiac for stallions, so Ben Calvo says. He owes his cafe to his knowledge of racecourse matters so perhaps this will prove true.

The doors of the chemist shops had been locked but we walked as if they were open to our desire, arm in arm and by the Church of England graveyard where we stopped to kiss. Sex makes a man dishonest with himself, as is well known. I feared the slippery ambiguity of false feeling, of expediency, of things not being exactly true.

We entered the front gate of my house, and squeezed down the side by the hydrangeas, and I smelled her soft neck, imagining rooms and places beyond my life.

In the smudgy dark I spied my sleeping chooks, chalky lumps up on the roof.

"I'll clip their wings," she said, "before I go."

Once inside I was deaf with worry about the chemists and my disfigured shoulder. I drew blinds and curtains everywhere and she smiled at me and I wished she would not see my awful scar. She kicked off her shoes. I could not imagine what she thought.

Say we were in Italy, what then?

In the kitchen we embraced and she held me close and breathed my breath and said that was how you knew a person was right. She was so lithe and exceptionally beautiful and gentle and, with her hands clasped around my shoulderblades, she pulled herself up into my life.

I said we could not do what we both wished.

"That's for the girl to say."

"Not without a 'thing.' "

"You've got a very nice thing as far as I can feel."

Then my veins and arteries were full to bursting, but I would rather kill myself than play this game. Then we were on the bedroom floor, amongst the books, like teenagers, and I said, outright, plainly, the problem was the absence of the contraceptive.

She said there were lots of ways to skin a cat but she did not understand I was who I was because, once upon a time, I had been a boy. I had spurted in a second, like a sparrow. I spilled my seed, but not upon the ground.

I trusted my secrets to those glistening observant eyes. I confessed. Adelina Koenig and I had been just twenty years old when she got pregnant and we ran away to Melbourne. I had assumed we would have the baby there. It was Adelina, the nurse, who found the abortionist. I did not know such men existed.

"Poor children," Clover said, "how awful. What a lot of money you had to find."

I was touched she would accept my ugly secrets. I confessed that I had borrowed the money from Sebastian Laski who I did not know well enough to ask so much of, but who would, more than once, descend into the wreckage of my life to save me.

"You are an attractive man," she said. "You will always be forgiven."

She helped me remove my shirt and there was no choice but to reveal the scar, that brutal wound like a fissure in a concrete slab. She licked it, as deep as she could go. She loved me. She said so. She sucked my nipples like I was a girl. I moaned. I thought, the power of sex cannot be denied, stopped or plugged, is as insistent as water leaking through a roof, finding its way in darkness, emerging in the back seat of a car. There was nothing to be frightened of she said, no, I thought, only what it makes you do, clawing at the trees, splintering the bark like a tomcat, the blind and violent need of it, a joy, but who would not want to be relieved of it. I pity the Catholic priests suffering their sex, the stream of desire finding its way to the ocean without regard to good or evil, and if it ends up as evil then that is the relentless nature of it. The cat was flayed alive.

Hours later, still on the floor, we talked and talked, kissed and cried and my wound must be examined and my tumble from the kitchen window lived again and Adelina Koenig, also, must be described.

"It means King," she said.

"I know."

"But you must have had another baby. That's why you're hiding from the summonses now."

"He turned out not to be my child." Any moment, I thought, she will not love me any more.

"How could anyone be certain he was not your son?"

"Just say the baby was red-headed, and that my wife was not." I could see she was about to argue and I would not tolerate it. "And there was a red-haired bloke who was always at your house."

"What did Adelina say?"

I wished she would not use her name.

"You left her, is that correct?"

"You don't understand," I said, but I saw her face and it was clear she did.

"Poor Willie."

"I'm sure she suffered and he suffered too, the poor little blighter."

"How old are you Willie?"

"Twenty-six."

"You're too young for all this guilt. See. Look. You're ready."

In self-defence I summoned an urgent interest in my grandmother's coloured atlas of the Holy Roman Empire. I laid it before her and she admired it and listened to my unshakable belief that I did not belong where my mother had delivered me. I had no reason to be in the hot streets of wartime Adelaide, not when my true home must be in the atlas of the Habsburg Empire and the lands of Hungary. There was no map of Adelaide that could produce the longing aroused by the dense fibrous universe of that atlas, which, being hand-painted in a slightly unconventional if not eccentric manner, had the mellow colours of a closely woven Persian rug, in which our red Hungary had turned a greyish brown, Salzburg was the colour of dried straw, Croatia was pale pink. Bohemia like the other states was now foxed and speckled brown. The crumbling coast of Dalmatia in the south was what I believe is known as Spectrum Violet.

"But of course, dear man." She herself had not belonged in Dandenong.

There was her gorgeous silk skinned leg, folded beneath her dark private hair glistening with dew and here were all of these lands with their diverse peoples, Germans, Magyars, Spanish Jews, Romanies and Mohammedans, which had been a source of wonder to my childish imagination. My grandmother told me that an ancestor of ours, a Venetian nobleman, had been called to advise the Imperial Council in Vienna. What he had done there or what became of him we could never know but he was the reason that I had curiously splayed "Italian toes" and although blond haired as my father the pastor, would turn "brown as a Mediterranean berry" in the Australian sun.

Likewise, Clover was olive skinned but did not know, she told me, where she came from. She thought her grandfather had been in a poem by Wordsworth, perhaps in "Troutbeck" and she had read compulsively but never found either poem or boy. Her grandmother was a "real cockney" in Bow, but the address on her birth certificate had been bombed to dust in the Second World War. There were olive skinned Scots and Irish, she supposed. Her great-grandmother had hated de Valera because he would not take off his hat to the Prince of Wales. She had a magpie history, bright pebbles with no bedrock. "We know nothing. It is *l'État australien,*" she said. "Think about the red-headed child. What might he ever know of how he came to be?"

I told her the father was an American nurse at the Royal Melbourne Hospital, he had been our friend. He was a good nurse, I thought, a good friend, I had imagined.

"And fucked your wife," she said.

Dear God, how could I defend myself from that brutality?

"You should have killed him," she said, playing with my toes, rumpling the maps. "Who knows what murderers we descend from?"

You will expect me to be repulsed by this, and yet this imaginary murder was an expression of passion, an expression of support, of love, a renewal of unresolved desire, and Lord, well never mind, she drew a fine wet thread from my sex and there was more than one way to skin the cat and the walls were thin and I did not care how she snorted or shouted out to God.

When we finally rose from the floor the Holy Roman Empire was in shreds and, for the moment anyway, I really did not care.

# 16

WHEN MY HUSBAND told me he was off to "see a man about a dog" I assumed it was somehow related to the show-off Redex Trial. It did not occur to me, not for a moment, that after all I had said, after all he had said, he was going back to Ford to try again. It was predictable of course. This was how he was with his father, always going back to take another beating.

It was morning. Edith was in strife for handing in a drawing in which all the kids were purple. No-one wears purple, the teacher had said. She was allegedly old and crabby. And Edith was Edith. She had "just pointed out" that Barbara Radford had purple stripes in her sweater. Her teacher said Barbara Radford did not have a purple face. Edith did not wish to go to school.

Ronnie was stamping around the house. "Roundy bouty," as he liked to say. He had never had real boots before and he was mad with happiness, rushing outside to break the ice in the puddles and tramp mud back across the carpet.

I walked them hand in hand to school. I returned intending to make a trunkline call, to learn what Dunstan had said to Titch and what Titch had said to him.

At home I discovered there had been a chicken massacre next door. Huge white flowers, dead mounds of dusters, dead as dodos, and in the midst of all this sudden death in his vegie garden, wearing a woollen beanie in Bacchus Marsh colours, stood Mr. Bachhuber grasping a dead creature to his chest.

"We cut their wings," he said.

On their first flightless morning his chickens had been visited by next door's cocker spaniel. I don't see this was my fault, although I felt it. I did not ask him who was "we."

Titch was meanwhile travelling at ninety-three miles an hour towards new humiliation.

I was at home, busy on the phone with Dunstan. I asked him why had he given in about the Redex. He needs something to look forward to, Dunstan said. Wasn't a dealership enough? I asked. He laughed.

In Geelong the Big Noises asked my husband what he was doing back with no appointment.

"I have the capital," he said.

"That's nice, mate."

"Plus, I am going to win the Redex Trial."

"Yes, but we have the franchise allocated, all signed up."

"Unsign him."

"Mate . . ."

"No-one can match my sales numbers."

Why was it, they asked him, that salesmen always imagined they were the centre of the universe. This was not so. The Ford Motor Company required a Bacchus Marsh dealer with business acumen, as they called it, plus substantial capital, marketing know-how, promotional capability, real estate experience. Salesmen were a dime a dozen.

Titch was not offended, he said so. He had been insulted by experts in the past. If a dealership was impossible then he would make it possible. Doubtless he annoyed them, shouting, not knowing that his power was no longer what it was.

"Give me a chance," he said. "I've got the capital."

To tell the truth, his capital was not enough. Also, he might as well hear it from them: there was the problem of confusion about Bobs Motors.

"What confusion?"

"Your old man has opened up outside of Melton."

"No he hasn't."

"Yes he has."

"Opened what?"

"A motor business."

I can see his mouth, poor darling. "Well what of it?"

"Branding," they said, a new word that had to be explained. "We can't deal with two Bobs Motors. Can't do it. When you see the place, you'll understand."

Of course it didn't matter that Dan had gone and opened up his own used car business on the Melbourne Road. But it mattered to my husband. In fact, it winded him.

"Sorry Titch."

He should have come home to me. Instead he rushed off to chat to his tormentor. Forty-three minutes later he found the one-hoist garage with BOBS FOR FORD in fluorescent orange.

Of course Dan had no franchise, never had and never could. He was a crummy second-hand car dealer with one vehicle and the deposit written in whitewash on its windscreen.

"Why are you doing this to me?" Titch asked.

The answer was: the mongrel couldn't help himself. He took his well-dressed son around the back where, beside the battery shed, he showed him a propeller rescued from the Darley tip.

"After all I did for you," he said.

# 17

I WAS EMOTIONAL, yes, but not in the way Mrs. Bobbsey imagined. How could I have told her that, even as I dug the graves, I was happy. I was loved. I loved in turn. It was all I ever wanted, that was the immoral truth I could never tell a soul. I drove the spade deep, cutting off my own potatoes, and all the time I thought of Clover, those unflinching eyes bright behind her lashes, her tennis player's legs drawing me in deeper.

I stood my spade against the side wall of the house. I washed my hands. I scrubbed the floor and made the bed. I swept the front verandah and burned the legal letters demanding child support. I saved only the envelope marked "The Education Department of the State of Victoria." This I read as I dressed for the recording session.

"Dear Blah blah blah. As you have failed to appear as requested the tribunal has no choice but to suspend you without pay as of the date of the offence. Should you wish to appeal this decision you may present a sequestered defence at the meeting December 10, 1953."

What was a sequestered defence? I didn't care. I wished only to return to Clover and the studio.

And what a quiz show we recorded there, a dance in fact, floating in a field of jasmine and orange blossom. Deasy must have dealt the yellow cards but I hardly noticed him. It was not until the final minutes that I became aware of his ferocious stare. Had he been looking like that all through the show? Perhaps. But he was a strange man with a peculiar past and wide rings on his large fingers and I had never tried to really "understand" him. When Baby Deasy rewound the tape, Deasy invited me out for tea. That is, he pinched the sleeve of my jacket and, with no farewell to frowning Clover, tugged me down the stairs, all the way up Collins Street, not slowly either, dragging me up Spring Street and through the grand doors of the Hotel Windsor.

The waitress asked Deasy would he like scones and clotted cream.

"No scones," he said. "Tea."

"And you, sir?"

"He'll have tea," said Deasy and chewed at his moustache until the waitress departed. "Did you root her?" he said.

"What?"

"Root, fuck, bang. Did you schtup her?" He showed his big teeth and nodded his head ferociously. "You did, didn't you?"

I thought, what gives you the right to speak to me like this?

"Strike me lucky," he said. "I never saw a fuck so public. She's lost her spark. You have too. If I was a sponsor I'd take my advertising budget somewhere else. Jesus, Willie. Don't shit in your own nest. Not now."

I thought, I am not your dog.

"This is meant to be a contest," he hissed. "We don't fix the questions. That's the point. Neither of you know what's going to happen next. You want to destroy her, or did you forget? She wants to kill you. That's the point. That's why we cast her."

Frankly I thought he had gone cuckoo, with his great hands enclosing a soft pack of unfiltered cigarettes, crumbling tobacco onto the Windsor's white tablecloth.

"What are you looking at? This?" He held the pack, pinching it between thumb and forefinger. "What is it?"

"Philip Morris cigarettes."

"Do you know the slogan?" he asked. His eyes were far too bright.

"Nothing to lose but your smoker's cough?"

"Yes." He stared at me with eyebrows raised dramatically. "What would you say to a national quiz show called *Nothing to Lose*?"

"They're signing on?"

"I am *this* close. *Nothing to Lose,* brought to you by Philip Morris. We're going to have to record today's show again. I can't play them this lovey-dovey bullshit."

"There'll be real prize money?"

"Real cheque. Real money you can put in the bank. We'll re-record on Wednesday. OK? You want to kill her. *Comprenez vous?* You want a job?"

"Yes," I said but frankly I was not certain any more.

"Well piss off."

I thought, poor monster, sick with greed.

It was cold and drizzly on Spring Street but there she was, my darling, tucked into a dark doorway in her bright red overcoat.

"You waited."

"But of course."

I thought, she will wish to know what Deasy said to me. I was relieved when she did not. Her nose was cold and her mouth was warm and we bought two tuppenny fares on the 15 Tram and soon, minutes later, we were entering a Queens Road apartment building. Perhaps you know the type, always divided by a long thin garden path punctuated by blind white statues and melancholy topiary, one of those "Spanish style" blocks which had previously seemed so lost and loveless to me. We entered chastely, brother and sister as far as all the world could see.

Then the door was closed and locked and never mind the rest. Afterwards, Clover asked me if I was pleased to have my feathers clipped, and I said nothing about the murders. I told her that I loved her, and proved it once again. We lay on musky sheets redolent of jasmine, with her hair curling upon my chest. She kissed my nose. She had discovered Adelina was living in Prahran. She had seen her, she said, and my son as well.

Another man might have been alarmed, but I trusted jealousy.

"She's in the phone book, sweetie. Your red-haired boy," she said. "Oh poor poor Willie."

Thus she spoke to me in a code, and I could now trust her absolutely. She knew, now, certainly, my true history, and she showed me how she accepted my disastrous past. I lay drowsily in the perfumed bed and watched, with the pride and vanity of ownership, her slender athletic body as she moved around her tiny kitchen and then brought me mushrooms on toast and I kissed her earthy buttery mouth, at once so strange and so familiar.

Why would I ever want to kill her? I would rather lose to her in fact.

We moved from mushrooms to Sparkling Rheingold. In vino veritas, by golly, only half a glass. We discussed our savings, the cost of life in Italy. I was a balloonist cutting loose the ballast, and with every slash I rose until I was once again a teenager who might become anything he wished.

I told her that we had a sponsor. Somehow she already knew. We agreed we would spend weekends together. I returned to Bacchus Marsh with no-one to tell me how to spend my time. The education department had lost all power over me and yet, like many men who find themselves unemployed, I could not be idle.

Now, each day, I would arrive in Melbourne just after noon and enter the State Library of Victoria when Sebastian Laski was at lunch. That is, I would not face the map librarian just yet or justify my inexplicable occupation. And as he never manned the desk and stayed in his office above Little Lonsdale Street, I was able to call for maps of the pastoralist properties which lay like a lethal patchwork on top of the true tribal lands. Here, beneath Norman G. Peebles' gorgeous dome, I was at peace transcribing the co-ordinates of the famous properties of Deanside and Rockbank. It was a map of murder, of course. What else was I to do?

In Bacchus Marsh I removed an entire wall of books and tacked tracing paper on the plaster. My dining room became a bombsite of homeless volumes, a destruction that permitted the future to exist.

We re-recorded. What a show. Clover attacked me and Deasy was beside himself. He was an auctioneer, conductor of the philharmonic, a prancing villain in a cloak. Then, as he had promised, we signed real contracts. When that was done I sat in the control booth while Clover recorded the first commercials. "Nothing to lose but your smoker's cough." Oh Lord she had the voice for it. Do I root her? Deed I do.

Now we did shows with real prizes. The cheques all cleared. I spent my weekends in sweet tumescence, my weekday afternoons in the library, and on the road to Kororoit where the guards at the ICI factory had recovered from their early panic and obtained permission to guide me to certain trees whose bark, they believed, had been used by Aboriginals to make canoes.

Being so occupied with my own happiness I saw little of the Bobbseys and I only learned of their own adventures when Missus called on me.

"Cough cough," she cried knocking on my kitchen door. "Nothing to lose." They had heard me on the radio, she told me. They were so proud to know a famous person.

Her excitement was not solely the product of my own success. She and her husband were now Holden dealers, or almost. They were planning to be heroes of the reckless Redex Trial. Imagine that. Around the whole continent, followed by newsreel cameras and photographers.

I revealed my ignorance of matters Redex and she was happy to educate me. The quotidian brands, Ford, Holden, Plymouth, would take on a gladiatorial persona, armoured against bulls and kangaroos. They would be sticking ugly decals all over a brand-new car. Castrol Oil. SPC. Lucas Battery. They would have Bobs Motors written right along one side. She had to go to the solicitor's. Cough, cough, she said. Bye-bye.

I set off to bicycle to Kororoit Creek with my notebook.

The wind was at my back as I sailed down the highway, giving myself entirely to this symbolism. For almost ten miles I flew, until, on the long plain near Exford, just where those inexplicable foreign cactus plants grow in the corner of that sheep paddock, my bloody tyre was punctured and I fell and grazed my knee. But even then my luck was good for I had come to ground exactly opposite a motor garage that seemed to have been freshly decorated for my arrival. Here I found a single Caltex petrol pump, a two-tone Ford Customline, violent yellow paint splashed everywhere about the concrete forecourt. Bold whitewash had been applied excitedly to the windscreen of the Ford: *Low Deposit Finance Available.*

As I approached, an old man emerged from the office carrying a ball hammer. He wore heavy oil-stained boots, and was disguised by a pale grey shop coat. When his thin white hair lifted in the wind, I recognised the famous aviator.

"It's you Jimmy," he said. When I did not immediately follow him around the corner, he turned. "You need me to carry you?"

Thus I beheld what had been hidden from my view: the eastern Day-Glo wall with red letters taller than a man: BOBS MOTORS. Here also was a tap and hose, a big steel bath of the type used to locate air leaks, an air compressor, and a battery shed against which leaned the propeller Mrs. Bobbsey had so cruelly amputated.

"Come here Jimmy. Hold this."

He already had the front wheel off my bicycle. The tyre was just as swiftly liberated. He called for the air hose and inflated the tube and, not without a grunt, kneeled to submerge it in the tank. We watched the air bubbles escape the puncture while the westerly wind whipped dust across our faces. Looking at his stern countenance I thought of Boreas, the god of wind, a sometimes violent old man with a billowing cloak. In the case of Boreas, it was said he had snakes instead of feet.

"There you are," he said. "I suppose you've got your own repair kit."

"Sorry."

He did not criticise me for my lack, and yet, when he disappeared into the battery shed, I felt myself severely judged. He returned without explanation and set to work, drying the tube, washing it with petrol, marking the leak with a white X, and clamping a small black device to the wound. He threw me a box of matches.

"Make yourself useful," he said.

I lit the match and held it to the patch, startled to see the conflagration thus instigated, like a fuse on fire, hissing, sputtering, dancing around the device.

"That's a vulcanising patch, did you know that?"

"No."

"I thought you were a schoolteacher, Jimmy."

"I'm Willie."

"I know who you are," he said. "You think I would forget you?"

He draped the snaky tube across the seat and while the vulcaniser cooled we stood with our backs to the vast sign gazing out across the volcanic plain. The tarpaulins on the passing trucks cracked like sails in a storm but the wider view was blocked by the battery shed against which the amputated propeller continued to cause unhappiness.

Of course it had been a beautiful piece of design. It had been maliciously damaged. I could not help but feel guilty for my part in that.

"How's my boy?" he asked at last. He held me with his rheumy grey eyes. "I miss the little bugger."

"I think they're OK now," I said.

"I heard he ran off to GM. Going to sell Holdens."

"They seem happy."

"Do they now? You never drove a Holden."

"I'm not a driver, no."

"Yes, I know that. I had a fellow in here yesterday, Jim Woodall, from out on Long Forest Road. I said to him, how's the Holden handling? (You might not know this, Jimmy, but with the light weight in the rear end of a Holden, the handling can get a little hairy.) Jim said he had been exceptionally unhappy with the handling but then he laid a couple of bags of cement dust directly over the rear axle. That almost did the trick. So then he thought, why not, so he took out the rear seat and filled up the well with cement, gravel, water, like he was laying a garden path. When it was set hard he put the rear seat back and Bob's your uncle. You might pass that on to little Titch," said Dangerous Dan, as if he were about to smile. "He might pass that on to GM if he wants to make a living. Woodall bought a Ford last week. And by the same token," he said, "does he have any bloody idea of how he's going to feed himself?"

"I believe so. They seem happy."

"Happy, with Miss Lesbefriends? Did you clock the way she dresses?"

"They're going in some race. There's big excitement in the camp."

"What race would that be? Not the Redex?"

"That's the one, I think."

"What a circus." Dan ground his cigarette into the ground. "How could they afford that?"

"Perhaps I'm wrong."

"In a Holden?"

"I think so."

"Think?"

"I'm almost certain, yes."

Dan picked up the tube without a word. "He's not a driver's bootlace," he said. He looked to me. I kept my counsel. He inflated the tyre and flung it into the bath.

"Do you think you can manage to put it back together?"

"Do you have a couple of tyre levers I could borrow?"

"Borrow?" He stared at me.

"Sorry."

"It's a piece of shit," he said, producing the tyre levers from his coat pocket. "The FJ Holden."

"Thank you, Mr. Bobs."

"Are GM helping him financially?"

"I don't know."

"Whose idea was this? Who did this to my propeller? You knew what you were looking at when you first saw it. You knew its value, I know you did. So tell me, Jimmy, can you imagine what a father feels? I'm the one who raised him. Don't ask about the mother. Don't ask what it cost. Years of sacrifice, thrown back in my face. I keep the prop here so everyone can see what I put up with. People are shocked. People who thought they knew him. They thought they liked good old Titch, but then they look at this. Good luck to them," said Dan, and I saw he was once more talking of the Bobbseys. "How can they go in the bloody Redex Trial and have two children? Don't tell me Miss Lesbefriends will stay behind?"

"I don't know."

"Here, give me that bloody wheel."

I thought, why is everyone suddenly speaking to me like this?

He fitted the tube and brought it to its proper pressure with the air hose.

"Listen to that. You hear that? That's the compressor. They call it Free Air," he said bitterly. "They come in here. Don't want to buy any petrol. Can I just have some free air? Listen to the compressor, does that sound free to you?"

Go root yourself, I thought. I smiled. "How much do I owe you, Mr. Bobs?"

"I'm a Ford dealer," he said, although this was not true.

"Yes."

"Come back," he said. "Tell your friends."

I suffered his handshake and set off towards my original destination, blown forward on the gusting wind, but the further I went, the more I thought of how this benevolence would turn to punishment when it was time to get back home. I turned and came once more past Bobs Motors, with my head down low, my bum high, my legs in agony already. There, beside the Caltex pump, was Boreas, bringer of winter, the devouring one with his gown billowing. What a miracle was Titch, I thought, to rebound against that force.

# 18

AT TEATIME every Friday we Bobs gathered round our wireless and listened to the quiz and ate toasted cheese sandwiches and were very pleasantly *livid* that the dumb high school had fired our famous neighbour. He was a "gebius" as Ronnie said. But who would have guessed it to see how he lived? His narrow weatherboard cottage was sad as suicide. The roof was rusting, its paint peeling. There was no sign of fame visible from the street, and in person he was just a bachelor with old-fashioned bicycle clips to keep his trousers from catching in the chain. You might see him in the co-op buying butter, or pushing his Malvern Star up the Gell Street hill, or trundling a wheelbarrow full of manure he had collected from the sale yards. He was top heavy in the chest and shoulders and although shorts revealed a pair of thin and boyish legs, he would, in normal costume, have been mistaken for a labourer from the brickworks. But when Titch took the trouble to add up all his winnings, it was clear our next door neighbour must be a wealthy man.

I was sorry when he began to spend weekends away from us, in Melbourne with his "fiancée," as he called her. Who was she? When we heard Bob Deasy ("Now knock that off, you kids") we guessed that Miss Cloverdale was his intended.

Bachhuber was our neighbour but we knew him better on the wireless, and *Nothing to Lose* was our family entertainment and our education. It was why we invested in that dictionary and fought for its possession.

"He hogs it, Mum. He can't spell cat," etc.

If anyone ever wondered why a person of Titch's education might say "It's a cardinal error" it was from his study of that dictionary. "Ubiq-uitous" was another word from there. He brought the dictionary into our bed and I was often awoken when it slipped from his grasp and exploded on the floor.

I loved the dictionary in spite of this, but I was *fascinated* by the com-petition between the man and woman on the quiz show. Deasy clearly favoured Bachhuber. He was the king. I was never one of those who wished him to lose his crown but—fair is fair—I was dying for Miss Honeyvoice to get a break. I will not say Bob Deasy taunted her, but he certainly brought out something in her opponent—lovely as he was— that suggested it was his man-born right to win.

You better marry that fiancée, I thought. She is every bit as smart as you.

I barracked for Miss Cloverdale so loud my family teased me for it. When I noticed her questions getting harder than his, I said so. For example: *In what year did Australia have an inland sea?*

Miss Cloverdale's answer was *sixty thousand years ago, before the land was invaded by humans from the direction of New Guinea.* What clever children they will have, I thought. But no. Her answer triggered one of these dreadful sound effects, a slow creaking noise, then an explosion, like a tree crashing to the earth.

"Mum?" protested Edith. "Mum! They're ganging up on her."

"Wrong answer," Titch cried. I did not see why he should be happy.

"What says the king?" cried Deasy.

"The correct date is 1827."

Bob Deasy's voice was so happy, I hated him. "What do you say listeners, is it yes or is it no? Australia with an inland sea? Get on the blower. Give us a tingle. You've got nothing to lose."

"Call them," Edith begged me. But we were not rich and would never make a trunkline call for fun. We gathered around the glowing dial, hearing telephones ringing thirty miles away. The popular vote was all for Clover which was pure ignorance we learned.

"The king is sorry," Deasy purred. "You should see his face, listeners. He's sad to be correct, to defeat the pretty lady. He's sorry to the tune of five hundred pounds."

He then had Bachhuber educate us: a certain Maslen map had been drawn in 1827. It included an inland sea where, in real life, there were only blacks and desert. There was no inland sea, not ever. Yet because the madman's map was in the State Library of Victoria so the inland sea existed, and our neighbour was judged to be correct. What tosh.

There were bad fires at Bullengarook and Mount Macedon in early summer. The siren rang all day, and the hot wind blew from the north. During these few weeks, when you could smell the smoke inside the hairdresser's, the tide of local opinion turned against our neighbour. The new judgement was freely expressed at the co-op and the post office. Bachhuber was a good bloke. He'd had a great innings. Now let the lady win.

Mr. Dunstan, obviously, did not follow the quiz show. As to the significance of Friday, he had no clue. He assumed there was a place for him at our dinner table, which would have been true on any other night when he might arrive with his plans, contracts, cashflow charts, spare parts inventories. Then I would be quiet as a mouse and listen to him talk and I would fill his beer glass and not be disgusted by the froth which gathered in his fat moustache.

When I demanded silence for *Nothing to Lose,* he was offended. Then, when he finally paid attention to the wireless, all he noticed was the prize money.

"You should have told me," he said. "You're living next door to a bank."

"We would never take advantage."

"That's correct," my husband said.

"Jeez." Dunstan looked to Titch as if he should get his wife in order. "I'm only speaking from a cashflow point of view. We could always use a little more investment in the firm."

We? I thought, but my husband did not catch my eye.

To be fair, Dunstan did us favours. He found us sponsors for the

Redex Trial. He released us an FJ Holden demo model before the franchise was officially in hand. Titch used that demo to sell a record-breaking seventeen vehicles. So thank you, Mr. Dunstan, I suppose, although our success stressed our family to its sleepless limit. In those days we had to drive forty miles to General Motors and pick up the cars ourselves. If we were getting one vehicle then OK: I would drive Titch down with a set of trade plates and then we would both drive a vehicle back. To pick up two cars meant the train to Melbourne and an expensive taxi to GM. We could have used another driver in the family.

On account of this we missed the quiz show twice. We must have been somewhere in the industrial dark on Dynon Road, past the West Melbourne Stadium, when poor Willie Bachhuber lost his throne. We did not even notice it had happened, only that he was suddenly in his back garden pulling down his chook house and stacking the wire and broken timber up the front. If we had even read the paper we would have known what happened to him, but we had our own worries, not least my sister claiming she had been reduced to penury by me forcing her to sell the Geelong house. She said she now was forced to live in a caravan at Barwon Heads.

Meanwhile Miss Cloverdale had become the champion and Willie Bachhuber had been replaced by a new challenger. How could I live next door to him and not know? His heart was broken. His life was destroyed, but my main concern was that Ronnie fell out of the walnut tree and broke his arm. Also Edith was trying for her *Herald* learn-to-swim certificate.

We were sometimes forced to drive the new Holdens home over roads just sprayed with tar, a small enough thing until you understand the value of a new vehicle and the damage this risked. When we hit the wet tar we crawled at five miles an hour, but not even this could save us from those little bits of bitumen sticking to the lower body then hardening as we rushed down Anthony's Cutting towards home. What a nightmare. It was all hands on deck and a rag and a bottle of eucalyptus oil for every one of them. I did not hesitate to rouse up our genius next door. Cough cough, I cried, not understanding how that must have hurt.

If he appeared reduced, I did not notice. I had a rag and a bottle of eucalyptus ready for him and it was a presumption, I said, sorry, my husband would pay him for his time. We had to remove the tar before it set, under the wheel wells, hubcaps, rims, lower parts of doors.

I worked on the front mudguard while Bachhuber did the door.

"That 'cough cough' business," he said.

"We're very proud," I said.

"I'm dead in the water, Mrs. Bobs."

And then Edith and Ronnie arrived, Ronnie in his plaster cast, crying because I had not picked him up and he was forbidden to walk home alone and Edith had twisted his good arm and made him walk past the Catholics, the sale yards, the house full of illegal communists.

I dried my son's tears and cooked the tea and tried to help Edith with her long division. I returned to find Bachhuber squatting on the grass thoughtfully removing specks of bitumen.

"You're not going to let that woman beat you, Mr. Bachhuber."

"It's done, Mrs. Bobs."

I thought, it's not too bad, she is his fiancée. "Keep it in the family," I said, but I saw his face and then the penny dropped. Dear God, I thought, why is life unfair? It was not for me to comfort him. That was why I brought Titch into it.

After tea, the kids were clean and calm and happy and Titch got off the phone and read to them and they both snuggled up against him in Ronnie's tiny bed. Our neighbour was at home, I could see the light. I washed the dishes then found my family all fast asleep like creatures in a burrow. I woke Titch and gave him a fiver and a bottle of beer and sent him visiting next door and I crept outside and stood in the driveway in the dark and I could hear their voices, on and on. Then Ronnie was Mum, Mum, Mum. He had wet his bed, poor sausage. When he was once more dry and sleeping I fired up the copper in the laundry and had all the time I needed to wash his sheets and jamas, put them through the mangle, hang them on the line, forget the dew and pray for sunshine.

I was in bed with my face cream on by the time Titch lay down beside me.

"What a fascinating bloke," he said, but he had learned absolutely nothing about his broken heart.

# 19

HERE'S A KNOCKING indeed! Knock, knock, knock! Who's there, in the name of Beelzebub? Knock, knock! Who's there at the back door? "It's me," called Mr. Bobbsey.

Why not the front door then?

My sad bachelor kitchen was piled with dead and dying dishes, the roasted leg of lamb—what shade of green was that?

Knock, knock. "Mr. Bachhuber."

I saw the shadow. Birds, I thought, a tumbling troupe of them. But no, dear God, I had a conjurer visiting.

"It's only me."

Only? It was the marvellous midget juggling three oranges while he wedged a beer bottle between his tiny knees.

"Mr. Bobs," I said. "Please enter."

"Puss in Boots," he announced, pausing to present a single orange then heading politely up the hall and into the front room where he set the beer down before my private map. Up and down the street all windows were open to catch a little breeze, but I was securely locked and my front room was as humid as a henhouse. Titch Bobs, a gentleman, did not even twitch his nose. He had sold cars to Irish bachelors with no time for housekeeping, that is, he was not in the judging business. He came to me as an angelic presence, luminous in his lemon yellow pullover, dry and sweet as Johnson's baby powder. His cheeks were wide and freshly shaven, his hair smooth and black and his eyes alive with mischief. I thought, he is like a girl, so pretty and light, the way he listens to you before you say a word about your failure.

"Beer first," he said, "and oranges for pudding."

I never drink without regret, but he had already lifted my heart and

I found two clean glasses and a bottle opener and he was immediately busy with his wallet. He offered a fiver which I declined and he used his hands with inscrutable good humour until, finally, like a child at a birthday party, I found a five-pound note behind my ear.

"That's for good luck," he said. "You've had some bad luck I hear."

What had he heard? What did he know? That I knocked on Clover's door and found her in the company of an older woman eating my tuna casserole? No-one moved. No-one spoke. It was impossible to fully understand the situation except: I was not liked or wanted.

I later discovered that Clover had been a shop assistant not a school-teacher, but had I known it at the time I would have loved her just the same. On the day Titch found me I was still living amidst the ruins of Jacob Burckhardt and *The Civilization of the Renaissance in Italy*. That exquisite phantom head was resting on my imaginary chest.

I was slow to realise he had come into my house with no more motive than you might expect of a kind-hearted child of the Great Depression, ready to pay a homeless man to chop a stack of wood. He sat companionably cross-legged on my floor and poured two glasses. Why had he mentioned Puss in Boots? He didn't know. He did not recognise Puss's famous lines: "Costantino, do not be cast down, for I will provide for your well-being and sustenance, and for my own as well."

And yet, surely, he wanted something. He was quiet in the way someone might be silent with desire. If he had been a girl I would not have doubted what was up, but he was not a girl, and he did not wish to go home, and I finally understood that he had seen my map-in-progress, and was waiting for me to tell him what it was.

I had not touched my beer and surely he saw that too because he filled his own glass twice, but not before insisting I take an orange and he watched while I peeled in the way my dear pastor always had, making a spiralling snake, an action which produced its own sweet homesickness.

"We've all been down on our luck from time to time," he said, but he had become distracted, peering around my sweaty front room which must have seemed a Loony Bin, with its interesting slogans, thoughts and quotes pinned against the blameless wall. For instance, A VAST, OBSCURE COUNTRY, words which Alessandro Spina had used to evoke the Italian view of his own bleeding Libya but of course I had meant it in another way. Titch Bobs approached my map like a stalking cat, refilling his glass without looking down. My cartography included a dimension not normally suggested on flat paper, I mean the layers of time, the way the tree with the canoe scar sat in relationship to the effluent discharge. Being aware that he had abandoned school for ever on his fourteenth birthday, I did not expect him to be curious about such scholarly annotations, so how could I guess that he was being drawn, almost physically, across the carefully rendered car park of the Deer Park Hotel and up the Ballarat Road and hence along the corrugated gravel leading to Diggers Rest and Sunbury, up the driveway of Kippenross, the farm in Melton where the Robinson twins had played such tricks upon the doctor who could not find an appendix scar he had caused just the week before.

"You're a surveyor, Bachhuber?"

"Good Lord no."

He finished another beer and refreshed it without losing interest in my wall. "What are you going to do for a crust now?"

"I've got some savings."

"Would you do something for me? It will sound a little odd. Do you have a set of bathroom scales?"

"I do."

"Would you take off your clothes and weigh yourself?"

I laughed. I did not understand I was in the presence of a salesman, which is why I soon found myself walking with him down the hallway, not believing that I was about to stand nude before him and he, being closely focused on his own objective, would have no interest in my actual body, my privates, my skinny legs, my scar. He produced a stubby pencil and wrote down my weight.

"The thing is," he said when I returned to join him in the front room. "The thing is, Bachhuber, the three of us would weigh less than a two-man crew."

I would later learn that it was quite normal for Titch to omit certain steps in his thinking process. In his own mind, he had already proposed that I join the Redex as a navigator. So when I asked him what was this about he was already one step ahead of me.

"Petrol," he said. "Miles per gallon."

For this I had removed my clothes?

"Me, the missus, you. The three of us together. Two drivers, one navigator. We would still weigh less than Lex Davison and Tommy Fox, you get it?"

I was the we?

"Don't tell me the high school will take you back."

"No."

"Is there a quiz show that wants you?"

"No-one wants me."

"I want you," he said. "We want you. You are the bee's knees."

Good grief, I thought.

"I could use you to pick up vehicles from GM."

"I can't even drive."

"I'll get you a licence. Don't worry. The thing is, mate, you are expert in the required field. You can read a map."

"Surely your wife?"

This was where he revealed a second bottle. "She'd cook my balls with the bacon if she overheard. I mean, she wouldn't take it well. You must never say I said this, but Irene cannot read a map. You've heard the expression, woman driver?"

I had.

"Driving a car is all in the bum, and her bum is a perfect instrument for the job."

Was I blushing? Could he see it?

"Driving is like an art," he said. "Not everyone is physically or mentally able to do it well. My missus is a better driver than any man I ever rode with."

I did not wish to think about her bottom.

"Do not repeat this, ever. We do not want her to be the navigator."

He had been haunted by this thought, he confided in me, mate, from the day he picked up the Redex entry forms. It was an issue that must be confronted, and he dared not give offence in the female department.

"And here you are." He raised the glass, a jam jar with jonquils printed on it. "A bloody miracle is what you are: a chap who can read a map and also—and also what? Tell me."

"What?"

"Also speak *clearly.*"

"My mum was hard of hearing."

"There you are: a reason for everything on earth. As for the map business, you have obviously inherited it."

I did not reveal that neither my mother nor father had any sense of direction and my Nazi brother was forever getting lost on the way to meet with his fellow Aryans in the Barossa Valley. Instead, I allowed myself a glass of beer and suffered a dreadful hangover which endured into the following afternoon when I found myself reincarnated as the navigator of an FJ Holden while Titch Bobbsey drove like a maniac through the dirt roads of the gnarled Brisbane Ranges, stones ricocheting off the sump, huge trees flanking my vision as he slid through lethal corners. We streaked down long straights into hidden bends, or hairpins with dizzy drops awaiting us. He executed a handbrake turn above a precipice and I came to rest with my head nodding like a plastic dog.

Through all this "training" I was expected to hold the stack of notes he had supplied me with and to read them out loud above the engine roar.

"You see," Titch said. "It's in your blood."

# 20

BEVERLY SAID she could never live in the Marsh. She would die of boredom. For me it would be perfect, she allowed, because my life was one straight line. I was Mrs. Average. Her life was like a wrong 'un, googly, bosie, a cricket ball that looks like it's going to break one way but then does the opposite. That was her, she thought, but in the end it would be me who was Mrs. Wrong 'un. I wish it was not so.

No-one ever came to the Marsh without thinking, what a pretty town. It was a secret, almost, tucked down at the bottom of Anthony's Cutting. If there is a prettier war memorial than our Avenue of Honour, I never heard of it. Every tree in the avenue was planted for a local boy who died. Every trunk had its own name. The dead boys are now huge elms and they join together above the road and give a very calm impression. This is how you enter the town. You drive beneath them, up the aisle, beside the apple orchards, the shire offices, the lawn bowls games in progress.

You can dawdle through the wide streets and get some glimpse of our boring life. You will find no more exciting noise than the ding-ding of the blacksmith's hammer. On the other hand, there is nothing to warn you of the possibility that Mrs. bloody Guthrie at the state school might release your children to the care of their grandfather.

On the day Beverly arrived the police were out searching for my kidnapped children. My kitchen was so quiet and fretful that our tinny ticking little Westclox was getting on my nerves. And then, by jiminy, all quiet was murdered. Metal ripped and wood splintered and I felt the floor shudder in my shoes, as if some vital part had been removed by dental pliers.

Outside I discovered, three feet from my back door, a car connected to a long aluminium caravan the side of which was peeled open like a sardine can.

Two sulky-looking boys climbed from the car. I was stunned to recognise my sister's sons. Phonsey and Theo surveyed my house as if they hated it. They were darkly tanned, and had their swimmers on, as did the driver, Beverly, who modelled a bright pink one-piece with no accessory other than high heeled shoes.

She had scraped her caravan along the full length of my house.

Meanwhile Bachhuber was at the fence, raising his battered hat to her. Men are fools. My sister smiled and nodded, lifting that little nose she had been complimented on too often.

"Yoo-hoo," she called to me.

Yoo-hoo? I waited for an apology, an explanation. And what were her first words when she reached me?

"That's a good-looking man," she said.

Even when I drew her attention to the damage she announced I was the lucky one, compared to her. For while her caravan was seriously hurt, my house only required a lick of paint. The phone began ringing. I thought, police. The phone stopped. Bachhuber was staring, I thought, at Beverly's neat bottom. Was he blind to the implication of the caravan? Couldn't he see the warning written across her forehead, the way her whole body was leaning towards me, like a creature looking for a snack, then retreating (rearing, pulling back alarmingly) from the possibility of dire affront? Any listener to the quiz show knows that certain fruits signal their poisonous content to birds. You would think a quiz king could read my sister, but no: he removed his hat and smiled. So this was how Miss Clover stole his quiz show from him?

*And off he goes,* I thought, Mr. Handyman, riding to repair and rescue, lowering his stepladder on my side of the fence.

I drew my sister inside my kitchen where she could cause no more public excitation. She did not ask about my kids which she should have. She was deaf until she had located the wireless and settled herself at my kitchen table with an ashtray and her cigarettes. When I spoke, she hushed me. She just had a horse race she must listen to.

Her boys vanished into the shed where a freshly detailed FJ Holden sat waiting for their smudgy fingers.

I made a pot of tea and listened to my sister lose her bet. If I had had half a brain I would have understood why she had no money.

"Is he single?" she wished to know.

I said our neighbour was a teacher, meaning his wages would be insufficient for her purpose.

"He has women coming in and out of there," I said.

And then here was bloody Bachhuber, tapping at the flywire door. He had his ladder and a toolbox and was ready to do the neighbourly thing to my damaged wall. I would rather not have brought him in, but there was Miss Geelong, clip-clopping across the lino in her clever little shoes.

"Beverly Gleason," she said.

She was thirty-five years old, in her bathing suit.

"Willie Bachhuber," he said.

"What a musical name."

"As in Bach, you mean?"

Beverly smiled and frowned at once. I told Bachhuber that Mrs. Gleason and I had business to attend to and I dragged the little tart into the living room.

"What are you doing?" she hissed.

I told her to stay away from him. He had suffered quite enough.

So then, of course, I must have a crush on him, and I could have slapped her face but the telephone rang and it was Constable "Lurch" McIntyre who had had a call from Ron Durham to say Dangerous Dan Bobs was causing a nuisance at the Lerderderg River.

"Are my kids OK?"

"No worries," he said. "They're with their grandfather."

He was a moron. He knew nothing. I rang off to deal with my sister and her dirty smirk. If my face was red it was nothing to do with what she thought it was.

I asked her outright: "Where are you off to?"

In other words: please leave.

"Caravan parks aren't as cheap as you'd think."

"Bev, I got the same money you got. You can't have spent it all yet."

"I took your advice," she said, colouring as she was bound to. "Everything's tied up. So where am I even meant to live? Tell me."

And of course she was my flesh and blood. I had to let her stay here in her bloody caravan. She would be no trouble, honest. But she would suck up my electricity and eat my food. Her kids would fight with my kids. She would clutter up the yard which was, for now, our showroom.

Constable Lurch phoned again.

"Are you acquainted with Theodore Gleason and Alphonse Gleason?"

"You can tell their mum," I said. "When you get here."

Throughout this conversation Bev dramatised her poverty, counting out the small change in her purse. I wished Titch was here to read her the riot act, but he was in Footscray to inspect the second fuel tank which was being tailor-made to fit inside the boot.

He therefore missed his father's invasion of our kitchen. With him came our kids, head to heel in mud. Then Constable Lurch who wouldn't say no to a cup of tea. Then Theo and Phonsey with their smudgy upper lips and smutty teenage eyes. Last came Bachhuber himself.

And they all shoved into my place without any invitation and then, without permission, as if he were a miracle himself, the mongrel Dan upended a chaff bag full of fish.

I wished his son had been a witness to the act.

# 21

MRS. BOBBSEY WAS STARING daggers at me.

The God of the Wind was spreading out his arms above his catch.

They were redfin, by golly. Twenty of them, thirty. Beverly Gleason got a big one, ten pounds at least, gleaming olive green with broad vertical bands of anthracite across a deep body and bright reddish-orange pelvic and anal fins. She slid her fingers in the gills and lifted, and I saw the pale smooth underside of her brown arm.

"Do you want to feel the weight, Mr. Bachhuber? I never knew they grew this big."

Did it matter that this same fish had been the constant companion of my tumescent adolescence? Of course. Why else would I be suddenly transported to the weed-rank banks of the secret River Torrens where it snakes along the edge of Payneham, hemmed by thistle, and rusting corrugated iron, and stinging nettles, and sappy fat paspalum, musty with our amateur desire?

I had been too young to buy a "French letter" in the chemist shops—they would have laughed at me—but there was a newspaper seller on King William Street, Bert, who would flog them to us boys in ones and twos, not without a dirty joke. He had thinning red hair and a sweaty head. Like putting a sock on a banana, he said.

The redfin *Perca fluviatilis* which now covered the Bobbseys' lino floor was the same fish that colonised my childhood river. My pastor papa taught me to catch them with a rod and tin of worms. He never knew how close we stood to the site of fornication. He showed me how to skin a redfin (not judging it necessary to kill them first). There was something very disturbing in the shuddering convulsive flesh.

"Put it *down*," Mrs. Bobbsey instructed her sister. "Go wash yourself," she told her son. She turned on the policeman whose little finger was crooked delicately around the handle of his cup of tea. "The orchard called you to complain?" she asked him.

"They started it," said Edith. "We were just fishing."

"This is not fishing. This is slaughter."

Edith hugged her chest with her skinny muddy arms. "The Durhams were there, Mum."

"Yes. The river goes through their property."

"We were just mucking around, staring in the water at the fish and Grandpa said, could we eat them if we caught them and Mr. Durham said, good luck mate, no-one ever catches them. They're too smart for us. They hide out down in the snags."

"Help," cried Beverly as her redfin slithered free, sliding across the lino.

"Quit it," said Mrs. Bobbsey. "Act your age."

Beverly Gleason kneeled before her fish. Only the deep gut prevented it from vanishing beneath the fridge.

"As I was saying," said Edith, "before I was interrupted. They gave us their permission. Grandpa told them he's got this bubbling thing to attract the fish . . ."

The God of the Wind had been briefly distracted by Mrs. Gleason's kneeling form but he paid attention when his name was mentioned.

"Grandpa," said Mrs. Bobbsey. "You will have to leave."

"Grandpa said the fish would come look at the bubbling thing."

"Grandpa threw the bunger in the creek," cried Ronnie.

Was I the only one who didn't know they were discussing dynamite?

"Everyone likes a bunger," said Dangerous Dan who would later say the same thing to the *Sydney Morning Herald*.

"Explosion is not an activity permitted by a fishing licence," said the constable. "Not that this applied in your case, Mr. Bobs, if you get my drift."

"You wash yourself," Mrs. Bobbsey said to Edith. "You too," she told her sister.

"Grandpa bombed the creek," cried Ronnie. He shoved his hands into his crotch and lifted one foot in the air.

"Go now," said Mrs. Bobbsey. "If you have to pee, go now."

"Boom," cried Ronnie. "Boom." And ran out down the garden path and banged the dunny door behind him.

The mass murderer of fish was bathing in his glory. He stood in the midst of his harvest and rocked back on his heels and thrust his hands deep in his dustcoat pockets. He raised a flirty eyebrow at Beverly and, from his dustcoat pocket, produced what might have been a sausage wrapped in fatty brown paper, my mother's *Landjäger* to be precise. If there was animosity towards him, he did not seem to notice.

"Everyone likes a bunger."

"Oh Jesus Christ," said Mrs. Bobbsey. "Edith go to the bathroom. Now. Go. Dad, a word outside?"

"Come on." Dan tossed the *Landjäger* to his granddaughter. "It's not dangerous."

"Get out."

Mrs. Gleason was staring at me and I looked away.

"Only teasing," Dan said. "Bachhuber you haven't spoken."

"Leave Mr. Bachhuber alone, all of you," Mrs. Bobbsey cried, at the same time trying to wrest the *Landjäger* from her daughter.

"It's just gelignite," Edith said. "It's not dangerous, Mum. Grandpa could blow up the dunny while Ronnie was sitting on the seat."

"You could, could you, Dad?"

"I've played some pranks. No-one ever hurt themselves."

The air itself was unstable and Mrs. Bobbsey's lips were set thin and tight with rage.

"Dad," she said. "Outside. Now. Chat."

The God of the Wind put up his fists. "You want a fight like a man?"

Mrs. Bobbsey held wide the flywire door. "Please, Dad, please."

"When you're in the Redex you'll wish you were experienced with gelly."

Mrs. Bobbsey let the door swing shut again. "How do you mean? What about the Redex?"

"I might be your competitor."

"You wouldn't dare."

"I was in car trials before you were even born."

Mrs. Bobbsey sat down. "You're not in the Redex."

The old man offered a tight wide grin. "We'll be friendly competitors."

"Can't you just leave Titch alone?"

"I was talking to my mate Murray—he was in last year's Redex. He swears by the gelignite I gave him."

"Let us have a life, Dad."

"Murray reckons the road from Cloncurry has a stretch about eighty miles long. It's so bloody narrow, and if a car breaks down ahead of you, you're stuffed without a stick of gelly. Take a carton. Learn how to clear the road. I understand you're nervous," he said to Mrs. Bobbsey.

"Get off his back."

"This won't hurt anyone."

"All you do is hurt."

"I've been doing it for years. You can throw gelly in the fire and jump on it. It's got to be detonated. So you've got your gelly with a poker the size of a pencil up the middle of it and then you buy the detonators. They're the dangerous things," he said to Ronnie as he came back through the door. "Dets, they call them. Keep those things apart and you're OK."

The God of the Wind laid a second stick of gelignite on the kitchen table. "Play with it," he said to Mrs. Gleason. "Go on. Give it a whirl."

Ronnie took immediate possession of the gelignite and danced around the room, hitting himself on the head until his mother slapped his legs and he dropped the gelignite and ran away in tears.

"I will clean the fish," I said.

"I'll help," said Beverly. "They must have a knife."

I had no choice but to stand close beside her as she turned her attention to a kitchen drawer. Her shoulders smelled of coconut and I pointed out a wooden handled knife and she placed it in my palm and closed my hand around it.

The children were sent out of the room, and I set to clean the fish, standing at the table. Mrs. Bobbsey was in the garden. Dan explained gelignite to Beverly who signalled her understanding, step by step. Just the same, it was she who went to find the flour for dredging. I made a sharp cut along each side of the spine. I caught the dorsal fin between thumb and blade, and then, like a faith healer, held it in the air. Then I drove my fingers into its body and lifted out all the flesh and peeled the skin away like a sock off a foot, and I paused a second as Mrs. Gleason excused herself to Dangerous Dan. She took the fillet from me and dredged the sweet white flesh in flour. Feel the weight, I thought, not certain what was happening now. It was impossible.

# 22

WE HAD DAYS and days of fuss and bother. Bachhuber passed his driver's test at Bacchus Marsh police station where they asked him what colour an orange was. He helped deliver new cars to customers and was useful in many ways, although not always available when we wanted him.

Finally it was revealed he had been at the library in Melbourne, researching the Redex route, particularly the road north of Rockhampton because, he said, none of us had ever driven it. This was a presumption, but correct.

After dinner he produced maps and notebooks. My sister was stimulated beyond all decency. Now she had a bloody *pointer.*

"This is of more than academic interest," he said.

Titch fastened onto "academic."

"As a matter of academic interest," he would ask Bachhuber who never knew his leg was pulled.

The Redex certainly gave my husband something to look forward to but, as a "matter of academic interest," I also loved to drive. Sometimes I fretted I would be left behind. On sleepless nights I imagined myself speeding across the floodplain Bachhuber described, the brigalow scrub, the flying rocks kicked up by other cars. This was my adventure, on the "Crystal Highway," named for all the broken windscreen glass scattered along the verges. It was corrugated, guttered, crossed by creeks. When we heard it was also known as the "Horror Stretch" we assumed it was on account of the road conditions. Bachhuber did not suggest otherwise until the kiddies were all in bed. Then he gave it to us, no holds barred.

Titch left his beer untouched as he listened to these sickening stories.

"This is really true?" he asked.

Beverly nodded vigorously. I thought, what could she know?

Bachhuber said families had been forced off cliff tops, gunned down, babies brained with clubs. At Goulbolba, more than three hundred people had been shot or drowned which was called a "dispersal."

"This really happened?"

No, it was black people. It happened centuries ago. To me it was like a horror in the Bible. It was not from our modern time. *Now therefore kill every male among the little ones, and kill every woman that hath known man by lying with him.*

"God help me," cried Titch who would get upset listening to the story of the crucifixion. "What use is this to us?"

He gave his full attention to the hundred and eighty miles through the Kimberley, from Mardowarra to Halls Creek, eight pages of strip maps, each sheet depicting a vertical black snake of track cut by fine straight lines and warnings of heavy sand and water crossings and gates across the road.

"We know which way the gates open," cried Beverly, as if she made the map herself, as if she had flown on her broomstick two thousand miles across the red desert to the Kimberley, as if she understood the significance to us drivers who must confront these time-consuming obstacles. Just the same: if we knew which way they opened we would also know exactly where to stop, reverse, go forward.

"Well blow me down," my husband said. "You clever bugger, Bachhuber. How could you know this? The postman?"

Bachhuber's eyes crinkled at my husband and I thought, he'll be the navigator and I'll be home being mummy. I admit to feeling double-crossed by Titch. At that stage everyone was in love with Bachhuber, including, I have to say, my sister. At night we could hear them through the fibro walls, across the drive. Of course it was nothing to do with us, but we were the married couple and all the stress and tension of the Redex had dampened our affections. How sad it was to lie there, on our backs, not touching. I thought he had betrayed me.

He rolled away and I mourned those years we had held each other all night long, our good life which we wrecked by bringing the Redex into bed. I could feel Titch beside me, wide awake, not liking me but wanting me.

Beverly and Bachhuber woke me up. It was four in the morning and I went to the kitchen and made tea. Sooner or later she would go sneaking back into her caravan. I opened the back door and waited. A mopoke cried. The moon crept from behind a cloud. A smudgy cat stalked mice amongst the canna lilies. Finally I heard the soft pat of Bachhuber's flywire door and then the rusty hinge of the garden gate. I turned on our back light so she would see me walk along the path to the laundry and wait beside the copper.

She arrived barefoot, carrying her dirty bunched up stockings. Her makeup was smeary. She had ratty bird's nest hair. I took the stockings from her and laid them in the concrete tub in silence.

"He's very frail," I warned her. "Anyone can see that."

"Frail?" She smirked. "He's twenty-six years old."

"He's been hurt."

"Poor Irene," my sister said. "I'm sorry."

And I was reminded of why I always fought with her. I had wanted an older sister who might have looked after me, but that had never been the case, and she would always take what she could get, and put me down. I suggested she would be better having her social life off the premises.

She stared. I stared back. Once upon a time I would have pulled her hair.

"Alright," she said at last. She fled across the gravel to the caravan and I was left with just her filthy stockings.

The very next day she began to make a contribution to the household. She shopped. She cooked. She swept the builder's sawdust off the new showroom floor and removed the "Pilkington" stickers from the plate glass windows. She was not going to be denied Bachhuber. That must have been the basis of her thinking.

She was still annoying, of course, but now she helped the kids with their school projects. The Melbourne *Argus* had produced colour sup-

plements for the Royal visit and Beverly got down on the living room
floor with cartridge paper and a pot of homemade paste, cutting out
pictures of the "Royal crown," the "sceptre" and the "orb."

She also had her hair done so as to solicit comments on her physical
similarity to the Royal person. She and the boys dug a pit in the middle
of the back lawn, without permission. Here she cooked a lamb on hot
stones as had been described in the *Women's Weekly* as "Maori style."
This never cooked right through, but fair is fair: she was earning her
keep.

Bachhuber then encouraged her to believe she was an expert on
maps. He allowed her to lecture us on *The Australian Map Compen-
dium*. I admit this contained curiosities, not least the map with Australia at the top and Europe at the bottom, also explorers' maps with Bass
Strait missing and Tasmania joined to the mainland, the Maslen map
of the inland sea, and the entire country shown as a quilt of pastoral
leases.

"It's as educational as a dictionary," Titch said, but he never did like
education.

Also, we had to listen to them from our bedroom. That made me
sad and I tried to show Titch how I loved him, how he was always, for
ever my husband, but we failed, somehow.

In the dark I heard him say, "I've seen how you look at him."

I did not dignify that with an answer. All night my mind was full of
Redex. I thought about the Holden air cleaner which would clog with
outback dust. I decided I would put the kiddies into boarding school.
In the morning I was ashamed. I took Beverly's filthy stockings, and
put them in my handbag and drove down to the part of Simon's garage
which was becoming our new showroom. I lifted the bonnet and there
was that bloody air cleaner, a big black cylinder with a wing nut on the
top. I wasn't even in overalls, just a pleated grey skirt and blue cardy
and I could feel the apprentice watching me, wondering what was
the silly woman doing. In actual fact, the woman was being a genius.
She unscrewed the central wing nut and lifted off the lid, removed the
mesh cylinder, detached the main unit from the valve cover, poured

the oil away, tucked her lovely linen hanky into the open carby, washed the filter and main unit in petrol. Then, everything being shiny clean, she retrieved her hanky, stretched her sister's dirty stocking over the cylindrical mesh, and—Bob's your uncle—reassembled an air cleaner that would do the job.

I found the silent apprentice by my side.

He asked, "Does your husband know what you are doing?"

Being a man, he will have forgotten that by now.

# 23

THE BOBS BOY LAY on the backyard grass looking at the sky. I knew exactly how he felt, or so I thought, watching a transport plane drone through the clear unclouded sky. This was the utter desolation which colonised my childhood afternoons. This sadness was always lurking and could be triggered by something as inconsequential as small black ants, beings with no possible knowledge of my existence, hurrying across a concrete slab with what purpose who could know. I felt a similar sadness exploring my grandmother's musty atlas, those patchwork European nations whose lovely reds and violets were my natural home.

Then Germany declared war on me. We Lutherans were loyal subjects of the British Empire but my older brother was excited by his German blood. You could see his muscles fighting with themselves. He was lean like the pastor, but much taller, and stronger, and his constant rage left his neck pushed forward. He bought a motorcycle and rode to meetings. He celebrated Hitler's birthday by marching up and down the main street in Hahndorf. He spat a great bubbling tarry mess on our framed portrait of the King of England, and dared to smile while my father prevented my grandmother—frail and pale as china—from cleaning up his crime.

I wet my bed. I was compelled to fight at school. My father wrote away for the 1943 *National Geographic* map of the world which he imagined might bring me peace of mind. By the time that arrived the war was over and Carl had finally, after so much effort on his part, become one of the two native-born South Australians to be interned.

My parents suffered him, then I added to their pain, fleeing our home without a word of farewell or explanation. (I think of this most days.) My life was fear and chaos, but when I arrived in Melbourne it was to maps I turned, as to a parent.

When I entered Sebastian Laski's office, I thrust the door wide and closed it so energetically that Tindale's precious sketch maps rose into the air and sailed perilously close to the open window.

"Willy-willy," he called me, when he heard my name. I doubt I ever showed such energy again.

Sebastian was the Map Librarian of the State Library of Victoria. Such was the library in those years, when there were no proper cataloguing guidelines and very few shelves to accommodate the library's treasures, it is likely that this grand title was one Sebastian had granted to himself. He was a broad chested man with legs like fence posts which he displayed bare in all weathers, even when there was frost upon suburban lawns. He had a long jaw, and wide high cheeks and close-cropped silver hair and an ugly scar stretching from the corner of his mouth almost to his eye. I imagined him a warrior who had been compelled, by some failure or disgrace, to be reduced to this sedentary role.

Sebastian hired me to be his assistant. Lord knows what he might have finally taught me if I had not fled again, this time from Adelina who was the reason I ran away from Adelaide in the first place.

I was twenty-one years old. Sebastian briefly loved me, I think, in the way of childless men. He shared his reading of maps such as Willem Blaeu's "Terra Sancta quae in Sacris Terra Promissionis olim Palestina" which his erudition layered with the ghosts of other charts, including population movements, abstracting the cruel invasion of the *Homo sapiens* into the lands later fought over by Christians, Jews and Muslims. In those faded sepias I saw the extinction of the Neanderthals who had been moved, not through any restless desire to explore the world, but by the need to flee a ruthless enemy.

I had only known him for a week when I asked him to help me with the crisis that had caused us to flee from South Australia. Where else might I have turned? What other reckless path might I have chosen? I requested a loan of fifty pounds to procure an illegal abortion.

Sebastian brought Adelina and me home to meet his wife. We must have appeared to them as orphans, as indeed we were. They fed us soup with spoons so large we could barely fit them in our mouths.

It was to Sebastian I divulged not only my guilts and agonies but the unsettling emotions engendered in me by maps. This was grief, he said. He offered Jung: *I feel very strongly that I am under the influence of things or questions which were left incomplete and unanswered by my parents and grandparents and more distant ancestors.*

*It often seems as if there were an impersonal karma within a family, which is passed on from parents to children.*

*It has always seemed to me that I had to answer questions which fate had posed to my forefathers, and which had not yet been answered, or as if I had to complete, or perhaps continue, things which previous ages had left unfinished.*

My father never learned where I had vanished to. I owed him so much more.

Sebastian drove us to the abortionist's in his rusty Hillman Minx and then delivered us home again. He left us with a pot of stew and dumplings. In that blessed time I was his protégé and he introduced me to beer and his opinions of the relative virtues of both Freud and Jung which I remember as the subject of our conversations at the Albion Hotel in Carlton. Here, every Friday afternoon, when I was still a happily married young man, I learned much of value, including the error of standing on an ashtray which might close around my ankle as fiercely as a rabbit trap. It was at the Albion that I heard him say, "Don't give an old digger the shits." (Because how else would anyone know this odd foreigner had fought for Australia in the war?)

It was established I had no head for alcohol, and must stop at one. Those seven fluid ounces lifted my inhibitions sufficiently to reveal things to Sebastian I had never told a living soul. He seemed astonished to hear I sometimes became a river in a dream. He asked permission to make notes. Who else on earth would have talked to me like this? Through Sebastian I understood that Freud had mistakenly thought the unconscious is the filing cabinet for those repressed sexual desires which cause pathological or mental illness, but it was Jung who was his man. That was my good fortune, he said. It would have been traumatic to confess my snake dreams to the opposition, but a Jungian could recognise them as blessings. My giant snake was a reflection of *the Omnipotent and Omnipresent power of "God"* that lives within every human. My snakes often had whiskers which caused him to clutch me to his bosom and, such was his strength and size, no-one in the aggressively heterosexual Albion dared say a word.

Freud thought religion was an escape and a fallacy, Sebastian said. The correct view was the total opposite. Religion was a "direct line" between all peoples, from us to blacks and others known as "savages." Although all religions differed, he said, the archetypes and symbols remained the same. "Your snake is not your penis," he said, "it is a god."

With hindsight I suspect he was a member of the Polish aristocracy. How astonishing that I never asked. I ignorantly imagined his wound was a war injury when it was clearly a duelling scar from Heidelberg or Bonn. He was from an old family, I suppose, and had carried those huge soup spoons across the earth for some reason I could never know.

He told me that Jung had dreamed the First World War in November 1913, before it started. The great man had dreamed a map, in fact, a great flood and the death of thousands. He saw blood covering the northern and low-lying lands between the North Sea and the Alps. He saw mighty yellow waves, the floating rubble of civilisation, uncounted drowned bodies in a sea of blood.

I remember coming out of the Albion one yellow winter evening. I can still see the corner of Lygon and Faraday streets, and still retain whole sentences of Sebastian's recitation. I have searched but never found them on the page. Did he invent them himself? Was my mentor possibly unhinged?

That afternoon was in June 1950. Sebastian and his diminutive wife were two of our three good friends in Melbourne, the other being Madison Lee, the first male nurse and the first black man I ever knew. What a rarity Madison was in that year when the White Australia policy was in full effect. A few years previously the government had dithered about letting black GIs come ashore, but Madison had been granted residence as a "person of distinguished merit" which he claimed was a misunderstanding. The truth, Adelina said, was that he had saved an Australian general's son. In any case, he worked the same shift as Adelina. He was her friend and my friend. He cooked spicy dishes from Louisiana using yabbies from Merri Creek. That must have been *étoufée* although we had never heard of such a thing. He sang too, after dinner in the East Melbourne flat. His "Mona Lisa" was better than Nat King Cole's. Once or twice he brought a girl around, but his manner was that of a dedicated bachelor. I mean, his grace, his delicacy, his exquisite cleanliness, and the pain and yearning of his velvet voice.

I was relieved he was there when Adelina's waters broke and comforted that he came with us to the hospital. He was my companion in the waiting room where we ate meat pies and drank Fanta with all the careless innocence of boys.

But then the gowned obstetrician emerged and it was clear, immediately, something had gone wrong. I saw it on the doctor's narrow sculpted face, a twist, a sort of anger, and I thought, they screwed up, she's dead. I looked at Madison and he had seen what I had seen. The doctor wished to speak to me.

"No," he said, "alone."

I followed him along some corridor hating his thoughtless squeaky shoes. I don't know where we went. Was it an "examination room"? I remember a bassinet, an unhappy nurse. They both looked at me with awful pity. I thought, I will bring this baby up alone. I will care for it for ever.

But then I saw that this was not our baby. He was black with wild black hair.

The doctor said he was sorry.

My head was filled with storm and sand. I left the room and was lost inside the hospital. I emerged in a kitchen, and then the street and the cruel tram lines were wet with summer rain. I was a moving storm of rage and grief, a willy-willy, twenty-one years old, about to perform an action which would take a second and last a lifetime.

# Sydney to Townsville,
# 1300 Miles

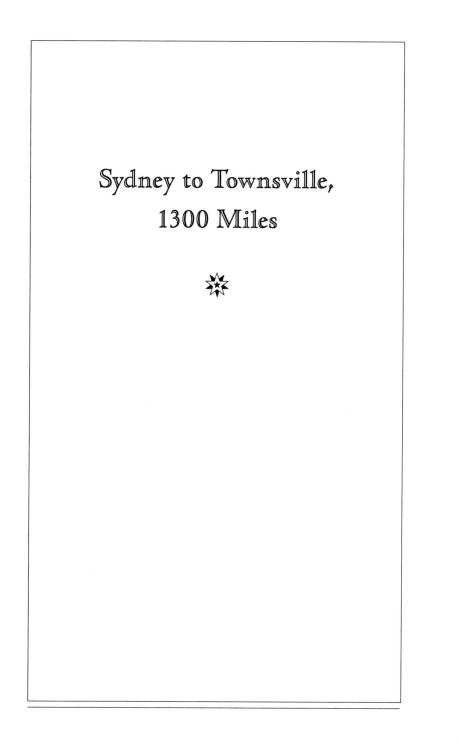

# 1

IN TWO WEEKS the Redex cars would depart from Sydney. Thus we moved from a private simmer to a very public boil. Our showroom was a work in progress, a temple to Redex Car Number 92. Once a polite suburban vehicle, our demo had become a brutal beast, four-eyed, with mesh protected headlights. We fitted a massive bull bar and applied the decals for Caltex and SPC bearings. Titch worked off the floor, taking orders in his spivvy charcoal suit. No-one seemed to understand I might be a driver too.

The car was bound to break a spring or two. To fit a new one would lose us points. At night it was back to overalls and drills, changing tyres, replacing leaf springs.

At night my husband did his Marine Corps exercises in his underpants and I lay in bed and watched him and wondered how much money would persuade Beverly to stay with the kids. I lay in the dark and imagined her face, the pleasure it would give her to refuse me.

Ah, she had been waiting for this, she claimed when I broached the subject. She understood the trap, she told me. I had used Bachhuber to keep her in the Marsh and now she would be compelled to be my babysitter. Well she was sick of Bachhuber. What did I think of that?

I said that was sad, of course.

Was I a dummy? she wished to know.

Yes, I thought. I was a dummy. I would have to stay at home.

"What diff does Bachhuber make?" she asked me. "Go on," she said. "Go and swan around the country. I've got nowhere else to live."

Thank you, God, good kind Jesus blessed be thy deliverance.

Bachhuber wore shorts into the colder weather and my sister was critical of his legs. Titch taught him how to remove the shackle bolt from the leaf spring, put a block of wood between the spring eye and floor, then jack the spring up so the eye moves along the wood to the spot where the shackle can be fitted. I was going to drive. I was really going. I made sure we had spare clips on the second leaves, to take the recoil and weight of the back axle when travelling over jump-ups and corrugated roads.

The Russian spy defected and the newspapers were full of photographs of Moscow thugs trying to drag his wife onto an aeroplane. Ben Calvo came running across to the showroom with the latest news, going yes, yes, yes, "Don't worry about the Russians. Look at this."

It was an attractive woman with her chest stuck out. This was Glenda Cloverdale the champion of *Nothing to Lose*. I would not have trusted her a moment.

Apple season ended. I made a huge map of Australia for the showroom and Beverly stole it from me. "Sorry," she said. "I just think I'd be better at this." Then she took my kids to help her paint it. I was very pleased at first.

Ronnie and Edith's cousins finally took an interest in them. Together they painted a window sign REDEX TRIAL 1954 in Day-Glo orange. They made small green flags to show the progress of Car #92 through blackfellah country no Holden ever crossed before. I did not like my kiddies cuddling with their aunt and of course she knew it. But I had got exactly what I wanted, hadn't I?

After teatime local families stood in the dark street staring through the showroom window while the kids added details to the map, GRID, GUTTER, CREEK CROSSING, DUST BAD etc.

I collected shillings for the public telephones along the road. I hid gifts so the kids could discover them every day I was away: ribbons for Edith, say, or a pretty little ring. I bought a sheriff's badge for Ronnie. I splurged on *Sparky's Magic Piano,* a real "album" with three ten-inch records, six sides, a total playing time of twenty minutes.

Titch did not want to carry spare tyres on the roof but we had no choice. The extra fuel tank took up too much room, we couldn't help that either. Titch rationed every inch of space. We laughed at Bachhuber, packing his grandmother's atlas and a book called *Answer to Job*. He owned the first drip-dry shirt I ever saw.

Dunstan was still in our hair but I expected we would soon be quit of him. Bachhuber packed no trousers, only shirts and shorts. He preferred bare feet to sweaty shoes.

Ours was the country that had killed the white men who dared to cross it, poor Burke and Wills and Leichhardt. Now we would face the killer country. We would face roads with dust two feet deep. We would circle the whole of our murderous continent in the same car Joe Blow drove to work. We were not pleased to hear Bachhuber compare us to dogs marking out our territory with pee.

We were front page in *The Bacchus Marsh Express:* Titch and me together with all the Holdens we had sold so far. It was a thrill, I admit it. I imagined that was fame. The Melbourne *Argus* telephoned me. They had a statement from a female competitor known as Granny Conway. "My motto is never touch the engine," she said. "You always strike trouble when you start lifting the bonnet."

So would I make a public comment on this nonsense?

I refused and Titch was angry. He said, "Get real, Irene." We were in it for the business. I should be prepared for Sydney where there would be no denying I was a woman driver. In the business of being written up, of course, Titch was his father's son, and when we finally left the Marsh for Sydney, he arranged for a convoy of new Holden owners to follow us out of town through the Avenue of Honour. He reckoned that might "make a story."

I wanted the kids to come with us for those first few miles. But then it seemed Edith and Alice Tudball were making Girl Guide uniforms, and Ronnie and his cousins could not be found. I did not let this spoil things. I was not offended that our navigator crawled into the back and studied the Redex rule book, as if reading would have us win.

"You'll get carsick," my husband said.

"No I won't," said Bachhuber.

And in this dull way the Redex Trial began, as tame and ordinary as a Sunday drive. I did not know what Titch had been up to. We rose from our lovely fertile valley, and I could not know that I would soon become a *wrong 'un*. Ahead of us was the climb from the flat country up Pretty Sally, a dormant bald volcano, a radiator-boiler of a road with an accident "black spot" due to a sharp turn near its crest. I was thrilled to feel the "go" in our engine.

There were no freeways, just the Hume Highway with yellow gravel verges, broken fanbelts, semitrailer skidmarks, a two-lane track with bridges too narrow for two vehicles to pass. The highway led us through streets of prosperous small towns, Euroa, Violet Town, Benalla, Glenrowan, Wangaratta. We arrived in Yass, in New South Wales, the road chock-full of all-night truckies' cafes and spare-parts garages and panel shops.

"See that," Bachhuber said at last.

He indicated a signpost.

We did not respond.

"Sixty-three miles to Young. That's Lambing Flat."

"Is that a fact?"

I never knew about the so-called "riots" at Lambing Flat. Why would I? They had occurred a century before, apparently. There had been thousands of Chinese miners just down the road at Lambing Flat.

"Poor buggers," he called them with emotion in his voice. The nasty white miners had knocked apart the Chinese tents and stolen everything inside. There was gunfire and police sabre charges and one man was left dead.

I thought, oh no. I squeezed my husband's hand, but still he stopped the car.

"Get out," Titch told our navigator. "Yes you. There's something I want you to do for me."

"Of course."

"Just walk around a bit. Tell me what you see."

I thought, he's going to drive off. He's going to leave Bachhuber in Yass.

"No, don't," I said.

Titch was waiting behind the wheel.

"Please?" I asked.

Meanwhile Bachhuber was on the footpath staring in the window of the baker's. Then he was in the middle of the double lines with the traffic whizzing past each side.

"Pretty town," he said when he came back.

"So?" Titch asked. "What did you see?"

"Nice goldrush buildings," he began. "All the money in the courthouse and the pubs."

"Any Chinamen?"

"Not a one." And he was grinning, his teeth very white in his tanned face.

"Any blood?"

"Not a drop, I'm pleased to say."

"You're the navigator," Titch said. "You tell us what is happening *now*. I could not give a fuck about what happened a hundred years ago."

I was embarrassed. I smiled at our poor navigator so he knew I liked him.

Titch pulled back into the traffic. "I was a chauffeur for a Chinese herbalist," he said. "My father sold him a Model A. Then I lived with the family in Little Bourke Street. Mr. Goon, his name was."

I thought, here it is, one more torture he never told me.

"He was a clever man, the herbalist," my husband said. "He had a little velvet cushion and he would lay the patient's hand on it and touch it very gently. The Goons wanted me to go back to China with them. If my dad had not needed me, I would have gone. So when you tell me about all that business back there, you haven't got a bloody clue what I think. I have never seen children treated so kindly in all my life."

And then I loved him, more than I ever knew I loved him. He had grown up with no mother, been raised by a cruel father. He was a wonder, wresting love from dung. And now he was in the Redex Trial. It was impossible. The road markings changed from white to yellow and we were in another world. We travelled together towards the start, along the rain-slicked narrow highway beneath clouds like greasy wool, through wide wet sodden winter farms, the unrelenting green of paddocks, the distant mountains of the Great Dividing Range.

At Mittagong—seventy miles from Sydney—I saw sunstruck sandstone, gum trees with skin like elephants, I was in driver heaven. It was exactly at this point we first heard an engine roar. Not a truck, but something big. It sounded like a tractor doing a hundred miles an hour.

It was then we saw him pass, the bastard, the devil, like a wasp from a mud nest. Dan Bobs, the enemy of my husband's happiness. Behind him came a police car, blue light flashing. Bastard, bastard. I would have killed him if I could.

## 2

I HAD WRITTEN away for my own copy of the Redex rule book and had also purchased an expensive Curta calculator to prepare for my role. The Bobbseys teased me about the book because they thought the rules so obvious, and as for the Curta calculator, they had never heard of such a thing.

The Curta was beautiful in the way of a Zeiss lens and was a thing I would not normally have had any excuse to buy. Fortunately the Redex was a contest where average speeds were everything. As the officials kept saying, it was not a race but a gruelling test of machinery in the "outback conditions."

That is, we must prove our car reliable. If we arrived a minute early we lost points. Ditto if we came in late. The purpose of the Curta was to constantly recalculate the speed required to arrive on time. I entered the prescribed average speed, official mileage, odometer reading, corrected speed in miles per minute. No-one joked about it in the end.

The rule book decreed that reliability was the only issue. There could be no major rebuilds of engine, transmission, chassis or suspension. Components were sprayed with a special paint visible under a mercury vapour lamp. There were scrutineers waiting for us everywhere, as annoying as policemen in their way.

As for the police themselves, they hated us. They knew what the rule book would not admit, that the drivers were all maniacs, gathered to race, to burn each other off, to "do the ton," to get ahead, to make up time, to sometimes create breathing space for adjustments and repairs but always, no matter what they said in interviews, to make the other fellow "eat my dust."

We entered Sydney at 30 mph.

# 3

NEITHER TITCH NOR I had ever been to Sydney. Don't laugh. We'd never seen the Harbour, the Bridge, a Bondi tram, a ferry, never even bought a pound of prawns. As my husband told the street photographer, we were business maggots from Bacchus Marsh.

We ate Oysters Kilpatrick for the first time. We almost forgot what we had come for. It was a shock, in late afternoon, to roll into the Sydney Showground and see what we were up against: two hundred and sixty-seven hardened competitors, armoured with massive bull bars, done up in war paint, arranged on the dirt speedway ring inside the parade ground. Lex Davison, Jack Brabham. *All the cracks had gathered to the fray.* The press were there, camera flashes erupting in dense clusters like a battlefield. A cat could look at a king, we dropped in on Jack Davey's crew. He said, "Hi ho, everybody," like he does on radio. Two cars over was a swarm of flashbulbs dying for the fame. It was Dan Bobs still in the race, with his false teeth and his false smile and his arm around two pretty girls, the *Women's Weekly* crew.

"Got to hand it to him," his son said. "He doesn't give up."

Give up. Throw up. In the rubbish bin I found the morning's newspapers:

### MAD DASH FOR STARTING LINE

Mr. Bobs had hit a stone and damaged the back plate on his differential which lost its oil. In Benalla he filled the diff with heavy oil and made a dash for Mittagong where a new differential was fitted. He made up lost time thanks to Sgt Coady and Constable Withers of the Highway Patrol who had escorted the former aviator to the showgrounds where he had admirers waiting to assist.

Dan Bobs, I read, was "well known to the motoring fraternity." I don't think this was true. He was also a "wily prankster," a joker, a character, suspected of playing pranks with gelignite in previous car trials, a habit which had him named Dangerous Dan.

The reporter had learned of the existence of a second driver Mr. Sullivan ("my little Englishman" according to Dan Bobs) and also revealed the former aviator had a daughter-in-law in Holden # 92.

"Women can wear overalls all they like," Bobs said, "but they can't teach their father-in-law to suck eggs." He reportedly had little patience for women "cluttering up the contest."

"Don't worry about it," my husband said. "Forget it."

As usual he did not understand his father would destroy us any way he could.

Bachhuber found a boarding house, ten minutes from the starting line. The landlord had had a stroke and would not give up his best chair by the wireless. As we could not hear the ABC news the landlady undertook to provide the papers in the morning for a shilling each. Likewise we were refused the use of her telephone and I was forced back into the showground where the red phone boxes were lined up by the toilets, offering a full view of the only person I did not wish to see.

Dan, surrounded by his subjects, removed his hat and bowed to me.

There were a mob of drivers crowded around the telephone boxes, rattling loose change in their pockets as if their private parts were made of silver. These same jokers thought it amusing I was wearing overalls. I did not care. I waited. It was only when I got to the phone I saw that my father-in-law was in the next door box, making a show of saluting me. I turned my back and heard Ronnie had gone down the shops to buy lemonade and Beverly was still at the hairdresser. Dan was now kneeling, tying up his boots, not caring about who might be waiting to call their wife. I ignored him in favour of Edith who needed help with the recipe for golden syrup dumplings. We were just mixing in the butter when there was an enormous bang.

I did not know what world I was in.

Dan's phone box jumped in the air. It fell over on its side. I saw the receiver lying on the grass.

My phone was dead. Poor Edith, I thought, poor little girl. I ran into a shower of flashbulbs blinding me. I was in tears when I got back to Titch.

I told him his father tried to kill me.

I was told to relax. Blowing up toilets was Dad's favourite trick. Did he kill me? No he didn't. If he had wanted to he would have.

I lay awake for hours and hours, thinking my husband should stick up for me. I woke to find my photograph on the front page. An ugly woman in overalls, her mouth like a torn rag.

REDEX STARTS WITH A BANG.

I was Irene Bobs co-driver of Holden # 92. I was by "sheer coincidence" the daughter-in-law of Dangerous Dan Bobs. At the time of yesterday's explosion, Mr. Dan Bobs had been in "serious conversation" with Sergeant "Dick" Worthington of the New South Wales police. The two men were some considerable distance from the telephone booths involved.

The reporters had already used up all the male contestants. They went off to Granny Conway (Car # 28) who was very pleased to give her opinion of me. I should quit pranking. I should wear a skirt. I should drive carefully and then I wouldn't need to copy all the men who raced ahead to make repairs before the checkpoint.

The journos found me working on our vehicle. Would I comment? No I wouldn't.

My father-in-law had a low opinion of women drivers. What did I think of that?

Seeing he tried to blow me up, I said, he must be a bit worried.

Did I plan to beat him, they wished to know.

I said I would destroy him. If I had been a footballer that would have been OK, but now I got us named the FEUDING BOBS.

Titch, it seemed, heard none of this. He wanted to buy me a pretty dress for the photographers, but we had to attend a road safety lecture by the Road Safety Council, and the Police Traffic Branch. We checked air, tyres, water, oil, and tightened everything that might shake loose. I put on some lippy for the photographers who never came.

The front seat must be adjusted to the driver's legs, so the navigator must conform and Bachhuber's knees were therefore bent and pushed against the dashboard where they would be locked in place for eighteen days. He was hard at work with a tricky gadget, calculating how to maintain the 22 mph average required.

We departed at ordered intervals of one minute, after which we must suffer the hysteria of the New South Wales police. Being forced by law to crawl we were overtaken by Sunday drivers and hoons in lowered Holdens with three-quarter grind camshafts. Their younger brothers manipulated the crossing lights to make us stop and sign their autograph books.

Bachhuber began updating instructions based on his Curta calculator. We saw the sea at Newcastle, and then were winding through the bush, overtaking semitrailers. Then the country changed and slow brown rivers looped and snaked across the gaudy green. There was heavy rain between Taree and Coffs Harbour then pineapples and bananas, like in a foreign country with bright green hills, the highway as muddy as a pig paddock. The locals turned peevish and changed the road signs, but credit where credit is due: the Curta was a beauty. Titch drove. I drove. The navigator was calm and level.

I checked us into Brisbane, six hundred miles of Sunday driving. Titch had fortunately missed my comments to the Sydney press. That night I dreamed I had a baby which the court ruled must be taken from me. They would not say my crime.

# 4

THIS WAS the tropics and all that suggests. For hundreds of sweaty miles I had breathed Mrs. Bobbsey's neck, her familiar sister skin. It was a cruel road of boulders, dry creeks, tidal creeks, ruts, deep holes, scrubby floodplain, a few hills, although the toughest obstacle was sorting out the confusion caused by two conflicting official maps. In this schemozzle, fifty cars were unfairly penalised, and their crews lost twelve hours of rest time while they appealed injustice and ineptitude. My two drivers, on the other hand, were free to find a boarding house and telephone their kids. The navigator gained great kudos.

Now it was time to sleep chastely beneath the cooling car. No-one knew my dreams. With morning came the Bobbsey husband, smooth cheeked, fragrant with Old Spice and baby powder, his black hair flat across his perfect head. Did I sleep well? Like a madman, I did not say.

"Good man," he said. Today the road would be a nightmare. He had no need of average speeds.

"What about secret checkpoints?"

"Eff the secret checkpoints," he cried, pulling on his yellow chamois gloves. Machinery would get murdered now, he said.

The official map described the road as "undulating" which meant it was a series of ramps which had the vehicle airborne half the time. It "undulated" its way through dreary subtropical brigalow, brownish grass, sleepy creeks whose murderous alter egos had previously ripped the banks apart and left jagged descents and rocky beds I would never have dared to drive across. I had the utmost confidence in Titch's ability even though his eyes were only inches above the steering wheel. The map said WATER CROSSINGS and SUDDEN DROPS and I kept my head on my shoulders as we slid and drifted with the wheel sliding through the driver's perfect yellow gloves.

On a straight stretch of 2.5 miles we were overtaken by Frank Kleinig in a Peugeot 203, then the Humber Super Snipe works team who were nice enough to wave.

Mrs. Bobbsey forced a stop. She was concerned about a blowout due to increased tyre pressure in the heat. They released forty pounds, husband two tyres, wife the rest. We were overtaken by Ken Tubman's team.

Now Mrs. Bobbsey was at the wheel. She had a lovely bump on her nose. She reported the "old bugger" was on our tail.

"Let him go."

But hers was not a nose to yield.

"It is not a race," her husband said.

We were in Tubman's dust and Dan, the old grey shark, was charging at our rear. The road was narrow, bumpy, decorated with broken windscreen glass. It had spongy edges that I feared would roll us over. Titch was clutching the front seat with an eye peeled for kangaroos.

Mrs. Bobbsey's eyes were watery with dust or domestic issues.

Titch said let him pass, let him pass.

"BEND INTO DEEP DRAIN," I said.

She got it perfectly, sliding gracefully to the side so the grey Plymouth edged slowly by. Her high colour travelled all the way below her buttons. Who would have guessed it would feel just like a dance, even with the dust and danger and her husband breathing in my ear.

"ROUGH ROAD. 9 MILES," I said.

I thought, this is it. This is my life at last.

Then came a mighty percussion and I recognised the brutal slap of gelignite. My innards came into my mouth and the whole rear end was smacked sideways across the road.

"Controlled explosion," Titch said. "Take a joke."

"GRID in two clicks."

Now a corrugated road, in the Plymouth's dust. I waited for the second explosion as we shook and rattled at sixty miles an hour while Mrs. Bobbsey shouted F and C and B and S like a woman giving birth.

My Lord, she stirred me up. I would not have missed it for the world.

# 5

BY NOW, I thought, my reported comments to the Sydney journalists must be wrapped around fish and chips. If so, that was not enough to save me from my punishment. My husband had read the Sydney press in Brisbane. He had not said a word. He had stewed in private for four hundred miles. Not until we were dealing with overheated tyres did he judge it time to speak.

He was disappointed, he said.

It was not so much what I had said about his father. It was the damage I had done to the value of our name. This was why we were in the Redex, apparently. I had thought it was so he would have something to look forward to, but I must have been wrong. We were in the Redex to "merchandise" our famous brand.

He stank of Dunstan.

He said there was a knack in talking to reporters. It was one thing to criticise his father but perhaps I could learn from Dan and how he used the newspapers. There was a definite art to it.

Art. Fart. He pulled the rug from under me and never knew what he had done.

We stopped at Toolooa, some place spelled like that approximately, just a few miles inland from a lovely beach I never saw. There was an abandoned petrol station and a working telephone box. It was in this place I discovered Ronnie had the measles. Beverly was waiting for the doctor's call so please get off the phone.

I asked my husband what we should do now. He said we had to make up time.

They reckon Gladstone is the gateway to the wonders of the Great Barrier Reef. I remember the smokestacks, and my despair on learning that the doctor had still not arrived in Bacchus Marsh. We were now twelve hundred miles away from Ronnie. It was the day I drove the so-called "Horror Stretch," well named for every minute of what lay ahead. The unexpected comfort came from Bachhuber. I was so grateful for his reassuring hand as we dropped down into a creek and slammed the armour-plated diff against the rocks.

"Nicely played," he said.

Then Titch was driving, pushing the speed, but he drifted wide around a bend and nearly hit Dan's Plymouth: on its roof in the middle of the sugar cane. Don't stop, I thought. We don't have that luxury. How bloody sad to feel him brake. He was still his father's dog.

# 6

THE FIRST ABORIGINALS I ever saw were rocking Dan's Plymouth back and forth. As I crossed the road the car rolled upright and stood on its wheels again, swaying, steaming, in a nest of sugar cane. The red-headed co-driver was already back behind the wheel.

While Dan checked all the vehicle's windows, his new friends pressed around him eagerly.

What conversation took place between them was difficult to know although the voices of the rescuers became progressively higher in their pitch.

There was also a quieter fellow, perhaps sixty, not tall like his boy-ish comrades, but broad shouldered and barrel chested, with a deep furrowed brow, hooded bloodshot eyes, grey stubble and a mischievous disposition. The younger men were a flock, in persistent negotiation with a moving but resistant centre. This was Dan who had, he said, no *baksheesh*.

The older man showed no interest in this altercation. All his atten-tion was on me.

I held out my hand. He took it.

"Where you bin grow up?"

"Near Melbourne. Far away."

"Bloody Yarra River," he said, not inclined to release his hold. Then, suddenly, he tugged my fair hair. At the time I thought this strange. I think it even stranger now.

"Proper whitefellah," he said.

"I'm Willie. Willie Bachhuber."

"Bachhuber no way," he said.

My scalp was stinging, but he was smiling. I had my driver's licence and I showed him.

"Proper whitefellah," he smiled. It would be days before I realised he knew more than I did. In any case, I would never have allowed the possibility that he was being sarcastic.

I thought, dear God. Perhaps his grandparents had been killed by white men. "Goulbolba?" I asked, because this was Goulbolba country on my mental map.

"Bachhuber," the man said.

Perhaps I mispronounced Goulbolba. "Goodbye," I said. The Plymouth's engine roared. The air was full of violent dust. My shins were stung by a shower of gravel. The young men threw a stone or two at the fleeing Plymouth and then turned on Titch whose hand was already in his pocket.

The old man had another go at my hair, but I was ready for him, and he laughed when I clamped his wrist.

Back in the car I arranged my clipboard and my map. I said nothing about the tragic history of these men Titch was calling "boongs."

10.2 MILES. LEFT RIGHT BEND ON CREEK.

It was hard going. It took all of eighteen minutes before we reached the place where I glanced upstream and saw, to the west, amongst the tangled flood-washed tree trunks, another Redex car, a Holden, decked out in violent racing livery with decals and a number it is wisest I not mention. The car was pitched nose-down, almost vertical, pointing into the dribbling creek. Rolled vehicles would soon be a common sight but this second one seemed impossible. Its back wheels were in the air, leaving its springs as naked as a corpse's private parts. Titch quietly braked and killed the engine. He indicated we were to leave both the car and Mrs. Bobbsey.

We called "coo-ee." Otherwise the creek was quiet with no birdcall except a mournful currawong crying, as usual, like a lost child. We clambered over the snaggy tree trunk flotsam and saw, through the open driver's window, strip maps scattered front and rear, and the key in the ignition. There was a strong smell of mashed bananas.

The crashed vehicle seemed so perilously arranged I would not have gone anywhere near the radiator, but Titch, having placed himself in a position where he might have been crushed to death, announced the radiator was almost cool.

There was something oddly furtive about him now, and he climbed up a mouldy tree trunk to the floodtime bank and stood, like a yellow-gloved wood spirit, with his left hand supporting his right elbow, and his right hand across his bright red mouth.

"Tell her to bring the car down here," he said at last.

"How?"

"Along the track we walked on."

"She can't drive there."

"Just tell her, Willie."

It was the first time he called me by my Christian name.

# 7

THE CAR WAS STOPPED, my husband vanished. Bachhuber was at my open door apologising for waking me: there had been an accident. Would I kindly drive our vehicle along the track beside the creek. I did so, imagining we were on a mission of mercy.

But then Titch announced we were to remove a set of rear leaf springs. I asked would he make his wife a graverobber. He winked, and I saw he planned to somehow cheat.

Bachhuber and I worked on the teetering carcass exactly as we had done the drill in Bacchus Marsh. There was a bad smell of rotting leaves around the scene, and it was still clinging to our clothes later as we hid the looted springs and clips beneath our own rear seat.

No-one told me that we would be able to re-use these springs without penalty. My husband kept that secret from me. The Redex scrutineers had used radioactive paint on the original components. So if we used these stolen springs the Geiger counters would not know. Witnessing this deceit I thought of Mrs. Markus.

We still had six hours' drive to Townsville, and when we had stowed the springs it was come on, hurry, come on, pedal to the metal. I said I must attend to a call of nature. He told me to be real. I thought, he has wasted time to help his father, now he can waste some time on me. I deliberately took along my front page interview to wipe my bottom. If he noticed he did not comment.

Being a man the navigator was surely thinking like they do, that I must remove my overalls and be nude as Eve just up the track. So I went a long way up the creek, amongst a nest of broken sticks and leaves and timber smashed up by the floods. I carried our little garden trowel, until I came upon a huge tree ripped out by its roots so it left a crater six feet deep. That saved a lot of digging. I teetered over the crater, naked as the day, clinging to a mud-crusted tree root.

My call of nature was just a whisper. On the crater walls, only a foot from the surface, I saw the roots had grown around dead bones. The first crumbled in my hands and I saw there were so many others, a graveyard, sickening. That is, these were not animals. There were so many, they must be blacks.

I extracted a human jawbone. I retreated. I rushed back into my overalls. I was an interfering woman. I climbed down into the excavation where I was able to lift a human skull from the broken soil.

It was just a tiny thing, as fragile and powdery as an emu egg. I was a mother. I knew what it was to hold a tender child and I knew this must be a little boy, and all these bones around him must be his family. He was quite clean, and very light, and it seemed he might turn to dust if I was clumsy. So I tucked the digging tool in my back pocket and held him in both hands, then carried him, as carefully as if he were a bowl of water, back through the dull shrubs and grasses.

When I arrived at our car I showed them what I had.

"It's OK," Titch said, "I'll drive."

He had nothing more to add.

The navigator opened the back door for me but then he stood in front of me, peering down at my little fellow, so long dead. Bachhuber had a pencil stuck behind his ear, as always, and now he removed it and I moved the little head away from him. But no, he said, he wished only to point out the round hole, right where the little ear had once listened to the water of the creek.

God knows why I cried about something so long ago. My husband did his best to understand but this was not our fault. We never knew this piccaninny.

I didn't drive for the next six hours but I felt the angry corrugations on the road as big as railway sleepers. I smelt the leaves from the riverbank like the abattoirs and tanneries from my childhood. Poor little boy, I held him like a mother does, with my palm around the back of his head. Then the road was deep between the shivering sugar cane, twelve feet tall it seemed. We were insects speeding through the secret grass. Sometimes we had horizon, sometimes not. Then we idled in the morning dark as farmers set the cane on fire. Ash blew through our open windows. "Burdekin snow" they called the cinders. I held his little smudgy head and listened to the cane fire in full roar.

I nursed him as we passed through endless cane fields. The tropical towns had smokestacks and lumpy mills and grey worn-out houses built on poles. There was rambling bougainvillea so big and old it was pulling down its trellises.

Finally, at dusk, we checked into the Townsville showgrounds. In the giant fig trees above our heads, hoards of lorikeets squabbled over who would sleep with whom and where. It was a foreign land to me.

When my husband was informed I intended to take the skull to the police station he ordered Bachhuber to accompany me.

I would have appreciated it if he could come along himself.

No, he had to see a man about a dog.

Careful he doesn't bite your bum, I did not say.

The showgrounds were in Townsville's West End and the police were at least two miles away. So the locals had plenty of time to gawp at me. There was a woman wearing overalls. Well, blow me down. The police station was as big as a factory and here we found a sergeant grappling with a black man the worse for wear and we had to wait until he had been escorted to his "sleeping quarters" before we could state our business.

I will not say the sergeant laughed or smirked but he was certainly discomforted and had great difficulty in knowing how he could assist the Redex crew.

So what was I meant to tell him? Was it really such a puzzle? A crime had been done by someone.

Bachhuber pointed out the bullet hole.

"Your boyfriend has forensic knowledge?" the policeman asked me. Then, to Bachhuber: "It looks like you might have a personal interest in the dusky races, mate."

"Oh really?"

"Just looking at you, mate. It's obvious."

"What do you see?"

"It might not be obvious where you come from, mate. Up here we have what you might call an educated eye."

I asked him what this had to do with dusky races.

"You're from the south, Missus? Your boyfriend is a white man in the south?"

I thought, we'll have a good laugh about this tonight.

"Then good on you. Good luck to you both. As for this matter." He pushed the little head towards me. "You should consider it a souvenir. It may even be worth a bob or two down there. What's so funny, Jimmy?" And he stared at Bachhuber until he looked away. "Now," he turned to me, "here's what we'll do about your lost and found."

From deep in a drawer he produced a large receipt book with many sheets of carbon paper. He fetched a steel nibbed pen of the type you see in post offices and on the form he wrote: *Abo infant skull found near Funnel Creek/Finch Hatton.*

I did not question how he knew the child had been Aboriginal or how he guessed the placenames and I had no choice but to accept the piece of paper together with the skull. He had no room to store it, so he claimed.

I carried the small cardboard box into the tropical night and I suppose we were both thinking the cop must be troppo. I was embarrassed, so I held my tongue. The air was rank with flying foxes and I saw them blanket the sky above the showgrounds like bombers on a raid.

The Redex crews had gathered at the West End Hotel where small bats were feasting on the insects around the lights. The pub was like a glowing wedding cake, built in the ornate style of years gone by. The public bar was on the ground floor but the crews were all upstairs, crowded on the wide verandah, leaning over the floral cast-iron balustrades. My husband was in a jolly mood, calling down to us to join him.

I felt foolish with my cardboard box and hid it beneath the stairs. Then the only obstacle was a green frog, as big as a dinner plate, sitting bug eyed on the landing. I politely stepped around him. Upstairs I found a barmaid who demanded I name my poison and I said I'd have a beer and asked Bachhuber what he'd have.

"You got your certificate?" she asked him.

"We're not from here," he said.

I said I had no certificate either.

"You don't need one, love, but he knows what I mean."

Of course I ignored her nonsense. I ordered a beer for me and a lemonade for my navigator.

"Well he can certainly have that," she said, and whatever tickets she had previously required, she did not want them now. She must have seen how warmly we were accepted by the crème de la crème, famous drivers with their war stories e.g. a Hillman somersaulting three times before sliding to a halt on loose gravel, a Vanguard flying from a jump-up and landing with such a thump its rear window fell out. We were an elite crew who had not lost a single point. In less than a minute, I would be inches from Lex Davison and Jack Brabham who would soon become our mates.

And there he was, in the midst of all his towering heroes, the very complicated bloke I married. Handsome Titch Bobs was once again illuminated by inner light, a leader in the 1954 Redex Trial, pushing his finger into Jack Davey's chest.

He got the usual laugh for being a "business maggot" from Bacchus Marsh. He was understood, celebrated, high above the Townsville showgrounds, and I saw no reason to dwell on his deceit in the matter of the looted springs.

# Across the Top End,
# 1600 Miles

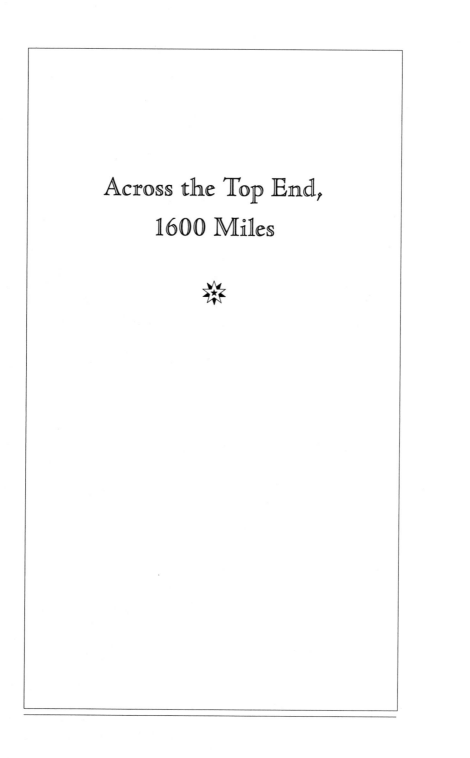

# 1

THE BOBBSEYS HAD PRE-BOOKED a room for themselves in the hotel. I was allocated a cot in an abandoned wartime barracks where I cleaned the frog droppings from the floor, squeezed lemon juice on ears and toes, pulled the sheet over my head and stretched my legs out straight at last. By the time the drunken crews returned, my brain was far away, filled with endless looping roads.

My ears were itching from mosquito bites. In my dream I had become a black man in a court. I suppose this was set off by the idiot in the police station, driven hysterical by his own white purity. In my dream I was accused of being a spy. I was brought before a judge who was a "connoisseur of race," the ugly term stays with me. He thought I possessed knowledge of all routes, paths, roads, ancient and modern tracks like veins and arteries and the viscera of prawns. The Curta fell apart. I scrambled on the courthouse floor searching for the screws, impossible, too small to hold.

There was a farting competition in the barracks.

Meanwhile, in my dreams, I had hundreds of maps but I was no longer sure which was the official route. Beverly was somehow there. She made a dirty joke about "route" and "root" and "rubber." She gave me an eraser and I must rub out all these Vacuum Oil and Shell and Esso routes or I would be disgraced. Mrs. Bobbsey was present, whispering that she would kill to win. She showed me a peculiar screwdriver, in confidence. The crumbling eraser destroyed fierce lines of bluish black crushed ants. I called the turns in a foreign language—*ahe phlupwa*. I thought, I must remember this.

My face in the shaving mirror, white as it ever was.

It was the men's opinion, at the self-serve breakfast in the barracks, that Mrs. Bobbsey was up herself. She had drunk too much. She had boasted she was going to win. I fled the barracks for our car where I napped amongst the backseat jumble until Titch arrived with blood-shot eyes and Alka-Seltzer. I accompanied Mrs. Bobbsey to the news-agent where we found ourselves amongst the favourites. There was a telegram for Mrs. Bobbsey and one for me.

PLEASE REPORT ANY GIANT WOMBATS. BEV.

That is, she was threatening to report my night vision problems to her sister. I should have revealed them anyway, but you could ask any semi driver, or simply examine the skidmarks on those long straight stretches of highway where weary brains had projected hypnagogic nonsense on the road ahead. I was a good navigator, it was proven. Sometimes at night I saw things that were not there.

As we came back to the showgrounds, the cars were leaving at one-minute intervals and the motorcycle cops were revving their Triumph 500s. Our departure slot was in twenty minutes' time.

"Just watch me go," said Mrs. Bobbsey, beautiful, bloodshot, with tangled hair.

# 2

AS WE CUT ACROSS the continent from east to west, the little boy was safe between us in his cardboard box. Bachhuber navigated me across dry beachy land, hills and flats, arid plains of reddish kangaroo grass. There were more trees than I had expected. God knows what murder was buried there, curled up in their roots.

Two level crossings.

At 29.5 a CULVERT and a LONG SINGLE TRACK.

Then a talcum powder dustbowl. Then a switch of soil. We cut between grey banks. We banged over baked clay, into long ruts spiked with rocks and roots. It was said the real Australia is beautiful, but not by me.

My father-in-law was defeated, done, dusted. He had already lost a hundred points but now he was filling up my rearview mirrors. There was no room to let him pass, not even if I wanted to. The edges of the track were piled high with sand.

He charged at me. I braked. He sat on his horn. My husband ordered me to take it easy, keep my panties on.

"Don't speak like that," I said.

Bachhuber touched my knee. "Bear left," he said.

I did so.

There was a worrying suggestion from the exhaust valve, although how could I hear anything above this clatter?

Titch instructed me to let his father pass. "He's just having fun."

Ha bloody ha, I thought.

"Pull over for him. Let him pass."

"No."

"It's not a race, Missus."

The road now widened and the Plymouth pulled around us and I saw the cockney sidekick was at the wheel. The big boss was rolling down his window to the dust. I could see his mouth opening and he was signalling for me to wind down my window.

"He wants to tell us something."

Bachhuber nudged.

"DIP OVER CULVERT," he said.

"You're driving like a girl," called Dangerous Dan as we both hit the culvert and I swung the wheel, so close you could not fit a razor blade between the vehicles.

"I'll murder him," I said. "Next stop, I will kill him."

"Puss," my husband pleaded for his father. I thought, not that. Not now. I have fought for you for years and years. "You bloody well support me," I said. "I'm your wife." He patted my shoulder and I thought, you have no clue what I am feeling.

Bachhuber called, "GRID."

The map showed a road but nothing was so definite in real life. It was a cleared strip through scrub, punctuated by washaways, long stretches of sand, sudden jump-ups, blind crests, cattle grids and kamikaze cattle. We had Dunlop on-off road tyres, thank Titch for that. Thank Titch for Mrs. Markus too. He expected everything to be overlooked. We could not escape potholes, dead kangaroos, and dust, bull-dust they call it. We passed more broken cars than I could number. If dust was fattening I would have weighed a ton.

There was petrol in eighty miles, at Charters Towers. The town turned out to be as lost and broken as those abandoned cars. The main street was occupied by rusty old emporiums, piles of mullock overgrown with weeds and rubber vines, weary unpainted houses set on stilts. The petrol station was an old mill burned down in tragedy, with just a lonely petrol pump remaining.

As we pulled in I saw the old buzzard's Plymouth stopped across the narrow street. There were the usual rubbernecks standing on the footpath but I had the tyre lever in my hand. I planned to serve him right.

I knocked on his filthy passenger window, just to have him pay attention to his punishment. There was the little Englishman. My father-in-law was behind the wheel.

At that moment I did not know about his heart attack. How could I? When I whacked the windscreen I thought he was alive. That should wake him up, I thought.

I was set upon by rubberneckers. Some oaf got his hands upon my shoulders. I squirmed away, but it was a cattle town with drovers' men and station agents and they had no trouble removing a tyre lever from a woman's hand.

Finally it sunk in: he was dead. I thought I did it to him. The windscreen glass was in a thousand little bits and when they laid him down, I heard the sound of his threadbare skull against the footpath. His false teeth were nowhere to be found.

There was a great clumsy lump of policeman, in shorts and long white socks, assisted by the co-driver. Must be a wig, I thought of the little Englishman, of all the things to think at such a time.

I saw my husband was laying his head on his father's chest. The old man's eyes were wide and staring, his mouth open. Death had not improved his looks.

All my married life I had worked to protect Titch from his father's malice and his father had done everything he could to keep his sonny in a cage. It had been the purpose of my life to make sure my husband knew the comfort of being loved. Now it seemed all this had been for nothing. He threw himself on the dead body, in public. There was nowhere left to hide his relentless secret love.

I did not grudge him his grief but I felt none myself. I was a driver in a race that I had sacrificed my inheritance to enter. When I crossed the road to our car I knew we could spare an hour for mourning. But then I discovered our car would not restart, the battery was dead, the regulator not functioning.

I told the little Englishman to find an undertaker. He had blue blue eyes, but they would not look at me. A crowd had gathered, God knows where they had come from. I asked Bachhuber to find the undertaker and he returned to escort me into a dusty store with hats and boots and a wrought-iron balcony around the upstairs floor where she-in-charge-of-haberdashery was also the funeral director.

I had buried my parents within a month of each other. I knew what must be done for Dan. I chose the coffin and the handles. I wrote a cheque for embalming and then we had another three-quarters of an hour to spare. Bachhuber went off to arrange a jump-start for the car.

The haberdasher was cursed with very white skin and was the most sunburned undertaker you could imagine. I wrote her a cheque to ship the coffin to Mrs. Donaldson in Mordialloc. Due to embalming there was no ice surcharge. I paid cash for a telegram to Melbourne and I admit I did not wish to be the one to break the news on the phone. That was wrong, I know it. I was not in my right mind.

It was the middle of winter but hot in Charters Towers where, in the shadow of a mullock heap, I found my distraught husband in his nice yellow sweater and his driving gloves lost to all the world.

I held him, but he did not want holding.

I told him everything I had arranged, and that Dan would soon be with Mrs. Donaldson.

"What sort of person do you think I am?" he asked.

I said I loved him. I would give my life for him and his ambitions. Had done so since day one.

"I can't just drive away and leave my father."

A better woman would have granted this. A saner woman possibly. But I could not permit Dan Bobs to defeat us as he wished.

"You can't give up," I said.

"This is my duty."

I said his duty was for himself, and the family who had sacrificed everything so he could win.

People were listening I suppose. But why should I care who heard me in Charters Towers. I asked my husband what sort of person did he think I was. I had left our babes, for what? I had spent our inheritance for what? Not so I could give up halfway through.

"Alright," he said, "then go."

His eyes were foreign and I thought of my sister who I never understood before. You could be married to a man and not know who he was.

"Piss off then," he said, for the first and last time in his life.

"Yes, I will."

"The regulator is up shit creek," he said, as if that were an apology.

I said I would look after that and not to worry and I saw we were really going to be separated and I had never spent a night away from him in fifteen years and I had waited for him in my kitchen, waited for him to come home from Morrisons or Ballan or Wallace or Buninyong, all these years I had held him in my arms. Now I was a cane field roaring in the night, consumed by fire.

My father-in-law had died. My husband had told me to piss off. A willy-willy came down the middle of the main street of Charters Towers, not a big one, only ten feet high or so, a red dirty whirlwind that danced and swayed and seemed to release a stockman from its centre, although doubtless he had simply limped across the street as the willy-willy descended on him. He came to join us on the footpath. He was a black man, tall as Bachhuber with a clean tartan shirt and white moleskin trousers, one leg shorter than the other. I noted his interest in my navigator and saw them talk to one another, the black man being very insistent even as he looked over Bachhuber's shoulder, with his one good eye.

I made nothing of it, but when the awful moment came, when I abandoned my husband in the street, when he would not even say my name, when I returned to our car to win the race that was not a race, I was slow to realise the black man was in the car.

He had been drinking, I certainly smelled that, and I was frightened of him and Bachhuber would not tell him to get out and so I left Charters Towers, driving very fast, my throat an ache of grief, because I was the wilful one who must do what she had set out to do.

I was in the wrong. I was a bitch. I bawled my eyes out at fifty miles an hour. Bear left, bear right, bear left and level crossing. Two creeks and bend across the railway tracks. My navigator must protect me now.

# 3

LORD WHAT HAS HAPPENED to me, I thought, I have a crippled blackfellah in the rear and a weeping white woman driving at speeds beyond the law.

Between Southern Cross and Homestead she turned back twice and I thought, both times, thank the Lord, we will all be returned to kiss and make up, and there will be a proper funeral and the children will have parents. But no, no, no she had to win. She spun the wheel and we were once more in the Redex, heading through the dust clouds for Mount Isa, and I had no choice but to call the odometer clicks for the same awful grids and drains. We sped past vehicles fresh from showrooms, now destroyed. We shook and rattled like pills in an Aspro bottle but lost nothing except a door handle, also the speedo cable which might have mattered if the driver had any interest in average miles per hour. My bones were slammed into my bottom. My crown split off my head. We were airborne on the jump-ups and the leaf springs still held out. At Pentland there was mud like sticky toffee, a dozen competitors up to their doors, two extortionists with tractors offering to set them free. Amongst the local picnickers there was a low-slung drover type with a sign: UNDERTAKER PREPARED TO DO ANY DIGGING JOB.

The blackfellah leaned forward expectantly and I caught his yellowed bloodshot eye and thought, I cannot imagine how he sees me. But perhaps that could also be said of Irene Bobs who was roaring down into the field of battle, low geared, high revved, as we growled and banged across the hidden rocks and hurled wet mud over everything behind us, including the crew of Vanguard Spacemaster 53 who had been our mates last night in the pub. So far so good.

There was a post office in Betts Creek est. 1884. Not a soul in sight. Due to the state of the regulator, Mrs. Bobbsey left the motor running and rushed inside to make a call to Beverly. The engine had an occasional cough and I thought, no-one will stop to help us if we stall. I put fresh stockings in the air filter.

Dwarfed behind the wheel, Mrs. Bobbsey was coughing and spitting and we had four hundred miles to Mount Isa, creek crossings and—worse than that—certain competitors who had disconnected their brakelights to cause accidents behind. No competitor on that leg will forget the dust coating every surface, the drumming violent gibber stones like a malevolent spirit with a sledgehammer clouting the bottom of your car. Back in Townsville they had seemed to think I was a black man. Were they ever-vigilant for the signs of impure blood? Confronted by this "education" I had never felt so lost.

Our rear seat passenger indicated he would be happy to take the wheel which induced Mrs. Bobbsey to speak at length, lecturing him on his weight, how much fuel he was using, how little he was doing, and why he would be better off walking in the dust with "your mates." It seems likely she used the term "dead weight."

When I next caught his eye he had turned off all the switches and there was no human signal I could detect. "All else being equal, individuals of a given race are distinguishable from each other in proportion to their familiarity or contact with the race as a whole." So said someone, long ago. I would wish this was not ever true but at this point of the journey our passenger looked only like a blackfellah and I could see no more except, sometimes, the possibility that he had suffered some surgical incision in his tongue.

We proceeded through desolation, twisting and turning through copper coloured hills. If this was our country's heart, I never saw anything so stony, so empty, so endless, devoid of life other than predatory kites, circling, while we sat separately contained, our webs of pain and history hidden from each other. We arrived at 89.3 miles from Mount Isa at that dangerous time of day when the roadside cattle spill like underwater shadows and the deep purple of the sky drains into the mineral rocks and the most balanced person might see phantoms. We were at 50.6 CREEK CROSSING 49.8 L/R BEND ACROSS CREEK.

Mrs. Bobbsey would never drive into water without first walking it, and for this reason she had changed into her shorts and thus I spied her lovely calves in the pale uncertain yellow headlights, so like her sister in a different situation. The water was almost to her knees.

I needed no-one to instruct me that we would, in normal circumstances, with a functional regulator, have removed the belt from the engine fan. Now it would spray water all over our electrics. We had crossed plenty of creeks since Charters Towers and some of those had been risky, but she had always first walked the creeks, had always plotted the safest course across. When the water had sprayed through the engine, Titch's treatment of the electrics had been enough to keep our tinder dry.

Now we lurched lopsided down the bank and I felt the sudden water flood over my feet. And yet we would get through, it seemed. We bounced once, twice, then stalled.

"Oh no," she cried. "Oh shit and fuck."

There seemed no point in rescuing the strip maps which we left floating on the floor. We abandoned ship and I sat beside my tiny driver on the bank, listening to the engine hissing in its bath. There was wood smoke in the air but if it was from a bushfire there was no light to be seen, and we were passive victims, watching the dusk swallow up our victory. Mrs. Bobbsey slapped mosquitoes on her unprotected legs and asked where was that blackfellah hiding.

I assumed him gone. Why not? It was his country. My reading suggested that he would not die of thirst or hunger. He could get a feed from this red earth as if it were a grocery store.

Soon our Redex competitors came charging at us and we faced another danger. I exhausted our precious torch batteries waving them away from our vehicle. Of course they did not stop to help us. We watched their red tail-lights with the secret panic of children abandoned after dark. They fled from us across the ridge, their headlights washing out across the scrub.

Later there would be a moon, but when the human noise came from behind us, it was pitch dark. Then I smelled the backseat breath. When I realised he was not alone the hair rose on my neck. I sat very still while our former passenger firmly removed the torch from my hand and popped the bonnet and stared at the battery. Mrs. Bobbsey grabbed me urgently. In that moment of extremis I still had room to feel her chest against my upper arm.

"Tools," our man demanded.

"Don't give them to him," said Mrs. Bobbsey. "They'll sell them."

I did not wish to betray her, but I surrendered the smaller of our two kits. Then I watched as he selected an adjustable spanner and removed the leads from the battery.

"What is he doing?" she cried, although she had pushed in very close and knew the answer. We were being relieved of our battery.

"They'll sell the lead."

"Madam," said our former passenger. "We warm him."

"Bachhuber," she cried.

I understood my job as a man, but what was I meant to do? I gave up our torch to the "robber" as we followed along the creek and then down into what might be a billabong in wet season but now must give good shelter from the wind. Here I made out a band of blacks, perhaps a dozen including children, camping around a fire and two scrawny dun coloured dogs finishing their late afternoon meal.

Our passenger placed his burden beside the fire.

"Battery he no good," he said. "Gotta make him better."

Even if I could have overpowered him it would have made no sense. His two accomplices—one no more than a teenager, the other a sturdy bearded older man—were clearly not afraid of me. They were now dragging some queer wiry logs out of the scrub. These they placed parallel on each side of the fire and on top of this a piece of rusted corrugated iron.

"Don't let them," said Mrs. Bobbsey, pulling at my arm.

I thought, don't let them what?

Our passenger picked up the battery and held it out, like an offering, above the fire.

"Stop him. Willie."

It was nice to be called Willie, but it was an impractical request and I could do nothing more manly than stand inquiringly beside him.

"Bush generator," he said to me. "We stop and fix him, bush doctor." It was the first time that he smiled.

Mrs. Bobbsey pushed closer into the firelight so her face was illuminated in a way that would have had Clover talking of Caravaggio. Later she would say she had been frightened, not just by the danger to the battery, but the hostile eyes around her, peering from the dark.

When the Lucas battery—Lucas, Prince of Darkness, as the saying goes—when the Lucas 12 volt was placed on the corrugated iron her shoulders dropped and the firelight revealed a most profound exhaustion on her dirty face. It was then that two children, two girls, perhaps five and ten years old, were sent to drape a blanket around her shoulders. Clearly she feared the dirt. The girls, in any case, did not thrust their sympathy at her. They observed her from the middle distance, squatting, with their arms around their knees. And only when the moon rose, throwing tangled melaleuca shadows across their faces, was it possible to see their good intentions.

The battery was finally removed from the heat and placed on the dirt before us. We were told that "he" (i.e. the battery) was strong now and I finally understood they had used heat to get some bounce into the electrons.

When our "robber" returned the battery it was almost too hot to handle. I rushed it back through the moonlight to the car with Mrs. Bobbsey close beside me whispering.

"What is he? Medicine man?" she said. "What next? What do they want?"

Just the same it was she who was the boss. He might know the magic but it was Mrs. Bobs who must reattach the cables. The battery sparked violently and she was suddenly angry.

"You coming or not?" she asked her benefactor.

"We sit down this place," he said, I think.

"No waiting," she said. "Mount Isa next. Big hurry."

"Start him," ordered our passenger, making a motion as if cranking up the engine.

And of course it started, and of course the generator ran the lights.

"Lochy Peterson," he said and shook her hand.

"Irene Bobbsey," she said.

One hour after our engine had failed, we were back on the road again, just me and Irene Bobbsey and her small white knees.

# 4

THE SMELL OF a rally car, the stink, the whiff, the woo, you will never find the recipe for this pong in the *Women's Weekly* but ingredients include petrol, rubber, pollen, dust, orange peel, wrecked banana, armpit, socks, man's body. I drove into the night on the ratshit regulator. My headlights waxed and waned depending on the engine revs. Beneath us was bulldust, two feet thick. It was always smooth and soft-looking but the Holden banged and thudded like an aluminium dinghy hitting rock. It is a miracle our suspension didn't melt. Sometimes I saw the shock absorbers on a car in front, white hot, glowing like X-rays. Cattle loomed from the blackness and if I had rolled or hit a roo, if I killed us all, what then? What would my son and daughter say about me? *What did Mummy imagine she was doing? She must have been so selfish, up herself completely.*

Dunstan came into my mind. I did not imagine I also was in his.

My thoughts sometimes left the road, circled the little black girls, their precious blanket. I had not even folded it. I had not thanked them. I imagined myself behaving properly, walking across that bare hard earth and laying the neat blanket at their feet. I ate caffeine tablets and raisins.

The FJ Holden had a bench seat and my navigator was sometimes pushed hard against the cardboard box. I thought about the little boy and what we were obliged to do with him. I thought, Bachhuber wants me. I was certain. You cannot be so close to a man and not think about these things. I had lain in bed and listened to him with my sister and imagined things I should not have.

He was on the caffeine too. He cried wolf for a giant snake as fat as an oil drum. He was seeing things, reporting abos running beside the road in long white shirts. We almost missed a culvert. White groundsel seed floated in the dark like broken pillows. The seed that made my babies had blown against my door. I never regretted it, never wanted any more. I had never expected I might have laughed so much, or felt so much, and what we did with our bodies was unimaginable. Titch was the first man on earth to put his mouth down there. I thought he had invented it.

What was his plan when he married me? He taught me to drive. He was popular and funny but who can guess what's going on inside the human skin. He wore long-sleeved shirts, always buttoned, to hide his scars. Cigarette burns. These were for me to see, to cry for on our wedding night. So this is why he shines, I realised then. So this is why he jokes. I held his perfect head against my breast, and had no clue about the damage.

We never spoke about what had been done to him, and he would reveal no more about his injuries than he did about his mother. The perpetrator was either Dan with his constant ciggies, or it was Dan leaving him alone with priests or bachelors. In terms of scars, how many had it cost to teach each customer to drive? Had this made him cunning?

I thought it was my job to save my husband from his helpless sonny-love. I was his wife, his protector. I had always honoured that sacred vow. But when he wished to give up the Redex on account of that cruel skite, no, no, never.

I destroyed a spring on a rocky outcrop 38.9 miles from Cloncurry, clearly marked. And why was I not warned? Because Bachhuber had been drunk on caffeine, seeing "megafauna." Whatever that was.

In order to repair the spring we must perform the drill Titch had taught us, lying underneath the car together. We were close by necessity, shoulder to shoulder, sliding the shackle bolt from the oily spring. There could be no such thing as manners when he shoved a block of wood between the spring eye and floor, and his rough arm was against my cheek, and then we jacked the spring up and moved the eye along the wood until the shackle could be fitted and then my mouth was on his mouth. Dear Jesus, that's enough, not even thirty seconds of my life.

"We'll never speak of this again."

He returned to calling out GRID and CURVE and CREEK and two hours later we were at the Mount Isa Control with only the oil stain on my chest to tell the tale of those minutes when Bachhuber, his hand above my bottom, had pulled me hard against him. We signed in. Then I was the boss lady, giving orders for refuelling. I ran a check on engine compression which was a waste of money. The Redex drivers with the narrow waists and rolled up sleeves were much less slick than when we saw them last. They waved. We gave them the false impression that Titch was sleeping in the back. I located a telegraph operator named Mr. Gilbert, working late as a special favour to the drivers. I wrote: TITCH BOBS c/- MASSON'S UNDERTAKERS, CHARTERS TOWERS. I LOVE YOU SORRY ARRIVING DARWIN TOMORROW.

The navigator slept beneath the car, me in the back seat, as everybody saw.

In the morning I called the kids from the post office. Beverly was comforting. Mr. Gilbert came round the counter to deliver a telegram from Titch. DO NOT ENTER DARWIN CONTROL WAIT AT WATER SUPPLY LINE BERRY CREEK 181.1 MILES ON STRIP MAP T-D 14. T. BOBS.

I thought, thank God. He is coming to get me, but how will he pay for an air ticket? I telegrammed NO POINTS LOST but would not pay for LOVE.

There were outdoor showers at the caravan park. There I spied the top half of Bachhuber bare. An awful scar, a scoop from his flesh, a wound made by something like a melon baller.

I rolled up coats and blankets in the back seat so Control would imagine the third crew member was fast asleep. We got a push start from some blacks and paid them ten bob which they thought was not enough.

As we drove out of Mount Isa the navigator touched my cheek with the back of his broad hand.

"Don't get ideas," I said.

A Jaguar went past at ninety miles an hour. It would be every pedal to the metal until 181.1 MILES ON STRIP MAP whatever was going to happen there.

# 5

BACHHUBER WAS a nervous driver. It was only kindness that made him offer to take the wheel between Mount Isa and Darwin. The road was bitumen, as he pointed out. And I would have let him, I should have. It was my own fault that I must drive for hours without a wink of sleep. I lost time. I was slowed by mobs of cattle, four hundred at a time, on their way to a ship in Darwin and thenceforth to their deaths. Our supposed average was 44 mph, but you could not hurry through the bullocks, and the abo stockmen walked them at the speed they wished to go.

These beasts got off the road at night, but there were still stray bullocks and roos and apparitions visible only to my navigator. He said the country had once been occupied by wallabies twenty feet tall.

As we approached Darwin I was slowed once more by cattle. Their escort of blowflies came to feast upon my sweaty face. It was in their company I arrived at the rendezvous described by the telegram: WATER SUPPLY LINE BERRY CREEK 181.1 MILES ON STRIP MAP T-D 14. Here I stopped the car.

Due to the jiggered regulator I had to leave the engine idling. I waited. I saw nothing but red earth, a lonely barbed wire fence, a cluster of old signs LIVINGSTONE AIRSTRIP, HUMPTY DOO NOT THIS WAY, which I did not understand. There was also PILOT'S MESS, an open-sided shed strangled by allamanda vine, bright green and yellow flowers. Boys must have died here, Japanese or Australian or both, and now their so-called Pilot's Mess had been invaded by a mob of blacks and piccaninnies. The steers and drovers pushed on past.

So I waited for my husband. The bullocks bumped against the car and I felt their warm soft shoving. The passing abo stockmen could not have guessed that the sweaty white woman could always judge a bullock pretty fair.

We brushed and slapped at flies as the minutes passed. Finally a vehicle came towards us, its lights shining through the dust. Could this be him, in a Volkswagen? He stopped in front, nose to nose.

Not him. Where was he? This driver was a dork and dill: brand-new Akubra hat, tight shorts, fat legs, brand-new elastic sided stockman's boots. This was what is called a Southern Wonder.

"Open up," he cried.

It was not until he was in amongst the toolkits and fuel cans that I recognised him.

"Mr. Dunstan."

"No, no." He winked into my rear view mirror. "I am Mr. Shearer from Ballarat."

But it was Dunstan, as pale as a funeral director with that fat moustache occupying all his upper lip. He was pressing something on me, a small purple crepe paper parcel. I was, of course, reminded of an earlier occasion when he had wished to show his "appreciation."

"Can you fit a new regulator?"

"You're still at GMH?" I asked him because I was honestly bewildered by his presence so far from his proper place.

"If GMH knew about this I'd be a dead man."

I asked had he spoken to my husband.

"You'll see," he said, and I thought, what new deceit is this?

"You've spoken to him?"

"No-one has seen me or spoken to me, OK? Including you. Can you fit the new regulator? It's painted with the proper fairy dust, if you get my meaning."

"This is a regulator?"

"No, it's a string of bloody pearls."

"I'll need a jump-start afterwards. Yes, I can fit it."

"By yourself?"

"Where is my husband?"

"You must be the only competitor who would leave their driver stranded."

"Where is he?"

"Don't get your panties in a twist. He's on his way. Now. Can you fit that regulator? Do you have the tools?"

As Dunstan asked this last insulting question Bachhuber twisted in his seat to fetch the smaller kit.

"As for your navigator," said the Southern Wonder, "he is wanted by the law."

Willie tugged the toolkit free and set it on his lap. "That is a misrepresentation of the situation," he said quietly. He lifted the lid and offered me my choice of tools, holding the red metal box as if it contained shortbread or chocolate biscuits. I selected what I needed for the job at hand.

"What if you win, Mr. Bachhuber?" Dunstan asked. "The newspapers will represent your situation just as I did. Have you thought of what damage this would do? Have you considered your position as a member of the crew?"

I told him we had already lost a driver. Did he intend we should dismiss the navigator too?

"You have not lost a driver, Mrs. Bobs."

"Last time I saw my husband he was in Charters Towers."

"Yes, and the next time you see him you will be very bloody nice to him. That will be in Broome. If anybody asks, he never left the car. He will be there when we cross the finish line."

We? I asked him why is a man from General Motors in a Volkswagen, and why is he three thousand miles from where he should be?

"I'm a backer."

"No you're not."

"Ask your husband when you see him."

I thought, I have been a dupe. I have been made a mug of. Everybody knows I have been deceived.

"Who got you your sponsors? Do you even know?"

No I didn't know. I could have wept but I would not, not in front of this creature who would not know a regulator from his bumhole. I turned off the ignition. I popped the catch on the bonnet and took my tools and the regulator. And of course my navigator was going to assist me with the hot electrics, and I welcomed him, his gentle familiarity and his restraint. I trusted his feelings for me. I trusted his honour and his calm.

"You!" said the venomous pencil pusher in the back seat. This was how he addressed my dear and decent friend. "You are Willem August Bachhuber?"

I told Dunstan to get off the poor man's back. We had driven twenty-four hours and if he would just stop yammering a mo, if we could ever get a jump-start, we could still make Control on time and let the battery charge.

"You placed your crew in jeopardy," he said. "You are in arrears with child support?"

I asked him was he still employed by GMH.

"There are more important interests in this car."

"Your name is Dunstan, not Shearer."

"Shut up," he said, and turned to Bachhuber. "Your life is a grubby mess. When we win the reporters will find your wife and son. Do you really want to do that to Mr. and Mrs. Bobs? You're shitting over everything."

"You've got the wrong fellow, Mr. Dunstan," he replied, and I was pleased that he stepped out of the car, and pleased also that he walked away, up the road. He picked up a stone and threw it far ahead. I had never seen him lose his temper but I judged it would be a fair explosion when it finally happened. I told Dunstan to piss off and leave us. It was a first for me.

# 6

THE LAST THING I required was alcohol, but beer was the Bobbseys' cure for every ailment and Irene asked would I please accompany her to the pub because she was "not comfortable" with Dunstan.

I said she should stay away from the schemer.

That was no-can-do, as she expressed it. But we could drink here, she said, meaning the old Larapinta Hotel, of which she had, moments before, been loudly critical. (She had never seen a place so filthy. I was lucky I would sleep in the car.) It was true, the hotel was a rough and dirty place, perched on long fat legs across from the railway yards, in a sour effluvium of meatworks and flagon wine. It advertised "sea views" and there it was, indeed, beyond the broken scrub and grass, the misty Timor Sea disappearing in the dusk. In the foreground, across the street, a sign announced there was to be NO DRINKING, NO GAMBLING, NO HUMBUG, although this was obviously intended for those behind the rear side of the sign, scattered groups of blacks gathered around their smoky fires.

Mrs. Bobbsey's presence made it necessary for her male companions to drink in the so-called Virgins' Parlour. Thank God, I thought when I beheld the public bar crammed with argumentative hard-faced whites. I wondered about the single blackfellah in their midst. He looked exactly the same as that battery doctor fellah who had saved our skin. It *was* him. It must be. He was staring at me across the bar. Better leave here, I thought.

Then the toxic sweaty Dunstan told Mrs. B that he hoped she had locked her vehicle. If not, it would be stripped clean like a chicken carcass. I offered to attend to it.

That damned stare was waiting on my return, no longer in the public bar but in the Virgins' Parlour where the black man positioned himself with his long back against the wall. He raised his beer to me.

"Battery doctor?"

"Mr. Redex."

Of course I shook his hand.

A penny flew across the room and bounced over the bar. Only later did I think I was the cause of it.

"You got along the road pretty fast. Lochy? Lochy Peterson?"

"Lochy. Come drink with me."

Of course I did not drink, but I would not give offence. I turned to find the wall-faced bartender was already paying close attention.

"Dog tag," he demanded.

"He's with us," called Dunstan. "My shout."

"Doesn't matter if he's with the Prince of bloody Wales. I need to see the certificate of exemption."

"I don't understand," said Dunstan.

"Why would you?" said the bartender, speaking over his shoulder as he filled the glass of a young woman who had tattooed herself with nails or darning needles.

"Woof woof," she said, and laughed.

"Look here," said Dunstan.

"It's alright, mate," the bartender said, "I can see you're from down south. All I'm asking mate, does this chap have his pass, his dog tag?"

I turned to find myself the subject of Lochy Peterson's bloodshot yellow eyes.

"Better you come," he said.

"You're serving me," said Mrs. Bobbsey. "You can serve my navigator too."

"Show them, Lochy," said the bartender and the black man paused, considered me, and finally produced, from deep in his trouser pocket, a crumpled piece of paper which the white man, careless of the wet surface, spread out beneath his hand so I could read: *General Certificate of Exemption. This document entitles the bearer, HALF CASTE Aboriginal known as LOCHY PETERSON (1) to leave Quamby Downs Station,*

*(2) to walk freely through town without being arrested, (3) to enter a ship or hotel (individual may not be served—at proprietor's discretion). N.B: Speaking in Native Language prohibited.*

"Drink nother place," said the black man. He jerked his weathered handsome head whose creases all pointed to the joining of his forehead and his nose. "Much better drink nother place, come langa me."

Irene had let her mouth drop open. Dunstan suffered a shudder of impatience. My driver ordered the barman to give me anything I wanted.

I fancy I will not forget this moment, turning my attention from one actor to the other, at first amused by the size of their mistake. The tattooed woman had barked like a dog when the penny had been thrown. But why? The barman affected great busyness with his beer gun while he kept his secret eye on me.

"Come with me," whispered Doctor Battery, although that is an approximate quotation and I am not sure what he said, then and many times afterwards, for his diction was rather soft and indistinct, sounding more like his melodic language than my own. He spoke again and there was such a bad-blood odour in the bar, such malice, that I did not have to understand a word, only that there was nothing here to laugh at.

The hotel was built high on stumps capped with tin, and the time it took me to arrive at the dark sour earth-floored place at the bottom of the stairs was insufficient for me to grasp my situation except I had been ambushed, by whom or why I did not know. I had been set on by an expert, you might say, for it was a Darwin barman's job, just as it had been the Townsville policeman's, to exercise the finest discrimination. He had "read" my physiognomy, I suppose, with the same confidence as the previous barmaid who had agreed to serve me lemonade. All this was incredibly upsetting.

"You gimme five quid," Doctor Battery said to me. "We drink in camp."

You rascal, I thought. I opened my wallet and, as I never kept my money there, it was as empty as I had expected.

Irene had arrived at the bottom of the stairs. "Come back up."

"No good for him up there," said Lochy. "Don't like blackfellahs there."

"Don't be silly," she said, small and neat and frightened. "Come back, Willie. I can't be with Dunstan alone."

"Me two fellah stop here, Missus. You gimme five quid. One flagen six beer. Poor fellah come drink langa camp with me."

"You don't even drink," she said to me.

"He come back, he stop with me, look one thing."

"Willie?"

The drinkers upstairs made their own distinct warning thunder, shuffling their railway worker boots across the floor. I looked at Irene's sweet face, her big wet eyes and saw she was even more frightened of Lochy than she was of Dunstan.

"I'll do what you want," she said. "I'm on your side."

She was so tiny in her pale bleached overalls. "You really want me to pay for a flagon?"

"Plagen port," said Doctor Battery. "Six beer. Twenty-seven shilling."

"Do you know what you're doing?" she asked, counting out the money into that large pink-palmed hand.

In fact I was about to be a special guest of those citizens of Darwin who this afternoon were gathered at campfires by the sea, just up the bumpy Bagot Road.

As he limped down onto the sand, Doctor Battery explained it was not the best day to come, but never mind. These old men had been waiting all day to get "that old fellah" from the morgue. There they had been met by a big mob of police who would not let them have the body of their relative, a Law boss and much respected. The cops wore white socks on their hairy legs. They said the dead man was still a ward of the state. He was a "government aborigine," and they would deal with him dead as they had had cause to deal with him for "disorderly behaviour."

The flagon and beer were produced and all seals were checked. Now Doctor Battery, who was neatly dressed in his elastic sided boots and moleskins, chose a place beside an old wild-haired fellow sitting cross-legged in his dirty sandshoes and dusty pants. To me he was courteous but not friendly, but he and Doctor Battery were immediately whispering to each other close up while their fellows, most noticeably, looked away as if the last thing on their minds was to eavesdrop. Finally the flagon was given to the next man who passed it, still unopened, down the line, beyond my ken.

The six beer bottles were a different matter. They had definitely become the old man's property and he would dispense them according to a system very clear to him. He opened the first bottle and poured it into a large enamel pannikin. I imagined the drinkers' seriousness was all to do with that sad "dead body business" so I sat respectfully to one side, cramped, uncomfortable, bitten by sandflies, not grasping that it was I, Willie Bachhuber, who was the object of all these frowns and worry. When I was instructed to illuminate myself, to place my face close to the fire, I was like a drowning man who is surprised to find the distance from which he views his present situation.

I heard the soft wash of the ocean and thought of Indonesia, out there, beyond the smoke. I heard glass break. Two men were fighting by an isolated campfire, rolling into the flames. Lochy stayed beside me all this time, sipping constantly, quietly. He spoke and was listened to and had a great deal to say. I heard the word Redex and wondered if he was telling the story of the sick battery he had cured. I was not prepared to become the subject of examination. It was distressing, the sudden, unexpected touching of my face. The mob held lighted sticks to better see me. I saw them as well. Indeed some looked as white as I did. A woman wept. I called to Doctor Battery but it was he who now set on me, tugging at my shirt and I felt myself ripped from time and place and I curled myself into a ball and rolled into the sand which is where the flashlight found me and I was attended to by brave little Irene Bobs who had come out in the unknown dark to find me.

# 7

YOU WOULD THINK Dunstan was married to my husband, the way he spoke. He knew all Titch's secrets, more than me. He was in charge, OK? He forbade me to follow Willie when he disappeared into the night. I would be raped, he said, snatching at my wrist. I would be chopped up with an axe. He rushed at me, then fled the consequences. "Wait there," he said.

What had just occurred I did not know, except the whole bar had slammed the door on my dear friend and crew member. They had been ignorant and vicious, like a clique at Geelong High. You're in. You're out. You're not our friend. It was almost closing time. I waited for Dunstan while he consulted with two policemen but then he raised a glass, the mongrel. Clearly I was on my own. I pushed through the six o'clock swillers as they spilled out onto the street, straight into the headlights of exhausted Redex drivers cruising for a hotel bed. I ran across the mown government grass, towards the sea, entering the yellow sandy track which snaked down through the inky ti-tree scrub.

"Irene," Dunstan called.

Alright, I was relieved. That he was behind me. Better late than never. He's going to look after me, I thought, but no—he handed me the bloody torch.

"Watch your feet," he said. "There's broken glass."

Yes, I was afraid of black people. I did not understand what a police torch meant to those who appeared in its white beam. I blundered around the ti-tree. At last I found the Aboriginals, like photographs in *LIFE:* another race, caught in a moment of thoughtfulness. But when I saw Willie I did not recognise him, why would I? A bare chested white man curled up like a seahorse, dried out on the sand.

I thought, he's dead. Perhaps I shouted. Immediately I was surrounded by murmurs. "Don't cry. Don't cry. They bin look after that fellah." Everyone was eager to lift the white man to his feet, explaining to me, not quite accurately, but very seriously, "That fellah go mad. He bin drinking."

What else made sense?

All the while the waves lapped gently. The smoke was sweet and the air soft and sickly with plonk but they "bin look after that white lady" which, I was slow to realise, was me. Thus we were escorted, nudged, encouraged all the way up to the road, and politely safely back to the hotel. I mean, the concrete guttering on the opposite side of the road. The bitumen was no-man's land. On the far shore stood a moustached white man who should have been told, years ago, don't wear shorts.

"You're off at four a.m.," Dunstan said.

Thanks for telling me my job.

Now he followed me without invitation, and although he did not say a word his *tch tch* was close behind me like an insect in the night. How could he possibly think himself in charge?

I knew the way without his help, up the fire escape, along the mesh-floored catwalk high above the leafy yard where, between the mud-caked Redex cars, a solitary vomiter was hard at work. Dunstan followed me inside and chose one of the beds.

I told him get off. That was for the working crew.

"Irene, be sensible."

In the toilet I found the bowl occupied by another huge green frog. It would not be flushed away. I returned to see Dunstan had shifted to my bed, hands on his potato knees, staring at the man lying opposite him.

"You are clean-sheeted," he said angrily. "Did you know that? Everyone else has lost points."

"Why wouldn't I know?"

"You simply cannot drive solo for another twenty-eight hours. I forbid it."

"That's for me to decide."

"No, it's not. I'll meet you by that old airfield after you've checked out of Control. At Berry Creek. We can co-drive to Broome."

"We'd be disqualified."

"Only if they knew. They won't. Titch will land in Broome an hour before we get there. No harm done."

"No."

"And then your navigator leaves the race."

"That's not your decision."

Willie was gazing at Dunstan without particular expression.

"For God's sake," Dunstan said to him, "make yourself decent. Irene, can you hear a word I say?"

"Mrs. Bobs to you."

"You can win if you don't muck it up. Your business will be famous. Your life will change for ever. I'll help you drive until Broome. Once Titch lands you can check in at Control. Then, Mrs. Bobs, I require this fellow to withdraw."

"He's the navigator."

"He's a bloody liability."

I thought, here is a pencil pusher, wishing to dismiss the most talented member of the crew.

"Mr. Dunstan, do your bosses understand what you are suggesting?"

"Bosses? Which bloody bosses? There are more serious interests in this car than General Motors. If you come in first there are a number of interested parties." His moustache and open mouth looked like a smirky sea anemone. "Irene," he said, "you were very long odds when you left Sydney. You were a great investment."

"Titch has put my money on a bet?"

"Maybe don't tell Titch I told you. We've got bigger problems now. Put your bloody shirt on, man."

Willie opened his mouth wide and dragged at his lower eyelids with fingernails.

"He has a black son he has abandoned. He is probably black himself."

My navigator groaned loudly, rolled over twice and sat upright, staring at me.

"Irene," said Dunstan. "Did you understand what happened in the pub?"

"Mrs. Bobs," I said.

"He is half-caste, Mrs. Bobs, don't you get it? He is being sought for child support, he is a known adulterer."

"Ha-ha," cried the navigator and drummed his bare feet on the lino floor.

"He has been seen consorting with the worst elements in Darwin. The police know who he is. He's a half-caste or a quadroon or an octoroon or a macaroon for all I care. If you were the Redex sponsors would you want him representing you?"

"There's a black man on the two-bob stamp. His name is One Pound Jimmy."

"Oh shit, get real, Irene. You've got seven hours to sleep."

"I thought this was 'Australia's Own Car'? You can't get more Australian than that. In any case, you better leave."

"You want me to tell your husband what you're about to do?"

I thought, Dunstan is a shameful disease given me as punishment for infidelity. "Yes," I said. "Yes I do."

He slammed the door behind him, his brand-new heels thumping along the catwalk.

"I'm not black," my navigator said quietly. "I can't be."

He was seated with his sheet wrapped around his shoulders, his thick fair hair standing as if electric-shocked. I thought, who cares what they think in Darwin?

"I know who my father is, my mother, grandparents. I look like my father. I am his son, you see. Why is everybody trying to drive me mad?"

"Of course you're not black. It doesn't matter to me."

"You think it doesn't matter to me?"

Now I looked at him I saw the deep black worry showing on his forehead, the same corrugated frown I had observed amongst the drinkers on the beach. "If you were black you'd still be the best navigator in the Redex Trial."

He had begun to weep, slowly, gently, making dirty trails on his travel stained cheeks. And then, really honestly, there was nothing left to do but turn out the light and cuddle him. "Come on," I said, "squeeze over."

"Darwin to Christmas Creek," he said. He meant the nightmare tomorrow.

"I know."

"Eight hundred and seventy-two miles. Then Mardowarra, Broome, Port Hedland."

"I would trust you with my life."

"I won't let you down," he said and I would not let him down either. I pushed up hard against his back and I massaged his head, his neck, his knotted shoulders. I made him sleep.

Gently, gently, back in the bathroom I took down the shower curtain and managed, finally, to wrap it around the frog. He must have thought his death had come but I carried him outside and left him to find his freedom.

I double locked the door and lay back down beside my dear old navigator. I was all roiled up.

# Darwin to Broome,
# 1200 Miles

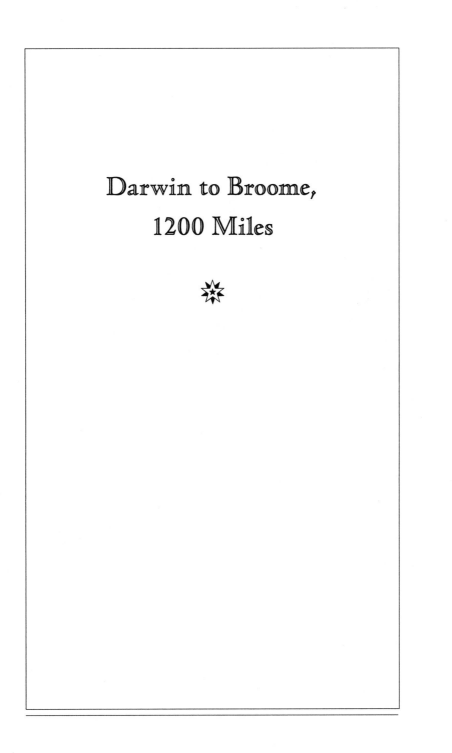

# 1

MUD-CRUSTED AND CRACKED like a dried up waterhole, the leading car in the 1954 Redex Trial had been broken into. Mrs. Bobbsey was showering when I found it, at four in the morning, beneath the brilliant stars, its back door swung wide, a pair of elastic sided boots, neat and parallel, resting by the rear right tyre. Someone was asleep inside, not quite snoring.

The twelve-volt ceiling light revealed Doctor Battery on the back seat, slender ankles crossed, peacefully asleep. It was my unenviable task to now explain, without being rude, that he must leave his bed. The Lord knows, I thought, how he will take this.

And yet he woke pleasantly, in no way embarrassed that the normal odours of a trial car had become those of a public bar. Indeed he was all business, pulling his boots onto his unexpectedly delicate feet and thoughtfully assessing the stubble on his long chin. No, he had no plans to leave. He come you two fellah.

I explained we had a Redex Trial to win.

"Sure, sure."

"No room," I said.

Now, as he returned his white stockman's hat to its usual place, I saw there was no escaping the strength of his will. His bad eye was soft and vulnerable, but that good eye had a determined character which would make it difficult for me to insist on Irene's concerns about passenger weight and petrol consumption.

It had been a long night in which my lovely driver squirmed and whispered and apologised to my back. What torture it had been, to feel so much, to do so little. Around three o'clock I summoned up sufficient character to take the second bed. Perhaps she felt this to be rejection. I didn't wish her to.

And now, hours later, here was that dear face in public, tilted up to me, apologetically, defiantly, showing her puffy weary eyes, her bruised blue lips, the smudge of a smile as she turned her head away.

"What the hell," she said. "Let him come along. He can play the part of Titch."

To Doctor Battery she spoke in the form of English used by southern whites in this situation. "You hide under blanket," she said, and was miraculously obeyed.

She wound down all the windows and then settled her neat body in the navigator's place. Now I would drive for her because she needed rest. It was a piece of cake, she said, the first stage south: long and straight like the road from Bacchus Marsh to Melbourne. I installed myself behind that high thin steering wheel, beside the Edgell emergency rations and a second box (Ardmona Pears in Syrup). That is, when the starter motor spun, I was in the company not only of Doctor Battery, but a child's skull, the victim of ignorance and murderous technology. As we crossed from the car park to the road I was aware of that physical object shifting inside its box, and as we passed through Darwin Control I was overly aware of it, sensing its historic essence, like a "wrong." Battery, thank the Lord, remained unaware of the taboo that we were breaking. He stayed quiet beneath his rug, playing the part of a sleeping co-driver.

Soon I was following the funnels of the headlights down the empty bitumen, pushing back the curtain of the dark until the torn edge of horizon emerged in the east. The bewitching Mrs. Bobbsey murmured in her sleep. Doctor Battery sang, softly, with sufficient authority, it seemed, to lift the sun up from the sand, suck the shadows out across the plain. If the definition of desert (*Away he goes*) is an area with rainfall of less than 9.75 inches per annum, this was not desert, but the soil was red, the scrub sparse and that horizon very very far away. Later there would be rough conditions, corrugations, bulldust, bone-breaking rock, but for now my only enemies were the hypnotic undulations of the blacktop, and the tendency of wandering bullocks to lay ambush inside cloud shadows. The danger was to let one's concentration drift and of course, inevitably, I did. I was already dizzy with sleeplessness and a sort of existential lightness in which my Self had slipped off like a shade.

Of course I did not require a certificate to prove to an ignoramus that I was a German. The foundation of my life was not so easily threatened but, like a sodden hillside after rain, I felt the danger of a slide. Yet everything would turn out to be OK, I felt. We would get to Katherine, then Broome. Every mile brought us closer to a stable place, not here. This landscape could never be mine, nor would I have wished it. My treasured childhood maps showed a German village every eighth of an inch but here I drove two hundred miles without the sight of a human being. I could not begin to imagine where that human might rest, sleep, eat. It was easy enough to say, as my dear grandmother often had, that the blacks lived by hunting kangaroos and eating seeds, but how often might you see a kangaroo and who would conceivably eat those dry grasses or those gnarled trees with their grey branches and rubbery leaves?

Doctor Battery's songs did not bring me peace. Each time I thought he had retired, he started again, only pausing during those periods of intense vibration that felt like an out of balance wheel but were caused by the tracks of someone else's "bar tread" tyres. After a final fierce eruption he leaned forward to rest his scarred forearms along the top of my seat.

He wished to know, were we going to Quamby Downs.

Quamby Downs was a pastoral lease thirty miles from Mardowarra. It was on my map, but off our route. I passed him the strip map which he seemed to read.

"My country."

We had left the bitumen and now the track bifurcated constantly. Here the map was useless and I found my way by trial and error, through an eruption of low rocky hills. I thought, we will slice our tyres to ribbons.

"Maybe you go to Quamby Downs," he said.

We should never have had him in the car.

In the rear view mirror, I glimpsed that half closed eye, that brooding brow. I slammed the sump against the armour plate and the "Ardmona Pears" rose and landed on the floor. Immediately Irene's eyes were open, Doctor Battery was at her. We go to my place, Quamby Downs. And so on until she shouted, "Christ."

In the rear view mirror I saw Battery's eyes, unrelenting. "By and by," he said.

No bloody way, I thought.

# 2

FIFTY-FOUR VEHICLES WERE BOGGED to their axles in a creek bed twelve miles before Katherine, but it was weariness, not mud, that would leave my children orphaned, I thought, as I waited in the Katherine post office for my trunkline call to Bacchus Marsh. I had just learned that a driver (E. Roberts) and the navigator (R. Gibson) in a Morris Minor (New South Wales) had been injured when their car crashed into a tree. Gibson was found unconscious by a Ford crew, who took him to Wave Hill station, where he was treated by Sister Kettle, of the Northern Territory Medical Service. Roberts received broken ribs. Might have been me (I. Bobs). Nearly was. In my case, I had been jolted awake by a stalling motor and found myself behind the wheel in the middle of a blacks' camp, dogs everywhere and dark faces squinting into the headlights from all directions. Irene, you are a danger to yourself and others.

"Go ahead Bacchus Marsh," the operator said.

"Ronnie?" I asked, and I heard his voice, the huge hurt choking. "What happened lovey?"

His response was like water in a twisted garden hose. "Give back."

Then Edith snatched the receiver. She said the cousins had stolen something from him. It might be his best marble.

"It was the TOMBOWLER," he cried, first from a distance, then weeping loudly in my ear. "They bust it with a bloody hammer."

"Don't swear darling."

"Mum, they bust it on purpose."

"What does Aunt Beverly say?"

"She's seeing Uncle Kevin."

"Who is Uncle Kevin?"

"An uncle. How would he know?" said Edith, not sounding like herself. "Mum, you've got to come home. Please come home. You've got to be nice to Daddy. Poor Daddy. He was crying."

"Oh darling, what did he tell you?"

"I'm not an idiot, Mum. You know what happened. Grandpa died."

"Yes, it's very sad."

"You don't like Grandpa."

I thought, I will kill that little bugger Titch. "Darling, we'll be home soon. It's only eight more days."

She did not hang up on me. She never would. "Eight days," she cried, and something crashed and then I lost the connection, and my bladder was already bursting and I kept the Peugeot crew waiting while the operator tried to reconnect but I think I offended her when—all that water, a gallon every day—after all her efforts, I had to go. When I returned, the Peugeot boys had taken over and I was told our petrol tank was full again (although it wasn't, as we would later know).

There was a good gravel road out of Katherine and Willie drove and I should have slept but I could not stop thinking about what Titch had told the kids and we were then two hundred miles from Broome and the so-called Doctor Battery was attacking the emergency cans of Edgell's product with our can opener. I was hungry too but would not tolerate a sticky steering wheel. Then Bachhuber ran over a length of ³⁄₈" wire rope. It was then I learned that Doctor Battery was a motor mechanic at Quamby Downs. I lay down on the hot ground and fell asleep while the men untangled the rope from the back axle and springs.

I woke to the news that the brakes and springs were undamaged. I took off at speed, careless of the likelihood that I would crash and die and my children would hate me for my selfishness and would grow up believing I had abandoned their father in his hour of grief.

We passed the turn-off to Quamby Downs. No-one asked to leave the car. Soon after that I nodded off, just for a second, and woke with a fright. I ordered Bachhuber behind the wheel.

When I woke next time, Doctor Battery was driving. I was too weary for surprise.

Next time: the motor silent, crows cawing. I was told we had run out of petrol but that Doctor Battery had just begged a gallon from a passing car.

Bachhuber was wide awake, calculating that we would be at the airport early for the plane. I thought, I have to drive, but I woke still in the navigator's seat. This time we were stopped in the scraggly outskirts of Broome.

Doctor Battery had finished off the Edgell pack and opened the box of Ardmona canned pears. There he discovered the skull of a poor dead baby boy. Who knew this was personal to him? But I had broken laws. I had been wrong way. I was crazy kartiya. The car was stopped at his demand. Now he stepped outside. I slipped behind the wheel and saw him fleeing evil spirits in my rear view, carrying his elastic sided boots, walking through the dust back the way we came.

My problem was not evil spirits. I almost missed the airstrip, not surprising given that the biggest sign said TOILETS. Behind this was a Nissen hut and a strip of bitumen where a solitary creature (with his gut bulging in his too tight shorts) marched up and down. God knows how he got there before us, but it was Dunstan.

"Back in a mo," said Willie and headed for the toilet sign. Dunstan chased him inside, with what intent I did not care. I would fix Dunstan in more ways than he could imagine. For the moment it was the car that took priority. I would not be criticised for its filthy state and as there was a tap and garden hose outside the toilet wall, I got to work. There is a definite satisfaction to be got from blasting off the clogged-up dust and dirt, the filthy skin of dead creatures, moths, wasps, bees, seeing the crapulous waste pouring out from beneath the mudguards. Was Broome short of water? Perhaps it was, but nothing could have made me leave the vehicle unwashed except, of course, an aircraft engine, and the sight of a galvanised iron box, labouring through the onshore breeze. Dunstan bumped his way past me, carrying his self-important bum out onto the edge of the strip and he was still standing there, waiting like a faithful dog, as the aircraft came in over a barbed wire fence, hovered in the air, and then dropped onto the bitumen so hard its undercarriage bent. It was about as lovely as a dunny colliding with the earth.

Taxiing, the single radial engine aimed straight at us, forcing us to retreat towards the shed. The door opened before the propeller stopped. There were as yet no steps or ladder and the passenger was not inclined to wait. Suitcase in his hand, he jumped, stumbled, and—intending to run—limped violently towards us.

It was Titch.

I had not known what I would feel to see him. I had forgotten he was beautiful, with a grace that could not be destroyed by pain or injury. As he came towards me I thought, oh Titch, dear Titchy. I was tired and dirty and I stank, but I had no doubt we would now, in spite of everything, be gentle with each other. And then he ran straight past me, and Dunstan too, and flew at Willie Bachhuber who was emerging from the Nissen hut, with nothing on his mind but how to dry his hands.

Titch flies at him, through the air it seems. Soon they are rolling on the ground together. Titch is trying to punch Willie's head and Willie has caught him by the wrists. Dunstan intervenes, then leaps back, sucking on his hand. It is left to the filthy sweat-stink woman to hose them down like dogs.

Do not say thank you for being saved from your own childishness. No, of course not.

Bachhuber was sodden with his white shirt revealing physical details that were normally hidden. Then, addressing me as if I were an umpire he held out his arms, like a boy protesting blatant injustice. It was in this state of holy injury he disappeared inside the Nissen hut. I waited. A taxi, a bright green FJ Holden, left an orange plume of dust across the dreary half used paddocks. As it turned onto the highway it did not occur to me that my one true friend, the navigator, might be inside and that I would now be left alone, with no support, to confront my marriage to Titch Bobs.

# 3

I HAD LIKED Titch Bobs but I was not going to be locked in a car with a pugnacious little ferret who blamed me for doing what I had not done. The taxi driver left me in a hot street of one- and two-storey timber shanties, all hiding their real business in the deep brims of their verandahs. Broome was a foreign land to me. The pavement was red earth, the buildings silver, worn down by a century of salt and sand. Shops and warehouses and general stores perched anxiously on three-foot pylons, awaiting the king tides, tied down against cyclonic winds. This was where I left the Redex map.

The taxi disappeared around a distant corner and I heard a blasting truck horn—no, it was a peacock, strutting down the street, screeching until, before the Roebuck Bay Hotel, it displayed its feathers in a wild priapic shudder.

This hotel—long and low with a deep verandah, the sort of roman-tic outback pub you might see in a Drysdale canvas—recalled that unpleasantness in the Larapinta bar. I felt the eyes of the hidden drink-ers heavy on me. No, I thought, you will not ask to see my dog licence. I became an actor with urgent business in a lane, and I fled into Sheba Alley without knowing what it was. I could not read the Asiatic signs or those particular mixed race faces which withdrew as I approached.

CHENG LOONG DEP BOARDING HOUSE. PAY FIRST.

Had he not been settled in his Rangoon rocker, the proprietor might have retreated from me too, but he was a desiccated old man and his chair was slung very low, and he remained where gravity demanded.

I pointed at his sign.

"Roebuck better," he said.

That surprised me, but I could not trust his word.

"Better you go there," said Mr. Cheng Loong Dep.

But I would not be put off, not even by the smell of drying prawns. I climbed the verandah steps to Mr. Cheng whose face had more creases than a walnut shell.

"What your work?" His eyes were small and dark and very lively.

"No work. I want a room."

"OK, plenty room."

He was a little man with strange appendages, fleshy ears as large as abalone.

"What work?" he asked as I followed his huge feet. "Meatworks?"

"No."

"No pearling," he said. "Pearling all gone to hell."

By now we had entered the polished shadow of a hallway and I understood him to be saying that his normal customers had been pearl divers of all nationalities, deckhands and cooks. "Prastic brutton," he said. The plastic button had killed the pearl shell business. He now had vacant rooms, no worries.

"You pay now," he said and his hands were like his ears and feet and I paid him plenty, but then he wanted another two bob to rent a mosquito net and I would not be taken advantage of.

"No net," I said.

"OK. No knocking in the night."

I thought he meant no nookey. I agreed.

He gave me a heavy iron key and allowed me to discover that my "clean room" reeked of cigarettes and grog. From the open window I could see the vertiginous jetty and inhale not only drying prawns but sweet wood smoke and ginger. My God, I thought, what have I done to myself this time?

There was no furniture except a single cot and there I lay, reading my savings bank passbook, wondering what would happen to me next, thinking of lovely Irene Bobbsey on the road south towards Port Hedland. The Lord knows what she would say to her husband when they were all alone behind their headlights.

I slept for hours. So then it was night and I could see yellow hurricane lamps on decks and cabin tops, the sand dunes, blue and black as night.

I drifted back to sleep and woke to confront the great mess I was making of my life. I would soon be twenty-seven and I had fallen off the edge again. I was unmoored, with nothing to cling to, to say "this is who I am" with this job, this business, this belief, this wife, child, future. I was not one thing or the other. I had no driving passion, for God, for instance. When I imagined my life with Adelina I had seen a suburban house and a life somehow spent with books. The library, in this way, had been perfect and in the time I worked with Sebastian I had imagined that this would be it, and he and I, together, would establish a sensible system of classification—why not us? No-one in England had done it properly—and we would finally build, with our own hands if need be, a map room where our cartographic holdings would not fit the accommodation offered to the dominant culture of the book.

I heard the soft clatter of mah-jongg tiles and the music from a gramophone and a concertina and beery singing. This is what I see when I hear "Heartbreak Hotel." I was so lonely I could die.

I had once been a quiz show king. I had been the master of a book-filled house. Now that was lost to me. I tossed and turned wondering how I could retrieve my poor treasures from Bacchus Marsh—my grandmother's atlas, a painful letter from Adelina—before the Bobbseys both returned.

Someone was burning joss sticks. The mosquitoes bit right through the sheet. My mind would not leave the list of my disasters. There was one thing I would not think about.

By midnight I was prepared to pay anything for a mosquito net, and I knocked up old Cheng. But he would not open.

"You no nookey," he said. "I sleep."

I returned to the mosquitoes *mano a mano*. They were fat with blood. I murdered them. I would fly to Perth first thing tomorrow. Why would I stay here where they would argue with me about who I really was? Who gave a damn about expense or the pain it took to rip through space? A thousand miles down the coast to Perth. Then slice like a razor across the bottom of the continent, across the Nullarbor. Would it take a day or two days? In any case I would arrive back in green and normal Bacchus Marsh where I would be understood to be a white man once again.

I wrote churning, looping letters in my sleep.

Next morning Mr. Cheng pronounced there was no airline office in Broome. I fancied he enjoyed himself, to see my astonishment. But no, he said, of course I could buy my tickets from his friend the German pearl dealer.

He led me to the pearl dealers where the proprietors had not yet arrived. Instead I met the clerk, a young Englishman, a boy in fact, whose every word made perfect sense to me. How I cherished his clarity. When he said it was within his power to sell me as many tickets as I should require, I reached to shake his hand.

He was Toby. He was tall and blue eyed with a long top lip and curly smile. How sweet and familial he seemed. He had a veritable bible of airfares to study and he went through them with a ruler and wrote numbers on an envelope which (although he was shortly to go up to Oxford University) involved a great deal of crossing out and starting once again.

Poor handsome chap, I thought, he is a dunce.

I did the numbers in my head and Toby was relieved to hear the total was too much. He crumpled up his envelope and dropped it in the bin.

"Honestly," he said, "it's highway robbery. I don't know how anybody pays." He suggested I simply cross the road to the Shell petrol station where I would find plenty of chaps filling their tanks for the trip south. "Anybody will be pleased to take a white man," he said. (Ah, I thought.) "Someone to talk to. That's how I got across the Nullarbor myself."

Soon he was busy with a plastic airline bag which he was stuffing with the contents of the office rubbish bin. "A gentleman always travels with his luggage," he said, throwing in a weighty pencil sharpener that had previously been clamped onto his desk.

"Good luck," he said. I liked him. I did not know him. I never would. Toby was a flipper in an existential pinball machine, a god who sent me pinging towards my fate. It will be OK, I thought.

I walked across Carnarvon Street to the Shell petrol station where I did not have a happy start. That is, I presented myself to men pumping petrol, to men filling radiators, to the open windows of men about to leave. I made my request. I found myself inspected and rejected. Granted, I had not shaved. Granted, my eyes were red, but it is a hard thing for a shy man to offer himself up for this type of judgement. I felt myself a relation of that Redex Ford which a tow truck had clearly dragged in overnight. There it lay against the wall, windows broken, blood smeared grill attesting to a kangaroo or bullock in the night.

I was approached by an older type of gent, a tall khaki chap with a big nose and large red lips.

"I'll take you," he said. "I can take you as far as the Roebuck Roadhouse. It's a start." Later he claimed it was my business to remind him. It was not his job to stop, to remember what he said.

"I am Garret Hangar, by the way."

"I am Willie Bachhuber."

We set off in his Morris Minor which had a roof rack full of tyres and the back seat crammed with cardboard boxes. He was a Public Servant, he soon confided, employed in a boring job with the government of Western Australia. He spent his lonely days, like this, "going round the traps," he said, "delivering stationery."

Garret's nose had suffered many years of sunburn but his blue eyes were youthful, enormously inquisitive. "So tell me young Willie Bachhuber," he said, "how you got to Broome."

Thank God, I thought, he is curious. This will be OK. If it were not for his tendency to engage with me rather than the road, I would have found him an unalloyed delight.

I readily told him what I would have revealed to no-one else, firstly the whole business with Bennett Ash and my dismissal from my job, a story he applauded loudly. "Oh good for you, Bachhuber," he said. "If only there were more like you."

Thus he encouraged me in my recklessness.

He had always admired schoolteachers he said, but we would never have good teachers if we did not allow for genius. He declared that I clearly had that quality, and I confess I was happy to be flattered and we rattled on down that corrugated road and I was less attentive to the road than I should have been.

I revealed that I had, until yesterday, been a navigator in the Redex Trial. He said he would have given anything to be in my shoes.

I told him I had a falling out with my crew.

He said he was not surprised. He had thought of entering but had never found anyone he could get along with on the road. He had some jokes about expelling wind. I really didn't mind.

He wanted Redex stories. I gave them to him, gelignite, batteries, ice to pack a coffin, cable tangled in the brakes. He loved it all. He thought he and I should consider entering next year's event and I was careless and happy and agreed with him. Why not?

The course of our chatter led us to my father's occupation and he was again delighted.

"A Lutheran missionary," he said.

I told him I had uncles who were missionaries but my father was a city man.

"You might be wrong there Bachhuber," he said.

"I would know, I think."

"You should bloody know, absolutely," he said. "I agree." And thus he revealed that character which, presumably, made it hard for him to find a co-driver. He would not give up on this business about my father. Finally I told him we should quit it.

He offered an orange Lifesaver and I accepted.

The road had by now degenerated. I observed, as he dealt with one particular creek crossing, that this was eerily like the road from Mardowarra. Completely déjà vu, I said: that dead beast, that broken fence.

When he laughed, I found myself annoyed. "It's not déjà vu," he said, "this is the same road."

"No, this is the road to Perth."

"The road to Perth was back at the Roebuck Roadhouse."

"But that was where you were to drop me."

"Oh, you should have said."

"I didn't see it."

He laughed at me again. "Dear God man. Did you not see it? There is nothing else between Broome and Mardowarra and you didn't see it."

"You said you had to drop me there."

"Well I forgot," said Garret Hangar.

"How could you?"

"How could you?" he mocked then softened. "Mea culpa, mate. La Condition Humaine. And so forth."

"But what am I to do?"

I expected the answer would be an offer to drive me back, but he didn't change his speed. "It will all work out," he said, and smiled with red annoying lips. The lone and level wastes stretched far away.

# A Fork in the Road

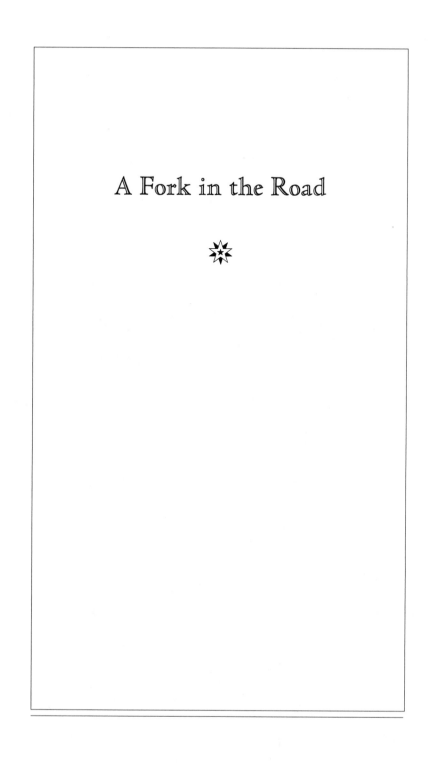

# 1

NO-ONE TOLD ME the Nullarbor Plain would be so cold. But then again, what about my marriage? Who would have predicted that turn in the road?

Five hundred miles east of Perth I peed by the rear wheel and listened to my husband "tidying up the vehicle." Translation: chuck out anything that Willie Bachhuber has touched. Any skerrick, any chip packet, caffeine pill, etc., pecking at the shadow of the other male. Nothing had happened with the navigator, but my husband clearly thought otherwise.

This behaviour had begun in the warm red soil of the Kimberley. It continued south to Perth. It turned left across the bottom of the continent, onto these grey treeless limestone plains. Peeing beyond sight of the sea, I could hear the spooky ocean moaning. Sometimes I felt the phantoms surging through the caves beneath my feet.

Titch unearthed a pair of Willie's oil-stained shorts. I told him I had done nothing wrong. He threw the item in the dust. This would not be the end. There were always reserves of dried up orange peel for instance. He would have chucked the little boy's skull away, except I would not permit it.

Alright, give it to the abos, he said. But the blacks feared the evil spirits sleeping in the bones. I passed this information to my husband. In response he made jokes about mumbo-jumbo, voodoo. He was merciless, on and on. In Perth we heard the stupid hit parade, a song about a box that a woman can't get rid of. He never heard a song so funny, especially when he changed the words.

*As I strolled one morning on Bondi's tropic shore*
*I spied a huge Ardmona box like I never saw before*
*I hauled it in and looked inside to see what I could see*
*And there was a great big beep-beep-beep staring back at me*
*Oh, there was a great big beep-beep-beep, it was a mystery.*

Titch *looked* like he could sing, with his bright eyes and appley cheeks and that dark neat hair. You could imagine him a crooner like Sinatra, but he couldn't hold a tune, he never could. Even when I loved him without reserve his voice was hoarse and broken. Now, on this grim plain, with a hole in the muffler which made conversation difficult, his rasping voice seemed cruel and taunting.

"Take a joke, Irene," he said.

*I picked up the box and ran to town to pawn it in a shop*
*The broker saw me coming and hollered I should stop*
*He took his key, he turned his lock, and shouted through the door*
*Oh, get out of here with that beep-beep-beep, before I call the law*
*Oh, get out of here with that beep-beep-beep, before I call the law.*

There were so many verses. It went all the way to the pearly gates, and of course Saint Peter would not let him in.

I had expected the Nullarbor Plain must be a scorching desert, and I had still thought so back in Perth, even when I had sat in the post office shivering in shorts, listening to Titch, on the phone, amusing the kids with new stories of the rascally wombat. He did not say he had run over a wombat and that we had to pull it off the road, the poor thing, dead and mangy with pus-filled eyes. These were our babies, and he had only love and cheer to offer them, and it was such a contrast with what he felt for me, I had to walk away and leave him to invent an excuse for Mummy. I could not have pretended happiness. I would have cried to hear their lovely voices, so I turned my back, and hid myself amongst the people looking up numbers in interstate directories. If I opened the Adelaide directory, it was only by chance. Of course I was pretending, and I looked up the only name I knew in Adelaide, and there he was, Bachhuber the pastor, and I did not have a pen so I just tore out the page and shoved it in my handbag.

Our car was on the front page of the Perth *West Australian*. Just the same, I did not feel like I was winning anything and when we pushed west to the town of Coolgardie, the small city of Kalgoorlie, we were not the first cars in the pack. But we were still ahead by points, and when we arrived at lonely Norseman at four in the morning, we found its single street crowded and the shops all ablaze and I hated how people smiled at us and waved. They had stayed up all night to see us. It was wrong to hate them for grinning at the ruination of a family.

"Get used to it," my husband said. "This is the future." I did not trust him any more. I thought, he will divorce me once we get back home. For what? For nothing.

When a flashbulb popped it seemed as if his face popped back at it, and he would be luminous with popularity all the way to Sydney. I would not get used to it, and I was outraged that he should trust vile Dunstan who had obviously filled his head with lies. I wished I had been guilty of adultery. I might have had some fun.

Peeing on the desolate Nullarbor, no sign of human life, I heard a jet plane high above the clouds. I imagined Willie was in it. He would not laugh at what I felt.

On we went, and on, Titch and I shouting at each other above the roaring exhaust, digging ourselves deeper when all we wanted to do was climb out of the hole we'd made. We drove through bright moonlight with windows closed uselessly against the limestone dust which drifted like smoke through the gnarled scrub and hurt our eyes and nostrils. Our feelings were like things previously unknown to us, moaning from beneath the road itself.

I peed again. I took the wheel.

"Am I a partner?" I asked him. My boots were splashed and I felt disgusting and unlovely.

"You are meant to be my wife," he answered. Meant to, I noted.

"Yes, but not your partner?"

"Say what you mean, Irene. We put some money in a syndicate, OK?"

"Whose money?"

"The odds were long," he said.

"Who else is in this syndicate? It's those Ballarat geezers isn't it? Joe Thacker? And that man, the bookmaker?"

This was a dumb guess and I was frightened to see that it was right.

"You notice I'm not asking you questions?"

"Ask away."

"I wouldn't lower myself."

"Perhaps you should."

We passed the Vanguard Spacemaster, abandoned, lonely in the headlights, wrapped around a grid post. A mile later we got our third puncture and it was all hands on deck. The wind whipped the sand into my eyes and I thought, if Australia had a bottom, this would be the place it did its business.

Of course Titch never thought like that.

"There must be something can be done with this," he had said, earlier. He meant the Nullarbor, that there must be something useful to be done with this sand, this gnarled and stunted scrub, myall and mallee and mulga. "With careful and sympathetic organisation," he said.

If I was irritated I tried not to show it. This was how he looked at everything and I had loved him for it.

Ceduna is a small fishing town two thousand, three hundred miles from Broome, twelve hundred miles from Perth, five hundred miles from Adelaide. There were few garages and every one was full of Trial wrecks, including Wally Bishop's Plymouth which had been in second place. No-one could fix our exhaust.

As we left Ceduna the rain began to fall and I thought, thank goodness, that will lay the dust. But the road was soon a slippery mess and the rain was beating in gusts against the car.

At dawn we passed miserable groups of poor blacks, families wearing rags the colour of cement. We were so tired, sleeping half an hour, driving half an hour. "Don't muck this up," he said. I thought, what does he think has happened to us? Who will live next door in Bacchus Marsh?

The city of Adelaide seemed so perfect it might have been dry-cleaned. We were two hours ahead of time and found a garage in Klemzig to do the muffler and perform a grease and oil change. I removed the Ardmona box from the back seat and felt my husband's eyes upon me.

"Where do you think you're going?"

Ah, I thought, you're frightened.

"Seeing a man about a dog," I said and he stood by the petrol bowser with his mouth open and watched as I hailed a taxi.

Boom boom, I thought, to you.

Of course the driver was excited to have a Redex driver in the car, not least because he recognised me. Mrs. Titch, he said, but fortunately he had very little curiosity. What he wanted was to tell me about the three-quarter grind camshaft he was fitting to his car at home.

Then this was Payneham where, as I would soon learn, Willie had loved the girl, at the back of these simple suburban cottages, between the Italian market gardens and this house from the phone book, with its screened in sleepout and its flowerbed and two long strips of concrete at the end of which an old Ford Prefect rested undisturbed.

I could not say exactly why I was so pleased, but I knew I could take my little boy here and he would be well treated. I did not know what it meant to me, but when I finally walked down those double concrete paths beside the hydrangeas and saw the old pastor with his high wiry grey hair and his round wire glasses and that long and solemn chin, when I saw he was carrying mandarins in his hat I trusted him completely.

# 2

MY SUNBURNT DRIVER WAS like a long legged bird, forever poking at whatever worm or beetle passed his way. Perhaps he would turn out to be a "character" or perhaps he would end up being a bore, but until we passed the roadhouse he had seemed curious and garrulous, ingenuous, provincial, friendly and it did not occur to me that I should fear him.

"I'm not the navigator," he said. "That was meant to be your game."

"Can you take me back please?"

He licked his lips and I thought of a dog, nervous, withdrawing from a fight. "I live in the here and now," he said. "But where are you?"

"I've got business in Perth."

"Relax. You're too young for business. You're in the here and now. What's that over there?"

"You mean those hills? Could you slow down please?"

"What you're calling 'those hills' are ancient coral reefs. That's your 'now' you're not even seeing. Compared to this," said Garret Hangar, revealing sincere and agitated eyes, "Perth is nothing. You would have been bored in a day. This is for you," he said more gently. "Here, have another Lifesaver. There is nowhere like this down south. Did you talk to any human beings while you were in Broome?"

Irene Bobs would not have tolerated him. Not Clover either. "An old Chinaman," I said.

"Well how many old Chinamen did you know before?" he said, surging forward, laying a great plume of yellow dust across the dreary scrub behind. He told me the Indonesians had sailed their prahu to Broome for hundreds of years. They had caught bêche-de-mer and smoked it on the beach. There were pearls and pearl shell. Japanese and Malays dived for it. The Chinamen traded it. The whitefellahs did all the usual business which included clubs that excluded all the dusky brethren. So that gave birth to a certain Sunshine Club. I should listen to Seaman Dan. He slowed a fraction and then sped up.

*"Saturday night at the Sunshine Club / Doing the waltz and the jitterbug,"* he sang. "Nothing like it anywhere. Hindus, Muslims, Christians. Sometimes they all live in one house together, men, women, children, all politely observing Ramadan and Christmas together. In Broome they can see your family history in your nose and earlobes. Why, man, you're blushing. Did you have female company? Of course the whites might be nervous of you."

"I beg your pardon?"

"No-one wants a throwback, do they?"

"You mean a black child?" I asked directly.

"There are beautiful mulattos," he said urgently. "They'll like you just to look at you. You'd be at home in Broome, blondie hair and all. You're a fetching young fellow. They'll go for you. The fair hair goes down a charm. And anyway. And anyway. The manager at Quamby Downs, you'll meet him presently. He's a blondie, pure merino, fresh from down south. Do you play cricket? Can you bowl?"

"More of a spinner," I said. My mind was no longer in the car, but in Melbourne long ago as I saw the pity in the eyes of Adelina's obstetrician.

"He'll love you," Garret said.

"Who?"

"Of course this one won't last. That type never do. But you get a good manager in place and everybody's happy. You'll be happy. There's a million acres and fifty thousand cattle."

"Where are we going?" I asked and he somehow understood I was defeated.

"You can travel for days and never leave the property," he said. "The blackfellahs will take you fishing and shooting. Lovely people. You'll help them get bush tucker, they'll be your friends for ever. Have you got a camera? You should get a camera. You should teach them proper English. No pidgin in the classroom, but you'll love them, fabulous kids.

You won't believe the things you'll see. Ask them to show you Geikie Gorge."

He did not tell me that the teacher at Quamby Downs station had suffered a nervous breakdown.

By now the sun was at our backs as we wound in between the raw red bluffs that mark the entrance to the station and I was a plump ripe teacher, fresh from the south, someone readily acceptable to the sahibs in Perth.

"This is one of the biggest cattle stations in the world."

"To which you are delivering your stationery?"

"That's it, chum."

We threaded our way between red iron outcrops and emerged on a vast overgrazed plain dotted with ant hills and divided by a single brutal line of fence. Ahead was a lonely tree like a huge fat-bellied jug, and beneath it was parked a car, the fire-blackened corpse of a once familiar Redex Peugeot, number 62. The back door swung open as we pulled up and from the wreck emerged a passenger.

Doctor bloody Battery. Bloody hell. He limped to Garret's open window and performed a mock salute.

"I heard you gone walkabout," my driver said.

Doctor Battery crouched at the window, waving flies away, looking off into the distance. "Back now, boss."

"You seen old Cricket?"

The black man's grimace suggested this was not to be desired. "Yeah see that fellah by and by."

"Maybe he let you fix my brakes?"

"He say he shoot me next time."

"Maybe he growl that fellah."

Captain Battery tipped his hat at me and I thought, how can a limping man be here so soon? I thought of A.P. Elkin's "clever men" who can run more than a foot above the ground.

"That is Mr. Bachhuber," the driver said.

Battery gave no sign that we had any previous acquaintance.

"He bin go mad, that short one teacher," Doctor Battery said. "He in hospital."

Garret lifted his great nose, a movement precisely understood by Battery who grinned.

"This fellah here? He bin teaching?"

"Hop up," Garret said.

"Maybe I see old Cricket nother time."

"Jump off when you like."

The old fellow disappeared and I did not understand that he was riding the rear bumper and holding the roof rack as we entered a site of abandoned trucks, untidy sheds, a bulldozer, some empty stockyards. He rode like a general inside a cloud of red dust, between the sorry iron buildings, past the workshop cut into a knotted limestone bluff, through the shanties of a blacks' camp, between a line of women carrying kerosene drums on their heads. Having driven straight through a burned out shed and without having seen one of those fifty thousand cattle, we arrived at the "Big House," a low wide-roofed structure with walls of corrugated iron protected by a barbed wire fence. Behind this barrier stood the manager of Quamby Downs, a blond haired, sunburned farmer whose good looks were quite destroyed by his parrot nose.

"Where the fuck have you been you mongrel?" he said to our passenger and of course he was Carter nicknamed Cricket. He slapped his leg with a fly swatter. "We're in the middle of the muster. I've got the fucking Chev out of order for three fucking weeks. Lochy, mate, you can't do this. I had the cops out for you. Exemption or no exemption, you're lucky you aren't in the lockup."

I climbed out of the car with my airline bag, but although the manager had come out from his wired enclosure, he was not ready for me yet.

"Mate, you can't just piss off when you feel like it."

"Sorry boss."

"What you doing now?"

"Need parts, boss. Fix up that Chev."

"I got you your bloody parts. We flew them in. They've been here ten weeks. Where you think you're going?"

"Talk that old Chev."

"Chev's not down there."

"No boss. This way."

So saying he limped back along the rutted track, and the manager, with nothing to distract him, turned to meet me formally.

"Who the fuck are you?"

"This is Mr. Bachhuber," said Garret Hangar, "a schoolteacher straight from Melbourne."

Carter beamed. He shook my hand and took my "luggage" and escorted me into his enclosure where, on his generous verandah, he introduced me to a slight girlish woman, also blond, who was watering a hanging plant.

"Melbourne," he said by way of introduction.

"Mrs. Carter," she said.

We assembled in a wide dark room smelling faintly of kerosene and the recent application of a damp mop. At its centre was a claw-legged table presided over by a huge black chair studded with pearl shell. A large rectangle of grimy calico—a punka—was suspended above the table, and this swept continually back and forth, distributing the unappetising smell of beef and fat. In the shadows stood its engine, a very black fine-faced man pulling on a rope. From this individual's glittering eyes I shied away.

I "pulled up a pew" as instructed. The school inspector, for that is what the scoundrel was, produced a "little something" from his Gladstone bag and the boss studied the bottle as if it were a rare and precious stamp. "Alice," he bawled. "Alice." In response there appeared a much laundered Aboriginal woman with a fortress face. She placed a glass before me which I had no choice but to push away.

"Not for you, Bachhuber? You're not going to be homesick for the opera are you? No. The last fellow missed the opera," said Carter. And I saw the Punka Wallah listening closely so I knew he had his hearing, unlike those fellows in the British Raj who were famously recruited from amongst the deaf.

"Poor bugger," said Carter. "Your predecessor was what you might call an idealist. Are you an idealist Mr. Bachhuber? No, it's OK. I'm not a monster. Of course, I blame the state of Western Australia, the curriculum or whatever you want to call it. No-one wants to teach these buggers anything practical. If the education department could see what Garret sees, they'd change it. Garret knows what I want, don't you Garret? Give me a kid at twelve and he'll be a working stockboy two years later. It's alright, mate, I won't kidnap them. We'll get on. I can get on with anybody. Of course the grog is a problem here. They can't take it like a white man."

"So," I said, "I take it there is a position here."

"Don't worry," he said. "I'll show you the ropes. You've got to get to know the characters, the communists. There used to be five of them, but I took to shooting out their radiators. Not one of them has got a job himself, but there they are, riling up my people about getting paid. You know how many people I feed? One hundred and bloody fifty. The day I have to pay them I'll kick the whole lot of them off the property."

I felt the Punka Wallah was the only one who guessed my resistance. At that time I imagined him to be Tamil, with his sharp and slender nose.

I sat at Carter's table in the gloom and darkness and then the kerosene lamps arrived and he carved a huge roast beef by the smoky yellow light. Two quiet fair haired children came to join us but I was not told their names.

Garret sipped his good share of rum and allowed himself to defend the education department as he was expected to.

"See, Mr. Bachhuber," said Carter, "I can get along with anyone. Ask the missus. Tell them, Janet. My bark is worse than my bite."

Mrs. Carter bestowed on me her weary smile and I knew there was no force that could keep me captive in this hell. I would rise early and stay by the Morris Minor until the brakes were done.

# 3

PERHAPS IT WAS the damage to my marriage that made me cry, or perhaps it was the tension of that endless Redex Trial. More likely it was the frail old pastor carrying his mandarins exactly as his son had once offered his welcome gift of eggs. He was Willie's father and so, of course, he comforted me, his hand as light as a leaf upon my arm.

"Dear lady." He relieved me of the cardboard box. "You clearly need a cup of tea."

He turned without knowing who the hell I was. I followed. His figure was erect, narrow shouldered, his gait a little rusty. I snuffled behind, down the concrete path, beside a powdery sun-damaged Ford Prefect, then the compost heap, and then into a garage which had not seen a vehicle in many years. It had become a standard model "Dad Shed," given over to carpentry, and garden pots, and incubators and drying plants like rooster tails hanging from the rafters.

He shifted a large wooden plane with his elbow and placed the Ardmona box on the workbench. What the heck was I to tell him?

There was a wobbly card table and a stool and kitchen chair. He gave me the chair and took the stool and poured black tea into a screw-on thermos cup. There was no sugar and no milk.

"So?" he asked.

When he saw I wished to open up my box, he produced a bone handled pocketknife, old and yellowed, and cut the electrical tape my husband had used to bind it shut. Then I knew I must speak quickly.

"I am Mrs. Bobs," I said. "From Bacchus Marsh. Near Melbourne."

But the flaps were already open, and he saw.

"I hoped you might give him a proper burial?"

His jaw was long, his lips compressed. I apologised.

"You came from *Melbourne?*"

"I know, but his own people will not touch him."

He cupped his freckled hand over his mouth and chin. "His people?"

"Aboriginal."

"And you are from Melbourne. But you have come here?"

"I'm so sorry, Mr. Bachhuber. I had no-one else to ask. You see we are in the Redex Trial." (This last was a mistake, leading only to confusion which took some time to untangle.) "I know your son," I said at last.

He spoke sharply. "Which son?"

"Willie."

"How can you know Willie?"

"Just days ago. In Broome."

He looked stricken.

"We are in a car race."

He turned to the cardboard box and removed the skull from its bed of crumpled newspaper. "But this," he said carefully, "this is a little child."

"Might we not bury him?"

He did not answer immediately. "You know our Willie?"

Who, of any age, would not suffer confusion? He did not know me from Adam. He had never heard of Bacchus Marsh or his son's presence there. Did he even know Willie had turned into a teacher?

"Poor Willie," he said, running his hand around that skull, as smooth as an eggshell, hesitating at its hole. "I did not serve you well dear fellow."

His pale eyes wanted something from me which I could not have named.

"It was an awful thing for a Christian to do. I think about it every day."

"I'm so sorry."

"Yes," he said impatiently (he had not wanted sympathy). "But you see, he was so at home here, so contented, truly. He ran, oh he ran, Mrs. . . . Would you like to see his room?"

I couldn't spare the time, but yes I must see the room, and the pastor was now very certain in his manner as he lowered the skull back into its nest. He closed the flaps and laid the wooden plane across the top. He then took my arm, not at all impatiently, and guided me out into the sunlight. It had rained not long before and the drops were crystalline on his silverbeet and the new back steps of his cottage were bright and yellow.

He need not have told me that his wife had died. The sad state of the kitchen, the little plastic bags hanging on doorknobs for the scraps, was enough to say "I am on my own these days." He hurried me into a hall, and then a musty room where he raised the dark brown holland blinds to reveal, like a faded photograph taken in the days before Kodachrome, a bare and tidy bedroom with tarnished athletic cups, a scuffed up cricket ball, and three volumes of the children's cyclopedia all arranged on long shelves above a tiny desk. A much used teddy bear rested on the pillow and on the wall above there was secured, with rusty flat-headed drawing pins, a black and white picture of a castle. I supposed it was from a fairytale but frankly it gave me the heebie-jeebies.

"Germany?" I asked.

"His castle on the Rhine."

I thought, where are his toys?

The old man was already lowering the blinds. "I did not trust him enough to tell him," he said. "And somehow he must have felt that, don't you think? He was sweet and affectionate but he could not rely on our love. It's clear, isn't it? Why else would he run away with the girl? We would have loved her too. And all their babies, every one."

The room was gloomy but he showed no inclination to leave just yet.

"I could not tell him he was not our natural son."

"I see."

"No, I'm afraid you don't. He is Aboriginal. You see the problem? Mrs. . . . ?"

"Bobs."

"Mrs. Bobs, why would I bother him with that when he fitted in so well? In Adelaide? I thought I was sparing him. But then he gave the poor girl a black baby. What did he think? Where did he go? We saw her afterwards, but never him. All those years we loved him, cared for him, and at the same time we were white ants at the very foundations of his life. We were destroying him."

His eyes, startled, frightened, accusing.

"I wish I had brought him back," I said, thinking how it might have been if he were still our beloved navigator, how different it might have been to see that pair united.

"Then what is that in the box and why have you come to taunt me? I should have told him. I should have found his people for him. There was a letter inquiring, you know, from Mardowarra. Frankly, I could not see the point of it. He was a baby very badly treated, you know. When he came to us he had a dreadful infection. He could have died. Really. I thought, why trouble him with what he can't remember?"

"This was the injury to his shoulder?"

"Ah, you know about that? He did not know what caused it. We invented a funny story."

"But then he had the child."

"If only they had not run away. If I had been there, if only I had been there. What a mess I've made."

He escorted me back through the house. My time was short.

"Mr. Bachhuber, may I use your telephone?"

"I am retired from the ministry. When people need my counsel they drop by." And he smiled and I realised I could not call a taxi.

Back in the garage, he lifted the wooden plane from on top of the cardboard box. "At least you leave me this."

I thought, oh dear, he is gaga.

"Mr. Bachhuber this is not Willie."

"How could it be Willie? This is a child."

"Yes."

"To be perfectly clear, Mrs. Bobs from Bacchus Marsh, I cannot legally do anything for this poor fellow. We have no coroner's report, I assume, no death certificate. It's as if you found him by the road."

"Yes."

"We did horrendous things, you know that?"

"Yes."

"Not only Germans, you understand."

"Yes."

"Do you know, Mrs. Bobs, it often happened that a member of my parish would ask me to hold some thing, a letter, a little photograph, which they could not bear to throw away but were worried their family might discover when they died. Many times I have taken these burdens."

"Yes."

"So I will hold yours."

"But it's not the right thing."

"There is no right thing," the old man said, "there are just many, many wrong things and sometimes we can do no better than pray to be forgiven."

In the shed he drank tea without remembering it had been poured for me.

"You see, his son needs him," he said. "His little boy is disconnected. The mother has married again, some American chap, a black man I believe, what you would call a confirmed bachelor. Is that the right thing? Or the best thing?"

"Mr. Bachhuber, I am sorry. I have to leave."

He did not reprimand me, but he cocked his head and frowned. "I do not have a phone," he said.

"I know."

"Yes, but wait. I have a number."

I waited. I could not be late. He messed around on his workbench amongst wood shavings and jars of nails and offcuts of timber. At last he took a carpenter's pencil and wrote with it on an offcut piece of tongue and groove.

"If you have news of him," he said, "the boy should have it, or his mother. This will find them."

I didn't want it. I had to take it. I should have stayed with him. I had to go. I kissed him and I felt him go quite rigid.

"I'm sorry," I said, meaning for the unwanted kiss, for everything, my rudeness, my inability to stay. This was the guilty burden I carried with me up that concrete path, back to the empty streets of Payneham where, finally, out of breath, in a panic, I walked into a service station and there, in the grubby office, its door smudged with greasy fingers, I found my picture on the wall and a big fat oil-stained woman who was pleased to drive me to the starting line. When she kissed me I did not mind at all.

# 4

WHEREVER THEY TRAVEL in the Atlantic, the North Pacific, the Bering Sea, when it is time to leave the great oceans and go home to spawn, salmon have the ability to find their way back to the river of their birth. It is thought that they use magnetoreception *(Off he goes)* to locate the general position of their river and when they are nearly there they switch to their sense of smell to locate the river entrance and, from there, the spawning ground where they were conceived. *(Listeners, block your ears.)* Even bacteria can have this magical ability to turn themselves into active living maps. In these cases the bacterium demonstrates a behavioural phenomenon known as magnetotaxis in which it orients itself along the lines of the Earth's magnetic field. *(And you have nothing to lose but your smoker's cough.)*

It is reasonable to assume that Bachhuber the Navigator might have had a skerrick of magnetotaxis in his bones, but my experience suggests the opposite. For I had been accidentally delivered to my spawning ground and did not see or smell or even feel it. I had no clue. I was irritated and unsettled by these confident references to my race. I feared Carter and his rum. I was afraid of the loneliness, the dust and dirt, the red rutted roads emerging from the spinifex and acacia, the scalded soil. The huge diesel generator throbbed throughout my first night. The dogs were never quiet. I twisted and turned and the mosquitoes bit me and my gut churned up and I panicked that I would oversleep and miss my ride in the school inspector's Morris Minor. There was no question. This was the flaw in my human clay, to always flee.

But I would not be a teacher again, at least not in a place where they held me in a dusty mudbrick "teacher's residence," a pioneer's ruin with a corrugated roof thrown up across its eroded walls. There were plenty of nasty drafts but none sufficient to blow away the stink of something dead or dying, a snake I thought. There was angry shouting in the night, then some wild creature scratching at the wall. Of course I wished to flee.

With morning I discovered that my "bedroom" was a storehouse stacked with a jumble of old motors and all sorts of scrap. I found the outhouse which had eluded me all night, picked up my "luggage" and carried my fake belongings—the crumpled newspaper and pencil sharpener—out into the weary air to face that single limestone bluff, the survivor of four hundred million nightmare years.

I know, I know: life was all around me and I was a white man, a kartiya, who saw only death. I rushed through a failed plantation of species I did not know and, having contrived to open an ingenious gate, arrived at Carter's front verandah. The concrete slab which had been wet and clean when first I saw it was now littered with beer cans and broken glass and it was from this chaos I beheld Carter rising slowly to his feet. He was unshaven, of course, and his yellow hair was a nest of broken straw, but he tugged his trousers up above his hips and looked down his parrot nose at me and I understood, in that moment, the status of a schoolteacher on Quamby Downs.

I did not see the cricket ball, nor did he intend me to.

"Catch," he cried, and flung it hard. "Howzat?"

Lord, it stung my hands, but I returned it casually, as if assaults were nothing to a man like me.

"I wanted a natter with Mr. Hangar."

"Gone mate," he said, considering me in a more friendly manner.

"No," I said, "he's going to get his brakes fixed before he leaves."

"He said the exact same thing to me, mate," he said, hamming up his response to this "coincidence." "That was our point of contention now you mention it. Fucking amazing. I said to him, what do you think this is, a service station? Of course he's a servant of the Queen, and I don't mind feeding him, and all the grog he wants but I've got a business. And he wants a free mechanic? I've got two mobs on their way to Broome. Five hundred beasts. Eight miles a day. Five men to a mob. You know how many windmills we lost in the last wet? That's my bloody day, mate, putting oil in windmills, and not a useful man left here."

"Where is Mr. Hangar?"

"I didn't see the point of detaining him. He left you this to mail to Perth. Good luck with that mate."

It was a contract for me with the Education Department of Western Australia. Sign or don't sign, didn't matter, not to me.

"It's Sunday. Alidai-taim tudei," he said mockingly, using the only Aboriginal language I would ever hear him speak.

"What?"

"You might want to give your house a sweep. Go to the store, sign out what you want, and don't complain about the prices, they're decided in Melbourne. Get some mozzie coils. Set yourself up at home. Ask the house girls to show you the school. That was a nice catch," he said. "You'll fit in, I reckon."

Did I look so easy? He would not be the first man to make that mistake.

The schoolteacher's residence on Quamby Downs, like the burned out Redex car, like so many other pieces of machinery, windmills, generators, wells, so much failed whitefellah endeavour, stirred in me an immense melancholy and this was heightened by the more personal leavings of the previous incumbent, the single dusty shoe by the front door, the open can of "Two Fruits," its rim gone black with feasting ants, the trove of whisky bottles hidden in his chest of drawers, the wind-up gramophone with—no records—its needles spilled across the floor. Beneath the bunk I discovered *The Complete Stories of the Great Operas* which, like his dirty postcards, was black with mould, a victim of the wet season.

I found a broom and redistributed some dust. I drew water from the tank and scrubbed the filthy sink. I opened the refrigerator, and found the source of that sickening smell: rotting meat from which I fled, dry-retching.

Carter was not at the house to receive my complaint, and instead

I was interviewed by the so-called house girl, Alice Thompson, all of fifty years of age, with sharp shrewd eyes and stick thin legs. She had no shoes, but was dressed in a spotless floral dress and Sunday hat and pin.

"Kerosene bin finish," she said when I had explained the rotting meat.

"No, it's the refrigerator," I said. "It's broken. Bad meat."

She gave me to understand she would fix it.

"But I think you're on your way to church."

But church was trumped by white men, it seemed, and when she met me at the teacher's residence her church hat was missing and she carried a scrubbing brush and a heavy bucket of steaming water.

"What about church?" I asked although clearly there would be no church and she would drag out the putrid mess of meat and carry it, dripping, to the outhouse.

It was a kerosene fridge, of course, and it had run out of fuel and Doctor Battery had already been called to do what was necessary to fix it although, being Doctor Battery, he would artfully avoid any part of that operation he thought beneath him.

"You strong one?" was his first question of me, and I thought he was contrasting my indolence with the house girl's hard labour.

"I know," I said. "It's shameful."

Crabbing sideways in his distinctive style, the good Doctor carried a kitchen chair to the middle of the room. "This old leg no good." He grimaced as he sat.

"Too many young wife that fellah," Alice said.

The old man bestowed on her a roguish smile. "I plenty strong," said Doctor Battery. "Three wives," he said to me.

"Poor old man," said Alice. "Young Olive bin reckon she better get some young fellah do the job."

This lewd taunting continued back and forth for some time before I understood the subject. The refrigerator could not be easily refuelled. First someone would have to shift it to the centre of the room. Not Doctor Battery it would seem.

"You strong one Billy," he said to me.

Alice scrubbed the pale pink suds laughing and shaking her head.

But if I was being taken advantage of, I didn't mind at all. I would shift this one, no matter what it weighed. I would follow instructions to scrape and clean the lamp unit. After that I learned how to trim the wick, light it and move the monster back into its place without tipping it over.

"Next time I fit a hose for you," said Doctor Battery.

Of course there would be no next time. I would be long gone by then.

"Put him juice in the tank," he said. "Tomorrow feed him from this side."

Alice left and returned with a sheet of plywood on which she had bread and marmalade and some glistening butter all of which she balanced on the chrome-legged kitchen table. She poured me strong black tea and added sweet condensed milk. She insisted I draw up a chair to eat and waited until I did.

Meanwhile I could hear Battery going through the empty bottles in the bedroom dresser. I told Alice she did not need to serve me. She shook her head and grasped the knife and smeared the canned butter on my bread. Her fingers were very dark, and dry and worn. She caught me looking, and then suddenly she smiled, and a moment later her whole face collapsed and her mouth opened and she howled.

Doctor Battery came rushing back. Alice abruptly composed herself. Something very odd was occurring between them. Battery required I step outside and I resisted.

"Come with us," they said, each of them, together and separately. "Why?"

"You'll see," said Alice and laid her wet hand against my cheek. Her smile made no sense.

There was no shade, no relief. Not even the house garden had a tree, and there was the Punka Wallah with his ink black eyes staring at me from the laundry door.

A few broken stones marked our path which otherwise was no different from the bare earth all around it.

"Where does this lead?" I asked. I thought, what do they wish to do to me?

"You'll see."

The fierceness of their purpose did not fit the circumstances. I decided it would be convenient to have a toothache and Carter would have to take me to the dentist and that would presumably require a town and then I would get a bus or a ride. I would be OK, I thought. I placed my hand on my jaw, in anticipation of my tooth erupting.

## 5

YOU WENT BEHIND my back, I did not say to Titch directly. I did not ask, what do you think I did with him, with Bachhuber? What lies did Dunstan tell you? Are you aware that your so-called mate, the mongrel, pressed his thing against me in the dark?

I was your wife, promised until death.

You were my husband. You took my money to bookmakers in Craig's Hotel.

In the end there was my sister, only she to understand. My husband waited in the car, thinking I was talking to our kids but it was just me and Beverly. We can never see the future.

# 6

DOWN SOUTH I had been a man of great authority. I had never seen a gunyah but (*Off he goes*) knew it as an Aboriginal word for a small temporary shelter made from bark and tree branches, with a standing tree usually used as the main support. In Quamby Downs a gunyah was called a *humpy* and was not made of bark but of rusting corrugated iron and cardboard. You could not stand up in a humpy. You could not wash inside. You had no bathroom, nothing but a single standpipe in the camp, sulphurous bore water, pumped by the clanking Southern Cross windmill. In the wet season the humpies leaked but then there would be a creek and swimming hole to wash in. Now when the kids rolled down the creek bank they came to a stop on waterless sand.

I said my tooth was hurting but no-one seemed to hear. The changing wind delivered smoke and the stink of cooking bones and offal, the only portion of the station's beef provided to the camp. I sat in the hot dirt ashamed of my cleanliness, hoping to never know the texture of that fat bellied goanna, presently lying across the coals. Alice touched my wrist with the back of her hand and I thought, if not money, what does she require? She stroked my hand and the kids brought me strip maps from the crashed Peugeot # 62. They wanted autographs. Ah, I thought, so that is it.

"You write Uncle Redex," she demanded, and so I did and who could not be moved by those little boys, their smooth bright skin, running noses, their hope and shyness?

All the camp had seen the cars in the Movietone newsreels, said Doctor Battery. They had projected the films in that Jesus place, a bough shed with a tin roof and spinifex tied to the chicken wire on the open sides. The projector had been carried in by Brother Max who showed films about Jesus but also newsreels and everyone laughed and clapped at the Redex cars rolling, leaping, thundering through. So this must be my added value.

"Proper film star," Doctor Battery said, approximately. Actually, he said something like "him proper film star" or "'im proper film star" but I will spare you my own confusion.

Alice excused herself for "second church." I said I had a toothache and was given red sap to chew. When Alice returned Doctor Battery teased her about her bible. "Poor blackfellah don't have a book. Jesus all mili mili, peipa, buk. That way, Alice? He better than mongrel blackfellah?"

"Lochy you bullaman toilet," she said, and of course they had known each other all their lives.

Alice rested her bible in her lap and touched my cheek and pinched my arm and watched to see how the blood fled the skin and then came rushing back. Her own black skin did not act like this, she showed me. That is, we were different. Obviously. Many people came to demonstrate this truth.

Time passed, sometimes peacefully, sometimes not. The Punka Wallah passed by, a wound-up clockwork engine, stopping only briefly to stare down at me. I put off my toothache. I took pleasure from the children playing. The wind changed, and brought the offal smell our way, and we shifted crablike beneath the weeping gum tree.

I was prepared for discomfort and for boredom, but not what happened next.

Imagine yourself a man at his shaving mirror. You know what you will encounter. But then you see, not your familiar reflection, but a stranger's head upon your shoulders. You touch your lip, perhaps, frightened to see your finger reflected on a foreign face.

Or, try another route. Imagine you look into a stranger's face and see your mirror image—except that you are white and he is black. Would you not bite your hand, as I did, or prick it with a knife?

Might it not, as my father would say, shake you up like salt and pepper, to see the most demanding emotion in a doppelganger's eyes?

"He bin wait long time la you," Doctor Battery said.

The hair stood on my arms.

"Yes," I said.

"He dream for you." (" 'E dream for you," to be precise.)

Alice was crying openly. Doctor Battery wiped an eye.

The doppelganger then spoke to me. If I did not hear him cleanly it was because I was afraid and I did not know there could be such a name as his, that it was the custom for half-caste children to be named, not for their fathers, but for things left lying in the dirt.

"Crowbar," he repeated.

"Willie," I said and we shook hands.

Later I would know him as a camp fighter and obsessive card player with money to invest. Now, as his fearless smile made its first claim on me, I wished I could escape his eerie presence. His smile did not falter but his eyes welled as he laid his hand on my arm and then his slender fingers reached to my shoulderblade and I could not resist him or move away and when he arrived at my scar . . . what a jubilant cry escaped his lips.

The bark at the bottom of the white-trunked trees was like cracked mud, like crocodile skin. Crowbar embraced me. Alice wailed and hit her head. Battery removed the rock from inside her grip. I thought, what have I done? Crowbar patted my cheeks. Women hit themselves and rubbed sand into their open mouths. Their faces were intense and folded. Their bodies bosomy and broad. Together with lean Alice they made a choir of unearthly grief and dug into my wounded shoulder as if it were a side of beef.

Doctor Battery claimed Alice was my mother but of course I knew my mother.

I said my tooth was hurting.

I learned I had three mothers, here they were.

But I was from Adelaide. I told them.

No, I was not from Adelaide. That was not my country, this was my country here. I was born at the river by that bloodwood tree. I saw the tree, of course, but I also saw the sand, the discarded clothes, the sorry heap of corrugated iron, the starving yellow dog licking its sores.

When the women had released me Doctor Battery placed his handsome hat upon my head and somehow that was a comfort. Crowbar instructed the kids to bugger off and the women to be quiet. Then the Doctor soothed me as if I were a brumby who would bolt and break a leg if he was not handled right.

"Alice is your mother's sister, so she is your mother blackfellah way." If I were a horse I would have trusted that deep furry voice, the words all worn like river pebbles. Thus I learned my mother's name. She had been Polly. She had been promised in marriage to Doctor Battery's brother. She had been "plenty lively and up to mischief like a kid."

The boss at Quamby Downs was Big Kev Little in those years. He chose Polly to be a house girl. She was not paid wages, just flour and tea and sugar and calico to make a dress. She had been pretty happy, Doctor Battery thought. She was a proper "inside girl," in the cookhouse first but then in the Big House, making beds and sweeping and in the laundry hut as well. Once the missus gave her a Sunday hat to wear. She liked the missus. Nothing bad would have happened except the missus did not like the wet season and she went back to her people for a holiday.

Doctor Battery said that Big Kev did not care about right ways or wrong ways. He was the King of his Castle. He did exactly what he wanted. He shot a union organiser "by mistake" and nothing happened. Likewise, it seemed, he had seduced or raped my mother. "Like they always did," said Doctor Battery.

My stomach lurched.

"Everywhere, missionary fellah, schoolteacher, didn't matter. White-fellah too greedy for our women."

"Your Dedi" was what Doctor Battery called his brother (who was my uncle "blackfellah way" and also my Dedi too). My Dedi had gone up to the Big House to tell the kartiya he could not pinch his wife.

"I bin grow him up," he told the boss.

"Him?"

"Your mother. Your Dedi grew 'im up," he said.

"You mean *her*? He raised her?"

"Yes, yes. Your father grew 'im up. He put 'e brothers through Law. 'E mine."

"Polly was his?"

"Yes. Your Dedi tell the kartiya: 'E mine, 'e promised one."

I will save any kartiya readers the inconvenience of learning the convention of Aboriginal English wherein a woman is called he ('e) and referred to as him ('im). Just the same, the guts of the story was not so hard for a stranger to comprehend: Kev Little was a king sitting on his pearl shell throne. He was a rapist and an abuser. He said he was so sorry for the misunderstanding. He never knew the girl was promised. What a shame. He had one more job for her to do and he would send Polly home in the morning and his best wishes and so on.

The next day, Doctor Battery told me, Big Kev sent for my Dedi, my mother's promised man. He said he had a sick steer over by the number 60 bore and he needed his assistance. There were hawks circling far away, so my Dedi saw that this was true. They rode three or four hours to reach the bore. And there was the beast, already dead, and the hawks tearing it apart.

The boss then ordered my Dedi off his horse and shot him dead in front of witnesses who would not dare to tell. He never got off his horse, but ordered an uncle to cut the dead beast open and hide my Dedi's body inside the carcass. My relations got him later during the muster, when they had to separate human bones from cattle.

Doctor Battery's face was like a stone. "By and by," he said, "you was born on the ground."

When I was born, I learned, my mother had dug a hole and put me in it. She covered me with a mud of ash and termite mound.

"That's what they bin do, this Law, this place. You blang this country. You bright skinned baby, she make you black like coal. But better be careful, Welfare might come and steal that baby, take him down south and bring you up a white man. Too much babies were pinched from here," said Doctor Battery. "There was always crying in this camp. You hear the mothers in the night crying for their babies and Kev Little come out on his verandah and fire his gun and tell 'em shut up.

"You mother lost her old man, she not lose you," Battery said approximately, and all around me were her sisters who thought they were my mothers and they lived in squalor, without a bathroom or a shower or knives or forks or chairs and tables. They had seen me arrive on earth, they said, witnessed my body come slippery wet and wailing, into the world. I could not doubt them, but I still loved a mother who was a little white woman with grey hair who sipped pale tea from a glass cup, who scrubbed her kitchen floor with bleach.

"Your mother kept you close with her and her sisters, Alice, Betty, Junie, with them all the time, and when he went down to the springs (over there, you see them trees) to get the long rushes and small bush onions, he left you langa coolamon.

"That same day, Kev Little sent old Eric Porter off to find a beast, for meat, we call them killer. Eric got the cataracts. He could see OK for shoot bullocks, nothing much more.

"You were a baby and you cried and she was a mother and she had to keep on digging and she was filling up her basket and there was a bloody big wind, what we call a willy-willy.

"Them Christian mob say it was the devil but we know that eagle, we know her name. Wamulu, the wedge-tailed eagle. She picked you up in her sharp claws and took you off to eat.

"Oh what happened to our baby? The mother bin running. They hear you crying in the sky. Give our baby back.

"Eric had Kev Little's .303. I going to kill that eagle. Oh no, you will kill the bloody baby.

"Silly women, stop shouting. He fire and the bullet miss the baby. OK, got that eagle.

"The wamulu drop you. You fell langa bush. Little ones, kids, bin hunting snakes, baby bin nearly hit them, kids bin bring you back la camp. He special one this kid.

"You were special, but look out. There is still the Welfare fellahs, worse than any eagle. They come into the camp and the kids would get hidden. You know Moses in the bulrushes? Pharaoh's daughter finds the baby. OK, except no daughter but two coppers travelling in the horse and dray. They took you away from Polly, and growled her because your shoulder was hurt and they washed off all the good medicine and put you in the dray. Removal of a half-caste child. They said they would took you to the doctor. Your mother walk behind that dray all the way to Derby. Cruel buggers. They end up let her carry you, but only so they got some peace. For two hundred miles she must of hoped she get to keep her baby after all, but when you got to Derby they stole you proper.

"When she learn you were in the ship, your mother went wild. Soon she try to burn down the police laundry hut and they catch her and put her in jail and when she come back to us she was very thin. Even Mabarn could not help her. She got even thinner. Then she had another baby from a whitefellah and she had another try at burning down and then she was in jail. She bin washed up, died la prison. We done plenty crying in this camp."

Three little boys, Peter, Lenny and Oliver Emu, brought me home to the teacher's residence. We came past Carter who was inside his barbed wire fence, playing cricket with his boy and girl. He called out that I had better take a wash. I thought, he is standing where the murderer Kev Little stood. God take this knowledge from me. I was sick to know who I must be. I began to write down my understanding of myself but the sentences were tangled and knotted beyond correction. I still had my pencil in my hand when I hurled my guts down the outhouse hole.

# 7

THE BOBS CAR HAD covered nine thousand miles since we left the Sydney showgrounds. We were seven hundred miles from the full circle. Now, at four in the morning, we came down through the Pentland Hills, just twenty miles from Bacchus Marsh. This was territory we had covered so many times, through Mount Egerton, past Mount Buninyong, down across Pykes Creek Reservoir where Ronnie hooked a redfin in the bum, past the turn-off to Blackwood where we took the kids to swing on the suspension bridge and drank fizzy water from a rock, past the pub at Myrniong where Halloran could not drive the Jag, a different world to now.

Our kiddies would be awake, waiting for us at the bottom of Stamford Hill and I had not known how this would feel, did not know, even as it happened to me: the streetlights blazing before the sunrise, Beverly all gussied up, shivering in the cold. She had spent her remaining money on a painter employed to make the big portrait of me on the canvas sign. Of course she put Titch in, but smaller. WELCOME MISSUS AND MISTER REDEX. My smile was bright as a doll's. I hugged my solemn little Edith, and Ronnie charged and winded me. Could they feel what had happened to their mum? Did it feel wrong to them as well? Ronnie clung tight, and had to be removed so I could get a hug from Beverly.

The kids' classmates from the state school presented me with wildflowers in a peanut butter jar.

Edith asked me what the matter was. I did not want to stay. We were fifteen minutes ahead of schedule but suddenly Mummy and Daddy must tear themselves away. We left without even inspecting the construction of the garage. I drove down that familiar main street, police station, courthouse, Benallack's chemist shop in darkness, only Johnny Bird's bakery with lights on, and I entered the tunnel of dark trees, our Avenue of Honour, our war memorial, each tree had been a son.

Ahead of us lay fame. I didn't want it, even then, which made me different from my shining husband still alight from whatever admiration he had received in Bacchus Marsh.

In my handbag was a scrap of timber, tongue and groove, with Mrs. Bachhuber's Melbourne phone number inscribed with a carpenter's pencil. I felt no need to mention its existence. Ditto Titch did not say a word re his shopping list for Henry Bucks: the lemon lambswool sleeveless sweater, the Harris Tweed, the pork pie hat, the red silk scarf he would use in magic tricks.

Titch and the paddocks were dark and hidden. Melbourne was aglow on the horizon as we crossed the Kororoit bridge, the forlorn explosives factories on our right. I told myself that I must talk to Mrs. Bachhuber to set her mind at rest, but who was I kidding? Why would a supposed adulteress speak to the abandoned wife? Why was I always getting twisted up in other people's business?

The suburbs surfaced from grim dark, and we were in Footscray, with abattoirs on one side of the road and the Flemington Racecourse on the other, below that steep murky park with its evil yellow lights.

There was a phone box and I stopped although I had always thought this park a place of lurking murderers. Titch could not argue because we had time to spare. He could have spent those minutes with his kids, but now he might as well wait here as the new sun caught the muddy river and I dropped my pennies in the phone, pressed the button, A or B.

To myself I said that sarcastic wartime prayer: Don't panic Tex, remember Pearl Harbor.

"Hello," she said, a woman still asleep.

I told her I was calling in relation to Willem Bachhuber.

"What has happened?" she said, and she surprised me with her anxious tone.

"I have located Willem Bachhuber," I said.

"And you are?"

"I am Mrs. Bobs from Bacchus Marsh."

"Yes. What do you want me to do about that?"

"I'd like to talk to you."

"It's not even six o'clock."

"We are in the Redex Trial. We're leaving Melbourne early tomorrow."

Titch had left the car and was checking oil and water. He had the wrong idea of who I was talking to and why.

The woman was well spoken, like a girl with a convent education. "I don't really see the point," she said.

Adelina, I thought. "Perhaps your son would like to know about his father?"

"That would be up to his father, wouldn't it? He could have called us any time he liked."

"Fair enough. Of course. I was wondering . . ."

"Yes?"

"Could we meet? Could you pass along a picture of the little boy?"

"Why would I give you that?"

"I'm a mother," I said, although that made no sense.

"He's had six years. We never heard from him."

"Mrs. Bachhuber, I know what happened."

"Oh, I bet you do," she said and I imagined all the things she might imagine. "It was a cruel thing he did to his own boy."

"He misunderstood what happened."

"Yes, I know what he thought. You'd have to be blind and stupid to think that about your friend."

"You mean, the nurse?"

"Actually the doctor now. Doctor Madison Lee. Our friend. He owes Madison. We all owe Madison."

"Would you meet me?"

"Why?"

"Mr. Bachhuber was our neighbour in Bacchus Marsh. Then he

was our navigator on the Redex. We are Car 92. We became fond of him, my husband and I."

"That's lovely for you both, I'm sure."

"The parking point is in St. Kilda. The RACV depot on The Esplanade. It's."

"Yes, I know where you mean."

"There are probably cars there now."

"Yes. There are."

"It sounds like you can see them."

"Look, none of us want to get involved in this again. We're retired from Willie Bachhuber."

"Our car number is 92. It's a Holden. I am Mrs. Bobs."

"Goodbye, Mrs. Bobs."

I came back to the car to find my husband now behind the wheel. I thought nothing of it until twelve minutes later when the photographers swarmed him at Control. TRIAL LEADER they called him. I didn't mind.

I had previously reserved the Prince of Wales Hotel on Fitzroy Street, but the booking had got lost. So it was the RACV depot for us. I lay across the front seat of the vehicle, like a puppy in a pet shop window with idiots tapping on the glass. I dozed and woke to find my husband dressed up in his new clothes, and for the first time I saw the signature pork pie in full display. If you had seen his companions, you would have thought him right at home: Arthur Dunstan, Joe Thacker, Green the bookmaker, like criminals and racecourse touts posing for the camera. It looked like my husband must be their mascot, his teeth a perfect echo of the Holden's grill.

No-one told me that they had the final Melbourne–Sydney route cards which had been secret until then. They had written off the wifey, that was obvious, although with what authority I did not know. The day was sulky and overcast with big grey clouds blown across the bay from Williamstown and I was marooned on this sea of churned up gravel with the general public staring at me, my awful hair, bloodshot eyes. There was a slender woman with colourless eyelashes and a pretty face ruined by her frown. I thought, don't stare at me. There was a child beside her, a gorgeous-looking black boy in a tartan shirt and turned up jeans, and behind her a man who I supposed at first must be the father. His skin black as black could be, and he showed a sort of grace you would never think to see in the RACV patrol depot, or even Acland Street for that matter, and they were staring at me, the three of them, and I went funny in the tummy when I understood. My face was dirty, my nails oil stained. As I approached them, they waited, inert, not giving, not taking, as unrelenting as a fence.

"I am Mrs. Bobs."

"Doctor Lee," the black man said. American. Is it too soppy to say his hands felt kind?

"Mrs. Lee," said Mrs. Bachhuber and I was surprised because I understood the doctor was a bachelor, through and through confirmed. There was no doubting, however, his hand on the boy's shoulder. It was he who encouraged him towards me.

"I am the boy," he said in such a solemn way I smiled. He was Ronnie's age. He had Willie's whippy figure, and such healthy brown black skin, not at all like the doctor's whose black was almost blue. "My name is Neil."

And then I did not know what to do.

The wind off the bay was cold and smelled of seaweed. The boy's legs were as skinny as his father's and he shivered and I thought, what have I done?

"Have you ever seen a Redex car before?"

He shook his head.

"Would you like to sit behind the wheel?"

He referred this question to his mum who took his hand and I opened all the doors and sat him behind the wheel and invited all of them inside. The doctor seemed like he was reluctant to stain his lovely clothes but in the end he was a boy like other boys, seduced by the legend of the Redex. I decided I would take them for a ride, why not.

Of course I was filthy but it was too late to be ashamed. I put the boy and his mother in the front, and shook out a blanket for the doctor and

I began the engine with a mighty roar that had Dunstan leaping from the bonnet where he had been preening for the press. Titch looked on incredulously, but he was not owed an explanation when his wifey drove the car away. Dunstan was his secret. This was mine. I took them for a ride down the road beside Port Phillip Bay, all the way to Brighton and then back and we did not have to talk about anything except the car and how fast it went and if we might win and how many miles it was to Sydney and I wanted to tell the boy he was sitting where his father had sat, but that was not my place. I bought him an ice-cream, on Acland Street, and when we were back at the RACV I thought I must give him a memento and I found the strip maps and the navigator's notebooks I had hidden from my husband. I told him we were going to win and that these maps would be historic. I told him they had been made by the navigator who had wanted him to have them. I watched him take them in his beautiful hands and could see he had a bright feeling but I could not know exactly what that was.

"We have to go now," he said. "Thank you for the ride."

He was a polite boy and very good-looking and I knew no more than that, or what else I might do, and I watched the three of them, the beautiful blue black man and the blond woman with colourless eyelashes and Willie Bachhuber's solemn boy, threading their way through the crowds and cars.

# 8

WITH NO CAR I was condemned to be a teacher, imprisoned in a limestone cave previously used to store munitions in a war, a dusty schoolhouse without books or blackboard or even the usual map to show the far reaches of the Empire.

As chance would have it, my scholars had their own strip maps, from the Redex car. These they traded like paper scrip. In this they were just like the kids in Bacchus Marsh who gave such value to the Asian export labels from the condensed milk factory. The class in Quamby Downs could not read the maps any more than the Marsh class could write those Chinese characters. They could not even draw Australia in the dust. This, I decided, would be my gift to them. I would teach them something useful before I fled.

I borrowed an atlas from the unfriendly Carter girl and one evening after tea (as they called it) I whitewashed the smoothest cave wall. As my predecessor had hoarded bags of ink powder of varying brands, I mixed ink while the wall dried. Then I found a cutting-in brush on the verandah of my residence. Then I returned to the cave where I made a blue map of Australia that stretched from my feet in Tasmania to my head at Cape York.

The kerosene light brought annoying winged insects and also smirking Carter who came to comment from the peanut gallery. God knows how he got to be so noxious.

Had he been considered handsome in the Western District of Victoria? Did all the most desirable graziers have fair hair and parrot noses? What, I wondered, gave him such confidence in his ignorant opinions?

"They can't be taught," he said.

"Leave that bit to me," I said.

"You're not familiar with the animal, Bachhuber. The blackfellah, he's a bloody genius with directions."

I thought, what made a Victorian sheep farmer such an expert on the people of the Kimberley?

"It's like the world's his footy field," he said. "He knows who's behind him and who's ahead. He has a completely 360-degree sense of everything. He's like this in the bush. But give him a bloody map, mate, he hasn't got a bloody clue."

What joy it would be to prove the hateful creature wrong.

The cutting-in brush was perfect for lettering, for *Melbourne* in particular with all is clear straight lines. My *Sydney* was OK, *Brisbane* even better. By the end of *Townsville* my tormentor had gone off for another drink and when I had written *Captain Cook 1770*, I washed my brush.

I allowed two weeks for my geography sessions but before that time the Punka Wallah arrived with a message. He was to inform me that there would soon be a big mob of cattle, five hundred bullocks, rushing past my cave. I was therefore to let them little buggers go to meet their fathers, brothers, those kings and princes in their stockman hats.

The Punka Wallah's name was Tommy Tailor (or Tom the Tailor) and his arms were thin and wiry as the rope he pulled. I asked him would there be a cook travelling with them.

Them fellahs had to eat.

How did the cook travel?

He would have a bloody cart.

Escape, I thought, laying down my stick of chalk.

Thus in the heat of the day I made a comic spectacle, running between the bullocks looking for a cook who was already setting up camp a day ahead. It was Crowbar who rescued me and propelled me into the safety of the camp where, soon enough, he tricked me into playing cards.

Later, at the Big House, the boss chastised me: "I don't mind if you go sniffing round the camp, mate, but you can't come in my house with scabies."

I was distressed. I said I must see the dentist.

"Calm down," he said. "Wash your hands."

There had recently been, it seemed, a general infestation of scabies in the camp. Now no-one gained admission to the boss's table without first scrubbing with Lifebuoy soap. Carter practised what he preached, leaving his chair between every course. And what a chair he then revealed. It made my skin crawl, to understand this was the throne that had known the broad backside of the rapist who begot me. I thought, if Carter knows I am a half-caste he might let me go.

I asked was that chair from Big Kev Little's time.

"What would you know about Big Kev?"

Nothing, I decided. "He was the manager before you?"

"He was a Kimberley legend mate. Did you hear the flour story?"

Mrs. Carter shot him a tight look.

"It's alright, mother. He can tell this one in church."

The boy and girl had their father's hair and soft pink scalps. I never saw kids cut their food so small.

"This was thirty years ago, two managers ago," Carter said. "No, listen. Big Kev drove a truckload of the boys into Mardowarra after the shearing. He said come into the bar and see me and I'll shout all youse buggers a drink."

Mrs. Carter clicked her tongue. I did not wish to hear what followed.

"All youse *fellows*. And they were at the Crossing Inn until after midnight but in all that time not a single one of the boys had come to drink with him. This was for the simple reason that blacks were not permitted in the bar. But they were Kev's boys and he expected them to go where he ordered them to go. It was not reasonable in this case, but he was an emotional man. When he had finished drinking he paid his tab, as normal, but he was offended and that was preying on his mind.

"He starts up the truck and toots the horn until finally the boys all come drifting back, and he sets off without a word about anything. But it's a long drive home and by the time they get to the crossing at the Nine Mile his hurt feelings have got the better of him.

" 'Alright, you lot.' " He stops the truck.

"The engine was running. The headlights were on. He lined them up and dressed them down like a bloody sergeant major. And it was: you so-and-sos. And: you ungrateful pack. He was easily hurt, Big Kev. He says, I offer to buy you a drink, and not one of you shows up. And they said, ah boss, you know, we're not white. We can't drink in there.

"Ah, says he, is that all it was?

"Yes boss, we bin with the blackfellahs.

"So Kev strolls over to the back of the truck. And he yells to one of them, lift that flour over there, Hector. Put it in the light. Kev always had a knife on his belt and now he slices the bag and lifts it, a hundred-weight, and then he walks along the line of them and drenches each and every one of them with flour.

"Alright, he says, you can drink with me now.

"And he gets back in the truck and drives away. What a character, Big Kev Little. They don't make them like that any more."

Alice was my mother's sister. She filled the boss's plate with the grey beef and white potatoes. I saw her worn black hands and then my own, Kev Little's hands, with knife and fork. I thought, *The Hands of Orlac*.

I have read too much. I should shut up. I can be a bore with what I know. But *The Hands of Orlac* was directed by Robert Wiene in Austria in 1923. Orlac is a brilliant pianist. He loses his hands in a railway accident. His wife pleads with a surgeon who transplants the hands of a recently executed murderer and of course the hands have a life of their own. In truth I never liked the film but now I had Kev Little's hands and I must rush outside.

When I had believed I was a German I suffered a phantom homesickness that gave its distinctive colour to my soul. But now I was in my real birthplace and finally knew my father's name, that nagging feeling had become a searing pain. I slept badly. I woke in fright. Panic, like sheet lightning, continued through my day and night and soon it was better to sit at Carter's table than think of who I was. Better than this was to be with my pupils who came to fetch me every morning, who held my white hand as if they loved and needed me, who called me

Uncle Redex and chatted to me or brought me, say, a grass snake and taught me its name and showed me how it moved through the red dust and left its cursive script behind.

We spent our first hour of school with showers and laundry and then they changed into their school "uniform" which was nothing fancier than a pair of shorts and a shirt bought from Coles in Perth.

But I met unexpected resistance to geography. I was not used to failure and did not appreciate Carter coming to observe it. Once or twice, when my class had left for the day, he brought his boy and girl and drilled them on the names of states and cities. That is, they could do what my class would not.

Trees began to flower, a bush orange, a kind of wattle. I learned their names. We wrote them down. Then the crocodiles and snakes were laying eggs and I made an English lesson out of that and I used the opportunity to have them teach me their language. Only then did I discover how many tribal languages were in that cave, all those broken pots with all their shards swept in together, including little Charley Hobbes who was one of a dozen descendants of a slaughtered tribe. They were prisoners of a war not mentioned by the education department.

To my great white wall I added the road from Melbourne to Sydney and this had uses for arithmetic. The scabies epidemic passed leaving dull black marks on my children's perfect skin. They now drew pictures of speeding cars which they enjoyed. I constructed popular puzzles where the correct answer was a car driving at two hundred miles an hour.

I was nervous about snakes but took long walks by myself at dusk, a time when the campfires produced an unworldly glow and my foreign place of birth was as depressed and mournful as a prison yard. The pastor had known, of course, that my ancestral home could never have been a *Schloss* in Germany. Then what did he feel to see me pining over that engraving on my bedroom wall? Nothing cruel, of course, and yet he had suckled me on lies. Did he know that I had been carried in the talons of an eagle and dropped into a camp of humpies, bones of rusty cars with smashed out windows? Would he have been upset if he had seen me, finally, stumble into my inheritance, my family seat? Excuse my bitter joke. It was a back seat passed down from a smashed up car. It was here I sat, in the gloamin', in deep despondency because I had been unable to teach my class geography.

It had been a bad day for the hunters at the camp, or perhaps they had eaten in the afternoon as they sometimes did or there was nothing but flour and water to fill their guts. I found Doctor Battery sitting by his humpy with Oliver Emu who was his grandson, and shy tiny Charley Hobbes.

I sat. Doctor Battery turned his bad eye on me. "See longa that?" He was pointing to a fence that cut from the Big House to the horizon. "What that?"

"You mean that fence?"

"Blackfellahs got no fence. No fence, no bloody map neither." How that last bit stung. To hear my map attacked by friends. "Whitefellah have fence and map," said Doctor Battery.

"Whitefellah cut'em up my country," he said, counting with his long fingers. "Surveyor map. Whitefellah peipa. Western Australia. South Australia. Kartiya lock the gate. Blackfellah stay out."

I felt my colour rising.

"Why these kids need map?" the old man insisted and every teacher can imagine how I felt.

"So they don't get lost," I pleaded but he would not go easy on me.

"How can they be lost langa country? You know nothing Billy," he said, not kindly either. It was his job to be guardian of many stories. This one involved an ancestral being who seemed to be a snake.

Oliver took my hand and in his comfort I felt my failure, his sorrow for me, my loss of face. "Snake and man. Both, together," he said.

Doctor Battery nodded in approval. He flicked the dirt off a plug of camp tobacco, and tucked it inside his lip. He said his snake ancestor had been looking for a place to live. He had pulled boomerangs from his body and thrown them and tasted what the water was like in the places where they landed. With these boomerangs the ancestor made the floodplains then the creeks.

Oliver, all the time attentive to his grandfather, illustrated his story as he told it, drawing with a stick in the dirt. It was a map, I cried. A bloody map. Was not that a map?

"We don't need map," said Doctor Battery. "This my country. The story, 'e hold that Law, 'e know the waterholes. That snake man wants living water for his camp. That is called a jila. Whitefellah can't see that living water don't know story for country. Maybe that whitefellah die of thirst there, langa jila, langa living water."

Oliver grasped my hand again and I wondered if I was the stupid whitefellah or if I was the blackfellah inheriting the story. In any case I was the teacher. And I did not wish to be diminished by an elder. So I insisted the story was like a map to find water.

But the old bugger would not help me, and I left the camp knowing that Carter had been correct, and I had failed to teach third grade geography.

That night I set up the kerosene lamp and obliterated the state borders on my classroom map. And then I painted out the coastline and left a perfect field of white. Here I would have my pupils drawings the paths of ancestral beings from one place to another. I would not call them maps.

Next day I brought Battery into my class and invited him to draw his story for all of them. He was perhaps the first black elder to be invited to stand in that room and my students knew this and were very quiet and watchful. He broke bark to make a brush. He dipped it in ink and drew his Dreaming story on the wall.

Oliver Emu wrote the place names as his grandfather said them. Little Charley Hobbes did not know the alphabet but I noticed how seriously he traced his finger over the letters JILA.

Later I would make this lesson the subject of a 10,000 word essay, but at the time there were more important things to do. Foremost, I was obliged to invite Doctor Battery into my residence and explain how

I would wish him and the old men to help in class. I served him tea and Anzac biscuits and explained my teaching plan.

He listened very carefully and asked many questions, most particularly how much they would be paid.

I said I was sorry there would be no pay.

He had been a stockboy for Big Kev Little, he said. He was the best stockboy. He would be sent out on muster with no whitefellahs. He as good as ran the station in the end. After all of that, his horse fell and Big Kev had left him five days in the bush with a compound fracture in his leg.

"He finish me Billy. I could not walk no more. Maybe you buy a jeep."

Then I saw that was his price. He would come to my classroom and in return I would give him a jeep, which was his name for any motor vehicle. Then I could drive him to his country and he could do whatever rituals were required. Was he serious? Did he believe I was so rich? Was he simply putting a price on the damage done to him at Quamby Downs?

"If I had a jeep," I said. I stressed the "if." We agreed we understood each other perfectly.

# 9

IT WAS SOON decided that Doctor Battery would bring two more old men to my class and I would pay them a few shillings from my own pocket. These men were both drawn from what had become the "Uncle Redex shooting party" and included me (Uncle Redex) and Old Mick and Peter Stockman. I would never have thought that the rather haunted Punka Wallah would be welcome in this group, but clearly he thought otherwise and so came to hover at the edges of my class, uninvited, dressed oddly in a formal waistcoat, tie, and a pair of calico pyjama bottoms I never saw him wear in other circumstances. In any case, they ignored him and on each occasion, prior to his departure, he made an indignant speech in pidgin, which for all its incorporation of English words was as inaccessible to me as any of the tribal languages. I assumed his complaint concerned his treatment by the others.

Now I pushed my kids towards the subject of "blackfellah business." I discouraged them from drawing the cowboys and Indians for which they had expected praise. When the old men arrived in class my pupils, contrary to my expectation, lost their normal animation. When I gave the old men ink and a cutting-in brush the kids became very still and apprehensive and I thought, of course, they are overawed. They know themselves too young to be initiated in the mysteries of Law. But then, later, they came to me, one by one, in confidence, fearful I would be "growled" by the boss.

The old men, on the other hand, were clearly happy to have their great authority recognised in the white space of the schoolroom. Their presence meant that the class must now be conducted in a mélange of languages and I would have lost all control had not sixteen-year-old Susie Shuttle become my trusted interpreter. Susie's mother was from the river mob and her father from the desert so, apart from her very reasonable English, she was fluent in pidgin and the common tribal languages. It was she who made the class possible. She translated the old men's stories, and helped me read their stick talk, the concentric circles, the marks for travelling feet, the slithering calligraphy of the rainbow serpent. She was a natural, and not above administering her own punishments when she felt them called for.

I was, in terms of knowledge, the equivalent of four years old. Thus I was informed by handsome Old Mick (he with the splendid military moustache) that Doctor Battery was effectively my father and it would be his job to pass on information about my country. He would introduce me to the jila and then I would learn my ancient obligation.

I said I had a job to do.

He assured me this would take "a couple days" and in this time I would learn some lessons, but I better leave my whitefellah peipa at home.

When Doctor Battery arrived in the humid dark of a Saturday morning, I failed to tell him that all his careful plans for my education were a waste of time. I planned to flee Quamby Downs at the first opportunity. Thus, in effect, I accepted an engagement ring with no intention to be there at the altar, and it was with a very guilty conscience that I observed his wonderful good mood, his considerable excitement, as he packed a box of my matches and two empty cans of Sunshine milk powder into his rucksack.

Surely, you will ask, I must have expected that his injury would prevent him from performing his duty? But he showed no hesitation. He set off so full of beans, with a hip and hop and scarecrow rattle. It was me who was tentative. I was there to follow.

Only when he announced a sit-down did I understand. His leg was bugger up. He could never do this walk again. He sat in the red dust with his back to the station and I asked him how I could help him achieve his goal.

In considering my question he removed his hat. "You want to help me Billy?"

"Of course."

"One thing I remember," he said. "Maybe we try that."

"Sure."

"When I was a kid."

"Yes?"

"My grandfather him stomach no good, he gotta go lookim country." He pushed his hat back on his head. "My Dedi carry him."

I considered the hot scoured country and was sorry I had said what I had said.

"How many miles?"

"Not so far. Up to you Billy."

The homestead buildings were still very close. I could hear the generator and the barking dogs. Of course I could have turned back home and who would have blamed me.

Yet I had my hands of Orlac, and so I carried him, faltering, bitter in my heart, recalling the lost explorers, Burke, Wills, mad with thirst and hunger, white men stumbling towards their deaths.

"You ask, I tell you anything Billy."

"Thanks mate, that's very generous."

So the old fellah talked into my ear, I learned that the jila was normally dangerous to approach. It would smell me. I would be OK, he said. Don't worry, he said. Rub dirt under your arms. Nothing bad could happen to me then. He would tell me everything. My ancestor was a snake with a long beard. He could bring misfortune or even death. We would sing when we approached him. Not just any song but the correct song Doctor Battery had learned from his father's brother.

The huge sun became high and Doctor Battery's weight increased and I no longer liked him. There was a low saddle in the west he needed me to keep my eye on.

I was a good man, he said, strong and kind. He would care for me, teach me, keep me from danger. This was almost comforting until I lost sight of the low saddle. Then I must be blind as a bloody kartiya, he said, and I felt all my goodwill abused.

Then some time after noon—I felt it like a horse must feel its rider's indecision—he became uncertain.

"You're lost."

He did not answer.

"Jesus. Lochy. You are lost."

"No, this is devil-devil country now," he said. "Sick country. Look at those bloody wattles growing there. No good."

I imagined he was blaming me, and although he would never hold me responsible for the sins of my biological father, I did not know that yet. He was my father, taking me to meet the jila, passing on his knowledge so I could keep the country alive. Now it had been neglected. A bloodwood tree was missing. It was always near the jila. Now it had gone. Well, I thought, it is not my fault.

Then suddenly he was off my back and hopping and skipping into the mulga in such a way I saw his pain, like a spring that could propel him higher. He ripped off a branch which he used to sweep the earth between some rocks. These were dead children, he told me. So we would see the bloodwood soon. We would light a fire, to signal to the snake that we were coming.

As the white smoke ascended, a wedge-tailed eagle rose lazily from the mulga and then it seemed we must follow in the same direction. On the edge of the mulga, the country dipped and became sandier. I looked for the storied jila but saw no comfort, no certainty, no spring or waterhole. The only shade was offered from a burned stump of tree now sprouting shoots of green. I thought, I have let this crazy old man cause my death.

"There," cried Doctor Battery, pointing. "Bloodwood."

What a sad sight, but not to him. No, he said, he was not lost. He was where he should be. He stood very tall with his head held high. I noticed, for the first time, the extraordinary broadness of his chest. He sang, without preamble, with a passion that surprised and moved me.

Then he spoke, and I supposed he was introducing himself to the ancestral being.

"What you see?" he asked me when he had paused at last. His eyes were fierce and bright. He grabbed me by my shoulders and compelled me forward. "Look, look, what you see?"

The earth was dead with no suggestion of any damp, desolation everywhere you looked.

Doctor Battery moved on ahead of me, crouched, as if hunting, but singing softly. He gathered scrub branches, mulga needles, spinifex and set light to them, recklessly I thought, and then he danced around me, wreathed me in the smoke, white as muslin.

"You want drink, you dig. You want water, you dig." He produced a rusty milk can from his rucksack and threw it at my feet. But dig where? There was no wet sand, no green blade.

"Is it the right place?"

"You dig. You strong one, you dig."

I held my tin and dug until my fingers were raw and my throat was lined with dust and sandpaper and I entered darker sand and then, as the sun began to drop in the afternoon I was working inside a pit. At four feet I struck damp sand, at six feet water. Doctor Battery crabbed down to see me and we stood and waited until the water cleared. Then he took a mouthful and bent his head back and blew a fountain up into the air and clear water fell back upon his dusty whiskered face. Then he was naked. Then he took a second can and spilled mud and water on his head and ruined chest and body and then I—the shy one with the ugly injury—did the same. No-one asked me to or told me to. The mud was warm, then cool and then I squatted on the ground and drank the living waters of the jila.

There was no English word for this.

We lit a fire. Doctor Battery killed a big goanna with a rock. We built up the fire with mulga wood and hollowed out places for our bodies and when I woke, cold, in the early morning Doctor Battery was sitting over me. Perhaps he was asleep.

Today was Sunday, never mind. We must follow the path of the snake ancestor (whose name I must not say), continue wherever it led us, into country described in T. Griffith Taylor's maps as "Sparse or Useless." It had been much abused by cattle whose hard hooves had made cruel impact on the soil which had, in turn, been much eroded. We negotiated the perimeter of violent scenes, like bomb craters littered with fence posts whose monumental mortices announced the folly of whitefellah business. There was no choice but to carry my teacher and surely neither of us was insensitive to the symbolism.

Finally, in late afternoon, I saw smoke and, an hour or so later, a campfire, and then, impossibly, a car.

"You see him Billy? Jeep."

I could see a human being, by golly. In all that enormous solitude it was the strangest sight.

"Maybe you more happy now?"

The human being called to us. "Coo-ee." I thought, it is not a bloody jeep at all, it is a car. And I forgot all that delirium of water and mud, flakes of which were still adhering to my skin. I thought, I will soon be down in Perth. That was an intoxicating moment while it lasted, but soon enough I saw the damned insignia and recognised the burned out Redex Peugeot I had first seen on the road into Quamby Downs and wondered why I had to suffer such a trek to come upon it. Beside the car stood none other than the man who had robbed me in a game of cards.

Crowbar grinned and his lip lifted as my lip always lifted, the curious muscle Clover had thought was "sweet." He took me by the hand and walked me over to the Peugeot. I was hot and tired and perhaps hysterical. I observed Crowbar pull at the underside of the dash and withdraw a melted mess of wire and plastic connectors and condensers.

The wires stank of fire and burning plastic. I did not wish to touch them, but Crowbar pressed them on me as if they were some special treat, like the meat of an echidna, a delicacy reserved for senior men.

"We find his brother Billy," Doctor Battery called. "Then we make him bloody go."

Well, of course Crowbar was my blood relation but by "brother" the

Doctor meant something else: the brother of the Peugeot would be an identical model, in a wrecker's yard.

"We make you jeep," said Crowbar. "We get him brother. He in Derby. Cost sixty for same wiring. That's all. He good like bloody new."

I smelled the smell of oil and rubber and another life. That is, they would take me to the wrecker's yard and I would run away.

# 10

SEBASTIAN LASKI

*Appraiser rare books, maps, early manuscripts. 26 Glenhaven Court,*
*Box Hill, Victoria. Tel: BW-9628*

My dear dear Willy-willy, having worried about you for so
many years your letter was a source of great rejoicing—he
lives!—and, as you might expect, some irritation. Did you
never know we loved you? Did you have to make us wait five
years? Or is it more? How many times have we wondered
what on earth might have befallen you. You were always so
wilful and so unprotected.

Your Adelina suffered awfully, as you must have expected,
and of course we have kept in touch with her and done our best
to help her, in her difficult social situation. As a man who has
himself left women, I would not underestimate your feelings
of self-reproach, but please understand, none of your upheavals
have made us care less for you.

So now you have willy-willied yourself into the wilds of
Western Australia. You have discovered an unsuspected father
and become a teacher in a rather Gothic-sounding schoolroom.
We, who never dreamed we would end our lives in *Terra
Australis,* have some understanding of your present situation.
Sometime we can compete on whose life is the least believable.

Since we have seen you I have suffered a small stroke,
nothing too bad, but I now drive with a type of doorknob stuck
to the steering wheel, if you see what I mean. It will be no
trouble at all to take a spin up to Bacchus Marsh, and if there

is someone there to help me load the books it will be a simple enough matter.

My question is, what should be their final destination? This will be no ordinary library, I am sure, but you have not said what you want done with it. Dorotea and I have (interminably) discussed its fate and now have an excellent idea. I will write to you as soon as I know it is, as they say in Melbourne, doable.

I was hunting for the etymology of "Quamby" which seems to be Aboriginal, but not from that part of the world. How on earth did it move from Tasmania to the Kimberley?

I look forward to your answer and, just to please an old friend, a fuller account of all your triumphs and disasters.

We both send our fond wishes, dear Whirly-whirly.

Sebastian

# 11

IN SYDNEY THE CROWDS would be waiting for us, warriors clad in mud and grit and streaking windscreens. TO HELL AND BACK etc. First we had to cope with the Snowy bloody Mountains. Excuse my French.

The first two hundred miles were simple, due east along the highway. At Orbost we cut north into the mountains: another two hundred miles with snow already on the ground. "To drive more than 25 mph would be unsafe," said the police.

Dreary Orbost was slick with rain and cow droppings. We filled the tanks and I was informed by my partner that I could not navigate. It was not my strength, he said. In all our years together he had never spoken to me like that.

I drove. I drove well. The misty windscreen would not clear and I had no choice but to wind down the windows and speed along the mountain roads with the insides of my nose like a pack of frozen peas. Titch had been reincarnated as his father, drunk on glory, impatient, fidgety, already imagining the trick he would perform when we had passed the finish line. He failed to call a hairpin and I travelled sideways above a lethal drop.

He shouted. He blamed the map. And on we went.

I was criticised for being too fast. At the same time I was too slow. He forbade me to stop in Cooma where there was a post office where I could have talked to Beverly.

On the giddy road to Adaminaby the windscreen was scratched and streaked and dark. There were steep descents with snow and rain. Coming down Talbingo Mountain the brakes were fading and I was nursing the handbrake and using the gearbox to hold the speed in spite of which I was nudging forty, then fifty, then sixty miles an hour on greasy road.

"Jesus, Irene."

I thought, we are going to die.

Gently, gently, I edged against the guardrail but then there were no guardrails to slow us and I could hear the clay and rock walls of the cutting, ripping at the screaming Holden body.

Titch was rigid silence.

I flicked onto the wrong side as I came through a pass. My babies, my babies, you will spend your lives as orphans, with warts and ingrained dirt and lonely Christmas Days.

Titch's eyes: wet jelly, serve him right.

At least I have not murdered Willie.

I lost all traction and was sideways to the double line, bouncing off a mountain drain. There was a drop of a thousand feet. I stalled. White mist. Then nothing visible but four white rabbits which turned out to be the feet of a draught horse in the middle of the road. The mist opened to reveal, far far below us, a low wide building with *Talbingo Hotel* painted on its corrugated roof.

Titch left the vehicle and commenced a damage survey like an insurance assessor.

As I opened the door, the horse began to pee.

Soon we descended to the pub where they let me use the phone, right in the bar. I held the big black receiver with both hands shaking, listening to the operators talking to each other, one in Cooma, one in Bacchus Marsh.

"Why that's Titch Bobs' number," cried Bacchus Marsh. "He's away on that Redex Trial."

"Is that so?" said the Cooma operator. "Is that you, caller? Are you the Holden?"

"Oh Mrs. Bobs," cried Miss Hoare from the Marsh. I could see her as everybody saw her, with her pleated skirt and thick stockings bicycling up Gisborne Road, going home for lunch. "Have you won yet, Mrs. Bobs? We're all so proud."

"Where are you?" my unhappy daughter asked.

"How are you?" I asked, knowing Miss Hoare would repeat everything we said.

"You better come home," Edith said.

"We'll be in Sydney tomorrow."

"You tell Ronnie then. You tell him, Mum. Aunt Beverly has done a bunk. We're being looked after by the cousins."

Through the window, through the mist, I could see my husband. He had a bucket of warm water out and was cleaning up the battered car. Idiot, I thought. Leave the mud on. Edith told me that Beverly was with that "Uncle chap," whoever he was. I said I would find Beverly straight away.

Miss Hoare put me through to Constable Lurch of the Bacchus Marsh police. He was the chap who had taken home his ten-pound redfin.

"I don't see what I can do for you, Mrs. Bobs."

Why would I expect him to be snotty? He had been nice to me before, and here I was, putting the Marsh on the map. "Can you find my sister?" I asked.

"I don't think that's my job, is it?"

I was startled to hear his peevish tone. I should not have been: I was addressing him as if he was my servant. I was in the newspapers and thought myself superior. This was how he heard me when I explained that Beverly had left my kids alone.

"We could say the same about you Mrs. Bobs."

"I'm in the Redex, you know that."

"Endangering the welfare of a minor. That's it, isn't it?"

Oh Jesus, forgive me for needing you, I thought. I was agitated then and everyone could hear, on the phone, and in the beery bar of the Talbingo Hotel.

"Please Constable. I'm sorry. I think she has a boyfriend."

"Yes, we are aware of that Mrs. Bobs."

"Is there nothing you can do?"

"Just leave it with me Mrs. Bobs."

I could have asked him what he meant. I could have apologised for being on the front page in the Melbourne *Sun*. He hung up and I had to wait for the Cooma operator to call in with the cost and the publican saw my distress and poured me a shot of whisky.

I drank, booked another call and you could rely on Miss Hoare to recognise the number when I said it.

"Bachhuber, W.," she cried. Together we heard the phone ringing in an empty house.

"Are you alright, Mrs. Bobs? You sound distressed."

I thought it best to terminate the conversation.

# 12

IN THE PALE LIGHT of dawn I was cleverly enticed out onto the verandah of the teacher's residence from where I beheld the Redex Peugeot. Clustered around it were Battery and Crowbar, Oliver Emu, Charley Hobbes, my entire class as they always looked before their morning showers, their skin still dusty, hair matted, their camp clothes a yellowish sick grey.

It is true, as I must have said, that Crowbar was a black man with my physiognomy, but he also had a slim-hipped cowboy swagger all his own. He was my disturbing Other and he was an athlete, folding his whippy body behind the steering wheel where, obviously, the key awaited him. The metal monster backfired, blew flame, and then it was rocking on its springs inside a cloud of oily smoke.

Forever after the Peugeot would be fondly called the jeep. It was now stripped and burnished, with the brutal appearance of a rocket or a racing car or that great Australian machine gun, the Owen, with its grim metal magazine. I mean, the stock car had become a war machine. It had no windscreen. Fire had blistered its paintwork and turned it as iridescent as an oil slick. Its innards were as sour as smoke. The floor was metal, the gearstick had no knob, just a rusty rod waiting for my hand.

This was a presentation of sorts. Crowbar pressed the keys on me. Then Susie Shuttle (my star student, interpreter and assistant) came forward to present a painting on behalf of all my students: a portrait of ghost-haired me, the Peugeot, a bearded serpent.

I prepared to make a formal speech, but the motor coughed and stopped. The tank was dry.

"Tipon," said Battery.

"Siphon," said Susie Shuttle and I understood they could sell me more petroleum as required.

"Plenty more juice," said Doctor Battery and I adjusted myself to his gait as we all made our way to school, strolling past the wire-fenced homestead where Carter's kids were at "School of the Air." Each day the poor creatures sat before a pedal radio like little gerbils on a wheel and as my lot now ran and tumbled through the soupy air, I could hear the boss's kids singing their school song. *Parted but united, Parted but united / Is our school motto and pride of our heart.*

The Carter girl was serious and studious—she disapproved of me—but twice at dinner her little brother had undercut his father with a traitor's wink. I would have loved him in my class, particularly now. It is not grandiose to say I might have saved his soul.

Since my visit to the jila, the station had been given over to the thrills of horse breaking. At the same time the white wall of my cave had become the site of an erupting diagram which kept me mixing ink and improvising brushes from twigs and bark. The chart was bold and blue and forked. It showed the blacks at Quamby Downs were not one mob but many language groups, two dispossessed of their ancestral lands and all of them systematically humiliated by the pastoralists. I could not have taught this by myself. I learned it from them, and they from each other, and from Old Mick and Peter Stockman and Oliver Emu's grandfather Doctor Battery, who still lived on the country of his people. Most of my pupils never would. Their ancestors had been slaughtered, their country made unreachable. And of course I had finally seen that all Aboriginal culture was based on country, on journeys, or tracks now cut up by fences. So then I understood that Quamby Downs was a sort of prison where it was often impossible to honour the moral and religious obligations of singing country, and then the cause of the people's awful lassitude was obvious. They were exiles, denied the meaning of their lives.

If Garret Hangar had seen our messy diagram he would have been greatly inconvenienced by having to fire me on the spot. Indeed, the

Western Australian education department had given specific instructions that I was not to reinforce "backward beliefs." They paid me twenty pounds a week to erase the past, to modernise the blacks, to make them as white as possible in the hope that they would grow up as stockboys and house lubras and punka wallahs.

Having regained their natural authority, the old men made it clear that they would rather not have a woman as their intermediary, but that could not be helped. It was from Susie Shuttle that I learned the story of the wedge-tailed eagle riding on the snake's back and making the great river whose name I have now forgotten. It was she who likened the jilas to the "knuckles" of a goanna spine, each one a link in an ancient story not shown on any strip map. The rainbow snake made Geikie Gorge which she taught me to call Danggu. Now I had the jeep, she said, Uncle Crowbar would take us to see it and would put fat on the rock at Danggu. He would thus ensure there were plenty barramundi. He would show us the marks on the gorge wall from the great flood. It was clear to me that Susie, with her energy and barely hidden fierceness, was destined to be one of those schoolteachers who are talked about for generations, so it was shocking, at the end of every school day, to see her change back into her camp clothes and assume the robes of dispossession.

My day finished as it always did, with me sweeping up the footmarks and the limestone dust. Doctor Battery, I noticed, had stayed behind. Perhaps he had a story he would not let women hear. In any case, he had something on his mind which he would reveal when he was ready. Now he squatted in the shadow of the supplies cupboard.

I winked at him.

He scratched his long chin.

"Damn good jeep," I said.

He nodded.

I told him: "Now I can bugger off down south."

His mouth stayed straight.

"Thank you," I said.

The old fellow took out his baccy pouch but now he held me with his good eye. "You reckon you pinch that jeep?" he suggested.

Well, he had "pinched" it. Now I would too. I judged it time to smile. Then I turned to hang the broom on the wall unaware that the old devil was creeping up behind. When I turned, I got an awful fright to find him in my face.

He slammed me against the wall and I felt the powerful spring of anger in his arm. "Lochy crash angry," he said. "Nothing funny. You bloody white boss," he said and I smelled his camp smell, his heat. "Same thing always. Blackfellah give present. You give nothing back."

"I carried you," I said.

"I carry you," he mocked. He spat, nicotine yellow, a great gob on the classroom floor. "Bloody kartiya," he said and turned away, his limp exaggerated by the violence of his temper. He was heading back for the cover of the camp but I did not intend to let him go, until, that is, he stooped to pick up a length of corroded pipe and then I changed my mind.

The camp may have been my place of birth but it was driven by rules no-one could explain to me. Why, for instance, would a man stand still while he was speared in the thigh? Why would the loser of a fight be set upon by a crowd of women and then do nothing to defend himself from their fists and feet? Why this? Why that? I had already exhausted everyone's goodwill.

Smiles and apologies did not buy love. To hell with it. I returned to my residence concerned mostly with petrol, and how to get it. I was not at all pleased to find Cricket Carter in the driver's seat, smoking nonchalantly, waiting for me, of course.

"You've got yourself a new job, I see."

I was in no mood for a lecture.

"They'll keep you busy mate."

I asked him who he meant.

"You're the chauffeur mate. Swimming. Shooting. They're going to love you now. How much did you pay to get this car fixed?"

Sixty quid to get me out of here. I would have paid two hundred.

"Your predecessor had a Kombi van. He spent all his pay on petrol, poor bugger. They drove him mad, mate. Literally." He held my eye until I looked away. "You know how much petrol costs up here?" I didn't care. He supplied the number anyway. He smiled and ground his cigarette on the steering column and came to stand beside me. "They're playing you, mate."

"I know."

"Ah."

I thought, ah what?

"The missus has been worrying about you. What are you eating? You used to come to tea."

"Didn't want to wear out my welcome."

"Don't buy that marda-marda bullshit. You're a white man, mate, no matter what you think."

"What would that be?"

"Oh come on, Billy. Everybody knows the story now. Give the camp a rest, eh?"

"I am."

"What happened with your limpy mate? I thought you were going to come to blows."

"Nothing."

The hateful fellow gazed down at his biceps and his pack of cigarettes secured by a rolled-up sleeve. "Then come to tea."

He was my sole possible source of petroleum and therefore, arguably, the most important person in my life. So of course I went and was much relieved to find there was company. First, a policeman. That was Buster Thorpe who had arrived with mules and horses and a "boy" who was presently down at the camp. They were about to make a 700-mile ride over the King Leopold Ranges. In addition there were three young jackaroos, white boys of course, and the rather raddled pilot of the Dakota who had been stranded by a Derby willy-willy.

The policeman had noticed the Redex Peugeot. And I left it to

Carter to explain how it was there, abandoned, and to quiz the policeman about its legal status. When it was established that the vehicle could not be legally driven on a public road, Carter stared at me significantly. Did he know what I was up to? Frankly, I didn't care what he thought. I would depart in darkness and if the Peugeot served only to get me arrested, it would have served its purpose.

Buster Thorpe had a policeman's normal animus towards the Redex crews who he described as hoons.

I frowned and laughed when it was expected. I felt Alice look at me from the curtained doorway. She brought me food.

Until this evening Carter had never said a single word about the Redex. This was only remarkable because he was a great source of southern sporting news which he garnered from his pedal wireless, QED Quamby Downs.

Buster Thorpe told stories about the Redex cars, their foolish speed through country towns, and about Dangerous Dan whom it was clear he'd never met. Dan had blown up a showground dunny with a man inside, or so he said.

Mrs. Carter worried that someone might be killed.

Young Gwynn chose that moment to introduce Mr. Redex to the visitors. Had he heard of Redex from his dad? I doubt it. Perhaps it was in response to some private storm, or the simple wish to see the visitors marvel that Quamby Downs should be home to a celebrity.

"He won," he cried, blushing so intensely you could see his red scalp shining through his hair.

I thought, by golly. Is it possible?

"Won what?" asked the massive Buster Thorpe.

"One?" cried Carter, rising, holding a large beer bottle high while he counted off the empty glasses as he filled them. "One, two," he said, "and three. And four for you, and none," he said to me, "none for you, you wowser."

Mrs. Carter showed me her sweet gums and nodded. So, the small-town Bobbseys were national champions. The Carters must have known for weeks.

"You mean car number 92?" I asked the boy. "Bobs Motors?"

"You won."

"Go wash your hands," Carter told his son. "Go on. Hurry up."

QED, I thought, God bless bright-faced Mrs. Bobbsey, in her overalls, with her singlet showing. She had kissed my neck all night.

# 13

"OH MRS. BOBS, where is your lovely husband?" So said the airline hostess as she led me to my seat.

"What a bag of tricks he is," they said, checking out my swollen eyes. "Mrs. Bobs, you must be proud."

"Of course the kiddies must miss their mum," they said. "What a shame you couldn't stay in Sydney for the fun."

"Can you trust him, Mrs. Bobs?" they said (nudge, wink) and I knew they had seen the photograph in that morning's *Telegraph*. Titch Bobs at Chequers club, his face between the breasts of the so-called exotic dancer. WINNER TAKE ALL. And I was there when it was taken, at the table, not even included in the photograph of the support team, Arthur Dunstan, formerly of General Motors, Mr. F. Green, a well known racing identity, and Mr. Joe Thacker who now gave his occupation as *motel proprietor of Ballarat*.

I had ridden on the roof of the Holden waving to the crowds on Parramatta Road but I ended up in the hotel room, on the telephone talking to my children, I should say daughter. Ronnie was locked in the laundry "playing with the cat."

I was proud to have given my husband what he wanted. He was happy. He was over the moon, there was no-one who could know it had been a nightmare, the general public banging on the car, taking our windscreen wipers, souvenir of the 1954 Redex Trial. It was not a race but there was a chequered flag and Titch climbed out the driver's window—what a circus—and joined me on the roof where he publicly performed his red scarf trick. I grinned until my face was aching.

WINNER HAD SOMETHING UP HIS SLEEVE.

You can see him in the photos, stamping on the roof beside his gormless wife.

I had bought a special dress from Gowings. It was *à la* Travilla, they said, bright red with a fitted bodice and straps around the neck and pushy-uppy bosom. There was a great knees-up at Chequers. You can say I was stupid to leave early. I said it was the kids, but I would not grin like a ninny while he was a dirty flirt. In the hotel room I cried and cried. Dunstan and Green delivered him back to our room at four in the morning, covered with lipstick and smelling like a bar-room floor.

And he was the one in a rage. Imagine. I had made a fool of him.

The airline hostess offered tea and biscuits but I turned my back, ashamed to be this wretched sniffling thing when I had been, so short a time before, a heroine, down there, with wheels on fire, driving through those snowy mountains with no brakes.

Nervous Nellie had never been in an aeroplane before. And now she was frightened of the bumpy plane, a Vickers Viscount, same as the one that crashed in Hobart on Christmas Day.

I should have stayed at the dinner until the end. I should have stayed sitting between Green and Dunstan and shoved my chest out, but I was too busy being betrayed.

We landed at Essendon Aerodrome, a dark paddock and two taxis sitting in the rain. The first driver was outraged that I would ask him to drive thirty miles to Bacchus Marsh. He'd never get a fare back. He'd miss his tea.

The second fellow was no better.

"Where?"

"Bacchus Marsh."

"Oh I don't know about that."

"It's not as if I'm going to have a baby in the back."

How cruel the world seemed. How pathetic I had let myself become, standing in the headlights. I crawled into the back seat and wept.

"Are you alright love?" he asked.

How could I explain or justify myself? I said my husband had died and then I howled as if he really had, howled and snotted and blew my nose all the way down to Rockbank, past Dan's garage. We came into the Marsh through the Avenue of Honour. I got out at Lerderderg Street, at the sale yards where I breathed the damp cold air of my real life. It smelled of mud and panicked cattle and I thought of dear decent Willie Bachhuber with his wheelbarrow and his shovel and I saw our lighted windows but I passed them, and ran my fingers along next door's rain-wet privet hedge. Willie was back home of course, he must be by now. I felt it in my bones. So gently, gently I lifted the latch on his rusting gate. Slowly, so as not to make a noise, I swung it open. I was smiling, a real smile. His wet unopened letters lay on the floor of his front verandah, white as bones.

I knocked cautiously at first, and then could not hide my feelings any more.

# 14

WRITTEN CONFIRMATION OF Bobs Motors' Redex victory reached me courtesy of Alice who retrieved the Melbourne papers from the Big House garbage and delivered them directly to my kitchen table where she smoothed out the crumpled pages and—with her intelligent face made sweet with mischief—went through the stories and the captions to learn each individual's connection to me.

I made her sugary tea and she touched the photographs and then my face. It would not be false to say we shared a kind of love. We were certainly joined by mutual feelings about Carter who was "plenty jealous" of me. But she would be growled if she stayed, so she sighed, and stood, and I walked her to my gate. There I waited until I heard the dogs heralding her arrival at the camp.

It was a sweaty night and I was alone again, watching the insects committing suicide against the kitchen lamp. I had picked up that awful *opera book,* when I heard a step on my front verandah.

A moment later three visitors filed into my house, Doctor Battery, Crowbar, skinny dusty-haired Tom Tailor in his waistcoat and tie. As they entered I saw each one held two flagons, emptied of fortified wine and filled with a clear reddish liquid which must be petrol.

Molotov, I thought.

I had some rattan chairs but Doctor Battery, as usual, was more comfortable on the floor and I followed his example. Then, for the first time, I was introduced by name to Tom Tailor, that same intense presence who had for so many nights caused the punka to stir the air above my pink-scalped head. Now he took my hand and I was surprised that the glaring man had such a gentle and unexpectedly adaptive grip.

Apart from his two explosive flagons the Punka Wallah had brought a small hessian bag which, as he began whispering and making signs to Doctor Battery, he gently laid aside. As blacks were forbidden to visit the quarters of the whites, this deputation clearly had a serious purpose, one that kept the men huddled in a conference wherein there was much coughing and clearing of throats.

Doctor Battery, being most senior, began speaking for the most part in schoolroom English. He said that although they had given me the car they were all agreed it was not for me to pinch it.

Further, he said, I was obliged to remain in my country where I belonged.

No you don't, I thought.

Crowbar was perhaps less confrontational. He said that I could now be taught certain secret Law.

Tom the Punka Wallah said nothing. I assumed he had no English. As for me, I had a few pidgin phrases, words for earth, fire, good, bad, food, sit down, come here. I nodded to him but he remained aloof, and I finally saw this was the start of a negotiation: they would offer something and take something away, the latter being the car my future life depended on.

I showed them that I knew the value of what they were offering to give. I said I was honoured that they planned to instruct me. The three of us, I said, were joined by lines of blood, but I "bin growed up" without instruction in the Law. "Them Welfare fellahs" had made me a proper whitefellah. My position was such that I was "too bugger up" to receive instruction in the Law (i.e. their part of the bargain was no use).

Crowbar then spoke to the Punka Wallah, and I saw, by the repetition of certain words, he was translating my speech. I was alarmed to see the fierce little fellow laugh, and then speak rapidly, looking directly at me. I suspect that this had been very tough talk before it was reissued from Crowbar's lips. In translation he said that when the Punka Wallah was a boy he did Law business and the world would last for ever. Now the world would die. He was sorry I now had to hear what he must tell me.

Long time ago, Welfare had arrived in a utility truck with a cage on the back, like you might use for stock. The Punka Wallah had been maybe five years old. His mother told him run, run, run. He ran to his father who threw dust at him, and told him, go, go, go, piss off. He headed into the spinifex but the Welfare caught him and threw him in that cage. They took him to an orphanage in Derby. All the way he hollered. Where was his mother? Where was his father? At the orphanage they sprayed poison on him and stole his clothes. He lived in that place a long time without his people. Then the orphanage closed down and the Welfare took him to foster parents. The foster mother took them to a big room with a bed. He never saw anything like it in all his life. Even the Welfare seemed surprised. It was for a king. Then the Welfare left and the foster mother said come with me, and she took him to a little caravan in the backyard full of weeds she used to grow leprosy, he thought, maybe syphilis and other bad things.

That night a man came to the caravan. There are records of what he did to the little fellah, Crowbar said, looking at the floor. Night after night. It is written down in the judge's books, kept in Sydney or Big London or someplace. Those books never did anyone no good. Did I understand? He had been used and raped, night after night until they shifted him to another orphanage. He was already finished then. When he fought them, he was whipped. When he ran away, he was starved. When he left school he was a drunk in Derby and then he was a drunk in Mardowarra. He was in jail and out of jail until he finally found his mother but he had lost her language and all he had was mongrel talk.

I had to stay at Quamby Downs, he wanted me to know. I was not too old for Law the translator said. The old Law was forgotten by the young fellahs. He was the boss of a new Law. He would teach me that, but he would need the car.

You scoundrel, I thought. I was a reader of *Oceania*. I had read Ted Strehlow and therefore understood new Law was impossible.

Away he goes.

*The thoroughness of their [Aboriginal] forefathers has left to them not a single unoccupied scene which they could fill with creatures of their own imagination. Tradition and the tyranny of the old men in the religious and cultural sphere have effectively stifled all creative impulse; and no external stimulus ever reached Central Australia which could have freed the natives from these insidious bonds. It is almost certain that native myths had ceased to be invented many centuries ago . . . They are, in many ways, not so much a primitive as a decadent race.*

"There is no new Law," said the King of Quiz Shows.

"He say we're all bugger-up," Crowbar said. "He show you now."

The Punka Wallah removed his tie and waistcoat and revealed damage that made my own shoulder injury look like a mosquito bite. His glistening back bore the marks of a greenhide whip, criss-crossed, raised, woven into his skin. I was appalled, of course, and grateful when he covered himself.

"You teach them kids," he said, quietly, as he slipped his shirt back on. "I teach you new Law. You be learning from the boss."

"He no cut your cock," Doctor Battery reassured me. "His Law don't cut. He paint 'im on you, no blood."

"It is book Law Billy," grinned Crowbar. "You can read it Uncle Redex. New Law."

I was shocked by the evidence of torture, but it did not weaken my desire to keep my car. They wished to steal it from me. Their claim to having new Law must be made up to serve this end.

I asked them where this new Law came from. If it was a book it must be the Christian Bible.

"Out of ground," said Tom Tailor.

"Who give you?"

"Calsh."

Later I would learn the name Kalch was that of the esteemed anthropologist Arthur Christian Kalch. Bringing in the academics was more than I had bargained for but I would not be bullied about the car which was, obviously, mine by right. Besides, I was not such a fool as to involve myself in any secret knowledge, the possession of which might easily place my life in danger.

Crowbar uncorked a flagon of petrol. "Smell," he said.

"You help us Bill," said Battery, his expression becoming rather soft and thoughtful. "We help you. This is best for you."

"We show you country Billy. We still go hunting."

I pointed out that they would need far more petrol than these flagons.

"You give money," Crowbar said sweetly. "We find you plenty petrol."

Whatever bargain I had made appeared to be a slippery one. I gave them eighteen pounds which was all I had. Then, when we had all shaken hands I turned off the lamps so the conspirators could leave in darkness. I sat out on the verandah listening to a normal night at Quamby Downs, the discord of the camp, the insistent drone of Carter's pedal radio. Dogs barked. An owl cried. I made out another black figure at my gate.

It was Alice who had returned to tell me that Tom Tailor was a very bad man. Bad man for everyone. Christian, old fellahs. His Law no good. He crazy.

Then she kneeled and I saw that I was to kneel with her. Our Father, she said, who art in heaven.

Alone again, I set up the kerosene lamp and it was then that I discovered, abandoned on the floor, the sugar bag the Punka Wallah had brought with him. Having seen how careful he was with it, I knew this was not due to absentmindedness. He intended me to see the contents: a substantial bark wallet, decorated with white patterning and tied with what was certainly human hair. Inside the wallet I found a book, not a Christian bible but something thinner, puffed, bleeding, water-damaged which I finally understood, beneath its artful ink and ochre decoration, to be *Oceania* No. 43 Oct. 1952. Here, by means of frequent ochre markings, my attention was quickly drawn to "Nativist Movements in the Western Kimberley" by Arthur Christian Kalch, a learned paper frequently naming a certain "Tom the Tailor." I was, to say the least, intrigued.

# 15

WHILE ANTHROPOLOGISTS MIGHT frown on the practice, or deny the very possibility, I cannot believe this is the first and only time the subject of an anthropological study saw the final published paper or that the recipient of *Oceania* No. 43, like anyone living a quotidian life, was not affected by the sight of his name in print.

"Tom the Tailor" was certainly Tom Tailor or the Punka Wallah. The thrust of the paper confirmed that he certainly had a "new Law" and this was occasion, in the writer's view, for considerable amazement i.e. final proof that Aboriginal Australians were no different from other peoples who had suffered from colonial oppression. "Few societies under foreign domination accept that position in silence. Objections are indicated in a collectively anti-colonial mood, and in more specific movements of emancipation."

The article in *Oceania* showed how certain survivors in the West Kimberley had raided the Christian Bible, taken possession of Noah's Ark and turned it into an instrument of resistance against the white oppressors. I don't know if it might be called a cult, a Law, or a religion, but it was certainly in a "book."

It was ancestral beings, I learned in *Oceania,* who had appeared to Tom the Tailor and given him this ark. It was on no whitefellah map, but was said to be somewhere near the old trade routes beyond Mardowarra. In its hold were gold and jewels and crystals. The former mission tailor had declared himself the boss of the Law of the Ark which said a mighty rain would come to flood his country, that it would be a rain of Holy Water which would make the skins of blackfellahs turn white. The blackfellahs would be ready for the deluge and they would climb aboard the ark and all the kartiya would drown. This ark was not a made up story. It was attested to by sacred boards. It was a real ark in a real place and it was a secret, so dangerous that if you saw it accidentally you must be killed.

As he was not a popular figure in the camp, I doubted the Punka Wallah had many followers. Just the same he possessed a certain malevolent power and I was not pleased to find myself the object of his will.

Doctor Battery had a bad eye but the other one was good, and he was respected for his marksmanship, always returning to the camp with tucker for those whose totem forbade them to eat kangaroo. All he needed was a car to take him shooting in the bush. He could drive himself, as he often said, which was why I kept the distributor rotor in my pocket, so my precious getaway was safe in my control.

Crowbar also hunted but, more importantly, he was a father of four girls and thus had his own uses for my car. The other teacher—my poor predecessor—had driven girls and boys to the Fifteen Mile where there was a reliable swimming hole, even in the dry. As the weather had become unbearably hot, I had followed his Volkswagen tracks to water, and you would never guess how many pupils I fitted into that Peugeot, fifteen inside and more on the roof rack. During those happy days I would be quite astonished to see what my life had become—faster, faster, Uncle Redex—those bare feet hanging over the windscreen and over the side.

As long as I lived at Quamby Downs, there was no escape from this responsibility. Carter eked out petrol for us and sometimes it was a gift, and sometimes he charged me on my store account, but it was never more than four of five gallons, not enough for me to do a bunk. As a result we were forever running out, and filth was then sucked from the tank into the carburettor miles from home and the next week's work would all centre on getting the vehicle back to life, transporting Doctor Battery and petrol and a plastic basin in which to wash the parts. I was only one of many servants to the cause.

I had never had so satisfying a class in all my life, which does not mean that I stopped preparing for my escape, collecting my own bottles and flagons of petrol, stashing them behind a stack of timber offcuts in the storeroom where Alice, on some professional mission of her own, discovered them.

She took my hand and led me to my stash and, for once, I could not make her smile no matter how I clowned for her. She worried what might be done to me as punishment for being complicitous in Tom Tailor's bad business.

As for that particular business, I am still not at liberty to disclose any more than what is publicly known but I did discover, in my own classroom, more evidence of the resistance that white anthropologists had hitherto denied. This came from my shyest pupil, Charley Hobbes.

Charley was small and sleek and delicate with large dark eyes and, while generally displaying the most anxious disposition, had it in his power to lift your heart with his lovely smile. He chose to sit furthest from the front, closest to the outside, the hottest part of the room but the one from which he might effect a fast escape and where he had sat on a particular morning, with Oliver Emu close on one side and Susie Shuttle on the other.

Charley had come to the station with his father who had been employed on the company's other property. The story he brought into our classroom was like a leaf that had blown hundreds of miles from its source at Victoria Downs where Charley's family were descendants of survivors of a massacre. He was one of those of whom Carter said "he gives no trouble."

His voice was quiet as moth wings and I could not hear a single word he said. It was calm barrel chested Susie Shuttle whose ear he spoke into and Susie Shuttle who repeated every word in a good strong voice, doing him the honour I never heard her grant another child. I mean, she did not correct his English, or attempt to make his "Captain Cook" comply with the historical record which would have kept the Englishman skulking around the coast. She enlivened Charley's injured whisper with sarcasm and indignation and many other registers which never survived the class transcription but are horribly easy to imagine as you read.

Captain Cook came out from Big England. He got to Sydney. He git all the books from London, Big England. Bring a lot of men, a lot of horse, rifle, bullock. "Ah, this nice country. You got fish here?" Yes, we got plenty fish kangaroo everything. Captain Cook look around. "Very pretty country. Any more people around here?"

"Oh yes, there's a mob in the bush, looking for a bit of fish and tucker. A lot of food old people get easy."

Captain Cook got a big ship. He got a jetty. He roll down guns and he been shooting there for maybe three weeks. Shooting all the people. Women get shot shot [sic], kids get knocked out. Then he packs up his gear and gets back in his boat go up around Australia. Goes in this pocket there. Big mob of Aboriginal people by this bay.

"This we country. We never look at whitefellah come through here. We can be ready for you. Git a big mob spear."

Captain Cook put the bullet in his magazine, start to shooting people, same like Sydney. "Really beautiful country," Captain Cook reckoned. "That's why I'm cleaning up people, take it away."

Captain Cook follow the sea right around. "I'd like to put my building there. I like to put my horses there."

Captain Cook been sendem over shooting lotta people. Horses been galloping all over Australia, hunting all these people. Still, people been running away, still. Can't catch up. Horse can't gallop in over rough place or them caves.

That's right. We been ready for whitefellahs alright. Our people been really, really cranky. They don't want white people here. Hit em with a spear, kill em.

They been fight whitefellah. They been have a spear and whitefellah been have a rifle. If whitefellow been come up got no bit of a gun, couldn't been roundem up, killing all the people. They never been give him fair go.

Captain Cook reckons, "This no more blackfellah country. Belong to me fellow," he said. "I'm going to put my place. Anywhere I can put him." Him been bring lotta book from Big England right here now. They got that book for Captain Cook from England. And that's his Law. Book belong to Captain Cook, that means all belong to Captain Cook.

The old people really frighten for the white people coming from Big England. And they been really, really sad, poor buggers. Anybody sick, anybody sick in the guts or in the head, Captain Cook orders: "Don't give him medicine. Don't give him medicine. When they getting crook old people, you killem him first. When they on the job, that's right, you can have them on the job. But don't payem him. Let him work for free. Any children come round, you can have the stockman killem. We'll still hold that people, and don't letem go. Any man come sick, boy, anything like that, blind man, don't give him medicine. You take him in a dry gully and knock him."

Susie Shuttle touched Charley's little hand and whispered in his ear.

"And after that," she said (and Doctor Battery's grandson wrote), "women, women got a bit of baby, don't let him grow that baby. Just kill that baby."

Charley was shaking now, anyone could see that the carcass of his history was just too big for his skinny body and he began to weep and Susie Shuttle and Oliver Emu wept with him and my entire class became very silent and I was frightened of what I had done, but also emotional, and angry, and I promised them that I would do all I could do, that I would begin now and not stop, no matter how long it took, until I had completely inscribed the entire saga on the wall.

I was not thinking about Cricket Carter or the Western Australian education department. I was not thinking of anything but my own rage and so, blinded by self-righteousness, I had completely forgotten that I had inscribed CAPTAIN COOK 1770 and that it now lay hidden, like a landmine, beneath the kalsomine.

# 16

SEBASTIAN LASKI

*Appraiser rare books, maps, early manuscripts. 26 Glenhaven Court, Box Hill, Victoria. Tel: BW-9628*

Dear Willy-willy, *Oceania* daubed with blood and ochre?
Well blow me down. What would our favourite Collection
Manager do to get his gloved hands on that "votive object"?
I assume it is now beyond his reach (and your reach too,
which is probably just as well). You have shown an amazing
talent for finding trouble. I write "trouble" thinking not of
Adelina or your son—although they can never be absent
from my mind—but of our recent visit to your rentier in
Bacchus Marsh who we found in a state of great anxiety about
your arrears. He had already advertised your house, "vacant
possession," and was beside himself with relief when Dorotea
and I arrived to remove your library. He seemed a decent
enough chap (for a rentier) but he did find it necessary to twice
remind me that we would be paid nothing for our work. At
the same time he stressed that he lacked the legal authority to
grant me possession of your goods and chattels. He resolved
this by cleverly deciding that we had come as prospective
tenants and that he would leave the keys on his desk for us
to make our own inspection. Having said that, he typed up a
PERMISSION TO INSPECT and signed it and we drove up
the hill to Lerderderg Street presumably intent on larceny.

He had given us due warning of the condition of your
kitchen which seemed to me (if not Dorotea) what one would

expect of a desperado in your circumstances. In any case, we were bibliophiles not kitchen maids and it was your library we had come for after all.

To this end we had brought with us he who was to inherit it from you, young Neil. Dorotea had thought this a psychologically ill-conceived idea but Adelina had already told the little fellow what we were to do, and then he could talk of nothing else but you, his father, and where you had lived and all the books that would be now his to read or sell as he thought fit. I thought this normal, Dorotea peculiar.

He is only six but, having spent many Saturdays at his mother's table at the South Melbourne Market, is no slouch in the selling department. Your wife, as I am sure you have reason to know, has a rare eye and that cluttered table has always yielded treasure each time we have visited. We never bought from pity (as she clearly thought we did) but from amazement that such art nouveau might be found so far from Europe. In any case, there is little doubt that your books will soon find their way to that table and there serve a useful purpose.

It was the thought of his inheritance that had the little fellow so bright and jumpy in the rentier's dank office and that gentleman, for his part, could not take his eyes off the black child, the very first he'd seen, so he told me *sotto voce*.

Dorotea was irate but very quiet through all of this, standing close beside Neil with her hand on his level little shoulder, clearly imagining some great racist damage would be done to him, but it was not so at all. Once we were inside your residence it was as sweet as Christmas morning. What fun to hear his smart questions, about the bindings, for instance.

How, I wondered, can a boy love his father via the medium of a dusty book? Well, he can and does. He was also strangely curious about the value of his inheritance and I soon had to declare a ban on all estimates until the books were back in St. Kilda.

Dorotea, of course, continually prevented me from exerting myself, as if a box of books would cause a second stroke. That was patent nonsense, although I must admit to being a less effective machine than previously.

We were in the middle of our work when I had a new reason to reflect on your talent for finding trouble, for we were set upon by a pert little creature, by no means unattractive even if she was dressed for a square dance. This was Missus from next door, demanding to know who we thought we were.

When we declared ourselves your servants she as good as called us liars and demanded proof, which we obviously could not supply.

You were returning home to Bacchus Marsh, she said, as fervent as a Christian.

I said our information was quite otherwise and it then became embarrassingly clear from her tremor that you had formed some intimate alliance with her. Dorotea kicked my ankle and what could I do but insist on the veracity of my statement. Your neighbour left in distress and there was nothing for it but to fill the little van with books. I stood guard in the street waiting to explain myself to the police.

Instead the next door Missus returned, red eyed and contrite, carrying a pot of tea and cups and milk and biscuits on a tray which she set down on the front verandah. It was then Neil saw her and it seemed he had met her in Melbourne and she was a Redex driver and you, good grief, had been a navigator.

As far as we had known you could not even drive, so we were gobsmacked by this new persona. And then further surprised that the pert Missus was previously familiar with Neil and Adelina and the noble Madison. Seeing all of these connections I thought there could be no harm in giving her what she craved: your address in Quamby Downs.

Now my ankles are bruised blue and I am informed by my

wife that I am a grand old fool but I hardly think it likely your admirer will come knocking on your door.

Dorotea, who is very concerned for you, sends you a frowning sort of love. I have rescued a few *Oceania*s from your very sneezy house and, seeing you are caught in a new craze, will send them to you, together with some of A.B. Paterson's doggerel which will say better than I can that we miss you very much.

*I had written him a letter which I had, for want of better*
*Knowledge, sent to where I met him down the Lachlan,*
   *years ago,*
*He was shearing when I knew him, so I sent the letter to him,*
*Just "on spec," addressed as follows, "Clancy, of The Overflow."*

*And an answer came directed in a writing unexpected,*
*(And I think the same was written in a thumb-nail dipped in tar)*
*"Twas his shearing mate who wrote it, and verbatim I will*
   *quote it:*
*"Clancy's gone to Queensland droving, and we don't know where*
   *he are."*

Sebastian

# 17

IN BACCHUS MARSH, the nights turned hot. The fire brigade became busy. It being almost Christmas, pine saplings were tied to verandah posts of the Courthouse Hotel. The Courthouse introduced a bargain counter lunch (T-bone for five shillings) and I was happy being spared the job of cooking for Titch and his "associates." It was in this pub, supposedly, that Titch hatched the plan for buying Federal Tyre Discount.

This deal stank of Thacker, Green and Dunstan, and all those blowflies who had descended on our life. Left to himself Titch would be content to be a dealer with a franchise.

The syndicate had made big money on their bet, although the actual amount of the winnings went up and down according to the beer or the moon or the tides at Ocean Grove. Izzie Green patted my hand and said I was a nervous little mouse.

After that I shut my trap and did my best to make sure the Bacchus Marsh business survived all this fame and fortune. Many afternoons there was no-one but me on the showroom floor. Of course the customers did not expect to find a woman. Sometimes they could not see me. They asked to see a salesman and I said that was me and often they were deaf. This proved difficult for all concerned but I had a nice smile and I began wearing skirts and if I could get a cup of tea into their hand they would have time to learn I knew my onions. I never contradicted or argued. I never said it was me, Mrs. Bobs, who had been the co-winner of the Redex Trial. Nine times out of ten I would take the vehicle around to the prospect's house "after tea so your missus can try it on for size." Sometimes the house was on a potato farm at Bullengarook and then I took the kids as well. I was no Titch, but I was no slouch. My husband was generous enough to say so and I liked the praise. I also liked how busy I became, for the new demands of life took my mind off certain disappointments. I was almost thirty, and of course the honeymoon was over. Alas, the more capable I became, the more my husband felt free to be away.

I never thought life would be a fairytale. The trussed-up pine saplings wilted and lost their needles. The syndicate formed a Pty Ltd Company to buy the chain of tyre stores with five outlets in the Melbourne suburbs. Mr. Green explained that the mortgage was "self financing," whatever that meant. He had just made a fortune when Rising Fast failed to win at Flemington, but I was not convinced. I was waiting for a crash that didn't seem to come.

But finally, what the hell.

I let Titch hire an "office manager" who had been a teller at the National Bank. One week later he decided the new man was useless but he still felt free to leave him in the office and go speedboat racing on Port Phillip Bay. Allegedly this was "business related" being filled with Redex contenders like Jack Murray and Jack Davey.

Why should I complain?

Bobs Tyres had thirty-second spots on 3UZ, the same station as *Deasy's Radio Quiz Show*. "Titch Bobs has something up his sleeve" and there is nothing like a catchy slogan to make you popular at a barbecue it seems. He practised magic tricks at night and it wasn't as if he actually looked like his father, but these performances made him excited and he got a sort of glint in his eyes and showed a clean straight line of teeth.

I was on the showroom floor one Saturday morning, in no rush to take the order I would clearly get, when Edith telephoned with what she called "a mergency."

"Can't it wait?"

"Up to you," she said. "They're carrying stuff out to a van."

The prospect was annoyed and, as I later learned, went straight up to Ballarat and bought a Ford with cash. But I was home in a minute, finding Ronnie in the driveway in his sister's place. How brave he was, coming with me to confront the burglary. And what a wild and woolly lot the burglars were, a pair of Balts quite obviously. The man's face cut with ugly scars, his body twisted to one side. His wife was small and fierce as a fighting fish.

"This is private property," I said, and much else I can't recall but naturally I was agitated, and the more I heard their cock 'n bull, the more upset I was and it was my lovely dear Ronnie who dragged me off the front verandah and back inside where Edith was too busy with her telephone to make tea for the Balts.

"It's Janice," she hissed, meaning Janice Cox, the new best friend.

Back on the verandah the black child had unexpectedly appeared. What did I say to that?

"I am Neil," he said, and held out his hand as he had done previously. "Do you remember me?"

"Yes."

The Balts said they had come for his father's books. I made conversation as if I were a normal woman. I poured them tea and was embarrassed to see my milk curdling. They pretended not to notice but they did. Ronnie asked Neil had he ever seen a two-tone Cadillac and Neil said no, and so they went away, and returned with the glossy American catalogue originally supplied by Dunstan.

As Ronnie had a rough and rowdy side to him and as he had never seen a black boy in his life I was pleased to see how attentive he was to his guest.

That was when I must have thought it. I mean, feeling kindness ease my pain, seeing them on the dusty hallway floor, backs against the wall, caressing those glossy Cadillacs: the notion that we could have Neil to stay for a weekend.

I certainly did not rush into it as Titch later said. I certainly did not ask the Balts' opinion but anyone could see those boys were born to be each other's friend. I was not conniving or meddlesome. The opposite. I tested Ronnie's feelings first, then Edith's. At that stage she was perfectly amenable. The complaints began after the first weekend.

She then said I was embarassing. "The way you grin and fawn on him. Can you quit it, Mum?"

Who had heard of such a thing? A girl being jealous of a boy, but she resented any kindness I showed, big or small. She was outraged that I dared pat his little head, and that I drove all the way to Melbourne to pick him up and then drove him home afterwards. "Your pet monkey," she said, and I slapped her and she would not talk to me for days, and it was not until her father came home that she rejoined the human race, sitting in his lap and tickling him. She was lucky to have a father at all, I told her. This also was a cause of great offence, but I must say I did look forward to those weekends when Adelina lent us Neil Bachhuber, as I thought of him. It was a relief for her, of course, with her husband not really being her husband, and she working six days a week and selling bric-a-brac on Sundays.

I never, honestly, thought about the boy's skin colour. Of course it was a shock the first time I met him, but I was more disturbed by his stand-in father who was black and sissy, and smelling pretty, with hands so very soft and dry.

In the autumn I was quite often in Melbourne with the two boys and then I could not help but feel the world's opinion, in the back of a taxi, say, with the driver's eyes on me, thinking his dirty thoughts, imagining what I had been up to. How many times was I asked where I came from, what age the boys were, and where they went to school?

Ronnie was boisterous and bouncy and Neil was careful and exact but they were continually amused by each other. What a shame it was that Willie never had a chance to see them looking through his gold-stamped foreign language books. None of this was in my mind when I took that photograph. It was not a very good one anyway, like a million photographs taken with Box Brownies, two boys in swimming togs, a grey paling fence behind them, their arms around each other's shoulders, squinting in the sun. Yes one was black and one was white but no-one remarked on it when I picked up the Kodak envelope from the chemist shop. Of course, it is well known, they look through everything when the pictures are delivered. In any case, what bad thing could they think? I had been "up to something." But what? What possibly?

I placed the photograph in an envelope and addressed it to Neil's father. He had a right. I was claiming nothing from him. I was not related to the son. Please tell me what is so strange about offering solace to a lonely man?

# 18

I HAD WAITED for it, the wet season, through every blistering morning and the heated rocks of afternoon, and still I was not prepared, not for its density, immensity, the roar upon the roof, the obliteration of all distance, the air sucked from my lungs, as if it meant to kill me. This rain was the temperature of blood. It polished the tree trunks until they shone. A billabong appeared from nowhere, right by the camp. It brought the trombone cries of frogs, splashing, laughter. My cross-cultural scholars ducked and dived and brushed their teeth with broken twigs and arrived clean and shining at their desks. The Crossing Bridge was said to be in danger. The landscape out my bedroom window was a necklace of islands in swirling cack-coloured water. I thought of Tom Tailor and his ark.

It was at this unlikely time that families began to leave the camp to go about their ceremonies and other Law business in their countries. Oliver Emu did not have to go anywhere. This was his country and he would soon face his initiation and I saw his silent apprehension and excitement as the days passed. Then, suddenly, his desk was empty, and I heard he had run away to the missionaries who took him in to protect him from these "barbaric practices." Just like one of those girls, said his grandfather, they did the same to escape their old man husbands. All bugger-up, Doctor Battery said mournfully. The boy would get a hiding when he found him.

It was dry in the classroom but sometimes, in my dreams, I heard the water working inside the limestone walls. It had been water, of course, that made my schoolroom cave, not by erosion but the action of carbonic acid, water combining with carbon dioxide. *Off he goes.* I thought, all this slow evacuating was not simply finished because Captain Cook had come. Caves were being created still. The Kimberley was riddled with them. In one of these, I thought, the Punka Wallah had his secret ark and all its treasure. It was from caves like mine that the great Clever Man (AKA Pigeon or Jandamarra, or the black Ned Kelly) had conducted his lethal raids upon the Kimberley police.

Jandamarra had known "finger talk" by which language he spoke silently to his followers while they stalked the white police. I also had learned "finger talk" and "stick talk" and I encouraged my kids to make stick talk paintings while water rose in the billabong and creeks rushed down what had once been dry and rocky gullies. The pupils, boys and girls, could all imitate the tracks of animals and reptiles and I had them dip their fingertips in ink and print with them, always removing the paper before they mucked it up. When each child had a "best" painting I transferred it to the limestone personally.

"Like a public toilet," said Carter, when he saw these paintings on the classroom walls, the gorgeous blue and white like a willow pattern, the Saga of Captain Cook which I had transcribed, line by line, a pillar from the earth to heaven, also the maps of ancestral chases stretching horizontal across the clean white space that had once shown the bull-dozed lines of the whitefellah highway. "I can't wait to see old Gavin's face," said the manager. "He'll shit his pants."

He was as vile as usual, but there was something else illuminating the golden beaky countenance, a naughty boy's delight in mischief. He still judged me weak as water, a boong-lover, a half-caste if not quite a poofter, but he was impressed that I had not yet gone mad or spat the dummy. So he watched me, waiting, like I was a good story that had not reached its climax. He could not believe I had held his interest for so long.

Of course I would be gone by the time Gavin finally returned, but I too would have liked to see the inspector's compromised and weather-worn expression when he finally understood that a human place of education might be sweeter than a church. The dusty cave school had disappeared and in its place was—what? Like what? An ancient cha-pel made by Bosnian Christians hiding from the Turks?

As the rain continued Doctor Battery remained my instructor. It was, as he never ceased to tell me, not too late for me to be a proper blackfellah. I was his son and he would take me to see secret boards when our mob had granted their approval and in the meantime we squatted amongst the empty bottles in his humpy and he taught me, for instance, that the flying foxes are the Dreaming companions of the rainbow snakes. "When the snakes smell that flying fox he know it time. He is a young fellow, that old snake. He frisky Billy. He plenty busy now, sticking his head up out of the water."

Inside the humpy there was no escaping the stink of Autumn Brown Sherry and musky flying fox, and I could see the Rainbow Serpent in my mind's eye, his mouth sprung open, shooting out lightning and saliva.

"Tadpoles swimming in his spit," said Doctor Battery, communicating ancient Law or teasing me or both at once.

The spit was rain, he said. Now the lightning people were wake up proper. "See, Uncle Redex. The lightning women flash their lightning more and more. Lookem now. Steam up into clouds. Grubs and frogs them bosses of the rain. They sing to the rainbow more, more. Down it comes, the rain. The waters dark and muddy," he said and I was a silly bugger he added, and I better keep away from those whirlpools in case I got dragged in and drowned. It was mournful down in the camp with so many gone.

Carter came to my residence to stack the fridge with his extra beer. I asked him, very casually (as this was the best style with him), why the people had holidays at this time of year when it was hard for them to travel around the floods to their distant countries. Surely the wet season was a better time for the kids to be inside at school. Dry season would be a better holiday.

"Don't be a nong," he said. "We don't run this business for their convenience."

I was a nong, I thought. This was all for the bloody pastoral companies. Now there was so little station work they could have their precious holidays. This must have been a small saving for the station who had suffered the expense of feeding the people tea, sugar, beef, and weevil flour. But when the wet arrived my blood relations returned their station clothes to Annie in the store. She wrote each man and woman a chit and saved it in a Brockhoff biscuit tin so they could claim them on return. If the eagle had not taken me, this might have been my life, I thought, frightened of the naked truth of their revealed anatomies, tall, thin and fat, young fruit, male and female, wrinkled, with shocking unarguable facts and characters as distinct as the human face.

As the majority of camp residents departed the stockmen returned. Takman, as they say. The last to arrive had been three hundred miles from camp when the deluge began, and they had a slow wet ride back through rain, their shirts and pants soaked, the horses floundering in the bogs. Days were added to their journey by their diversions around the heads of newly flooded creeks. Their salt beef went sour. At day's end they squatted round their hissing campfire, holding their hats over the frying pan to keep their damper dry.

Mrs. Carter and the kids were far away down south on the dry hot plains of Corangamite where they would not see a black face from one year to the next. So when Carter invited the white stockmen for a Christmas booze-up my fridge would soon be emptied and there would be no moderating influence from the missus.

I had no choice but to attend, knowing pretty much how things would go. I would arrive early, when everyone was sober. At this stage, I would be thought acceptable, sometimes interesting, even admirable, but my job was regarded as a waste of time and it would not take long before someone felt compelled to tell me, no offence. It would be noted that I did not drink. It would be necessary for me to point out I was not a temperance wowser. "Did you never even taste it?" they would want to know.

It would be unfair for me to generalise about the races on Quamby Downs but there would always be, in any gathering of white men at this station, a certain number with pathological or psychotic tendencies, and it was these, it seemed, who set the tone. Perhaps this would have been different had I the spine to oppose them openly. It is perhaps a weak excuse to say that I could always rely on Carter to expose my secret thoughts which he did most effectively at the Christmas booze-up by taking an inspection party out to the caves. Thus, I suppose, he forced me to speak up. I should have been pleased by the shock caused by the writing on the wall, but I was unprepared for their crude hostility to the Saga of Captain Cook.

My exit was accompanied by a silence so threatening that when I returned to the residence, I locked the door.

Soon there would be a call for the beer in my fridge and I would have no choice but to unlock. Therefore I remained at the kitchen table, and tried to read the silly opera book. When there was gunfire from the Big House verandah I did not take it personally, but when a rock landed on my parked car, I jumped. Then there came a mighty bang above my head. A brick, I thought, but it could have been anything. Then came a knocking on my door, so faint and scratchy that all the hair stood on my arms. I extinguished my bright kerosene lamp and picked up my torch. The bolt would not come quietly so I slammed it open and flung wide the door which banged against the wall. It was Susie Shuttle in my torch beam. In her clean school clothes in the middle of the night. I thought, she has been into the school, she has dressed in her best clothes. How hooded was her brow.

"They need a doctor," she said.

My torch found a young couple with a baby whose left eye was closed and oozing pus. One side of its face was hot and swollen with infection.

Susie did not know that I had already used my stash of petrol taking her family hunting. She had no idea I was scared to venture out in this weather and I feared being washed away and drowned.

"This baby is going to die," she announced.

I introduced my silent visitors to my table where I had to order them to sit. Having directed Susie to make them tea, I carried an empty petrol flagon through the puddles, knowing, of course, that a flagon of petrol would get us nowhere but hoping that, in the midst of all the happy celebration, it would make the purpose of my mission clear.

Things were said about me. No need to repeat what they were. I waited while Carter defeated a young jackaroo in a knuckles contest which had already made the young fellow's hand a bruised and nasty blue.

"You're an idiot," he told me when he had his victory, but he gave me the key to the padlock that secured the petrol pump.

I then acted as if I would really drive to the distant hospital. I bundled the parents and their baby in the back and Susie in the front and I removed the sheet of corrugated iron which had substituted for the missing windscreen. As water poured onto my knees, as the engine fired, the rain began again and I did not think of anything but navigating to the station workshop.

I had spent many hours there with old Battery and of course he had found it very useful for me to learn the ways of the workshop generator. So now I brought the monster into roaring life, providing power for lights and then the petrol pump. I thought, Mrs. Bobbsey would be amazed by my competence. I applied the key to the lock. It did not fit. I thought, I am saved. I don't have to drown myself. But then I heard the baby's broken breath and became the servant of a different fear, that I would kill it with ineptitude.

Susie Shuttle was right beside me as we entered the Big House and it was she who led the charge to Carter, who paused with his beer bottle still inches from his pouting lips.

"What are you doing here?" he asked, and I was surprised that it was Susie he addressed.

"You gave us the wrong key, boss."

"Maybe the problem is the hole," said Carter, speaking in a manner that I attributed to drink.

"We need the correct key," I said.

Carter rubbed himself obscenely. "My point of view exactly."

There had been a great deal of hooting and barracking until then but now there was a silence. I expected to get beaten and was, in the midst of everything, surprised I did not care.

"Quit it," Susie said. "We need the bloody key. The baby is going to die."

Carter made a grab for her knee, but she stepped back.

"Barry," she said.

"What?"

"Where's your missus, Barry?"

It was impossible she would speak to him like this, not just raise her voice, but use this familiar first name which I had never heard before. She was my sturdy clever pupil, just sixteen years old, but her eyes were on fire and she was not afraid and I understood that Carter, somehow, was going to listen to her.

"You're a little bit pissed," she said gently, "but you can save a baby. Barry, please."

"Suit yourself," he said. What an odd choice of words, I thought, from a station boss to a camp girl. He dug into his pocket and then stumbled across the room to that mess he called his office. Here he fiddled with a filing cabinet, from which he finally extracted a single key ring which he dangled before my surprising pupil.

"But don't you make assumptions, girlie."

"Thank you," she said.

"You understand what I am saying?"

"Yes."

"You've got a real future, Susie," he said, and flung the key out into the night.

# 19

IN THE MOONLESS DARK, between the sick baby and the tiny hospital, lay the engorged Mardowarra River with its brown skirts frothing against the upstream edge of the old Two Mile bridge. Of course the baby's parents must risk this crossing. So must I. But there was no reason for a schoolgirl to venture out onto a structure that might be swept away at any moment. I told her to get out, I would pick her up on my return.

The Peugeot smelled of damp and mould and rotting rags. I took a breath, and engaged low gear. If my headlights and my eyes were full of rain I could still make out the luminous figure of that wilful girl walking backwards on the bridge, gesturing that she would guide me. The bridge, being always temporary, had no parapet but of course my sturdy student had lived through many wet seasons and must be familiar with situations just like this. I told myself, Willie, there is only an inch or two of water. Do not be a Southern Wonder.

Of the baby whose life we were intent on saving I honestly have no memory, only of the ghost girl in my headlights and my fear she would be swept away.

The current was strong. The water surged upwards on her shins. A floating log slammed against the rear and the back wheel shifted. The mother was behind me, speaking rapidly in her tongue. I clamped myself around the steering wheel and dared not shift my eyes until, at last, the front tyres were churning, and the object of my attention was scrambling up the track ahead.

I have only the vaguest recollection of the dark hospital and then the ferocious camp dogs who attacked me as I tried to find a nurse. I suppose I was drunk on adrenalin. I remember no particular satisfaction when the child was in safe hands. As far as I knew we did not have to risk the bridge again. I could have stayed there for a week (more likely two) until the flood subsided, and when I was back looking out across the flooded bridge again, this really seemed the wisest thing to do. But my passenger had her own private motivations.

"Hang on, boss," said the sneaky clever child as she got out of the car and shut the door behind her.

I was the teacher, she the pupil, but it was her country. I mean, it was not insane to trust her judgement that she might lead the way across. To me, the river seemed a different beast since last we crossed. Not only had the water risen, but there was more debris which now jacked the tyres, just a little, an inch or less, but sufficient to lose a percentage of traction and permit the water to get a better hold of me. In midstream, the edge of the bridge was not even visible and I was steering against the current, feeling how the Peugeot wished to float.

The girl took two careless stumbling steps and I thought she was gone but she recovered and from that point there was no option for either of us but to inch towards the shore. She tripped a second time and I thought her lost but then she grabbed the bumper bar and, as I watched, climbed like a river creature onto the steaming hood.

Then my tyres were spinning in the welcome mud and I saw her marvellous white teeth laughing and she crawled across directly through the absent windscreen and her clothes were drenched and pasted to her, like clay slip in a sculptor's studio.

She rolled forward into the passenger seat and poured water from her sandshoes out her window and I thought, one day, Susie Shuttle, you will be an important woman.

But then I was back at Quamby Downs and what had become my "normal" life.

My first business was with the Punka Wallah who I found sitting on a kerosene drum on the wrong side of my gate. At this early hour he should have been at work in the laundry, but Carter was away dealing with a broken windmill and my visitor had planted himself fearlessly at my gate. He faced my front door, knees close to the offensively named "boy wire." Why he was waiting for me he wouldn't say and, being the Punka Wallah, he was bad tempered because I could not read his mind. Would he like a cuppa? No he wouldn't. He rested a poor fragile leg across a knee, and I saw his starving childhood and was now alert to the scars across those barky shins.

When it was time for class I bade him farewell. He was still at his post at lunchtime, joined by curly headed Crowbar who was a distinct contrast to his wound up friend. Yes Bill, certainly, he would like a cuppa.

I returned with the tea things, and saw the kerosene drum had been placed in such a way that it became a table and I was provided with delicate shade from a half dead poinciana sapling.

My visitors each took a staggering amount of sugar which I was no longer shocked by, and there then followed one of those companionable silences I had come to know at Quamby Downs.

"Good car, eh?" Crowbar grinned at last, and I thought, of course he knows we drove across the flooded bridge last night.

Nearby, the Peugeot steamed like a bucket of old rags. "Good car," I said.

He arranged his hat. "Electrics OK, no worries."

"Thank you."

Crowbar pushed his brim back and explained what he had done to waterproof the electrics. This technical chatter was very welcome to me, but not tolerable to the Punka Wallah who spiked it with sarcastic-sounding commentary until—suddenly—he threw his unfinished tea onto the dirt. He stared fixedly away from me. He spat. He began a long belligerent complaint, then stopped abruptly.

Crowbar sipped his tea with his habitual equanimity.

The Punka Wallah's voice now entered a new high register and when he had reached the true climax of his indignation, he spat a second time.

OK. The quiet returned, I asked Crowbar what I had done to offend his mate.

He drew something in the dirt and flicked it away with his long fingers. He explained that Tommy had given me a gift of petrol. The Punka Wallah nodded and curled his long black hair around his fingers and knotted it and I looked into his yellow whites. Crowbar translated. It was a present, he said. Now I had used it up. If I was a true blackfellah I would know what was expected of me.

I explained we had to save the baby's life.

The Punka Wallah understood me perfectly. "Bullshit," he said, "I give you. You give me."

After some consideration he added: "Baby bullshit."

I placed my hand on my heart and said I would repay the gift.

He said he was giving me a chance no-one else would, not Lochy, no-one. He could make me a proper blackfellah. He would teach me how. Without this, I would be alone. No-one would want to marry me. No-one would like my kids. On the ark I could have many wives.

It would be difficult to exaggerate how fiercely this pressed hard on the raw nerve of my life, the midnight fear I would always be from nowhere. How lonely and exhausting it was to live inside my skin, to spend my nights gluing the pressed plants into a big notebook, transcribing the names my class had taught me, to wake each morning frayed, disconnected and know I did not belong.

I said I understood the value of what he was offering.

He leaped to his feet. He spat. He walked away. Then, as I had seen a man in the camp return to the source of his offence, declaring outrage, shaking a stick, or an axe, appealing to the witnesses to judge his case, he came running back at me and stopped a foot away.

Then all the hard features softened and the eyes were wet. He would siphon more juice and bring it to me. He would save a place for me on his secret ark. He spoke in English, very clearly. I could bring plenty books, too much peipa, from Sydney, Big London, what I wished. Plenty jewels and crystals on that ark already. I could bring more stuff from inside my house here. There was room for a wireless, kero fridge. If I did not bring these things they would all be washed away, my whole residence, Carter's Big House too.

I thanked him.

But did I understand what he was giving me?

I thought so.

Then he would tell me once again. Carter, Carter's kids, jackaroos, policemen, Welfare, all the kartiya would drown. Christmas trees would catch on fire. Anytime now, he said, and I imagined blazing Christmas trees ascending, swallowed by the clouds.

It was important that I listened to him. But it was essential I be in class. In making my excuses I was clumsy. I pointed to the sky. No rain, I said. All gone. I smiled, meaning we could discuss the apocalypse on another day.

"No rain bullshit," Tom the Tailor cried in perfect convent English. "Gone. Ha!" he shouted. "Ha! Ha!" He turned towards the camp and then came back. He ripped a branch from the poinciana and looked like he would whip me with it. Instead he stamped on it and trampled it down into the mud. "You wait. You see. Big rain. That girl, she be washed away."

"What girl?"

"That wife you got. She bin finished now. Old Cricket got her in the house. They drown inside his bloody bed."

To pay him back I asked him what about the bloody car, would that be washed away as well?

"You cunt," he said to me and I saw his coated tongue, like a cockatoo's in his dark mouth. "Poor stupid fellow, you. Better lock that door tonight."

Tom Tailor had always walked faster than was quite normal and now he scurried along the side wall of my residence and disappeared from view.

I asked Crowbar was it possible that the Punka Wallah had just threatened to sing me to death.

Crowbar produced a roll of chewed up stinky tobacco. He said a black man could only sing a black man. He selected a choice piece of baccy and placed it delicately inside his cheek. He said that if a white man could be sung they could be killed, so many kartiya been killed long time ago, Carter for instance. Big Kev Little would have his kidney fat all stolen, his insides filled with snakes and crystals.

But had he forgotten I was a blackfellah?

Ah yes, he said. He looked away from me, out to the eastern horizon where soft cumulus clouds were massing once again.

"Maybe you go with him," he said. "He teach you Law a little bit."

"Gammon Law," I said.

This was to claim more knowledge than I had.

"Safer you be mates with him Bill."

Of course I did not wish to face whatever dangers would be involved in becoming the pariah's follower, but nor did I wish such a fierce fellow to become my enemy. For this reason I soon paid the Punka Wallah a visit, crawling on my hands and knees through the tiny door, bringing a tribute of tea and sugar.

I expected to be offered tea. None came. Then—what choice did I have?—I said I would drive him to his ark.

He accepted but I saw no cuppa was forthcoming.

I returned to the teacher's residence and wondered when that petrol might arrive and who would bring it and who I might offend but all of these complicated anxieties were soon forgotten when my final visitor brought, not petrol, but her glowering daughter, Susie Shuttle.

Only now did I learn that Susie had a chance to be accepted at the Perth nursing college and her mother had insisted that she have Cricket Carter write the reference letter. Carter had been very keen to oblige. He had employed Susie on the spot, as a house girl for after school.

I thought, how disastrous, but then again I saw the mother's point of view. A teacher was a weak and useless thing but now, when the boss had not delivered, I was her only hope. Mr. Carter had the papers. They were sitting on his desk.

How could I not offer my assistance?

# 20

AN EXPLOSIVE INCIDENT like the one with Bennett Ash was the exception to the rule. I did not usually lose my temper. I had been, if anything, too much the other way. For instance, when called a kraut in Bacchus Marsh I remained my good natured self, waiting a decent interval before sustaining an "injury" that would let me leave the football team without offence. That was my social habit or disability. So I went to visit Carter that evening completely sure that we would conclude our negotiation amicably.

I dozed while I waited for him to return from his day's work and it was late when the lights of the Chev truck swept across my bedroom wall and I heard the workers' soft voices as they drifted back towards their camp.

I left him plenty of time to clean up and was surprised, on finally entering the Big House, to pass the filthy cake of Lifebuoy in the basin and discover, in the hiss and glare of the kerosene lamp, the boss alone at the table eating tuna from a can. His desolate face was smeared with grease, and his rum bottle was wet with soap and engine oil. Above all this the punka swung, and the tepid air moved back and forth. In the no-man's land between dark and light I found Tom Tailor's eyes.

Carter was already speaking as I entered.

"My old man," said Carter, "was a mechanic in Warracknabeal. I thought I was getting away from all the grease monkeys when I went on the land." It was only then he spotted me. "Look," he said and held his dripping hands up to the light. "Windmills. Bloody windmills, mate. Did you know Inigo Jones died?"

Inigo Jones, of course, was the most famous long term weather forecaster in Australia.

"Jupiter," he said. "Saturn, Neptune and Uranus. Your anus," he said. "Jesus Bill take a joke."

He wanted me to sit. I sat. He slid his tuna can towards me.

"God I miss them," he said. "I should have gone home for Christmas while I could." He drank. "Giddy up," he said and I thought him impatient for me to eat the oily fish but he was looking at the punka above his head.

He twisted in his vast pearly chair to address Tom Tailor who was standing behind his shoulder pulling on the rope. The Punka Wallah raised his chin and I saw his eyes much narrowed as his speed increased and I thought how much he must loathe the station boss. Did he nod to me? It's possible.

Carter, meanwhile, knocked his glass but managed not to spill it. Of course I should have returned to my bed but as it was obvious that he was in no state to write a reference, I imagined he might be pleased to have me perform that labour for him.

Was I not aware that he had already formed an unsuitable alliance with my pupil? Yes. Did I understand he would not wish to let her go? Yes, yes, and yes. Then why on earth did I choose this moment to tell him that I had received a letter from the nursing college?

"No you didn't," he said.

"They wrote to me," I said although I was unschooled in lying, already beyond my limits.

"If they'd written to you, bozo, I would have seen the bloody letter."

I said he must have overlooked it. They had written to me only because they had not yet received a reference for Susie Shuttle. He was laughing now and I was already tangled, knocking over my pieces on the board while he played his own loose anarchic game where everything could jump three squares at once.

"There's not a letter comes in or out of Quamby Downs without me knowing. Of course they never wrote to you. They never heard of you, you little needle dick. I know what you're up to."

So I had made a muddle of it, although this had the curious effect of making Carter happy. Indeed he began to sing "Late Night Susie" which was on the hit parade that year.

> *What you gonna tell your mother?*
> *What your daddy's going to say*
> *About your stocking ladders*
> *Now the milkman been and gone.*

It was not the tunelessness that made it awful, but the lascivious lips, the clear claim to carnal knowledge of a child in his employ.

A flood of bile rushed through my cells. I beheld the creature on his filthy pearly throne and could have killed him.

"You've come to make sure little Susie gets her reference. That's it?"

"I could write it if you're busy."

"Good man," he cried, rising from his seat and lurching towards his pigpen desk, leaving me to confront his vacant throne and its back support, a kind of escutcheon, where I made out the crude fretsawed likeness of a crab.

He knocked a weight from his desk.

"Help your bloody self," he said. "Sit back down. Relax."

He thrust a letter in my hand and I thought, I've won. But it was the request for a reference, nothing more.

"You think I'm a mug?" He was too much behind me, hovering.

"Never."

"She's a great root, mate. Do you think I'm stupid?"

The etymology of root is in rut, from Old French, meaning "noise, roar, bellowing" which, even after it has entered the Australian language, still summons up visions of raw sexual congress.

"A lovely juicy little root," he said and thus condemned himself.

I asked him how long he'd had the request in his hand.

Since the mail before last he supposed. The wet season had held up the last two deliveries.

There was someone lurking in the kitchen hut. The punka rode back and forth. Carter continued to stand behind me, shifting whenever I turned.

"I could write it for you," I suggested, "and bring it in for signature in the morning."

"Oh, you could bring it to me, could you? Have you lost your marbles too?"

"Just trying to help."

"It's called a psychotic breakdown. Just comes on you, out of nowhere."

"Why don't we sit down?"

"Why don't you back off? You lay a hand on her again, I'll fucking drop you."

"Barry, you've got it wrong."

"Mr. Carter to you."

"Mr. Carter."

"She doesn't want to be a fucking nurse. She's got a job at Quamby Downs. Why would she need another one?"

Finally, there he was, where I could see him. I was sickened by the pasty glow of his skin, the gut above his belt, the corruption of his body, but still I was in perfect control of myself. Even when he crumpled the letter I kept my cool.

But then he cuffed my head, and I found myself in a place I only vaguely recognised. I grabbed his arm and found it more muscular than I had expected. He dragged me upright from my seat but I tripped him up and he fell, heavy, on his back and we were rolling across the floor and I could see the Punka Wallah's bare feet and smell the rum and feel a disgusting intimacy as we rolled across my family history beneath his dinner table, and then he tangled in the chair which rocked and tipped and fell and I saw the inlaid pearl shell pop, like confetti, as the paper was forced into my mouth.

"I'll take you to the bloody hospital," he said.

I gagged. His upper lip pushed into his parrot beak, showing gums as pink as tonsils. "You know what we do with twats like you? You'll be in psychotic breakdown by the time I get you up to Broome. I'll have you declared insane. You don't know how easy it is. You'll have all the boongs you want in there."

The crumpled paper cut my mouth and blocked my air. I bucked but he had his knees on both my arms and he plucked at my nostril.

"You better say you're sorry."

"I'm sorry."

"Give up."

I said that I gave up, and he let me go but he had not expected this outcome and he was wild-eyed and frightened.

"You are the most pathetic little shit I ever saw," he said. He was standing very close and it would have showed weakness to move away. "You could do five years for assault and battery."

"Sign a blank sheet of paper. I'll write the letter on it."

"OK," he said and slammed his arm around my neck. I had always been as slippery as a snake and I took possession of his weight, his fat and muscle, and charged with him, his head first, towards the support post in the outer wall, colliding with Kev Little's pearly chair, which now revealed its hidden weakness and cracked and splintered and delivered unto me one heavy leg, a club with such a slender handle. With this I smote the bastard.

His white arm cracked like a mud crab, the fibula the same, and with that my entire life broke through its shell and revealed the hidden secret of its true and final shape.

The air was very still. The thunder crashed. Gently, the Punka Wallah helped me to my feet, and now there was but one course available to me.

Carter lay groaning while the rain fell like ball bearings on the metal roof. Then I was outside and in the downpour where Doctor Battery passed me a tobacco pouch. In shock, I watched Tom Tailor siphon the petrol directly from the Chev truck into the Peugeot and then I saw young Susie and my brother Crowbar and it was clear they were my friends and would not abandon me now. I fetched my notebooks. There was room for nine more flagons in the back. The ark must be my refuge.

# 21

I WAS EIGHTEEN YEARS OLD when I finally saw my father Willem August Bachhuber. This first meeting took place on an airstrip in Broome in the midst of an enormous downpour and was of a duration determined by an approaching cyclone and the need to refuel. After his two years of freedom, mostly spent in a cave in the Oscar Range, my father was a gaunt scarecrow in sodden shorts and T-shirt who was now alone and unprotected in the middle of the storm while his police escort waited for him in the shelter of a fogged up car.

I felt not the least connection to this strange white man with springy wheaten hair cut high above his ears and a habit of looking down when he might be expected to look up.

He had become, in a strange way, my duty and if it had not been for my extraordinary guardian, I would never have known he was my father at all. Madison, however, had grown up imagining his own father was his cousin, and, although he rarely interfered in my mother's very particular notions of child rearing, on this question he exerted great authority. I must know Willie Bachhuber. This was why I had been sent to meet his books at Bacchus Marsh and why I spent so many hours attempting to understand them. I sold them too, of course, when Madison made me see them as a source of sustenance like those infertile trophic eggs which certain beetles leave solely to feed their offspring.

To arrive at that destabilising meeting in Broome, I had travelled on three tedious flights from Melbourne with my friend Ronnie Bobs and his mother. As my own mum had no wish to ever see my father it was Mrs. Bobs who volunteered and Mrs. Bobs who paid for all the tickets and Mrs. Bobs, alone, who was not bored. On the contrary: she was hysterical.

My father may have been, as so many have suggested, a meddlesome well-meaning amateur anthropologist, but he was also a well-educated, deeply read man, an intellectual whose soul had been seriously contorted as a result of his country's practice of ethnic cleansing. He was not the sort of character you would think to connect with this weeping woman across the aisle. Yet I will say, in her defence, that she was always warm and affectionate with children. She was someone who made me jam sandwiches and took me and Ronnie to the Royal Melbourne Show. Obviously something very grown-up had occurred between her and my father but I still have no stable notion of what it might have been. As for Mr. Bobs, I really have no clue. He was a famous car dealer and radio personality, and was in the tabloids for a while, but I have no recollection of him except, of course, those awful television ads in which he starred himself. It is not original to say that he seemed acrobatic, shiny, more like a wooden puppet than a man.

Ronnie had stayed aboard our aircraft and I was escorted into the deluge by his mother. I remember that the rain was warm, and my shoes were flooded. My father had no umbrella and his hand was wet. He did not kiss me although it had seemed he planned to do so and then changed his mind. I have a strong sense he wished to say things to me but that Mrs. Bobs' bawling somehow got in the way. I was not angry that she denied me my natural meeting, but because she embarrassed me.

Most probably I reported her behaviour to my own mother who presumably put an end to all those spontaneous swims, and barbecues. If I did not see Bacchus Marsh again, it was certainly not my doing. This was a sad loss but not a trauma. More seriously I had to contend with the discovery that my so-called German father had carried the genes that made me Aboriginal. Thank God for Madison. He sacrificed much of his personal life to stand by me.

Impossible as this would prove to be, I did not wish myself to be known or restricted by the colour of my skin. For the longest time I was determined that this would have no effect on me at all and I was readily annoyed with anyone who suggested otherwise. When my mother wished me to study medicine, that is what I did, thoughtfully gaining the scholarship to pay for it. And what human could study medicine in Australia without thinking of Aboriginal people and therefore of cataracts, anaemia, heart disease, diabetes, asthma and pneumonia. I was so often exasperated by friends who concluded blithely that I chose my practice and my patients because of the colour of my skin. Might it not have been my Hippocratic oath or my sense of common humanity? Were these not factors they might reasonably consider?

My father was given ten years in Fremantle, the maximum sentence for Grievous Bodily Harm. I wrote to him regularly as Madison had determined I should and I suppose my letters were as dull and dutiful as a child in a boarding school. I read his letters with no more enthusiasm than I wrote my own and it had to be pointed out to me that my father wished to tell me about that "little school" he had made on Quamby Downs. Why was it so hard for me to show an interest? Was I ashamed of him? Was I perhaps frightened of his loneliness and need? When he expressed the hope that I would visit his old schoolhouse I doubt I even acknowledged the request.

I passed my Leaving Certificate and Matriculation with first class honours. I was accepted for medicine at Melbourne University. My father continued as a prison teacher and as so many of his students were inevitably Aboriginal he continued his practice of collecting stories, making his non-maps and diagrams. He also, as I later learned, wrote regularly for *Walkabout* magazine under the name of "Eagle."

Did any anthropologist read those columns at the time? These days they are much better known. Indeed it's hard to think of a writer so frequently cited and so constantly belittled. We would say now that he reported the secret cults of opposition to white colonisation. The expert view, at that time, was that such cults did not exist. To insist on them was to be a sensationalist or liar who could no more be believed than, say, Daisy Bates whose tales of Aboriginal cannibalism are still attributed to her need to satisfy the lurid appetites of the popular press.

My father was never one for lurid appetites. He was, rather, a man torn apart by two conflicting desires, one to record and the other to keep secret. That is he would reveal or allege an Ark Cult, or a Ned Kelly Cult or a Captain Cook Saga but then, the minute this vast wonder had been glimpsed, his only wish was to kick the whole damn thing out of sight. In my own experience this was maddening.

I was offended that he never thanked me for the time and money it cost me to finally visit Quamby Downs. By then the magical school-room had become a whitewashed storage shed with no sign remaining of his labours with the exception of the words "Captain Cook" whose component dyes had separated and risen to the surface, no longer Quinky blue, but a ghostly orange bleed.

Anyone aware of the continuing crisis in Aboriginal health will not be surprised to learn that Doctor Battery and the Punka Wallah were dead and Crowbar was in hospital suffering the extreme consequences of acute diabetes. Of course I understood my father's sadness, but I was his child and yearned for gratitude as well.

On his release from Fremantle, without me knowing it, he pur-chased a rifle and ammunition and returned to the same cave in which he had finally been arrested. Here he somehow fed himself.

By the time my friends in Derby led me out to the Oscar Range where Willem Bachhuber and I had our adult meeting, he had made a replica of that other cave, his schoolroom. He had done this only for me, he insisted, and it had been the "labour of bloody Hercules." (Thanks Dad.) Using whitewash, ink and twigs and brushes, he had fastidiously reproduced the Saga of Captain Cook and all the maps or anti-maps and diagrams with which his students had instructed him. Here also, in the country of Jandamarra, he learned many stories and Dreaming tracks and our first proper sit-down meeting took place inside a trea-sure house, a museum, the inside of a skull decorated with arcs and dots and lines of furry blue.

I took this for what it was, an act of love, a vote of trust.

Yet my father's trust had limits as I discovered when I came upon a rusted Redex Peugeot overgrown by wattles. The Redex regalia was still legible as was the number 62. Of course I was excited. But Willie's first inclination was to push this far away. It had nothing to do with his Redex. Only days later did he admit to me that this was the car in which he had fled from Quamby Downs.

Why would he not tell me that?

Well, it was not interesting.

The rusted wreck abutted a large rock outcrop which was distinct not only because of its shape but because, in that vast Devonian limestone country, it was rich in iron. It was a monolith, about the length of a football field, with smooth sheer sides like an axe blade or, as I later thought, an upturned rusty ship.

I am a doctor, not an anthropologist, but I have made enough inquiries to know that distinctive rocks often have a role to play in Dreamtime stories (of metamorphosis, for instance). I mean, what seems to be a rock is sometimes so much more.

With this in mind, I asked my father was that big rock in fact the Punka Wallah's ark. After all, the journey of the Peugeot had ended here.

Willie was not an overly jolly man, but at this simple question he exploded in laughter which continued far beyond any reasonable explanation. When he had gasped and spat and deary-me'd, he teased me for talking like a whitefellah with my mumbo-jumbo bulldust. He returned to his point continually, for days to come, until I finally concluded that I had been correct.

But what is a rock without a story? Without its Law? Its ritual?

It is my belief that my father had collected these arcane formulae. This was what was stacked on the shelves in his cave, in his so-called "mud books" and his C90 and C120 cassettes. These last had stretched and deteriorated so badly they appear to be beyond salvation and are therefore no more interesting to the "experts" than the "mud books" whose cores are generally thought to have been written during a period of breakdown.

I have the distinct advantage of having read those "mud books" which seem to me, far from being the product of a breakdown, to be driven by Willie Bachhuber's desire to preserve and pass down what he had found while, at the same time, honouring his obligation to guard secrets. He had written so explicitly about an ark, I was slow to understand that he was not referring to the secret locus of the Punka Wallah's cult, but rather his own hoard of notes, diary entries, tapes, accounts of a culture he has now spent a life protecting from malevolent destruction. If my father would not be clear, professor, it is not because he had a breakdown, but because he must record the truth *and* keep the secret. What may seem to be the signs of madness might be understood by someone familiar with alchemical literature as an encryption whose function is to insist that our mother country is a foreign land whose language we have not yet earned the right to speak.

# Acknowledgements

This book could not have been written without the generosity and faith of Frances Coady, that great editor who just happens to be my wife. I am also indebted to many others who first knew me as a stranger. Of all these no name is more important than that of the anthropologist Catherine Wohlan. When Frances and I travelled to the Kimberley it was Catherine who was our companion and teacher. Later, by means of a hundred emails, she became a dear friend. In Broome she introduced me to Pat Lowe and Howard Pedersen (and if that collaboration involved nothing more challenging than opening wine bottles, Pat and Howard's books have remained my close companions ever since). In Fitzroy Crossing (Mardowarra in its fictional existence) Catherine led me to Carolyn Davey, David (Bullen) Rogers and their daughter Natalie Davey. My tape recorder remains a memorial to those important meetings.

Later Catherine suggested Steve Kinnane would be more than qualified to read the manuscript. Steve is a Marda Marda from Mirrowoong country in the East Kimberley. He is Senior Researcher for the Nulungu Research Institute of the University of Notre Dame in Broome. He is also the author of a prize-winning memoir. It was there I met him, finally, in the elegant and moving pages of *Shadow Lines*.

Georgine Clarsen is an Associate Professor of History at Wollongong University. She has a PhD in history and the unexpected bonus of a certificate in automotive engineering. She has written widely about women and the Redex Trial and is currently researching the ways that Australian national culture and automobile culture developed together during the first half of the twentieth century. That is to say, she is and was a perfect source.

It was Georgine who introduced me to Hal Moloney just as he was finishing his history of the Redex Trial. She also knew the Adelaide historian Tom Gara who became a constant advisor during the writing process. When my own illness prevented our great planned adventure on the Nullarbor Tom took me on other journeys in the library, returning with, amongst other treasures, the work of Deborah Bird Rose who alerted me to those rewritings of the white narratives of colonisation, for instance Captain Cook and Ned Kelly. The Captain Cook narrative in this novel is taken directly from Hobbles Danaiyarri's account which Deborah recorded at Victoria Downs and later wrote about so tellingly. She assures me Hobbles would have been more than happy to see this story find a different readership. The portion I have used is lightly edited.

I should also thank R. Graham Carey, who was not only a warm and generous grandfather, but a pioneer in Australian aviation whose character could not be more different from that of the fictional Dangerous Dan Bobs. I owe apologies to Seaman Dan and Karl Neuenfeldt and to Mrs. Petrov for subjecting them to time travel. I am indebted to the poet Paul Kane who is the translator of those twelve ghazals by the Persian poet Hafiz, to Lois Zweck, to Kingsley Palmer, Miles Homes, Paul Carey, Leon Saunders, Ian Madden, Janice Carey, Trish and Ken Claringbold, Kate Matthews, Sue and Garry Smith, Rod Baker, and finally, L & J Builders for adding the second storey to the Bacchus Marsh High School in a single low-cost sentence.

## A NOTE ON THE TYPE

This book was set in Granjon, a type named in compliment to Robert Granjon, a type cutter and printer active in Antwerp, Lyons, Rome, and Paris from 1523 to 1590. Granjon, the boldest and most original designer of his time, was one of the first to practice the trade of typefounder apart from that of printer.

Linotype Granjon was designed by George W. Jones, who based his drawings on a face used by Claude Garamond (ca. 1480–1561) in his beautiful French books. Granjon more closely resembles Garamond's own type than do any of the various modern faces that bear his name.

Typeset by Scribe,
Philadelphia, Pennsylvania

Printed and bound by Berryville Graphics,
Berryville, Virginia

Designed by Cassandra J. Pappas